ALSO BY BETH BROWER

The Unselected Journals of Emma M. Lion

The Queen's Gambit
The Ruby Prince
The Wanderer's Mark

The Beast of Ten

THE

Q

BETH BROWER

THE
Q

Rhysdon Press

Published by Rhysdon Press
Printed in the United States of America

Publishers Cataloging-in-Publication data. Brower, Beth. The Q: Beth Brower; p.cm.
ISBN 978-0-9980636-8-3. Historical Fiction 2. Historical—Fiction. I. TItle.

Fifth Edition 2021
10 9 8 7 6 5

978-0-9980636-8-3

The Q is dedicated to some of the most
important people in the print shop of my life.

K
R, L
A, B, L, A, S, K, L, K, K
N, C, N, T, C, S, C, C

M, E, O, C, C
G, A, S, R
T, M, G, M
I, T, I
C, L

A, A, W, P, F

R, J, F

CHAPTER ONE:

The Q

Every time the door into the front offices of The Q opened, the sounds of Gainsford Street, business hub of Rhysdon, would come tumbling in on the heels of whoever entered. Clicking, turning, marking time, the rush and flow of the patrons was like the working gears of humanity's clock. These sounds all transformed neatly into the mechanics of The Q. And perched on a stool behind the front counter, conducting her business—waiting upon customers, efficiently taking questions for the next edition, studying figures and markets and profits down to each percentage and comma and dot—sat Miss Quincy St. Claire, chief officer of operations, self-appointed auditor of all accounts, final editor overseeing the team of typesetters, proofers, and printers, and, in general, the central gear in the workings of her great-uncle's business.

The bell on the door sounded, and Quincy looked up from her work to see a tall gentleman sporting a deep red overcoat, a top hat, and appropriately coiffed facial hair. Quincy herself didn't care much for these turn-of-the-century fashions.

"Good morning," Quincy said, looking back down at her work. "How may I help you?"

"Question please," the man sniffed, glancing about the office while taking his gloves off one long finger at a time. "Inquiring if there is a repair craftsman in Rhysdon, competent in the restoring of seventeenth-century Queen Sarah motif trim. If interested, please contact, et cetera, et cetera."

These words flew from Quincy's pen, appearing in her mechanical script on the blank Q form. "And what name would you like for the contact?"

"Mauffry. Lord Mauffry."

Unfazed by his title, and rather uninterested in the tinge of self-importance lacing his response, Quincy procured his address and informed Lord Mauffry that his question would be featured in *The Q* of the following day. "Is there any reason for us to advertise outside the limits of Rhysdon? In Mirshire, perhaps?"

"No, no. Rhysdon is sufficient."

"Will you pay in coin or by account?"

"*Account,*" he replied, as if it were obvious. Clearly this man wished her to understand that he did not carry any shillings or jabs in his well-trimmed pockets. Quincy St. Claire didn't care.

"Certainly," said Quincy.

Finally, he looked at her and stared—as did all customers who usually paid a Q boy to deliver their questions instead of coming into the office—while she finished his order. It was a shock, she had been reliably informed, to find her, the genius of Rhysdon business, sitting at the front desk during business hours, helping the customers in person. How she chose to dress did nothing to lessen the shock of it either. Or so Quincy had been told.

Quincy ignored the man's interest and finished his bill, handing him a Q stub. "Is that all, Lord Mauffry?"

"Yes, it is, Miss St. Claire." He paused. "It is *Miss St. Claire*?"

"Yes," Quincy answered with the tone she most often used with anybody, that of brisk business.

Mauffry looked at her once again, seemingly wanting to say more. But he hesitated, then frowned, as if he found the whole scene of great interest, before nodding, setting his hat back on his head, and turning towards the front door to let himself out onto Gainsford Street.

"I think you deserve every chilly encounter you receive for the rest of your life."

Quincy turned towards her right, where Fisher, her office manager and fellow foundling, sat busy at his desk—which was set at a right angle to her long counter, on the other side of the swinging half gate that separated the front office from the door to the sorting room.

After returning to her work for several more minutes, Quincy lifted her head again and looked at Fisher. "Why?"

"People are interested in you," Fisher responded as he shuffled the day's correspondence into their proper metal baskets. "They wish to know more. They hear about you, about your genius," he waved a stack of letters in her direction, "and your unusual sense of style. And, when someone gives you a cue to engage, you dismiss them entirely."

They looked at each other long enough for one thousand past conversations to pass between them, and then Quincy shrugged as the clock clanged six o'clock. Wordlessly, she slipped off her stool, walked through the swinging half gate and across the front office, and locked the front door of The Q. It was six o'clock on New Year's Eve.

Quincy had been with the establishment since the age of nine, becoming indispensible at thirteen, revolutionizing the business and scope of The Q at fifteen. By age eighteen, Quincy had completely taken over the daily motions of the company whose influence filled the streets of every major city, and of most towns, in the entire country.

For the business set, the operations of The Q were a marvel. Quincy's innovation, drive, and rather avant-garde marketing concepts had made it prosper. The Q grew so exponentially from her genius that she caught not only the attention and respect of the Rhysdon businessmen but also international interest from London, Paris, and even New York. Her skill at wooing every class into using the services of The Q was the trick that had brought her name not only to the cheap-streets and the middle-class shops but also into the parlors and dinner parties of the most elite of Rhysdon's aristocracy. All invitations for any event of note were, of course, issued through a well-placed question on The Q's society page. As it had become popular to host Q teas, every lady owned a tea set featuring one of the many stylized Qs. There were also

Q tea towels and cross-stitch samplers for ladies, playing cards and flasks for gentlemen. The publication of *The Q* had become the most contemporary expression of what a person *ought* to be.

It was with little interest that Quincy heard the news from her uncle Ezekiel—a man of society, of people, of parties and concerts, a man who thoroughly enjoyed life's offerings, and a general mystery to Quincy—that her story had become a popular topic among the elite: a girl of nine, working in a foundling factory, thin-boned, world-hardened, found by her great-uncle and brought to Rhysdon as heir to his wealth and influence, only to find later that Miss St. Claire was a magician with numbers and a virtuoso in the art of running a business. The great interest of others in her story was unimportant to Quincy, who felt that unnecessary human contact rusted the gears of a well-oiled business. She had little time for talk, and she had no patience for people. What Quincy had time for was The Q.

Fisher stood, layered his overcoat on his threadbare jacket, and pushed each button through its stubborn woolen buttonhole with his mangled hand, short of two and a half fingers.

"You really should get yourself some new clothes," Quincy said as she came back and stood before his desk. "I pay you well enough for it."

"I would if you would give me the time off to do it," Fisher replied, pulling his leather satchel over his shoulder. It bulged with the books he was studying for entrance to Rhysdon University. "Speaking of personal time," Fisher grumbled, "why did Arch, humble solicitor, receive permission for the half day off, whereas I begged for it, but didn't?"

"Because," Quincy answered, walking back around the counter and reclaiming her stool, "the last day of the year means finishing your tasks and you weren't finished. He was. Also, I don't have the inviolable desire to ring your neck every time I see you. With Mr. Arch, I do."

"Poor Arch." Fisher grinned. "You can't catch him any kind of break, can you? He has made only one mistake in the four months he's been with us, and you've condemned him to eternal penance. He's brilliant, in fact, if you hadn't noticed. And he's fresh out of law school."

Quincy didn't care. "One mistake is more than enough."

"You caught it," Fisher argued. "Everything was straightened out. What more do you expect?"

Quincy looked at him. "Infallibility."

Grunting, Fisher pointed towards a stack of mail. "That's all for the sorting room, by the way."

"I'll take it straight down to printing," replied Quincy. "Mrs. Graves and the sorters are all gone home. I told her I would catch the last batch. You remembered your key today?"

"Yes." Fisher patted the pocket of his waistcoat beneath his overcoat. "I'll let myself out. You doing anything to ring in the New Year?"

"Uncle Ezekiel has asked me by, for a lecture no doubt. But I'll be back in the office after that. I've work that can't wait, as you well know."

"I know," Fisher said, disapproving. "Happy New Year. I'll see you on the second?"

"I'll be here on the first, if you would like to join me."

"Oh no," Fisher guffawed as he retreated towards the door, clearly afraid of getting sucked back in. "I'm not working New Year's Day."

"Happy New Year, then." Quincy gave her signature shrug, the lift of a single shoulder, and left her stool to grab the mail from Fisher's desk. Then she headed back through the empty sorter and down into the print room as Fisher let himself out.

The sound of The Q's long print room was all clatter and clack. The new machines made such a fantastic whir that some evenings, after the front office had closed and Fisher was getting ready for home, Quincy found herself sitting on the metal stairs mounted to the wall, watching the quick windmills going back and forth, hearing the clang and clip as pages rolled endlessly against the set rows of type.

"You are going to lose your mind in all that racket," her great-uncle Ezekiel would say whenever he caught her in the act. But Quincy ignored the quips he delivered calmly over her shoulder. Uncle Ezekiel, though impressed with the ingenuity of the machines, was not impressed with their lack of poetics.

It had taken Quincy the better part of three years to convince him to exchange his cylinder steam-powered presses for Heidelbergs out of Germany. He had thought a series of Whitlock presses would suffice, but Quincy had opposed this with several comments regarding his antiquated ideas. And while uncle Ezekiel had mourned the loss of his steam-powered presses—with surprising attachment, Quincy had thought, considering that her uncle had run his business for years on simple jobbers—Quincy had reveled in the new electric-powered presses, seduced by their efficiency, their sounds, their grippers, their ability to load their own paper into place, and their crisp print impressions.

Clack, Click, Fly!

Quincy ignored her uncle's criticisms about their lack of soul; the poetry of the machine, the verse of progress and speed, and copies of *The Q* spreading farther and farther into cities and towns all over the country were as much rhyme and meter as she needed in her life. Hang all conventional beauty, and give her the machine, the gear, the endless circle of print. The accounts. The reports. The way business numbers yielded so easily beneath her hand.

Give Quincy The Q. Let the world keep its poetry.

———————

Uncle Ezekiel lived in a neighborhood twenty minutes of good walking from Gainsford Street and the offices of The Q. His town house was respectable if not posh. Quincy did not yet know if she disliked it, for she rarely went by her uncle's while having a mind free enough to assess the fashionable Rhysdon real estate. When fresh out of The Q, her mind was filled with the ranks of numbers marching, her thoughts weaving through the patterns of in-house concerns, expanding markets, the rising value of The Q's stock since going public to raise investment money for international expansion. And Quincy was always fresh out of The Q, so her mind was always filled with business.

This particular New Year's Eve, the sound of her boots on the pavement was the only sensation linking Quincy to the December night, the only sensation keeping her from living entirely inside the mental file room of her brain. It was a colder December than had been seen in Rhysdon for many years, according to the reports, and Quincy tucked her chin further into her thick red woolen scarf, dug her hands deeper into the pockets of her tailored black jacket, and curved her mouth into a low whistle.

Hers was a peculiar jacket, one with shoulders set at such a sharp angle they were much more like a soldier's uniform from a century ago than the approved female fashions of the day. She did dress a bit absurdly for a girl of her age: tailored black jackets; white men's dress shirts, also trimmed to fit Quincy's diminutive frame; young men's breeches—resembling the style of a schoolboy rather than of a man about town—and tall black leather boots with one-inch heels and thin laces zigzagging completely up the front.

But Quincy had no use for skirts and dresses; she worked in a printshop. Her schoolboy attire, with the occasional flair of black velvet striping the outseam of her trousers or a jaunty cut for the lapel on her jacket, was just eccentric enough, yet well made and well formed. It was her hair that really caught people off their guard. Quincy's hair was shockingly blond, queenly blond, as blond as her large eyes were blue, and it was cut as short as a boy's.

It had been that way since uncle Ezekiel had reclaimed her from the streets at age nine, and he had let it be, remarking that her slight, small frame, with its lack of any kind of inch to speak of, made her seem a creature of the woods.

"Half shadows and the like," he would say and then wave his hand. "A creature of faerie. A bit pixie you are, with those big eyes and tufts of blond hair following their own whims." He would pause there, moving his fingers about his own forehead, and then sigh. "You coif it feminine enough to know there's a girl underneath all those clothes. Don't deny you use some mysterious female magic to make it do your bidding whenever it'll obey. I like it," he'd conclude. "I daresay, if some sophisticated dame in Paris would too, we'd have a whole rash of hair just so."

Quincy pushed a shock of blond hair away from her face as she paused at a corner, waiting for a hansom to pass before stepping across the street. Turning one more corner, she found herself in Half Crown Circle. Uncle Ezekiel lived in number forty-three.

She rang the bell, and the butler—older than Moses by Quincy's count—answered the door. Bees—which is what Quincy always called the butler, never bothering to remember his real name. He took Quincy's hat. But before he could unwind the vermillion scarf from around her neck, Quincy was up the stairs, thanking the man with a string of backward greetings as she went towards her great-uncle's favorite drawing room.

Bees was so old that she wasn't certain he heard her at all. With the exception of Quincy, all of Ezekiel's personal surrounds were old like him, an ancient race of associates. Krankgill, the former solicitor of The Q and Ezekiel's oldest friend, had been the first to evaporate. He'd died in October only to be replaced by a young upstart Ezekiel had taken a fancy to at some social event—the pale, quietly disapproving, jawline-as-sharp-as-his-silent-censures-each-time-Quincy-was-less-than-courteous Mr. Arch.

Grumbling something even she couldn't hear under her breath, Quincy rapped her raw-from-the-cold knuckles on the drawing room door and then let herself in. The fire roared against the chill clinging to each windowpane and her uncle was seated near it, a blanket over his legs, a book in hand, opened but unread. Quincy walked across the room and her appearance startled him.

"My girl, my girl!" He set the book down on a side table, and Quincy leaned down to kiss his cheek.

"Uncle."

"Look at that. You've walked all the way from The Q with naught but a jacket, a slim little nothing. Where is your overcoat!?"

"You know I don't like them," Quincy replied, sitting in the pink velvet chair opposite her uncle.

"They make you feel constrained, or some such nonsense."

"Yes."

"You look at bit like my sister tonight. The eyes, at least. Lovely girl she was."

The housekeeper then entered with a fresh pot of tea and poured them each a cup. She was, of course, also at death's door, but, unlike Ezekiel's other surrounds, she had less patience with Quincy.

"Peppermint tea?" she asked briskly.

Quincy gave her approval.

The old man nodded, the loose skin from his jaw to his neck moving in agreement. He was venerable, wrinkled, and—if Quincy had figured right—was plotting something. He waited for her to be lulled halfway into her peppermint tea before clearing his throat in a manner that Quincy recognized as his opening move. She countermoved by speaking first.

"And why is Ezekiel in his drawing room on a New Year's Eve? Don't your friends invite you to their parties anymore?"

Her uncle practically scoffed at Quincy. "Don't think I don't know what you're doing. And, yes, I received several invites, including one from Lady Fothergil."

Fothergil. Quincy pressed her lips together and raised her eyebrows. Even though Quincy was less than impressed by others' status, the Fothergil family had been the single strongest political force in the country for the last five hundred years. They were called The Kingmakers for a reason.

"But you didn't go?"

"No," answered Ezekiel. "I thought I would spend my last one at home: visiting with you, reading, thinking. I've an array of events from December whose specters are keeping me fine company. Indeed, I've years and years of life and friendship; the final days are a time to catalogue it all, give thanks, be."

"Final days?" Quincy asked with some suspicion. Had Ezekiel been a normal geriatric, she would have possibly heard this before, but her uncle was full of more life than most anyone she knew, and he never spoke this way. Her suspicion was stirred not because she thought he was clamoring for her attention but, rather, because he was quite serious.

"I am going to die this week," stated Ezekiel.

Quincy blinked at the man. "Why?"

"Has it ever occurred to you that I am ninety-three years old? No, of course not. Your head is stuck in that office. I'm ninety-three, pixie girl. My life has been filled with all that one would ever want. That includes you. So, now I've decided the first week of this new year will see me out. I wouldn't have dreamed of going cold last week; I was never one for endings, but beginnings," he lifted his shaking hand, and his face crumpled into a smile, "they are the best adventures of all."

Pulling her mouth to one side, Quincy set her teacup on the floor and threw herself back into the chair, sitting crouched against the pink velvet. She began to chew on her fingernails while watching her great-uncle's face. The old man was an absolute serious. Quincy shifted again in her seat.

"Have you picked out a day?"

"Good heavens," Ezekiel laughed, "you know me too well. I thought Friday. My body is winding down, like an old forgotten clock. I can feel it. Perhaps it will manage until next Sunday."

"What is your purpose in telling me?" asked Quincy.

"I thought it might be nice to hear it from me, so you would know that I wasn't leaving you behind without fair warning."

Quincy grunted and sank further into her chair, stuffing her hands into her pockets, her head turtled down in between her shoulders.

"Are you nervous?" she asked after a long enough moment had collected.

"No."

"Hmm."

The silence between them, punctuated only by the flare and pop of the fire, said all that Quincy could think of to say.

"You will find," the old man said after a time, "that all of my affairs are in neat order. You will inherit all my personal wealth and this house, though I don't think you care for it—sell it if you like—but, ah, here comes the unpleasantness. You must promise me not to rant. No, you never do it aloud," he added as he saw Quincy quirk an eyebrow. "But inside that pretty little head you can scream loudly enough."

"What is it you're saying?"

"You see, I've decided something," said Ezekiel. "I am not going to leave you The Q."

"What!?" Quincy sat up, ramrod straight, almost falling off the edge of her seat. "But I love The Q!"

"*I* love The Q!" Ezekiel jumped forward in his chair towards her with equal ferocity. "I built The Q! I, as a young man selling newspapers, dreamed of connecting people in a way never done before, dreamed of knowing half stories, half admissions, half truths. I began its publication as a love letter to the people of this pulsing, living city. That is the soul of The Q. Not your profits and expansions and—" he waved his hand in the air while trying to catch a word, "and machines-before-people philosophies. I love The Q. You love the running of, the improving of, the mechanicalizing of The Q. There lies the difference."

"Mechanicalizing is not a word," Quincy snapped, staring him down.

"It should be," the old man huffed as he settled himself back into his chair. "There are so many bells and whistles used these days that it *should* be a word. Now, as I was saying before you didn't let me finish, I am not going to leave you The Q, unless—" Uncle Ezekiel said, looking harried, "unless you can, over the course of this year, fulfill a certain list of requirements which I've taken great care to draw up."

"Oh." Quincy, though still confused, relaxed her guard. "What kind of requirements? If you saw the reports I sent, the projections for The Q's profits are expected to rise almost thirty percent. There are several new contracts in the works, and I can get more. We should also see the profitable repercussions of going public reflected in the last quarter. This spring, I'll be choosing either London or Paris as our first international market. Does that satisfy you?"

"No." Uncle Ezekiel looked at her with pity, something Quincy despised. "No, it does not. I expect something else. Something more."

Sitting into the back of her chair, Quincy crossed her arms. "Fine. What are the requirements?"

"I'm not telling you."

"Not telling me?" Quincy wanted to ask if he'd gone mad. Or gone angry with her.

"My senses are still intact—don't deny you weren't questioning my sanity just now, my dear. I have constructed a list of twelve things—events, decisions, whatever you might call them—which you must fulfill over the next twelve months if you wish to remain the leading officer of The Q."

"How then," Quincy replied, tart and disgruntled, "am I to know when I have accomplished said items if they are to remain a secret?"

"I have appointed an individual to execute this aspect of the experiment," Uncle Ezekiel said, very near to smiling.

"A watchdog to follow me around and see whether I've satisfied your invisible list?"

"That is not how I would phrase it."

"Who?" Quincy demanded. "If Fisher knows of this, I'll wring his neck for not telling me."

Uncle Ezekiel blinked twice, then spoke. "Arch."

"Mr. Arch?" Quincy said, her voice sounding like the bolt of a lock falling home. "Mr. Arch? The Nonentity?"

Uncle Ezekiel cringed at Quincy's cold nickname for the young solicitor. "Arch is a very able solicitor, who has, on the whole," he held up his hands in defense, "performed in an admirable manner. Yes, Arch will supervise the experiment."

"The *experiment*?" Quincy shot up from the pink velvet chair like a cannon, landed on her feet, and locked her hands into place behind her back, a prerequisite to any serious pacing. She made a few rounds before pausing and looking at Ezekiel. "Uncle, I beg you—everything I have built, all the work and passion—"

"Passion?" Ezekiel's question was accompanied by a single-syllabled laugh. "Calculations, yes! Speculation and equations and marketing— that is what you call your new fangled ideas, isn't it? Brilliant, all of it, but *passion*? Not so. You, my beloved girl, are passionless and mechanical. I love you dearly, as you well know, which is why I cannot, in all good conscience, leave you with The Q, save you fulfill my requirements."

"Requirements to be checked off by the Nonentity? Requirements that I have no idea of? Really, Uncle."

The tall clock in the downstairs hall chimed. Quincy only took note of this because it was so different from her clock at The Q, which never chimed; it clanged. Again, she began to pace. The heels on Quincy's black boots left marks in the carpets as she walked from the window to the door and back.

"Be sport, Quincy," Ezekiel said, using the jargon of the day. "What is the very worst outcome? You lose The Q."

She swiveled away from the window to challenge his gaze. "The Q, Uncle, is all I have."

"That, pixie child, is precisely the point I am trying to make."

Some jovial revelers in the street, illuminated by the iridescent streetlights, sang as they passed beneath the window. The snow was now falling thickly, whitewashing the streets below.

"And you are so certain that you'll go this week?" Quincy spoke the words into the window's glass, staring at her own reflection.

"Undoubtedly."

"I'll be by on Thursday, the usual time, to say good-bye," Quincy said as she pulled away from the window and walked back to her abandoned chair, reclaiming her red scarf.

"Will you not stay with me until midnight? Ring the year in and all that?"

"Can't," Quincy replied, her voice sounding like the slap of a typebar on a typewriter. "I've got another hour at least to be ready for the year-end audit.

"We pay accountants to do that work, Quincy," Uncle Ezekiel chided, disapproval evident in his voice.

"I know." Quincy wrapped the scarf around her neck and walked to her uncle, kissing him on the cheek before straightening and slipping her hands into the front pockets of her black jacket. "I can't say I trust them not to mess it up. Thursday, then?"

The wrinkles on Uncle Ezekiel's face shifted towards a questioning look. "Will you bring your violin? Play a little for me?"

"Yes," Quincy said. "Send round to The Q if you need me sooner."

"In weather like this, you should be wearing an overcoat. You'll die of the cold, Quincy."

"Perhaps." Quincy turned to leave.

"It is one of the great arts of the human soul," Ezekiel said to himself.

Her hand on the door, Quincy shifted and looked back at her uncle's profile. "What is?"

"Staying with someone. Companionship is one of the great arts of the human soul."

And with those words in her mind, Quincy left her uncle to the companionship of his fire and the pink velvet chairs, slipping down the stairs noiselessly and letting herself out onto the street.

She returned to Gainsford Street, felt the familiar pressure of her key in the front door of The Q, and opened it. Then Quincy walked across the wood floor, slipped behind the counter, and was up the stairs to her matchbox-sized room above the offices of The Q. Quincy unwound her scarf, and laid it over a matchstick chair. Removing her jacket, she opened her creaking armoire and hung it back in its place. Rolling up her shirt sleeves, Quincy walked to her window—a single window that looked down on Gainsford Street—and frowned at the snow.

The Q was to be given away.

If she could not fulfill her uncle's obscure requirements, The Q was to be given away.

On either side of Quincy's window stood two bureaus, tall, with five drawers each, large enough to fit clothing, papers, and what few possessions Quincy found worth keeping. She liked them not for the plebeian practicality they offered but, rather, for the way that, when she pulled herself up on one and rested her feet on the edge of the other, Quincy found herself perched high in her window, watching whatever was passing on the street below. She did so now, feeling the gears of her mind catching, too disjointed by her uncle's words for their usually smooth, oiled rotation.

There was only one thing that could unwind Quincy at such a time, only one thing, that is, besides work and numbers and profit margins. She slid down from the tall bureau, touching the hard heels of her black boots to the floor, and crossed the room, reaching for her worn violin.

CHAPTER TWO:

Arch Enemy

"Mr. Arch." Quincy's tone, when she said his name, consisted of every impatient material in existence. "May we speak in your office?"

Mr. Arch paused mid step, his dark eyes flickering to Quincy's face. He was pale and tired, his handsome face looking almost awful for it. Quincy had decided that a conversation with her newly appointed nuisance was a necessity, as it was now the second of January and she'd already lost a day.

Mr. Arch did not appear to feel the same way. He braced himself before answering, "Indeed, Miss St. Claire." With a stiff bow, he stretched out his hand, turning the knob and pushing the door open before waving towards his office with what she silently accused of being unnecessary flourish.

Gathering up her fountain pen and a pad of cheap, gray paper, Quincy left her stool, walked through the swinging half gate near Fisher's still empty desk, and stepped past the silent solicitor into his office. She halted and looked around. He had—of all things—decorated it. She resisted the desire to snort aloud. When such an exorbitant feat had been accomplished, Quincy had no idea. But here it was: four paintings on the walls, a handsome chair not previously belonging to the original furniture set of the office, and two small busts—one sat on top of Krankgill's antiquated secretary, while the other dour faced individual brooded on the corner of Mr. Arch's desk, the one corner that Quincy could not see from her own perch behind the counter. She wondered if he'd placed it there on purpose.

By the time Quincy had taken stock of his office, Mr. Arch had closed the door behind them and had walked around his desk to his leather chair. "Please." He motioned to the chair opposite the desk from him.

"Who is the man on the secretary?"

The pale Mr. Arch paused, his eyes on Quincy, and—rather slowly, Quincy thought—raised his eyebrows in a hint of surprise at her question. "That would be Lord Crandall, famous poet of Rhysdon."

"And the dour figure encamped on the desk?"

"De Vere, an essayist." When Quincy showed no reaction, Mr. Arch lifted his chin professorially. "His mother was an English aristocrat; his father, a French street painter. He wrote satirical essays about class, human nature, et cetera, et cetera."

Quincy thought De Vere should have had his hair cut before commissioning a bust. As she sat down, Mr. Arch followed suit.

"I assume my uncle has spoken with you?" said Quincy.

"He has." Mr. Arch looked uncomfortable and seemed none too pleased about this emotion. Or, perhaps it was his new watchdog assignment that had turned his face sour.

"I assume he's given you strict instructions that I am not to be told the items on the list."

"Correct," Mr. Arch said, his black eyes on hers.

"And you agreed to it?"

"Ezekiel made it a job requirement," answered Mr. Arch. "If I wanted to keep my post, I had to agree."

"I'm surprised you wanted to keep the post."

Mr. Arch pursed his lips and shifted his shoulders, apparently trying to get more comfortable in his coat, which was, Quincy admitted freely, very well tailored. "Why are you so certain that I would wish to leave?" he asked.

"I've not made things easy for you."

"No, that you certainly have not."

"Blunt."

Mr. Arch squared his gaze on Quincy. "You've always impressed me as a person who prefers a straight answer."

Although Quincy had never trusted in what could not be seen on paper or before her face—invisibilities were, in her mind, always dismissible—she was forced to admit that, as she held his gaze, the tension, the pull of argument, and perhaps a mutual dislike hung so tightly between them that one more turn of the screw might cause the air to snap.

"True," she replied after several seconds had passed. "I do prefer a straight answer. Now, I'm also given to understand that you are the one who decides if I've fulfilled the extent of my uncle's list."

"Yes."

"And I can trust you to not botch this up?"

He looked affronted and gave no verbal answer.

"Very well." Quincy tapped the pad of paper against her knee, making a soft sound, and continued, "My plan is to write out a list everyday of what I have accomplished, and you, at the end of your workday, can assess if I've completed any of the requirements. You will then let me know what was fulfilled before you leave. I'm hoping to wrap up this nonsense as soon as humanly possible."

He smiled, Mr. Arch did, when she had said the word humanly. Despite it being small, a glint of humor on that pale face, Quincy had caught it, noted it in her mind, and then tapped her pad of paper once more against her knee.

"I am afraid," Mr. Arch began, "that this would not fulfill the requirements."

"Why not?" Quincy said, sounding far more patient than she'd thought she'd had the capacity for.

"Ezekiel is very strict in his rules. The requirements will only be counted if I witness the events."

"If you witness the events?" Frowning, Quincy stared Mr. Arch down. "Do you mean to tell me that, until I've fulfilled all twelve requirements, you are to be my persistent companion during the operational hours of The Q?"

He didn't look any happier about this than Quincy felt, and he cleared his throat, indicating there was more to say and that he was not going to say it until she asked.

To the devil with him. "What?" she finally snapped.

"I am under strict command not to aid you beyond any reasonable help, but I will tell you now that you might want to consider my company for other events, not just here in the offices of The Q."

"What?" Quincy leaned forward, setting her elbows on his desk as she glared. "Implying that I should not only have your company all day, the worst kind of shadow, but also string you along with me at other times as well?"

"I am not any happier about this than you are, Miss St. Claire." Mr. Arch's pale face was cold. "It may be hard for you to believe, but I have my own life outside of these offices. So I do not relish spending most of my year as 'the worst kind of shadow' to anybody."

Hearing her own words given back so calmly—flat and chilled— caused Quincy to very nearly regret insulting him to his face.

"It seems the easy solution, then, would be to terminate you from your post, effective immediately," Quincy said.

"That you cannot do."

"Oh, I can't?" She sat up straight, daring a disagreement.

"The contract drawn up for your uncle's experiment clearly states that you cannot fire me or you automatically forfeit all stake and stock in The Q. Effective immediately. If I quit, the same stipulations apply, so you're forced to be civil."

"Never war with lawyers," Quincy muttered, clenching her jaw and slouching back again in the chair. "So, I'm stuck with you?"

"I admit I might stand to gain an odd satisfaction from all of this unpleasantness, Miss St. Claire." He leaned back as he spoke, his fingers playing with the latest model of fountain pen, his shoulders even and stiff as a metal slug of type.

"What's that?"

"Only that I can hardly imagine you do anything besides work at The Q, so I'm mildly curious to see what the famous Quincy St. Claire does in her leisure hours."

He looked half serious. Perhaps even three-fourths serious. The edges of his eyes even moved a hair's breadth upward in challenge.

Quincy guffawed, raised her eyebrows at him, and stood. Turning on her heels, she walked to the door, pulled it open, and closed it behind her, leaving Arch and Crandall and De Vere to themselves.

"This is the best bit of news that's come my way since the New Year," Jade said, grinning over a machine, her hands covered in grease as she finished the simple repair. This wasn't her job, but she helped Spense with the machines anyway, just as Quincy did. "I look forward to sheaths of good stories from this arrangement."

Quincy made a sound of disagreement and watched Jade work. She was tall, her brown hair bound up and out of the way, and her young face sported either a quirky smile or a serious draw of lines, depending on how smoothly the print room ran. Jade was The Q's master typesetter, keeping the mice—the junior typesetters—on task while Spense, a tall, red-headed, thick-armed man, ran the entire printshop.

Preparation for each day's copy of *The Q* began at three in the afternoon. Printing began between eight and ten, depending on the volume, and ran all night. As copies of The Q were printed, dried, and folded, they were sent out on delivery wagons traveling far into the outer counties, and were also sent with messenger boys who loaded up their arms with papers in the back alley to scatter all over the city of Rhysdon. One wagon delivered *The Q* insert for *The Times*.

Jade worked from five p.m. until five a.m., or later, with only the rare day off. Saturday nights she was free—often spending her time doing something with Jack, her husband, who worked all night in a bakery— for Ezekiel had always insisted The Q not run a Sunday edition.

Quincy continued to watch Jade's fingers move as Jade set a line of ornamental type for a special section with which they were experimenting. She then moved on to the front page.

"What did Ezekiel say again?" Jade said, pausing, letter stick in hand. "That it would be good for you?"

"Not in so many words," Quincy replied.

"And you have to work with Mr. Arch?" Jade grinned, then laughed, then went back to work, her quick fingers moving expertly among the cases of type. Quincy watched without really seeing, tapping her fingers in a frustrated cadence along the top of the cases.

"You'll figure it out, you know."

"What?" Quincy looked up, returning from her thoughts.

"You'll figure out the list," Jade stated, "and keep The Q." When Quincy did not answer, Jade shook her head. "Don't lose faith in yourself now, Quincy. Decide that you're going to do it and then do it."

"Yes. Well, I have work to do and so do you. Let's decide to do that. Tell Jack I say hello."

"I will," Jade answered. "Jack said to tell you he wants me to get a day off."

"Tell Jack to mind his own business and leave me to mind mine," Quincy called over her shoulder as she walked back to the stairs and then took them two at a time.

Jade's laugh followed her up the stairs and into the sorting room of The Q.

"Are you certain you're not going to see the old man today?" Fisher asked Quincy on Tuesday.

Fisher had been apprised of both Ezekiel's pending departure from this world and *the experiment* at work come Monday, leaving the offices of The Q immediately to pay Ezekiel a visit. He'd invited Quincy to come then. She'd declined, saying she would go on Thursday as she always did. Now he waited for her to answer his question.

Her pen cried a rather large ink tear onto her report, and she muttered under her breath, hitting the pen soundly against her desk before reaching into the drawer to find a new one.

"You should go soon," Fisher persisted. "Yesterday he didn't look well. Not well at all."

Wrapping her knuckles on the desk, Quincy looked up with a fierce gaze. Fisher was her oldest friend. They'd worked in the foundling factory together, inseparable as they operated the large machines in tandem, and had clung to each other late at night when they were turning inside out from hunger and fear. When Quincy's great-uncle Ezekiel came to find Quincy, to bring her home to raise her, she would not go without Fisher. But Uncle Ezekiel would not go with him.

"I will take you home, and if you still feel the same way in three months time, we will come back for your friend," her uncle had stipulated. It wasn't that Ezekiel wasn't kindhearted; he was. He, Quincy discovered later, did not wish to throw Fisher into a life that he might not want on the whim of a nine-year-old girl that Ezekiel did not yet know, only for her to change her mind ten days down the walk.

Ezekiel had already decided that he would find a home and family for the boy, send him to school, see him taken care of, and see what a doctor could do with Fisher's machine-mangled hand. In fact, as Fisher had told Quincy later, he had been taken in immediately by an older couple in Lester, the town nearest the foundling factory, and had been cleaned and clothed and sent to begin learning his letters during those three months they were apart.

Before Quincy rode away with her great-uncle, she wrapped her thin fingers around Fisher's wrists and promised that she would come back for him.

In the months that followed, Quincy sat at the window of her great-uncle's house every day, silent, waiting, marking the calendar one long-lived day at a time. Finally, they went back for Fisher. Quincy would have always gone back for him.

Their reunion, Ezekiel had claimed later, was one of the most moving scenes of his life. Quincy, wearing breeches and a shirt—as she'd insisted on since he'd found her—had sprung from the carriage just as Fisher had burst out of the door. They'd raced to each other— bones and skin, a flash of a blond hair, a flash of a brown—and when their arms went around each other, they sank to the dirt before the humble house and remained there, knees under their chins, their arms wrapped around each other in every direction, their heads tucked over one another's shoulder. And they did not move for half an hour. When Ezekiel asked Quincy about that moment later, when at fifteen she had such solid footing he knew prying would not dislodge her, she had simply replied, "It was how we slept, how we kept warm."

It was then, on that carriage ride back to Rhysdon, that Uncle Ezekiel finally saw his great-niece for the first time. She took Fisher's hand and, with great animation, told him about the stairs inside Ezekiel's town house: How many there were, how many nails could be seen, how many planks made up each step. That the treads were the color of wood, while the risers were white. That the banister was smooth and had thirty-seven balusters, which meant that there were two point four balusters for every tread. And that to have a similar staircase of one hundred stairs would mean you would need two hundred and forty balusters.

"And how fast do you go when you slide down the banister?" Ezekiel had asked her enthusiastically. Quincy had given him a look of disapproval for his intrusion, but also for his suggestion. She'd blinked her large blue eyes and brushed her blond hair from her face, as if she did not understand why one would slide down the banister.

Fisher had, of course, come home with them and been raised under Ezekiel's roof. He slid down the banister. Quincy did not.

And when Quincy, at fifteen, moved permanently into the old storeroom above the front offices of The Q, Fisher, then sixteen, took his wages and rented a small room in the student's quarter. For, unlike Quincy, Fisher desired to enter the university. That was when Uncle Ezekiel had moved from Linger Wood Street to the posh Half Crown Circle town house.

The three of them, having been thick as any thieves for six years, had each claimed their own territory separate from one another: Ezekiel, to a life fitting the socializing, the performances, and the people that he knew; Fisher, to a serious place of ideas and study; and Quincy, to The Q.

CHAPTER THREE:
Crow, Boy Blue, and Other Affairs

Wednesday morning, Crow came sauntering into the front offices of The Q. He was tall, quite tall, with broad shoulders and a trim waist. A series of meticulously arranged items of clothing denoted his haphazard approach to dress, topped off with a peculiar black coat that fell all the way to the floor and seemed to fit around his person so comfortably that Fisher had once remarked Crow must have been born in the garment. Crow's face was masculine and angled, his voice deep, his accent leaning towards the unknown places of the harbor. He had dark hair, a day's scruff on his jaw, and eyes as murky blue as quay water on a patient day. Each of his smiles held enough charm to cheat a cat out of its mouse. He was Rhysdon's most able smuggler.

"Quincy, my love," Crow greeted her as he walked to the front counter and leaned against it, his elbow resting just beside her report. He smelled as he always did: one third salt, one third soap, and one third something that Quincy had not yet identified, but it was musky and full and good. She never minded when Crow leaned across her counter.

"Crow. What question can I place for you today?"

"If the Crow flies in due course, who's foolish enough to flit circles? Will he never catch it?"

Fisher was watching, disapproving of how far Crow leaned over the counter, disapproving of how Crow's eyes knew Quincy's movements, and disapproving even more of how Crow was the only customer that Quincy never singed with her indifference. Well, she didn't mind Crow's attentions, and she liked to see Fisher flare. It wasn't as if Quincy had ever approved of the girls Fisher would moon over. Once, Fisher had placed a question in the personals section of *The Q* for some feather-brained female at one of the city's finishing schools. And, when Quincy found out, she wouldn't let him live past it. He never placed a question in *The Q* again.

"Crow, with a capital *C*, love," the smuggler corrected as Quincy wrote the question. "I'm a proper noun."

Quincy smiled as she crossed out the lower case letter and scribbled a capital C.

"Constable Catch is on my heels again," Crow explained. "And, when he searches *The Q* for hints and shadows of a smuggling ring— I'll pay for the extra question, of course—I want him to know that this is a present just for him. I believe it is his resolution of the New Year to see my virtuous soul behind bars."

A snort came from Fisher's direction, which Quincy ignored. Crow just raised his eyebrows and grinned. Crow was, Quincy admitted, rather beautiful.

"Capital C it is," she replied to Crow. "You really take pains to make that poor constable's life miserable."

Giving up on his grin, Crow gave Quincy the slow spread of a smile and motioned over his shoulder. "No more than I've seen you take with your solicitor."

Quincy tilted her head, considering, her eyes moving towards Mr. Arch's office. His door was open. He sat at his desk, his back to the street, which put his face in full view of Quincy, even when the door was closed, for it had a glass window. She saw from the set features of his face that he had probably registered the comment and agreed with the smuggler.

"By any way," Crow said as he slapped the counter, "he's tailing me now, Catcher is, so you'll have a visit if I'm not mistaken. Do forgive me." He reached into the pocket of his black coat, slapped a few coins onto the counter, then lifted Quincy's hand to his mouth and kissed it. Crow was also the only person Quincy allowed to touch her without her express permission, because he meant nothing by it and asked nothing for it. "Good day, my love."

He sailed out the door just as a gaggle of young ladies laughed— laughed? giggled—their way into The Q. "Ladies," said Crow, his voice smooth as he held the door open. This set them off in another round of hysterics. Quincy rolled her eyes.

After a few minutes, the young Constable Catch did indeed come into The Q, waiting as patiently as he ever did when he felt he was hot on some pertinent trail to expose the criminal underground of Rhysdon.

Quincy quickly served each young lady, taking down questions, seeing to payments, watching one dark-haired girl with an accent— French?—steal glances in Fisher's direction that were so sweet Quincy was surprised he didn't look up from finding the taste of syrup in his mouth. After the girls were helped, exiting the room in a cluster, all of them holding their Q stubs in their gloved hands—for Q stubs were becoming popular paraphernalia—Constable Catch stepped up to the counter.

"Miss St. Claire." He nodded, holding his hard hat patriotically beneath his arm, his uniform pressed to perfection, as if HRM, the king himself, were to inspect Catch any moment. Or Parliament, at very least.

"Constable Catch," Quincy answered. "Have you come today to place a question?"

"I have come today, Miss St. Claire, to question you regarding the movements of Rhysdon's most renown smuggler, whom I saw with my very eyes leaving these offices just moments ago."

His cheeks were always ruddy when he was on the trail of injustice. Not that Quincy was casual herself about the law. She, and the offices of The Q, were sticklers for its strict adherence: The Q, for reasons of integrity; and Quincy, for reasons of resenting anything that could lead to a lack of freedom. But she liked Crow.

"Crow was, indeed, in the offices of The Q, constable. Now, if you plan to question me, I am afraid that, unless an actual crime has been committed, with proof enough to warrant a breach of customer privacy, I can tell you nothing."

"But everybody knows Crow is a smuggler!" The young constable tugged hard at his jacket and frowned with great passion.

"Alleged smuggler," Quincy countered. "Has he ever gone on the books? Has he ever been proven guilty before the courts?"

"No."

"Well then. When he is, I will be happy to cooperate in any investigation. Until then, the only thing I can do for you, constable, is ask if you would like to place a question."

"No, Miss St. Claire, I would not." He put his helmet on so emphatically Quincy entertained the notion of feeling sorry. She liked him well enough, and she knew that catching Crow would be a career maker. She also knew that his main motivation was the law. But Crow's exploits were all speculation. Crow never even confirmed them to Quincy. And so, by law and by company policy, she was required to keep his privacy.

"Good day, Miss St. Claire."

"Good day, Constable Catch."

He left the offices of The Q looking more than a little dejected and turned right, presumably in the direction of the docks, where he would find no help. Poor Constable Catch.

Quincy laughed aloud, a rare thing, and both Fisher and Mr. Arch looked up from their respective desks at the sound, though neither made a comment.

The only other remarkable thing to happen on Wednesday was another question from Boy Blue. It came in on the heels of one of the Q boys, a straight-lipped, tight-fisted fellow called Spats, who ran not only his own route but also two others for the extra pay. He was always the messenger who brought in anything from Boy Blue. Jade had once cornered the boy, trying to pry whatever information she could about their romantic patron, but Spats would reveal nothing.

"Gainst Q regulations," is all he would say.

"But the question is in-house," Jade argued in response. "The Q is asking who this Boy Blue is."

"Sorry." Spats would shrug. "The only person wiff ability to make me speak is St. Claire, and she's done never asked."

"She hasn't ever asked," Jade corrected. Then he'd slip away before she could cuff him playfully on the ear.

The entire office of The Q was hooked on the malfated romance of Boy Blue and the girl he called Angel. It had been going on for over two years now, and every time a question was sent in by either of them, the entire staff would stop what they were doing and listen. It was worse than any serial story printed in the papers.

"Boy Blue is in for it," Spense would say, shaking his head and scratching his neck with his square fingers. "Boy Blue is in for it bad."

"You don't suppose she's of the upper class, forbidden to even speak to a lowly student?" Rebecca, the cleaning girl would ask, leaning on her broom and gazing around with large hazel eyes and what Quincy considered too desperate of an imagination.

"Hard to say," Jade would answer, studying the question before rewriting it and pinning the original to the board that held nearly every question the two had ever sent to one other. "The clues are there, but there is no definitive direction. At least, it seems to shift right when we think we've worked it left." Everyone would look at each other as if the match were some Shakespearian tragedy waiting to happen. And Fisher would always seem a bit moody after a question that exhibited particular longing or desperation.

Quincy, too, would listen, for she was usually the person Spats brought the question to, but she refrained from ever offering her opinion. The only other person who never spoke up was Mr. Arch. He had been introduced to the lovers three months back, upon his official employment with The Q, and came with the rest of the staff to listen, but he never ventured to speak. Afterward, he would disappear back to his desk and to his work—silent, pale, and dignified. Quincy didn't know whether he'd ever taken the time to read the board of Boy Blue and Angel's past correspondences. She didn't care one way or the other if he had.

So, this Wednesday, when Spats came in the front door at the end of his rounds—the only messenger with enough personal audacity to make a front-door entrance—he moved his eyes to Quincy, slung his gathering pouch around from his back to his side, dug a hand down, and, with the expert practice of one who had sorted through the bag thousands of times, pulled out a carefully folded piece of paper.

"Boy Blue?" Quincy asked, her eyebrows raised.

With a solemn nod, Spats set the question upon Quincy's counter—his eyes barely breaking the plane—and stood, waiting to see what she would do. Fisher came in from the file room and saw Spats standing there.

"Boy Blue?" Fisher asked.

Quincy nodded. "Yes."

Sliding from her stool, Boy Blue's question in hand, Quincy walked back through the sorter, out onto the stairs, and down into the print room, Spats and Fisher at her heels.

Jade, seeing what she called *the unholy trinity* descending, stopped her work and said something that Quincy couldn't hear because of the noise. They had not begun printing yet, as the mice were just setting the first boards, but these were still busy hours, filled with employees shouting, Q boys and sorters running in and out, up and down; and general organized madness.

Quincy held the question up in her hand, between two fingers, and everybody stopped their work to listen. Then she handed the slip to Jade, who lifted it with a definitive pleasure and called everyone's already given attention. Fading back from the crowd, Quincy settled herself on the ancient, one of the presses they kept on the west wall of the large print room. It was a relic but a beautiful machine in its own right. From this position, Quincy could see everyone clearly as Jade unfolded the paper with a sense of drama.

Mr. Arch had also come through the sorter's door and was standing on top of the stairs, leaning over the rail with a modicum of interest on his face.

An extra set of shushing ran through the staff as Jade cleared her throat and began:

"What earthly delights surpass any sweetness
I might have from thee?
What should I obtain of more worth than
thy praise, thy censure even, for it would
bring my face to your mind and you would know me?"

"That's it," Jade said, looking up.

"Read it again," Spense called out, and Jade obliged.

"It's a verse." Jade turned the paper around, showing the quotes. "None of these words are Boy Blue's."

"What verse?" Fisher asked. "Boy Blue never writes anything just because it sounds pretty."

What followed was a series of blank faces as each person looked to their neighbor. No one looked in Quincy's direction. They knew she wouldn't know any better than they did.

"It's Crandall," a voice called down from above. Mr. Arch had an earnestly pleased expression on his face. "Crandall, the greatest of Rhysdon's poets. It's an amateur verse from his *Student* collection and is taken from a conversation between a lost journeyman and a wood nymph. In this verse, the journeyman is pleading with the wood nymph to meet him by a set of falls blessed by the marriage of true lovers."

Everyone, including Quincy, just stared. This oration came so confidently from the mouth of their pale-faced, serious-minded solicitor that it was a trick to believe he was the same person.

"But what happened?" the cleaning girl cried up. "Did she meet him by the falls?"

Mr. Arch entertained a half smile and, with a shake of his head, pulled himself back from the rail and straightened his sleeves by the cuffs. "You will just have to read *The Student* for yourself to find out, won't you?" And with that declaration, he disappeared back through the door into the sorting room.

"Does the verse mean he's hoping to meet Angel in a certain place?" Jade wondered aloud.

General conversation persisted for a few minutes more before Jade declared, as she was pinning the question to Boy Blue's board, that they would find a copy of *The Student* later.

"Fisher can nose around the university," Jade decided. "It's time to return to work."

"Long night ahead," Spense echoed. "We've a high volume, and I want crisp work. The last messenger boy isn't yet in, so it'll be a scramble. Get to your jobs!"

With a wave to Spense and Jade, Quincy slid off the ancient and ascended the stairs, taking them two at a time and thinking about Boy Blue's message. Mr. Arch's professorial debut had been a surprise—and an amusing one at that. He most likely enjoyed knowing something the rest of them did not. She didn't understand any depth beneath the words, so Quincy decided that she would let the rest sort it out and would get back to her reports.

Quincy pushed open the sorting room door, passed through with a nod to Mrs. Graves, and returned to the front office only to see Mr. Arch standing in conversation with the late Q boy. The child's face was tearstained. He looked towards Quincy, and his lower lip shook and pulled down.

Mr. Arch put his hand on the boy's shoulder and told him to go down to Jade, then waited for the child to slip past Quincy and leave the room. He looked at her with regret and announced, "Your Uncle Ezekiel has died."

CHAPTER FOUR:
Funeral Expenses

Uncle Ezekiel had arranged for his services to be held in the Great Rhysdon Cathedral, a spectacle of stained glass windows and gray stone. Quincy sat by herself on the front row. She had tried to insist that Fisher join her.

"I can't Quince," he'd cried when she had asked him to be with her. "I can't. Not in front of all those people. Please don't ask me." And he didn't. He had found himself a place on the rear bench, his eyes red and rimmed and desolate.

The service wasn't particularly long or particularly brief, and Quincy endured. She had worn her best clothing: a jacket and breeches made of the finest materials, clothes far more feminine than anything she wore on a daily basis at The Q. Her own face was drawn and pale, but she did not cry. She did not speak. She sat and waited for the service to end.

More people than Quincy had imagined came to pay their respects. A few of them Quincy knew. Others she remembered meeting at Ezekiel's house on the odd Thursday night. Jade—actually wearing a dress for the occasion—had sidled up beside Quincy just before the service began to whisper that Lady Fothergil, *the* Lady Fothergil, was in attendance. She had listed several other names as well, but Quincy had paid her no mind.

She'd hardly valued her uncle's social calendar when he was alive, valuing it even less so now that he was dead. It wasn't because Quincy didn't care; it was that she did care. She cared about him and how she had lost him and how he had given her everything. More than everything. His loss had shattered the inside of Quincy, more so than she'd anticipated, and she wished desperately that she could join Fisher, mourning on the back row, emotions wild and raw, grief unmeasured by the public observers.

But Quincy hadn't cried since she was six years old. Not since just before she and Fisher had joined lots as children. The last place she would indulge in such a practice now was here, in front of hundreds of people who knew nothing about her and who she cared nothing for. The service neared an end. Something was read. Then the cathedral began to clear.

Ezekiel had left instructions to not have a graveside service, saying that Quincy could say good-bye in the warm, comfortable cathedral. "One can hardly stand at a graveside service in January without an overcoat," Ezekiel had written in his will. The side of Mr. Arch's mouth had drawn up slightly when he'd read that part to Quincy aloud.

A few brave individuals whispered their condolences. Quincy paid them no mind, waiting for the attendees to spill out of the cathedral and leave her alone. When they finally did, Quincy stood before the black casket, hands behind her back, a ruined pile of rusted thoughts and sharp emotions torn up and left in her empty chest. Such it was, Quincy thought, lifting a shoulder. Thank anything no one would disturb her as she stood here.

The guests would be making their way towards Half Crown Circle to take part in a luncheon held there in Ezekiel's honor. This was a Rhysdon tradition, and Quincy was expected to go, to be host for an entire lot of people she could not care less about. Jade had told Quincy to take her time, that the indomitable Mrs. Bulde, Ezekiel's housekeeper, and Bees, his butler, would see things right until Quincy could get there.

So, Quincy stood perfectly still before the casket, systematically distancing herself from every difficult feeling, like sweeping clear the storeroom in the back offices of The Q.

A sob accompanied by an undignified sniffle came at her back, and a hand rested on Quincy's shoulder. She looked up to see Fisher: eyes swollen, face stained from weeping, hair as askew as his necktie.

"He gave me everything; you know that." Fisher sniffed and wiped his nose on his sleeve for lack of remembering not to. "Arch said that Ezekiel even left me an inheritance. An inheritance! Quincy, can you imagine? Nothing so grand as yours, but enough to study, enough to get a house someday and set something by. He gave me everything."

Emotion burned behind Quincy's eyes and in her throat. She nodded in agreement, looking back to the black casket, covered in a cascade of white winter flowers. Fisher put his arm around Quincy and pulled her close. As he clung to her, he began again to cry.

She wasn't sure quite how it happened, but, as Fisher's knees gave out and he went to the floor in tears, Quincy went with him, until she found herself—knees tucked up, her arms wrapped in his, her head resting on his shoulder—feeling the shuddering of his body as he wept for Ezekiel. Only once, Quincy sighed, long and sad; but the sigh had begun to quiver, to quaver, and so she forced it down. The sound was too risky. The emotion too raw.

With a condemnatory fury, Quincy noted that there were more people at the luncheon than had been at the funeral. She walked through the front door, ignoring her role as host completely, and went upstairs into her uncle's favorite drawing room. A fire had been set but the room was empty. Quincy sat in one of her uncle's pink velvet chairs, pulling it closer to the fire—away from anyone who might take it upon themselves to occupy the other chair in an effort to console her—and gazed at the fire. She would wait it out, this open house.

It was not long before guests, food and tea in hand, discovered the comforts of the second floor and began to utilize the upstairs drawing room, the library, and the study, for a settle and chat.

Twice, Mrs. Bulde came to Quincy for instructions. She just waved the old woman off and talked to no one.

A few hours passed, and guests were yet coming and going, arriving and leaving. "Sorry," "how sorry" they were, Quincy heard them say. Most of them wisely kept their distance.

Only after the light had begun to fade and the Bees had stoked Quincy's fire did someone dare sit down in the pink chair beside hers and wait for her to acknowledge his presence. It was Mr. Arch.

"Is there anything I can do for you, Miss St. Claire? Anything I can get?"

"No."

His black eyes picked up the reflection of the firelight as he scrutinized her face. He looked older than she remembered him being. Perhaps it was his funerary clothes. They were very well cut.

"Are you quite certain?" he asked.

Breathing out between her teeth, making an awful sound, Quincy said, "You can turn all these people, who are here only for drinks and sandwiches, into the street. Make them go, make them all leave. I've no doubt there is no one from The Q still enjoying the delights of Uncle Ezekiel's wine cellar, and the rest can go hang."

Silence and a hesitant pause filled the space between them.

"If you really wish me to, I can clear the house for you." When Quincy did not answer, Mr. Arch stood and left the room.

It was not long before a swell of noise could be heard near the front door, and then the last of the conversation spilled out over the steps and was gone.

Mr. Arch returned to inform Quincy that she had the house to herself. "Fisher has gone to his quarters near the university," he reported. "Jade and Spense send their love. The messenger boys have all left with their pockets full of sandwiches and sweet cakes, which should make you happy. And your uncle's friends have been ushered out the front door. You are quite alone."

"Am I?" Quincy pulled her eyes away from the fire and stared at him. Mr. Arch, unsure what to say to that, nodded and placed his hands behind his back.

"I will leave you now as well. Is there anything of urgent attention that you wish me to care for at The Q tomorrow on your behalf?"

"No need. I'll be in the office come morning."

"Surely, Miss St. Claire—"

"Mr. Arch," she spoke the words very slowly, "I will be in the office come morning. You are now free to go."

From the corner of her eye, she saw him hesitate, bow, then disappear. His footsteps could be heard along the hallway and down the stairs. After he exchanged a few words with Bees—no doubt while donning his hat and coat—Mr. Arch was let out into the street.

Quiet. The house was now quiet.

Quincy pushed her chair back into its proper place, closed her eyes, and, without meaning to, fell asleep.

CHAPTER FIVE:
In Memoriam

They ran a special edition of *The Q*, with a biography of Ezekiel and a section where condolences were shared. It was the first edition that had not followed the strict format of questions only. For reasons Quincy could not understand, it became a massively popular edition to collect. And so, they did a second printing, selling it at twice the price.

"If they want a collector's item, they can pay for the inconvenience of it," Quincy grumbled.

The monthly board meeting was an affair of forced mourning. None of these men—the most stupid, self-important collection of men Quincy had ever known—cared for The Q. And, despite what Ezekiel had said, Quincy did. Scanning the table, she corrected herself. Haskins cared, and Vicks, for they were the old guard. Waits cared as well. But the others were middle-aged men who served on the board without, what Quincy considered to be, a single valuable thought in their heads.

Ezekiel had always run these meetings, and now it was Quincy who sat at the end of the long table. They didn't meet at the offices of The Q but, rather, in a building several blocks up from Gainsford Street. Quincy liked it that way. It kept idle hands out of her day-to-day operations.

She was not as charming as her uncle. Rather, she came in on the hour with her portfolio in hand, full of reports, of profits, of stock increases. Quincy began the meeting in a businesslike tone, and that is where she ended it. When it came time for questions, the board felt she had covered it so thoroughly and militantly that none of them needed any further discussion. They knew where The Q was, they knew where The Q was heading, and they could hardly think of anything to say. Only Rutherford and Levins, men whose methods had always run against Quincy's grain, exchanged a long glance and whispered to each other as Quincy packed up the materials of her presentation and marched from the room. Mr. Arch, who had silently attended and taken notes, followed.

January ended, but condolences continued to be sent throughout the first weeks of February. Quincy banned flowers from the front offices. So Mr. Arch placed them in the printing shop, the sorter, and in his own office without complaint. She mumbled that she needed a solicitor, not a florist. He only raised an eyebrow and then disappeared into his office with the latest delivery of white lilies.

Quincy had not yet fulfilled a single requirement on her uncle's list, despite the annoying presence of Mr. Arch. He followed her everywhere—on every errand, to every meeting. Each time Quincy stepped away from her counter, it felt like he was there, silent, waiting, flicking his eyes in silent disapproval as she stormed around The Q. He'd also developed a chest cold and a cough, which Quincy felt was inconsiderate. She wasn't in the mood.

Fisher hid at his own desk, went about his work, and disappeared promptly at six each night. Jade and Spense kept the print room running efficiently, as they always had. Crow stopped by one evening, just before close, to offer his condolences. He was sincere. It was the only time he did not call her love. It was also the only time he did not smile. Quincy was thankful for that. She could not find her balance or her bearings as it was, and pity-filled smiles were just the sort of thing that knocked her off her already shaken routine.

But mid-February brought the city of Rhysdon to a thaw. The snow was melting, leaving the city wet, and sunlight was falling onto the sidewalks. Much to the relief of the staff, Quincy began to thaw as well. She began to feel a touch more like herself. She could think without feeling angry. She was intellectually sharp. She gave even more energy into the business of running The Q. Her mind was spinning; her focus, well oiled; and her vision for The Q, as limitless as it had ever been.

Occasionally, Mr. Arch indicated that Quincy would never keep The Q if she didn't begin to do things differently. Quincy would either glare at him so fiercely that it would send him—silent disapproval and all—back into his office or she would throw a harsh string of words that were so severe he would have no choice but to disappear for an hour to keep his composure.

Mr. Arch always came back, although Quincy told herself that she wished he wouldn't. But if he didn't come back, she wouldn't keep The Q. She had poured over the legal document that outlined *the experiment* thoroughly enough. There was no way around it; there were no loopholes; there was nothing to bend or to work with. Mr. Arch himself had drawn up the contract, and it was as tight as anything Quincy had ever seen. This did not improve relations in the front offices of The Q.

One day, Fisher had come in with a small white flag, fashioned to stand up on the corner of his desk.

Mr. Arch did not smile when he saw it. Neither did Quincy.

———

It was a welcome day when the mystery of Boy Blue was again offered up as pleasant distraction for the staff. February had dipped in temperature again for a solid week, but on the evening of the twenty-fifth, just before close, a beautiful young woman—large amber eyes, brown curls falling from beneath her hood, her cheeks wide and rose blushed—entered The Q to place a question. Her voice was soft, her manner likewise; from her clothing, Quincy could not tell if she were rich or middle class, well bred or a native beauty born below her station. But, when Quincy asked for her question, she replied with a string of words that caused Fisher to drop his pen and stare.

"Why did you never come?" was her question, and it was to be signed *Angel*.

Quincy paused, her eyes glancing up towards the face of the young woman, before she finished writing the question. Fisher stared, his mouth open. Even Mr. Arch had paused in his work, and Quincy could see through his doorway that he was watching the front desk.

"Is that correct?" Quincy turned the Q slip around, and the young woman looked at the words in black and white before her. Angel's eyes rimmed with tears.

"Yes."

"Very well." Quincy finished filling out the Q slip, took payment, gave the girl her Q stub, and watched as Angel retreated noiselessly onto Gainsford Street. Once the door was closed, Fisher let out a whistle and Mr. Arch came to the doorway of his office, leaning against the doorjamb. Quincy sat, looking at the words before her.

Like clockwork, Jade came in from the sorting room. "Question on the services—" She paused, seeing the three of them frozen in place. "Oh, please don't tell me we've had another death. I can't handle working in this morgue one more day as it is."

Quincy moved the Q slip across the counter, and Jade stepped up, hands on her hips, to take a look. She read it once, picked it up, and read it through again.

"*She* came in just now? She came in *personally* to deliver the question?"

Quincy nodded.

"Poor Boy Blue," said Jade. "What must have happened?"

"She looked heartbroken," Fisher replied. "I want to ring the boy's neck."

"But what if something happened?" Jade defended. "What if he's sick or injured? Or worse?"

Nothing was said for another minute, no one moved, until Quincy slipped off her stool, walked around Jade through the swinging half gate, and turned the locks on The Q's front door. Six o'clock. Closing time.

"Better get these last questions to press, Jade," Quincy said, handing

Jade a stack from the final hours of business.

Jade nodded, still staring at the Q slip as her hand took the stack of questions from Quincy.

"Was she pretty?" Jade asked when she finally looked up.

"Beautiful," Fisher replied reverently.

"If they end things now," Jade threatened, her voice turning hard, "I'm not coming to work for a month."

"Amen," Fisher breathed out, leaning back in his chair.

Quincy half frowned and, after Jade had returned back to the print room, set about straightening up her counter and working out the reports for the day. Mr. Arch stayed in his doorframe a moment longer, watching, before returning to his own desk.

Uncle Ezekiel would have been heartbroken. Quincy thought it strange that she half minded herself.

CHAPTER SIX:

A Smuggler, Quincy?

The first of March was a welcome thing. The sun was fully shining, and the last of the snow had disappeared the day before, leaving the entire city in hope of spring. Mr. Arch sat in a chair before Fisher's desk, going over a long list of legal reports and contracts that needed preparation for the next board meeting, and Quincy sat at her counter, experiencing something that she didn't think she had ever felt in her life: restlessness.

It was under these circumstances that Crow sauntered in, as fresh as any sea breeze.

"I've been gone several weeks now," he offered to Quincy without her having asked. "Did you miss me?"

Pausing, Quincy shrugged. "I noticed you hadn't come in, that you'd sent one of your cronies, if that counts for anything."

"I'll take it," Crow laughed and then paused, his head tilting to one side. "Come out tonight with me, love. You look a bit overdue for it."

"What's your question, Crow?" Quincy did not investigate his invitation further, though her tone wasn't sharp.

"Nothing doing, love? Well." Crow leaned across the counter. "My question this morning is, 'Can a man love a woman without losing his soul?'"

"Probably not," Quincy quipped as she took down his question, her fountain pen jittering against the paper. She cursed, gaining a disapproving look from Fisher, and shook the pen until the ink ran smooth.

Crow laughed again. "I'll be at The Nest tonight, if you change your mind."

Fisher mumbled something under his breath—about guttersnipe, low-down scoundrels—which only gave Quincy the ammunition to aim and fire.

"I might," Quincy said, looking up at Crow. "It's been months since I've taken a night off, and with spring coming I could use an evening's entertainment."

Fisher's mouth fell open in full accusation. Quincy had never taken a night off, and never once had she ever desired an evening's entertainment. And he knew it.

"Good girl." Crow grinned, slapped a coin on the desk, pulled at his lapels, and turned towards the door. Mr. Arch and Fisher both followed the smuggler's swagger with their eyes as he slipped onto the street, his hands in his pockets.

Fisher's glare was soon transferred to Quincy. "Walking with a smuggler, Quincy? Don't even think about it."

But Mr. Arch leaned back obliquely, yet comfortably, in his chair, one foot lifted and crossed against his knee at the ankle, looking on with an expression of zero interest.

"Really, Fisher." Quincy threw Crow's question into the basket. "He's nothing I couldn't handle."

The bell on the door sounded, and a rush of noise entered from the street with a middle-aged woman.

"How can I help you," Quincy asked professionally.

"I've a question to place, for tomorrow's *Q*, if I'm not too late."

Fisher's glare returned toward his work. Mr. Arch's eyes flickered to Quincy once more.

The Nest was half tucked underneath a salt-ridden wharf. A rowdy cheer came from inside each time the door swung wide. Quincy entered, shouldering herself through the crowd, hands in her pockets, hat down, pressing into the familiar jostle and method of the low streets. Rude laughter and the scent of too many bodies filled the space, but Quincy didn't mind. She'd grown up scavenging along underbelly roads before being hauled off to the foundling factory.

A song about something unintelligible was ending just as Quincy pushed through the crowd, half looking for Crow, half considering never telling him that she'd come. The patrons of The Nest began to chant something she couldn't at first understand. She turned her ear towards it in concentration. There it was. She caught the anthem. The old man who had led the last song was standing atop a table, a drink in hand, chanting along with the group, "We want Crow! Crow! Crow!"

As if from nowhere, as if it were a miraculous appearance of the king himself, Crow materialized in the crowd and stepped onto a bench, then up onto the table beside the old man. A roar filled the tavern as the two of them began to string out a long introduction to a song that Quincy had never heard before. Soon, a violin struck up a tune, and the entire throng inside The Nest began to clap and to keep time against stools and benches and wooden floorboards.

It was a call-and-response song, with Crow and his friend tossing words back and forth between them only to welcome in the entire tavern for the chorus. Singing out and hearing their words echoed back, shaking the walls and their mugs of ale, their voices created a spectacular exhibition of noise. Quincy had pulled herself back, sitting atop a group of barrels in the corner nearest the door, one knee pulled up to her chin, the other dangling off the side. No one paid her much mind, which was its own relief. Anonymity suited Quincy; she knew how to keep it close.

The song ran through its verses, the entire tavern ringing with it, and Quincy found herself smiling as she sat, half hunched, half leaning against the wall, her fingers tapping against the worn wooden sides of the barrel. Crow was a natural performer. He sang the words with heart, an ironic smile, and an ability to draw out the crowd while leaving them wanting more of his presence.

When it was over and a cheer went up, Crow began to make his way off the table, laughing, calling out insults to those around him. As he stepped down to the bench and then to the floor, he caught sight of Quincy in the corner.

"St. Claire!" He passed through the crowd towards Quincy's temporary strong hold, pushing off a few eager friends and untangling himself from a young lady who was trying to catch his attention. "Miss St. Claire! You came." He grinned at her. "I just lost a sack of jabs, for I'd bet against you."

"Crow." Quincy tilted her head with the jaunty nod of a practiced street urchin. As Quincy slid from the barrel to the floor, the smuggler caught her by the arm and steered her through the press of The Nest's patrons to an empty back table with built-in benches. He motioned for her to take her seat, and rather than sitting opposite her, Crow slid in next to Quincy, his arm settling about her shoulders.

"Welcome to The Nest, finest of my establishments."

"Most legal of your establishments, I would guess," said Quincy.

"I wouldn't go that far." Crow grinned, hunching one shoulder down protectively, his height blocking Quincy from his riffraff customers. "Drink, love?"

And before Quincy could respond, Crow had already waved his hand and two drinks appeared, slamming onto the table. Crow grabbed one by the handle and took a long swig.

"Your genius concoction of a business saves me bundles on my overhead, darling. You can have free drinks anytime."

"That wouldn't sit well on the ledgers," replied Quincy.

"Is that your girl now, Crow?" someone yelled from across the room, and Crow tossed a look in their direction.

"Got a rich one, Crow?"

"She's my girl. Keep off." Crow turned back to Quincy with an apologetic look, "Sorry, love. I never said my patrons had manners."

Quincy shrugged and took a polite sip from the large glass before her. She liked Crow. She always had. Their friendship was comfortable, and although she didn't favor his choices in company or profession, there were worse.

"When do we marry?" he asked her from habit. The invitation had been offered half a dozen times since Quincy was sixteen.

"Once you start making as much money as I do."

Laughter came from a few of Crow's companions seated nearby.

"I'm closer than you might think, darling," Crow lowered his voice so only she could hear. "Closer than you might think."

"I'm not worried."

Crow laughed and kissed Quincy on the cheek before she could duck away. "You should be."

Grinning at his antics, Quincy began to shake Crow off. But, before she could, someone cleared his throat. Quincy looked up to see Constable Catch standing at the end of the table, his face red with prudish irritation as he stared down at Crow. And at Quincy.

"Catcher!" Crow lifted his mug towards the man. "What a pleasure to see you here. Sit now, have a drink with me and my friend."

"Miss. St. Claire." Constable Catch's polite nod was not very polite. "I admit I am a little surprised to see you here."

"Crow invited me down to celebrate the first of the month," Quincy replied. Still tasting the flavor of orphan, brought out by her expedition to The Nest, she leaned back and leveled a challenge at the young constable's face. "Last time I checked, there was nothing illegal in taking a night off of work and sitting down with a friend."

Catch pressed his mouth together and gave it a quick, irritated twitch to the left. The redness of his face now exceeded his usually ruddy expression. "I can't say you have chosen a very wise companion for such exploits if you value your good name or your reputation."

Quincy snorted, and Crow laughed.

"Catcher." Crow stifled his joviality as best he could, clearly enjoying the attention he was now drawing from the tavern. "Sit. Enjoy yourself. Let Miss St. Claire worry about her own reputation. Besides, whose to know, unless you spread the news yourself?"

Constable Catch pulled at the bottom of his uniform, and when he answered, his words sounded as if they'd been starched. "No thank you. I have simply come to inform you that we have found a lead that may sink your entire operation. If you value your life, or your freedom, I would recommend you come forth to lay claim on the merciful side of the law before justice is done."

A round of applause broke out when Catch had finished his speech, and Quincy felt sorry for the constable. Men lined up to shake his hand, saying how fine his words were, how perfect his articulation, asking if he would, indeed, be printing a circular of such exalted sentiments? Crow didn't take part in this charade but, rather, settled into the bench, the back of a smile on his face, obvious thoughts running through his eyes. Although, it was not long before he put an end to it.

"Thank you for your visit, constable. But now, I'm afraid I am quite busy." Crow raised a glass in signal, and before the constable could be certain of anything, he found himself being led out of the tavern in a friendly, yet definitive way. Waving off his friends gathered around the table, a bit of space began to form around Crow and Quincy, leaving them to private conversation.

"Do you think he really has anything on you?" Quincy asked.

Crow shrugged. "Nothing to worry about as of yet. But I might have to search my lines and make sure I've not a slicker in the group, ready to rat on me." He paused and turned towards Quincy virtuously. "That is to say, only if there was something illegal about my line of work."

"Do you enjoy it?" Quincy asked, pushing her fingertips against the worn, gouged corner of the table.

"Yeah." Crow ran his fingers along his jaw. "I enjoy my work."

"The adventure of it?"

"The adventure, yes. The challenge. The way you never know one day to the next. Ah, but I can see on your face that you wouldn't like that. You, Quincy, need the machine. You need the stability, the organization, your numbers and presses. You need The Q."

Quincy lifted one shoulder into a shrug. "I survived before I had The Q."

"Survived being the operative word. But were you living, love?"

Getting the sense that he'd heard bits and pieces of her story, Quincy shifted under his arm, setting her back against the wall, pulling her knees up before her, boots resting on the bench, facing Crow. "Yes. I was living. Some things are more or less the same. Besides, I find dreams to be overrated."

Crow took another drink and shook his head, in part disagreement, in part amusement, and in part worry. He seemed to do everything in threes.

"I disagree with you there, Miss St. Claire."

"Why?"

"Because dreams are what stretch you to find more, to be a better person, if you will."

Arching her eyebrows, Quincy found her face falling into a grin. "Did I just hear you say the words *to be a better person?*"

Crow dropped the humor in his face like an anchor and sat watching Quincy a long while. "What?" his deep voice challenged. "You don't think I can do it?"

It caught Quincy off her guard that he actually cared about improving his character and that he seemed to care what she thought about the idea.

"I didn't mean that," Quincy defended. "Of course I do, but—" She paused before continuing, "What is it you want, anyway? I mean, to expand your business? Triple the income? Buy yourself a castle in the south of Spain and leave Constable Catch endlessly running in circles?"

"Is that all improvement would be to you?" Crow's eyes narrowed as he surveyed Quincy's face. "Is that the pinnacle of where you would like to be?"

"Is there anything wrong with it?"

"No." Crow shook his head and shifted so he was facing Quincy straight on. "But is there anything right with it, love? Now, that's another question."

Flaring a bit and feeling self-admittedly curious, Quincy pressed him again. "What, then, is it you're ultimately looking for?"

"More than this." He laughed and took a drink, waving his hand in a combination of grace and foolishness through the air. "I've done it all, Quincy: the adventure, the danger, a riot here, a riot there. I've friends tucked round about, most of them none too real, but brash enough. And for a while, that suits me fine, but—" He paused. "How do I say this? I know my grandmother was the happiest woman I've ever known, and she was poor enough to keep the dirt sweepings in her cottage in case she, or anybody else, might need them someday. So, then, what did she have that I don't?"

Quincy waited for the answer to his question.

"Can't yet figure," Crow moved his knuckles against his lips, "but it's got something to do with other people, I'll tell you what."

"Other people," Quincy could hear the disgust in her own voice, "are the most unreliable investment one could make. It's a fool's game. That's how they would call it down at the exchange."

"Well, I'm friends with a smuggler chap who also has a bit of life experience, and you know what he says?" Crow lifted his glass as if he were proposing a toast. "The greatest risk can bring in the greatest haul." Then he made a mock toast with an invisible glass and finished the contents of his own in one solid draught.

CHAPTER SEVEN:

Q is for The Q

The following morning, Fisher was what Quincy termed *an awful nightmare*. He barreled into the offices first thing, stopping before her desk, ready to haunt.

"You went, didn't you?"

"I never knew The Nest could be such a good time," Quincy replied without looking at him.

Something slammed—Quincy did not look up to see what—and Fisher settled into his desk, making his presence so loud that she not only pitied herself but even felt sorry for the silent Mr. Arch, who deliberately closed his door only an hour into the day.

Quincy ignored Fisher's temper, and he in turn flirted with the gaggle of girls that had been in before. One particular beauty with a French accent, who had eyed him each time she came in, spent more than a few minutes in nauseating overtures with Fisher. Quincy filled out the girl's question with a singeing but professional glare, handing back the Q stub like the girl was the devil and Quincy was St. Peter at the gate.

This was how every morning went for the next two weeks. Not that the French girl came in each morning. She had appeared only once more, and Fisher had asked her name—it was Madeleine. But he couldn't forgive Quincy for "being so foolhardy," for "caring so little for her reputation," for "doing things in sheer stubborn spite." In return,

Quincy shut Fisher out, spending more time than necessary in the print rooms with Jade.

Just after midmorning, on the fifteenth of March, when Quincy could no longer handle the seething sentiments coming from her oldest compatriot, she decided to make a visit to Montjoy, the artist with whom she had collaborated on her unique marketing techniques. Montjoy had some new stylized *Qs*, a layout idea, and other random paraphernalia that he wanted Quincy to see for herself.

"Stop by anytime in the next week," he had told her confidently when he'd dropped in at The Q the week before. "I'm in office, and I think you'll take to the new ideas. They are, to put it simply, the most brilliant work to be seen in all of Europe." Quincy had looked up, amused. Montjoy was the best, and he simply had no compunction declaring the fact.

So, with a line to Fisher to mind the front desk, Quincy donned her jacket, shooting a glance at Mr. Arch with the nonverbal cue that she was leaving if he intended to tag along. He settled his desk and followed. Then Quincy, with her worst kind of shadow in tow, headed uptown and away from the inquisition of the front office.

Spring was spare but not shy. It had welcomed in the sun and sent rare patches of flowers shooting up bravely in the throng of the city. Many of the trees in Rhysdon's parks were also beginning to leaf out into a lacy cloud of green so cheery that even Quincy—who was accustomed to thinking about walking only as a means to an end or as a means to calm herself down before someone else came to an end— looked about her and came close to granting the walk some kind of virtue in itself. This lapse of mechanical judgment didn't last long, though, and soon she was reviewing everything she'd last discussed with Montjoy, forgetting, as she often did, that Mr. Arch even followed her at all.

"No need to come up," Quincy told him when they arrived at the tall building on High Queen's Street, where Montjoy's offices were. "Unless one of your requirements is tied to the process of looking over a possible new typeface?"

Mr. Arch shook his head and looked around. "I'll wait there." He pointed to a bench in the park across the street. "There was a place on the corner where one could procure a paper, was there not? That will keep me company enough."

"Most people simply *get* or *buy* a paper," Quincy said. "Why you feel it necessary to *procure* one is beyond me."

As was his custom, Mr. Arch ignored her comment and went his way as she went hers.

Montjoy had created a masterpiece—or so he spent the next hour trying to convince Quincy. His work was, as Quincy freely admitted, very good. Massively good. Many of the products he'd envisioned were sure to be successful. The brilliance behind his typography was, well, the best that Rhysdon had to offer. He was already splitting half his time in Paris, and Quincy expected London to follow suit.

"Yes, Montjoy, yes," Quincy found herself saying more than once. "This new concept is stunning, but I'm coming at this from a practical angle. The work you've done for The Q that is already in existence is working well. Nothing, in fact, could presently be better. Why then would I pay you twice or three times that amount to create this identity, which, yes, while it would be an incredible form of—" Quincy paused, "*art*, would not necessarily increase our sales? We are a business, not a museum. At The Q, art cannot exist simply for art's sake."

Montjoy's face fell, and he tucked his ideas into his portfolio, disbelief evident on his face. "I just don't understand, Miss St. Claire. If you, of all people, can reach a new level of excellence, why don't you?"

"The excellence I seek, Mr. Montjoy, is to run the perfect business. This, as of yet, does not help me get closer to that goal. Don't throw it away or burn it in some melancholy rant—Isn't that what you artists do?—no, keep it in my file. There may be a need for it someday. Now," Quincy said, waving her hand, "I do like the additional *Qs* you've produced for our product line. You said you had a new design that you'd placed on a teacup? Is the prototype at hand?"

"Yes," Montjoy said, recovering a little of his enthusiasm. "It's taken from an old Egyptian motif. I thought it would start the season as a big hit, especially if done in gold, with perhaps a silver option as well. The Q could stand to make a decent profit from it."

He went into a back room and emerged with a small cup in hand. It sported the most incredible *Q* Quincy had ever seen.

She took the cup in her hands. "Is that a sphinx inside the lettering?"

"Only the hint of one," Montjoy said, pleased with himself. "It looks beautiful monogrammed on tea towels, and all the other products I've designed, as well as on stationary for personalized Q slips. I may have already run a jobber's worth for your approval."

The letter had not been made with gold or silver for the prototype but rather with black, a shiny black against the fine bone white. Quincy actually took a fancy to it.

"I'd like to show Fisher, and Jade, to see what they think. Would you mind if I took this with me?"

"It's yours." Montjoy took the prototype from Quincy's hand and wrapped it in a piece of paper, finishing the job with a bit of string.

"Good work," Quincy nodded with a frown. "I like the new ideas for the merchandise you mentioned earlier, not just the tea towels but the calendar especially. And the ladies' fans? I never would have thought. It makes perfect sense, considering *The Q* is maintaining its reign of all things in trend. Keep your pet project tucked away."

When Quincy stepped back out onto the street, she blinked in the bare spring light and saw Mr. Arch sitting across the street on a bench at the edge of the park, reading his *procured* newspaper. His salary, Quincy decided, was too exorbitant for the work he did.

Crossing the street, prototype in hand, she nodded to Mr. Arch as he looked up, folded his paper, and tucked it under his arm.

"Finished?" he asked.

"Yes," Quincy said, and for some reason, she unwrapped the cup and showed it to him. "Montjoy has worked out some new products for The Q. This is his—"

"An Egyptian motif." Mr. Arch stood and took it from her hand, inspecting the cup. "It's a bit brilliant: not currently in vogue but never considered out. He does beautiful work, this Mr. Montjoy." Mr. Arch handed the cup back. "Make it expensive. The upper classes always like reminders of toppled empires they consider their peers, and the vine climbers will spend the extra money to be what they are not. I think you'll find success."

"Hmmm." Quincy shrugged, wrapped the cup again, then looked around her. "Let's cut through the park. It'll be faster."

"I can carry that if you would like," Mr. Arch offered.

Handing the cup over without much of a second thought, Quincy struck out across the street and into the park.

Mr. Arch followed, returning to his wordless self only after saying, "Spring is a statement season, even in the city."

Quincy jerked her head towards him then forced her eyes back to the pavement, trying to pay as little attention to him and to spring as possible, despite the feathery haze of green and the windswept piles of yellow pollen that gathered into light pockets, strewn along the wide brick walks like lace. Just as Quincy had stuck her hands into her pockets and set her shoulders in a manner conducive to thinking through the numbers of the day, Mr. Arch sneezed.

"Pardon," he said, his apology light and quick, given before Quincy could even remember that it was customary for people to utter *health* or *blessings* when someone sneezed. It was also customary, Quincy recalled, to inquire if he was feeling well. She did neither of these and attempted to settle back into her mind.

As Quincy began to move the numbers around, a butterfly—a white, light-winged, spring-wind sort of butterfly—flitted before her face. Quincy brushed her hand through its circles and kept walking. The butterfly, for whatever reason, was not deterred. After one more loop about Quincy's head, it settled itself on the lapel of her jacket.

"Bother," she muttered. Quincy tried to brush it away as she walked, but the butterfly hopped effectively to her shoulder. A few more attempts, and she gave up, placing her hands back into her pockets and blowing at a stray piece of blond hair that had fallen into her eyes.

Mr. Arch had noticed her attempts to dislodge the portable display of the season. And when it stubbornly positioned itself on the back of Quincy's shoulder, he did something that she had rarely seen him do before, he smiled. Quincy caught the expression by accident and thought it strange that, when he smiled, he appeared to be simultaneously younger and older.

The butterfly remained on Quincy's shoulder the length of the avenue, and not until they turned down Queen's Street did it decide she was not a hansom cab. With one swirl of wings, it disappeared across the busy street towards an establishment boasting rows of potted pansies.

"Congratulations, Miss St. Claire." Mr. Arch sneezed again, asking her pardon just as he coughed. His lungs rattled enough for Quincy to take notice that his cold had not yet vacated, the air having to scrape an uneven surface before it could come out of his lungs.

"Congratulations for what?" she asked as they stopped at the corner, waiting for an opening to cross Prince Street and continue down Queen's.

Once Mr. Arch recovered a clear voice, he gave her an answer. "You have successfully fulfilled, albeit accidentally, an item from your uncle's list."

Quincy halted abruptly. Mr. Arch, watching her face, stopped beside her.

"What?" She snapped the word at him like a whip, and he blinked from the invisible assault.

"You caught a butterfly," said Mr. Arch. "Or, rather, it caught you, but I deem it a success either way. You're one twelfth closer to keeping The Q."

"Do you mean to tell me that this *list* is made up of absurd, nonsensical items such as catching butterflies?"

The idea was impossible. Farcical even. If her uncle had expected her to run all over Rhysdon making a fool of herself, then he could give the key, lock, stock, and barrel, to that grasping, greedy board of directors, and they could all go hang.

The rest of the walk back to The Q did not register in Quincy's mind as she was busy berating every stupid thought in the world. Mr. Arch remained silent—a great wisdom, Quincy thought—and, when they returned to the office, Quincy passed the front counter, where Fisher sat, and directly disappeared up the narrow stairs to her matchbox.

Once entrenched in her room, emotions twisting and rising like a stubborn tide, she kicked her chair. It slid several inches across the floor, making an uncomfortable sound. Quincy looked around for another thing to kick. Of all the ridiculous—! What did she care for butterflies? Quincy was not her uncle, she did not need to prove to him that she had a heart, and, at that moment, she desired to throw her uncle's games into the gutter.

Why? Why must it be tied to The Q? If she could walk away, she would; her pride demanded at least that much from her. But Quincy knew that her heart beat with the rhythm of the presses in the back room, that her blood ran black with ink, and that her mind filled with reams of numbers and projections and plans. The Q was Quincy's only vital organ, so she would play the game. Not humbly, no. Quincy would fight. She would fight tooth and nail, and she would satisfy the demands of this experiment and win. And, once The Q was hers, she would fire Mr. Arch before the day was out. Good riddance.

Quincy paced, muttering and warring for what must have been hours. Finally, she heard Mr. Arch and Fisher exchange a few words. Then there was a slight shuffle of feet across the room. The sound of someone locking the front door echoed up her stairwell. She looked at her pocket watch; six o'clock and the offices were now closed.

At some point, Quincy had removed her jacket and thrown it across her narrow bed, rolling up her white shirtsleeves as she paced. She had also, rather ravenously, eaten away nine of her ten fingernails, feeling the sharp slivers of nail with her tongue just before she sent them out onto the floor with a burst of air.

Quincy reclaimed her chair from its temporary diaspora across the room and tried to sit at her table but to no avail. Her heart pounded stubbornly, angry and strained. No, sitting would not do. Neither would perching beside the window. And walking out through the streets sounded, well, awful. So she did the only thing that could draw her wound-up emotions into some semblance of peaceful control: she took her violin out of its case.

It was old, and the worn wood had a distinctly bleached quality that Quincy could not explain. She'd found it in a pawnshop three streets up from the dock. It looked dry and felt forgotten, but the instrument gave a rich, mellow sound despite it all. Lifting the instrument in her hands, Quincy ran her fingers across the strings, listening to the notes rise quietly into the still room. She turned the pegs until each string was perfectly in tune. Then she tucked the instrument under her arm as she picked up the bow and tightened it before setting setting the violin beneath her chin and touching the bow to its strings.

The music spread out of the *f*-shaped holes, spilling over the floor, easing and pulling, and Quincy gave herself to the personality of the sound. It was safe. It was straightforward.

The sound of the violin was all the humanity that Quincy could stand.

CHAPTER EIGHT:
Forgive Me? - Boy Blue

Fisher arrived early the following morning. Of course, Quincy was already working when he came in, and she gave him a sound of acknowledgement, although she didn't look up. She was reviewing distribution numbers when a branch slapped down over her counter: the young, long, muted green leaves obscuring the work beneath her. Setting her lips in a straight line, Quincy looked up at Fisher's face.

"It's an olive branch," Fisher said, tilting his head to the side, undeterred—as he had always been—by Quincy's glare.

"Meaning?"

"You need to read more." Fisher walked to his desk, lifting his heavy satchel from off his shoulder with a groan, before he settled himself for the day. "It means," he supplied a few minutes later, after Quincy had pushed the olive branch aside and continued her work, "a call for peace."

"It's unfair of you to be angry if I choose to spend time with Crow."

"How am I supposed to feel, Quince? You're the closest thing I have to family. And Crow is hardly the kind of man I want for you."

Quincy felt grateful and put off simultaneously. "Three sips of drink and a conversation hardly constitute a standing relationship, Fisher."

"I would be much happier if neither were taking place."

"I'll do what I like." Her words sounded like a piston releasing, but they deflated her defensive position, and Quincy put down her pen and turned towards Fisher. "Don't worry. I've got my head on. Crow and I are simply friends. But I appreciate that you care." She doled out a half smile, "Who knows, eloping with a smuggler might be on Uncle Ezekiel's list."

With a friendly scowl, he signified that he did not appreciate the joke. Then Fisher leaned back in his chair, his hands behind his head, as Quincy told him about the butterfly.

"You had to catch a butterfly?"

"Yes. Though, in reality, one caught me. Mr. Arch magnanimously counted the occurrence nevertheless."

A smile graced Fisher's face, and he looked like his old self, his chin jutting out in pleasure, his dark blue eyes catching the sparkle of the light off the street.

"I was wondering if that was the angle Ezekiel would come from. My curiosity has been renewed."

"Renewed is not the word I would use." Quincy leaned an elbow on her desk.

The door opened, and Mr. Arch stepped in, tucking his key back into his pocket. His eyes traveled to the olive branch on the front desk and then to Fisher and Quincy.

"Morning, Arch," Fisher said.

Quincy nodded a greeting but said nothing.

"Good morning, Miss St. Claire, Fisher." His mouth hovered above a smile as he noted the branch again before stepping into his office to begin his work.

———

Spense and Quincy were up to their elbows in a broken press when Jade sauntered up, newspaper in hand.

"Have you seen this?" Jade asked.

Wiping her hands on a rag, Quincy brushed her blond hair back from her forehead with her arm and took the newspaper from Jade's outstretched hand. It was a copycat version of *The Q*.

"*The Question Daily*," Quincy read the title aloud. Spense snorted and looked over Quincy's shoulder at the poorly dressed imposter. It was a mess, ill planned and unprofessional.

"Where was this circulating?" Quincy asked.

"One of the boys brought it up from Lester," Jade answered. "They've run the whole printing on a jobber from the look of it."

"Shoddy bit of work for certain," Spense grumbled, turning back to his press.

"Is it anything we need to worry about?" Jade asked, hands on her hips, standing with her weight on one leg.

"We've seen it before," Quincy dismissed. "As if any threat could come from Lester. But I'll check with Mr. Arch, just in case."

Jade grinned. "You said that as if you actually had faith in the man's abilities."

"I wouldn't take it that far." Quincy set the newspaper on the press, finished cleaning her hands as best she could, and then grabbing the copycat product, pushed herself through the mice, up the stairs, and into the front office.

Mr. Arch was standing before Fisher's desk—discussing something useless, Quincy surmised—when she came in from the sorting room. He glanced at her face a moment before his eyes strayed to her ink-stained hands and grease-marked shirt. "You fix the presses yourself?"

"I like to understand how everything works within The Q." Quincy blew her hair away from her face. "I have a few questions for you, Mr. Arch, if you're not too busy."

"Of course. Fisher and I can finish this later."

"Hours to go before we sleep, anyway," Fisher said with a melancholy look towards the street.

Mr. Arch opened his office door and waited for Quincy to pass before following her into his office. Quincy settled into the chair set before his desk.

"I'm not worried about the competition," Quincy began. "We've seen it before. A few of the upstarts were even successful for a few years." She tossed the shoddy paper onto his desk.

Picking it up with his white fingers, Mr. Arch studied the paper for a few minutes—at one point, giving a short sound reminiscent of a laugh—before setting it down on his desk. Then his dark eyes met Quincy's.

"An amusing piece of work," he said. "The paper comes from—?"

"Jade says it was brought up from Lester."

"We have a noncompete legal agreement with the local printer in Lester. We use him to print the local bit sheet of *The Q*."

"Yes, I know," said Quincy.

"It's unlikely this *Question Daily*—an awful name—is being printed somewhere else and brought in, so you can be sure that the printer himself is running a double deal and making an extra bit of profit. Do you want to do something about it? We can litigate if he refuses to stop printing it."

"There's no need to make it formal without first trying to scare him into keeping his contract."

"Would you have me leave for Lester in the morning?" Mr. Arch asked. "I should be there by the evening. There are certainly accommodations to stay the night, then I can return the following day, after I've had an interview with the owner of the printing establishment."

"Yes." Quincy stood, unrolling her sleeves, noting the ink on what was now a ruined shirt.

"Would you like to come with me?"

"To Lester?" Quincy looked up so fast her neck flared at the movement. "No. No."

Mr. Arch eyed her with his stern look, half of his mouth dropping like an uneven line of text. "You're sure?"

Quincy, back to the business of rolling down her sleeves, raised her eyebrows. "Does Lester fulfill anything on the infamous list?"

"You know I cannot say either way."

Quincy heard the second hand of the tall clock in his office click seven times before she answered, "I'll let you know at the end of the day."

After leaving Mr. Arch alone with his work, and setting Fisher at the front counter, Quincy disappeared up into her matchbox to change. It would be something Uncle Ezekiel might do, Quincy thought as she blew the dust of years off of her packed up emotions, this sending her back to Lester. It would be something Uncle Ezekiel might very well do.

CHAPTER NINE:

Lester's Ghosts

The road to Lester was far more comfortable than Quincy had anticipated. She had instructed Mr. Arch to arrange a driver from her own staff to take them, who would already be passing through Lester on his rounds; the two of them could—very easily, Quincy thought—have sat on the back of the wagon. Mr. Arch had other arrangements in mind. He'd procured a very comfortable carriage, with clean, cushioned seats, a smartly dressed driver, and a matched set of fine horses. There was also a footman.

"Despite what you need, by way of comfort, a wagon would not have done for me," Mr. Arch had stated firmly. Then he included the information that he'd paid for the extra expense from his own pocket, so she could have nothing to complain about. "And why you would ever think that, after a day's journey in a wagon, you would look respectable enough to handle legal matters is beyond me," Mr. Arch added, unnecessarily.

"We would have had the night at the inn to set ourselves to rights."

"With ruddy skin, smelling of horse and hay and who knows what else."

Quincy refrained from snapping back that he needed the color, saying instead, "The fresh air would have been nice." In all actuality, Quincy knew that, when riding in a wagon, your thoughts had plenty of room to wander and move and never bump into those of your companions. But in a carriage, with its confined space, people often felt compelled to speak with one another, even when their companion didn't wish it. And Quincy did not wish it. She thought that the truest test of humanity was riding in a coach and saying absolutely nothing to one's traveling companions. Few, if any, had ever succeeded.

Mr. Arch actually gave Quincy reason for surprise. He sat with his paper, a packet of legal paraphernalia, some reports that Quincy wanted him to review from the front office, and a pad of paper, where he occasionally paused to write down some thought that had captured his interest.

In her preparations to leave, Quincy had packed an overnight bag but had failed to think that she might wish to have anything for the journey. She was accustomed to working in her head—and intended to do so—but Mr. Arch seemed so pleased with his situation she couldn't help but let her mind and eyes wander to watch him on occasion.

The countryside was embracing the warmer weather, and meadows wearing vulnerable green ran the length of the roads in between patches of woods and the occasional village or town. They stopped for lunch at Saveaux, with very little conversation between them, and then, without much delay, pressed on into the countryside.

It was not until three in the afternoon that Mr. Arch finally spoke en route.

"I've noticed you doing a great deal of thinking," he said. "As you do when you walk the streets of Rhysdon. Is it all business? They say—" Mr. Arch paused, looking at Quincy a long moment, then began again. "They say you are quite capable of carrying all the numbers and statistics and percentages dealing with the business of The Q in your head, organized however you need them to be."

"They exaggerate," said Quincy, shrugging off his words and looking out the window. "But I do find I'm able to get a decent amount of work settled in my own mind before I have the necessity of using a pen and paper."

"Which is how you were able to find my error without more than a precursory run through of the legal document? It didn't match up in your head?"

"Error?"

"The small mistake I made two weeks into the job that you have exacted penance for ever since." Mr. Arch actually sounded irritated. Or something just short of irritation. He sounded miffed.

"Ah." Quincy said, lifting a shoulder. "Yes, well. It was an obvious enough number, and your having mishandled it could have cost The Q some money."

"It would have been caught in a second edit. You do realize that, don't you?"

Quincy looked away from the fields and directly at Mr. Arch. He sat comfortably, papers strewn about him, his face still pale, but his dark eyes brighter for the journey. "The probability was high that it would have been caught, but I would much rather have had a perfect go-around to begin with. Time is money, Mr. Arch."

"You don't have to call me that, you know."

"What?"

"*Mister* Arch. You could just call me Arch, like Fisher does."

"Why would I do that?" Quincy responded flatly.

"Would my own personal preference come under your consideration?"

"Probably not."

Mr. Arch shook his head and returned to the paper he was reading.

After a few miles of dastardly comfortable travel, Quincy could not help herself. "Who are *they*?" she demanded.

"Pardon?" Mr. Arch—Arch—looked up again, his lips pursed.

"You said *they* say I keep the business in my head. Who are they?"

"A few of the staff, the business community of Rhysdon, among others. Some of your uncle's friends."

He went back to his work, and Quincy went back to hers. Mr. Arch—*Arch*, Quincy reminded herself with a slight roll of her eyes— proved himself almost superhuman by refraining from conversing for the remainder of the drive. For an entire day's travel, they had spoken no more than two hundred and sixty-eight words to each other.

There might yet be, Quincy acknowledged, a chance of redemption for Mr. Arch—*Arch*. Quincy scowled.

When they rolled into Lester it was growing dark, and the coach took them to the front of the only establishment that appeared cobbled sufficiently together to stand through the night.

Arch pulled at the lapels of his coat as he let himself down from the coach, looked about once his shoes touched the dusty road, and then sniffed, offering Quincy his hand. But she was already shooting out from the carriage and onto the street, passing him without so much as brushing her sleeve against his fingertips.

Arch stood for a moment, his mouth pressed into a line, his hand extended, until Quincy saw, from the corner of her eye, that he closed his hand into a fist and collected himself enough to inform the innkeeper, who had come out to meet them, that they requested two rooms.

"Will you be using the dining hall this evening, good sir?"

"Yes," Arch answered.

Quincy paid them little mind, for she was scanning the street, the people, the old, sagging shops with few attempts at fresh paint. A lazy wagon with even lazier horses passed by, the farmer looking tired and ragged. Quincy felt the painful familiarity. The pang of having spent her early years scavenging on these very streets.

"Come on, Quincy," she said aloud to herself as she turned on her heel, away from the town and into the inn.

They dressed for dinner, and by no means was it upon Quincy's insistence. Arch had simply assumed that they would. In a fresh change of clothing, Quincy bothered to look at herself in the tarnished mirror above the washstand. She had always looked like a child—small, diminutive, hungry. And she always felt like an orphan. But her clothes were now nice. Quincy mussed up her face. She hadn't really looked at herself in such a long time and wasn't comfortable with her own serious stare.

A quick rap on the door caused Quincy to flinch and turn away from the looking glass, as if Arch could somehow see her self-scrutiny through the door and found it amusing.

"Miss St. Claire?"

"What?"

"If you've had sufficient time to dress, I thought we could go down together. An establishment such as this would surprise me if they kept the food warm for long."

In response, Quincy pulled her mouth to the side, breathed out through her nose, and opened the door. Arch was, well, not wearing black. He was wearing a fine, well-tailored overcoat of deep burgundy and was fiddling with the sleeve of his brisk white shirt.

"Good evening," he said, as if they had not been together all day.

"Hmmm," Quincy breathed out as she passed Arch and walked down the hallway.

The great room was not very great, with five tables—only one occupied—and a smoking fireplace. The room was warm, so Quincy chose the table farthest from the fire, in a dark corner. It made sense—but was unexpected—that Arch followed her and claimed the seat just across from her.

The innkeeper's wife was quick to bring out a meal that lacked in class but not in portions. Roast, beans, potatoes, winter carrots. Quincy began to eat, flipping through the files inside her brain to find some work to do. Just as she was about to settle on comparing quarterly expansion rates for the last three years, Arch said something.

Quincy snapped her thoughts shut.

"Did you say something?" she asked, her mouth half full of roast beef.

"Yes," Arch said as he cut his meat with movements that could have been the definition of propriety. "I asked if anyone at The Q had bothered to find a copy of Crandall's *The Student*, the collection Boy Blue chose his verse from?"

Quincy swallowed, feeling self-conscious of her manners with Arch looking at her so intently. "I really can't say. If Jade and the print room did find it, I don't suppose they would have wanted to share it with me. I've not been—I've been—"

"You've been grieving," Arch said, looking away. "When I lost my mother, I was a beast for the better half of a year and sinking ship for the other half." He returned his gaze to Quincy's face. "They've tried to give you space for the respect of it, I believe."

Pressing her fingers tighter around her fork, Quincy looked down at her plate.

"I ask," he said, "because if you are interested I could shed some light on the clue." When she gave no response, other than stabbing a carrot, Arch continued anyway. "*The Student* is an effort to dismiss the reality of love. Crandall wrote about our human obsession to turn into lasting mystery something that is only an illusion of the brain and the body. Love rises, overwhelms our decisions, and then, too late, we find we have been chasing a figment that we ourselves brought into existence, leaving us in sadness, denial, and despair."

"You said Crandall wrote this book of verses while still at the university?"

"Yes."

"It takes most people years before they realize that truth," said Quincy. "Some fools never do."

"You really believe that?" Arch asked, his eyebrows pulled together.

"I have Crandall to back me up."

The lines around Arch's eyes softened. "Not so. Within five years, he was writing about love as an enduring virtue, as the only true emotion. He died having left behind volumes of poetry dedicated to the reality and influence and power of love."

"What happened?"

"He fell in love with a woman and never doubted it again." Arch's words were calm, but they carried a current of tremendous electricity. He waited for Quincy to speak. She didn't. And a curtain of silence dropped between them, left undisturbed as Arch finished his meal, his fingers drawing invisible lines on the cheap glass that held even cheaper wine.

Quincy buckled after several minutes had passed. "So, what did Boy Blue's message mean, then?"

Arch looked up at Quincy, seemingly startled from his thoughts.

"You must have formed your own opinion," Quincy pressed with as bored of a tone as she could manage. "Being The Q's resident expert on Crandall, and De Vere, and the king knows what else."

Arch lifted an eyebrow. "I think Boy Blue is trying to convince himself, and her, that their love isn't possible, probably for reasons of class, station, or some other perceived barrier. Yet, he was holding onto one candle of hope, even if it was an illusion. So he used the verse of the hunter pleading for the unobtainable to tell Angel that they were chasing flickers and shadows of a flame soon to go out. But there is some part of his heart that still wishes he could believe they might win the gamble of illusions and find something solid and lasting."

The intimacy Arch created with his words made Quincy uncomfortable, for it was as if he could grant a soul to Boy Blue's love just by speaking of it. And his conclusions as to the meaning of Blue Boy's question felt layered and restless. This was opposite from her modus operandi of comfortably tabled ink and gears, and she did not like what she did not understand. So Quincy did what she knew always gave her the same results, she shut him out by locking her interior doors.

Standing, Quincy pushed her chair away from the table. "That sounds ridiculous. Good night, Arch."

He stood quickly, knocking the contents of his glass across the table. "Did I say something wrong, Miss St. Claire?" she heard him ask.

But she was already halfway out of the room.

———

The next morning, they met in the hallway, fully dressed and ready to confront the proprietor of the Lester Print Shop. Neither wished for breakfast, so Arch called for the carriage to be brought round, acting as if none of the conversations from the day before had taken place.

"It's ridiculous to rouse the carriage when we could walk there twice as fast," Quincy grumbled, pulling at her sleeve beneath her black jacket's cuff.

"Is it nearby?" Arch looked with interest at the tumble-down street. "None of the buildings seem promising."

"The print shop is three streets over, up against the river."

"Would you prefer to walk?" said Arch, not asking how she knew this information.

"I would prefer not to wait. Walking has nothing to do with it."

She headed down the familiar street, following the internal compass she had built into her body when she was orphaned and hungry. Arch followed, but Quincy paid him no mind at all. The smells of Lester's shops, the backstreets, the cobblestones—all these were the foundation of so many of her dreams. Dreams she had shared with no one, not even Fisher. Dreams of gripping another's hand in hers from the fear of not finding bread. Dreams of abandonment and of the guilt and shame that followed.

Quincy set her shoulders forward, her hands buried deep in her pockets, and dismissed these ghosts. As she stepped around the mess left by the horses—her black boots were polished, expensive—Quincy realized that she could now buy all the food in Lester. And they could all be damned. Every last one of them who could not spare enough food to feed a starving child.

So lost inside the memories and smells, Quincy hardly noticed that they'd reached the printer's offices.

"Good, then," Arch said to himself as he stepped forward and opened the door.

Quincy walked in.

Nobody was in the front office, and Arch courteously rang the bell on the desk. They waited, hearing sounds from the back room.

"Excuse me," Arch called out. It sounded like a question.

Folding her arms, Quincy leaned against the wall and tattooed the floor with her boot.

Arch tried again. "Excuse me?"

"Give me a moment!" came a hassled voice from the rear of the shop. Then there was a hard sound of metal falling onto metal, and a string of curses came from the back room.

Arch's skin tinged the faintest shade of pink, and he swallowed, clenching his jaw. "I am sorry you heard that," he said politely to Quincy.

He wasn't looking when she shrugged in reply. She'd heard everything, and had said most of it.

After hearing another burst of curses and a sound like metal rain falling to the floor, they saw a red-faced man come out of the back room. His hands were ink-stained, and he was wiping them with a rag.

"How may I help you?" he spoke to Arch gruffly. "Are you here to place a question in *The Question Daily?*"

Quincy stared, open-faced, at the familiar printer, the sound of his voice—yelling down the street, calling her a thief—lining the memories of Quincy's mind.

"Well?" the man said.

"We are here in regards to your *Question Daily*," Arch said, placing his leather satchel on the counter. "My name is James Arch, solicitor for The Q. This young woman," he motioned politely towards Quincy, who then peeled her shoulder blades away from the wall, "is Quincy St. Claire, proprietor of The Q."

The printer's face drained of its color under the soft weight of Arch's words. The man looked at Quincy for a half second longer than he apparently had meant too, almost catching a ghost of recognition, but not quite.

"The Q? Ah, yes. I print the local insert." He wiped his hands on his dirty apron, his red face shining from the sweat. "It's quite popular in our Lester paper. Very popular. I have records of the accounts, which we send with your drivers and Q boys, just like the contract instructs me to do."

A customer came through the door, a sour-faced woman, and the printer looked embarrassed, harried. "I'll be with you in just a moment, ma'am."

"Is there a place where Miss St. Claire and I could wait privately, while you see to your business?" Arch offered politely.

"Ah." The printer looked towards the ceiling a moment. "Yes. In the second office. One moment," he said to the woman as he invited Arch and Quincy into a small, cramped office, its desk piled with papers.

After the printer had left, Arch sniffed and rubbed his fingers together. "I hate to think what the first office looks like."

Quincy gave no answer. Rather, she just sat down and stared at the floor.

When the printer returned, Arch withdrew the contract from his satchel. "Here is a copy of your agreement with The Q, Mr. Andrews—

it is *Andrews*, correct? On the second page, you will see a noncompete agreement, which you have signed. Now we find that you are printing a copycat start-up, entitled *The Question Daily*."

"No, I'm not. I'm not. My nephew prints it, after hours. It's just that he uses my machines is all."

Arch's dark eyes narrowed. "Then, why did you ask if we would like to place a question in *The Question Daily* when we first came in?"

"He couldn't be here and asked me to take his customers."

"Wrong, Mr. Andrews. Those are The Q's customers that you are diverting to another paper for greater profits."

"There is no law that only The Q can run an enterprise in this country," the printer said, clearly flustered and irritated.

Arch held up the contract. "Sir, you've signed your name to this agreement. Any time you sign your name to a document, you open up some possibilities and close others. You cannot print a competing paper on your presses!"

"Well, I—!"

"Don't make me take you through litigation—"

"You—you can't—"

Quincy had now had enough watching. She stood up, leaned forward, and placed both of her hands squarely on Mr. Andrew's desk. The printer sputtered his last words back into his mouth and leaned away from Quincy. "Listen here, Andrews," Quincy began coolly. "Our contract gives us the leverage to not only fine you but also shut you down and take everything you have: your print shop, your house, the pathetic little jobbers you make your living by. These could all be taken from you. My solicitor is the best law mind in Rhysdon. He could find a way to take your life and make it a property of The Q. And I have no scruples about doing so, especially not in a place such as Lester." She took a breath. "Now, The Q pays its local printers quite well. But, if you are struggling for a profit, I and my solicitor would happily spend an hour or two helping you cut any costs so that you will not only recoup your losses but also begin turning a strong profit. Does that sound agreeable to you? Or, would you rather settle this in court, with the final act being debtors' prison?"

Andrews opened his mouth, twice. Finally, he said, "Lester's is not a strong economy. It's been difficult, you see. And I've got children to feed."

Grumbling, Quincy took off her jacket, laid it over her chair, and began to roll up the white sleeves of her shirt. Arch was watching her with a mixture of amusement and admiration. "Of course Lester's economy is strong enough for a successful print house. By the time we are done with you, it will be strong enough for two. Now, let's talk specifics while we get to work."

"Work?" Andrews asked, still wide-eyed from Quincy's well-delivered threats.

"Yes. It sounded like you've got a broken machine in the back. Let's set you to rights while we talk. Arch, there, can take notes for you."

"Certainly," Arch murmured, replacing the contract in his satchel.

"You're certain you can handle a press?" Andrews asked, eyeing Quincy's stature.

"My good man," Arch stood and picked up Quincy's jacket carefully, "you are looking at the woman who the king himself has called the brightest mind in Rhysdon. She can fix machines bigger than your entire shop."

"Yes, well, I am much obliged!" Andrews got to his feet and, somewhat bewildered, led Quincy and Arch into his print room. He had made a mess of his jobber, but Quincy could have worked out the problem in her sleep.

"Leave the machine to me." She waved off the printer. "I'll show you what I've done once you've picked up all that type scattered on the floor. Really, Andrews, if you can't maintain a cleaner room than this, you've no hope of making a profit."

Quincy set about her work, explaining what and why she was doing what she did in between asking Andrews about his business model. Arch found a stool, perched next to a counter, and began taking notes. Quincy did not look at him as she worked. She did not look at him when the job was done and the meeting with Andrews had ended with a handshake and a hastily scribbled business plan. And she did not look at him when they returned to the inn, packed up their things, and ordered the carriage round.

Neither spoke for the first several hours of travel.

"Thank you," Arch finally said, once it had become too dark for him to work.

"For what?"

"For calling me the best mind for law in all of Rhysdon, as fallible as I may be. Though, you certainly exaggerated, it was an unexpected compliment."

"Well," Quincy picked at the seat while staring out the window towards the fading day, "we both took liberties to line our threats. You said that the king thought I was the brightest mind in Rhysdon, which was bald-faced. Effective, though, as far as threats go."

"That wasn't a stretch," replied Arch. "He did say you were the brightest mind in Rhysdon."

"Uh huh." Quincy slouched farther into her corner, comfortable in her skepticism, craning her neck to see the moon rising. As if Arch had ever sat in casual conversation with the king. "So, what does this cross off the list? Me returning to Lester?" Quincy asked then grimaced; she hadn't meant to say the word *returning*. Arch, though, let it pass.

"I don't believe you crossed any requirement off the list while we were in Lester." By the way Arch had said these words, Quincy could tell that he was worried she would react badly to the news.

"Then why did you push me to come?" she replied with no emotion.

"I thought a day out of the city would do you some good."

Unbelievable. "Expect some kind of retribution for playing nursemaid, Arch."

He straightened himself in the deepening shadows and then said, "I always do."

CHAPTER TEN:
Quincy En Vogue

"Did you read this morning's *Q*?" Arch asked.

"Of course I did," Quincy answered.

As they walked along the street, a narcissus vendor intercepted Arch, throwing a full bouquet of yellow blooms in his face. While he stopped to fish out a coin from his pocket, Quincy continued walking. Eight steps into her abandonment, the thought entered her mind that perhaps buying street flowers was something on her uncle's silly list. She spun on her heels and watched as Mr. Arch tipped his hat and then continued towards her, the bright, sun-filled flowers in perfect contrast to his black attire, pale face, and dark eyes.

"Are you quite finished?" she asked.

"Yes." Mr. Arch fell into step with Quincy. "We were speaking of today's *Q*."

"*You* were speaking of today's *Q*."

"There were invitations to one of the biggest events of the spring sprint, the dinner at Lady Fothergil's."

"The *spring sprint*?" Quincy gave Mr. Arch a withering look, hoping to eliminate the awful phrase from his vocabulary. Really, where did he pick up such things?

"That's what they call the small season of events before things really kick into full swing."

"They?"

"The upper class," Mr. Arch supplied. "You do remember all those faceless aristocrats that you disdain with such fervor? Well, Lady Fothergil's gathering each spring is exclusive and a trendsetter. Did you read through the invitations?"

"Skimmed them to check for print errors." Quincy pushed past a knot of young women giggling about something.

Mr. Arch tipped his hat. Then he took a few long steps, to catch up with Quincy, and spoke again. "Did you see that you had your own invitation to one of the events?"

In record time, Quincy fashioned for herself a disbelieving glare. "My own invitation?"

"It appears that you have become quite popular among the social elite of Rhysdon, Miss St. Claire. You are *en vogue*."

Quincy snorted with indifferent disbelief.

"Believe what you will, but that won't stop the fact that you're becoming fashionable and being talked about."

"And how would you know who's being talked about among the social elite?"

"I'm your solicitor; it's my business to know."

Quincy shot Mr. Arch a sidelong glance. "You're my solicitor, Mr. Arch, not my spymaster."

Mr. Arch turned his face away from hers and laughed. It was the first time Quincy had heard such a thing from him. His laugh was a silver sound, smooth, exposing much more confidence than Quincy would have guessed. Perhaps it had to do with his chest cold disappearing and his face looking less gaunt.

"Are you planning on bringing those flowers into the offices of The Q?" she asked, looking for something to contradict the pleasantness of his reaction.

"They are for my desk."

"The corner that I can't see, I hope. They can keep De Vere company."

"I really think you should go to the Fothergils' party."

"Absurd."

"Imperative," he countered.

Halting so fast that Mr. Arch had to turn back around to look at her face, Quincy frowned.

"Will this fulfill one of my uncle's ludicrous requirements?"

Mr. Arch shrugged and—actually smiling—turned the corner from Queen's Street onto Gainsford. Quincy followed him, muttering.

The offices of Hewitt, Hewitt, and Hewitt, The Q's independent auditors, would be closed within the hour, and Quincy had been slow finishing the information that they needed. Fisher had gone home just after lunch with a stomach ailment, and Mr. Arch had finished his work and left at his normal time, while Quincy was down looking at a proof with Jade. There were no Q boys to be found, and when Jade offered to send one of the mice to deliver the papers, Quincy had declined, arguing that it would be better if she delivered them herself rather than take one of the experienced mice away from their work. The last two Q boys had arrived late and set Jade's work back as it was.

Donning her black jacket, Quincy grabbed her portfolio and headed uptown.

After Quincy left the offices of Hewitt, Hewitt, and Hewitt, she found she was a little cold and more than a little hungry. Her normal diet of stale biscuits and tea did not sound as palatable as her busy schedule usually made it taste. And so, Quincy looked about her and headed towards one of the plazas.

Here, cafés and restaurants catered to those just dearly departed from their day's work. As a result, the atmosphere of the plaza was always bright, the food decent, and the noise convivial. Quincy didn't stop here often. She was usually too busy and uninterested. But tonight the custom gas lanterns, the smell of soups and breads, the groups of diners surrounding tables inside and outside, the music of a man who'd braved the crowd and brought his cello down to earn some shillings and jabs—it all took her in.

She slipped inside the smallest café, ordering a cup of soup and two sweet pastries. The pastries she'd asked to have wrapped in paper, and for the soup, she requested an actual cup. Holding her prize before her, so as not to spill, her now empty portfolio tucked under her arm,

Quincy went out onto the café's patio and wove through the tables to a small brick wall outside of the circles of light. She set down her goods, pulled herself onto the wall, and swung her legs as she blew the soup cool enough to drink.

With nothing pressing the inner office of her mind, Quincy turned her attention to people-watching. Most of them were young, smiling, and conversing, debating, or arguing. There were some young women sitting with young men. There was a table of secretaries—women who kept their fingernails clean and their résumés cleaner—raising their eyebrows over some story as they shared the realities of their day with one another. Quincy paid special attention to them. For not many women worked in Rhysdon, and she was always curious to see what her fellow creatures were like. But mostly there were tables of young men—students, lawyers, bankers—men who assumed that they would have respectable work or who were already engaged in such work, men with no wives to meet at home for an eight o'clock dinner.

Quincy's eyes wandered from person to person, making judgments and calculations, but never with enough interest to linger. And then she saw him. Sitting at one of the more boisterous tables, surrounded by four other young men, arguing until they laughed. Arch. Her nonentity. Her staid solicitor with whom not much could be said for the grayness of it all. And, by the king and all his counts, he was laughing again.

Quincy fashioned a glare with both her eyebrows and took a long sip of her chicken soup. How utterly peculiar. Had she thought he could see her, she would have bolted right then and there: not interested in polluting the few private hours she had without her personal watchdog. But Quincy knew when a shadow was deep enough to avoid detection, and she never picked the shallower sort for sitting. So Quincy sat unseen, finished her soup, and worked her way through one of her pastries while watching her unaware solicitor.

All the other young men he was with were reasonably handsome, polished, and—if one could give value to their confident gestures— articulate. She overheard bits and snatches of their conversation, as they were really not too far away, though not close enough for her to follow every word. It was some discussion about the patent office and copyright law, from what she could gather.

The argument was passed back and forth across the table, the momentum behind each sentence filled with city codes and laws and precedents set by such-and-such versus so-and-so. They would each make a point and then have it refuted or angled and twisted. This would end in an explosion, and someone would laugh and shake his head.

Arch was certainly not the most gregarious of the set, his pale face holding a smoother, more stable expression. But when it was his turn for debate, he threw himself into it by shaking his hands and scowling through his opponent's argument. He seemed, from Quincy's vantage point, to be enjoying himself immensely.

They'd finished their light meal, emptied their glasses, and were soon served steaming cups of coffee with pastries and sweet breads. As the young man on Arch's left was commencing on an intellectually driven monologue, Arch took the white ceramic mug in his hands, lifted it to his mouth, and then pulled his face away, shaking his head and setting the mug down. He'd burned his tongue. Quincy smiled.

Just then, a boy darted past and reached his hand towards the tray of sweet breads, grabbing one and twisting away before much could be said. But Arch's friend was fast, and he half grabbed the little one by the arm, jerking the short-lived victor from his feet and pulling him back to face whatever law the young solicitors would invoke.

Someone said something, and the boy cringed. But Arch scowled, muttering something, and asked his friend to deliver the thief to him. Quincy's stomach began to hurt, and, although she was now finishing her second pastry, she felt the familiar pangs of hunger haunting her body. She gave a sympathetic cringe, worrying that they might call a constable, who would take the boy around the corner and cuff him hard. She swallowed and watched.

Then a comment was made about Arch, something about his heart, and jokes began to fly around the table as the red-handed street sparrow, still gripped quite firmly, was brought before Arch to stand trial.

Arch said a few things that Quincy could not quite hear. Then the solicitor reached for the tray, took a pastry in each hand, and wrapped them in a linen napkin from the table before handing them to the boy. The street sparrow blinked, moving as if he would run, then accepted the food with such surprise that he kept looking over his bony shoulder nervously, thinking it a trick.

Arch, who was still talking, finally secured the boy's attention after making the boy take a few sips of his cooled coffee. Arch seemed to be explaining directions of some sort and kept at it, until the boy nodded and made a reply that was satisfactory to Arch. Before the child could leave, Arch handed him a card from his pocket with a quickly sketched map on the back.

"Don't forget," he said to the boy before adding one more piece of sweet bread to the child's bundle and sending him off.

Confused and angry neither at Arch, nor at the hungry boy—but rather the fact her muscles still constricted around her heart and that her stomach still shrunk severely at the thought of being so hungry— Quincy slipped off her wall and disappeared around the corner, into the shadows of a small park, doing her best not to lose her dinner.

When Arch came into the office the next morning, he was his quiet self: outwardly cool and polite. Quincy watched her solicitor and wondered.

Spats brought a message in from Boy Blue that afternoon:

"Will you accept my company tomorrow evening,
if I bring the sonnets?"

BOY BLUE

Fisher was happy; he whistled. Jade joked with all the mice and even kept Spense laughing. Quincy felt no different than she usually did.

But, when Fisher turned to her, shortly after a stream of customers had left, and said, "Cities, foreign: Amsterdam," Quincy replied with "Berlin."

"Constantinople."

"Dover."

"Edinburgh."

"Fr—" Quincy paused. She always had to pause on the F.

"Ferrara," came Arch's voice from his office.

"Gaziantep," Quincy followed, allowing Arch into their game.

Fisher leaned back, his hands behind his head, and smiled, saying, "Hirosaki."

"Istanbul," came Arch's voice once more.

"Jakarta."

"Kandahār."

"Leipzig."

They made it to "Windsor" before a customer entered and the amicable game came to an end.

CHAPTER ELEVEN:
A Hunting We Will Go

Quincy was stuck. To try and work her thoughts loose she had been assembling the monthly report, hounding the accountants, the secretaries, Fisher, and, of course, Mr. Arch—her middle-ground solicitor turned prison warden turned sponsor of the poor turned surprisingly good contributor to her and Fisher's front office alphabet game. She was trying to work through the hard decision between expanding into Paris or into London first, detailing reports of which market would be most receptive—or rather, the most immediately profitable—so that she might convince the board that it was not only a safe way to use The Q's recently acquired capital but also one with vast potential in financial returns.

She still felt unsettled about the details, about the methods of innovative expansion she'd penciled into place. Something, some aspect of the plan was flawed, and the decision between the two cities remained fuzzy. She couldn't see the problem, but her mind could feel it. It was as if she were hearing the sound of a machine, one not properly oiled, rubbing slightly in the wrong way, causing production to slow only by seconds, but by seconds nonetheless. And seconds, Quincy knew, were the difference between vast success and medium impact.

Tapping the end of her pencil on her rough proposal, Quincy

looked over at Fisher. He was sleeping at his desk.

"Fisher," she said. He gave no response. "Fisher!"

"What?" Fisher slapped his hand on the desk and sat up. "Yes. Sorry. I gave you the tax projections for both London and Paris."

"I know. Do you need to go lie down, or can you stay awake long enough to watch the front desk and check the Q boys' arrival times?"

"It's a Q boy check day, is it?" he said, rubbing his eyes and trying to put his hair back in order. "Is the half-crown purse in the counter drawer?"

"Yes. Give each Q boy two if he's punctual. Mrs. Graves will give you their times. Those who are late must have twenty percent more questions to earn theirs. That includes Spats. Don't let him charm you into anything."

"The boy runs three routes."

"I know. And he does them all in record time, but he doesn't need to feel like he's got a free pass. Besides, I'm looking at setting Spats up for a promotion."

"Grease monkey in Spense's print room? Or a sorter?"

"Preliminary sorter, then mouse, once we can straighten his language," said Quincy as she packed up a brown leather satchel with a portfolio of loose papers and a few pencils. "He'll be a fine sorter and someday an able printer. Unless he proves his mind for accounting or editing and has a preference there."

"So he builds a career within The Q?"

"Undoubtedly."

The bell sounded, and two customers entered. Quincy and Fisher took their questions, and when they'd left Fisher motioned his hand towards her satchel. "Your mind stuck?"

Nodding, Quincy replied, "I'm on the edge of a solution. I just need some time. Remember that the Q boys will start coming in soon and that the sorters will be marching seventeen come Sunday. Man the desk, and throw Jade what she needs until I return."

Quincy looked towards Arch's office. The door was closed, as he was meeting with the editors of a medium-sized city paper from Hanspure, in the south. Quincy had, of course, been introduced upon their arrival the hour previous, declining to stay as Arch hammered out the details of their contract with The Q. He knew what he was doing by now.

"Have you now taken to waiting for Arch?" Fisher asked, and Quincy realized she had been staring at the lawyer's movements, at the quiet but determined set of his mouth in the conversation she was unable to hear through the glass.

"No," Quincy turned, "but neither do I wish to repeat something because I was too stupid to take him with me. The only progress I've made towards keeping The Q is catching a butterfly. Not promising. I'll take these back into the sorter," Quincy said, picking up the basket at the edge of the counter that held the day's Q slips.

Pushing through the back door, the stillness of the front office was replaced by the noise of the sorting room: sounds of bells and calls and feet. The sorting room was, between the hour of three and six thirty, like a child's toy that Quincy had once seen through a toy shop window. It had been a metal ball of sorts that was filled with marbles. Then, a small trap door was shut, and the child gripped a small handle attached to the contraption, which would cause the entire ball to spin in place. The marbles of all colors would hop and jump, creating the most spectacular sound of glass hitting metal.

This was how Quincy always thought of the busy sorting room. Q boys were arriving from their routes, the Q slips were being placed in their proper sections—be they trade Qs, invitational Qs, conversational Qs, et cetera—then, once every Q boy was accounted for and the front doors were closed at six o'clock, the mice would retrieve their assigned sections, and *The Q* for the following day would be set, with Jade breathing down their necks like some punctuation-obsessed dragon.

A retired housekeeper named Mrs. Graves ran the sorting office part-time for those afternoon hours. Graves arrived at ten minutes to three o'clock, waited for her small army of sorters to arrive, and managed the sorting with the same efficiency with which she had managed a large estate house in the country, chiding the Q boys if they were late, giving an approving nod if they arrived on time.

Once six o'clock rolled around—with every Q boy in, every slip sorted—Graves would nod to the sorters, say, "Good work," and then usher them out as the mice came in to collect their respective baskets. If the Q boys were all on time, then, by six thirty, she had set her hat with an antique hatpin, had placed her gloves on her hands, and was disappearing through the back doors of The Q's printing office, not to be seen or heard from until the next day at ten minutes to three.

Quincy was not the one who had hired Graves—it had been her uncle Ezekiel—but Graves was as efficient as they came and not wont to mother anyone except the youngest of Q boys. Now, as Quincy brought the basket in, Graves was overseeing the sorting staff, looking unruffled and serene despite the noise and clatter.

"Good afternoon, Graves," Quincy called as the bodies and noise parted to let Quincy through.

"Good afternoon, St. Claire." Graves dusted her hands as she turned primly.

"A steady day for office Qs." Quincy set her basket on the long counter in the middle of the room, where each Q boy would empty his Q bag. "Expect half this much at day's close seeing as how it's a Thursday."

Graves nodded. "The sorting room will do its job."

"I know," replied Quincy as she turned to go. "Thank you, Graves."

Then Quincy passed behind the front counter and went up the stairs into her matchbox room, where she finished a sweet roll she had *procured* the night previous from a baker who sometimes brought his goods into The Q's front office. She then checked her clothing for ink stains. Seeing her ensemble still sharp, Quincy nodded into her thin mirror and descended the stairs, licking her fingers and snatching her satchel. The door to Arch's office had just opened, and the Hanspure gentlemen filed out, sharing a few convivial words with Arch while he led them to the front door.

"A copy of the terms will be sent down tomorrow morning," Arch was saying as he shook their hands once more and replied to the men's niceties. "Good afternoon. Yes, yes, thank you."

Quincy slung her bag over her shoulder and slipped her hands into her pockets just as Arch closed the door and turned. "Going out, Miss St. Claire?"

"Yes. Is there anything you need to gather before we go?"

"How long are we to be?"

Quincy shrugged. She never knew how long fixing her own internal machinery would take.

"Who, then, are we going to meet?"

"It's not who, it's where," Fisher supplied as he filled out an order for more print ink. "You are being taken to the exclusive, known-only-by-me-and-Ezekiel Quincy thinking spot."

Arch looked interested. "What should I pack? An overnight bag filled with bribe money? A book on Himalayan parole terms? A rifle for hunting elephants, perhaps?" He had asked these all with such pleasant seriousness that, Quincy realized, when he'd stopped speaking and stared at her face, it was because she was grinning.

"None of the above, Arch. Though your places for thinking through a problem are much more interesting than mine, I think we both need to get out more. Bring any work you need to review, or bring a book to read. I don't really care."

"Well, then." He stepped into his office and filled his portfolio with some papers from his desk. Then, stopping near a shelf, he selected a book that looked well-used and well-loved. Placing his hat on his head, he closed his office door behind him and nodded towards Quincy. "Lead on, Miss. St. Claire. A hunting we will go."

"Good luck," Fisher called as he began an order for more paper. "Watch that the natives don't shrink your heads or some other such nonsense."

Instead of turning right, towards Queen's Street, as Quincy did just about every other time she left The Q, she turned left. Arch, perhaps thinking he'd already passed his quota of pleasant interactions with Quincy St. Claire for the month, was silent in a comfortable sort of way and refrained from asking questions.

Just before Gainsford made a ninety-degree turn, which led the street uptown, Quincy ducked through a small alleyway between buildings and worked her confident way through the backstreets. The route was abundantly full of refuse bins, forgotten crates, and various laundry, hanging from back windows. Several cats, the local monarchy that Quincy had long been acquainted with, were granting them passage while sitting atop the maze of half-broken fences. Quincy saluted a black female—the reigning queen—and passed through a slender passage between two buildings, leading them out onto Fair Street and its adjoining park in a manner of minutes.

"Really?" Arch said as much to himself as to Quincy. "That should have been an hour's walk through the city."

"Efficiency, Mr. Arch, is the game."

"So, I should learn all the back ways of Rhysdon?"

Quincy paused just then and turned half around to look at her solicitor in a discriminating light. "You're face is too pale. Your physique? Not bad, though you're trim enough you wouldn't pass for a bruiser of any sort. Your fingernails are too well kept. And the tailoring on your coat?" Quincy shook her head. "You pass through too many back ways alone, and I'll never get The Q."

"I'll be roughed up, you mean?" said Arch.

"You'll be dead."

When his chin pulled to the side rather quickly, Quincy saw he didn't quite believe her.

"What?" Quincy cocked an eyebrow. "You don't believe me?"

Arch's thin-lipped smile was dubious. "I would most likely be robbed then left worse for the wear, but alive."

"Hmmm." And Quincy turned on her heel, crossing the street into the park. Arch followed, as always.

"By any way," Arch continued, "your clothing is just as fine as mine. I'm almost convinced we have the same tailor."

"We do," Quincy stated with regretful admission. "I was hoping you wouldn't notice, but the stitches do tell. It's embarrassing."

"Why does it embarrass you?"

"How can you afford Favreau by any means?" Quincy half glared, while her mannerisms invited Arch into step beside her.

"I'm frugal on most other things," he said before turning the question back to his survival in the underbelly of Rhysdon. "You didn't answer my question. Why do you, dressed as you are, rich as you are—and known for it—get a pass from the muggers and thieves?"

"I don't always," Quincy answered. "But I know how to walk in a way that lets everybody know I've done my time on the streets. My own reputation is behind me, so they see me as one of their own. Local girl made good, as it were. And there's Crow."

"Crow?"

"It's known in certain corners that I am friends with Crow. And being friends with Crow is better than carrying the king's seal. No one wants to be on his bad side, and I'm on his good."

"You certainly are," Arch said. And his words sounded like a dictionary entry that had more than one meaning.

Quincy pulled up at the edge of the street, waiting for a carriage to pass, then crossed with a determined step. There, rising before them—tall, brass-lined, and glass-filled—was one of the marvels of the entire country: the Rhysdon train station. Quincy breathed in through her nose, and a smile flitted across her small face as the smell of burning coal filled her soul with the beautiful locomotives of Rhysdon.

She entered the station just as a gentleman came out, and took another deep breath. Forgetting Arch, forgetting tailors and backstreets and cats, Quincy lost herself in the magnificent architecture built to house even more magnificent machines. The train Quincy loved: its perfection of movement and speed and sound; its possibility and potential; its ability to efficiently transport the masses. It was here that Quincy always found the gears of her own mind worked loose, set back in place.

She did not stop at the ticket office but rather walked right past the line. A man in the ticket window waved, and Quincy lifted an arm in reply. She could tell that Arch was entertained by this abnormal turn of events, observing rather than speaking as if not wanting to startle Quincy now that he'd found out one of her natural habitats. Seeing as how she was almost feeling kindly towards him, she let the naturalist enjoy his work and set about her own.

Quincy felt a sense of reverence whenever she stepped into the grand station. It boasted rails, trains, comings and goings, weary and eager passengers rushing in every direction. She loved the sounds. The steam rising. The whistles. The cry of the brakes competing with the cries of the stationmasters. Quincy wove through all this with deep pleasure, her eyes lifting to the large swaths of diamond windowpanes that welcomed the day into this wondrous monument to progress.

She passed the main three tracks and came to a staircase built up an arch running over the fourth track. There was a velvet cord hanging across to prevent entry. Quincy pulled it aside, waiting for Arch to pass, and then put it back, continuing up the stairs until they forced her to turn right or left along the long wall. Again, Quincy chose left. There, along an iron-railed corridor lining the edge of the lower roof, was a bench.

It was here that Quincy sat, placed her black boots on the railing, and leaned forward with contentment to watch the train-station world spread out below. Arch settled himself beside her, careful to give her enough space that they would not elbow one another. Quincy approved.

Now that she was in place, her lungs filling with soot, she retrieved her notes from her satchel. Leaning back, she ignored everything written on her papers and, instead, watched as the three fifteen rolled into the station, black billows of smoke lifting, drawn upward by the clever contraptions that opened the windows in the roof and funneled the smoke away from the station. The locomotive itself was a brilliant beast, light flinging itself off the wheels, looking as if one eager fish after another were jumping to catch an ever-moving hook. Quincy closed her eyes and listened to the sound of several tons of machinery coming to a stop beneath the perfect control of well-maintained brakes.

The brakes released, and so did Quincy.

When she opened her eyes, she saw that Arch was watching her, a smile on his face.

"What are you reading?" she asked after a time.

Arch pulled his eyes away from his book and held it up. "The earliest collection of essays by De Vere that I own."

"He's the Frenchman who writes satirical essays on class and the like?"

"Yes."

"So he has other essays which have eluded you," Quincy stated. It was not a question.

"Why do you say that?"

"I did the math," she replied dryly. When Arch shifted his face in confusion, she explained. "You made a point of saying that this was the earliest collection that you owned. And, considering you are a disciple of the man, you wouldn't have added the extra words had you owned all of his works. It's a sticking point, enough for you to bring it up however inconsequential the conversation."

The dimple in Arch's cheek flickered. He watched her a moment before replying, "And Fisher says you don't understand people."

"I don't," Quincy snapped, but it wasn't at Arch, it was at the air before her. "They're emotional, unpredictable, and erratic; I don't like dealing with them. But words, once spoken, can be turned into an equation of sorts in my mind—each word receiving a value depending on its placement or emphasis—and then, I add it up and see what comes out."

"Your mind is amazing." Arch shook his head. "There's your obvious brilliance, but what you just said reveals more layers. It's one thing to understand the art of rhetoric, but to come at it the way you have, from a different discipline, yet work it into your own internal equations, it's—well, it makes me wonder what else you can put through your lens and see clearly."

"De Vere's earlier essays?" Quincy redirected.

Arch's face took on a wistful, romantic expression. "De Vere published one book of essays before his name was established. He only had enough money to make one hundred copies—gave everything he had to it, hoping to get the volume into the right hands and find a place for himself. The newspapers were only just printing his social criticism, but he'd saved his best work for his book. As fate, who is cruel to writers, would have it, there was a fire the day after he hauled the crate home. The books were burned, save the five in his possession. This was a crippling blow, and he was quite bitter over it. But, he eventually made his name nonetheless."

"And the book?" Quincy asked.

"Was never reprinted. The five surviving volumes were eventually sold at auction to private buyers for a pittance, to keep his family fed. They've traded hands rarely. No one quite knows who owns the copies now or even if they're still in existence. The owners have kept the volumes to themselves." He said these last words so sadly that Quincy felt herself frowning.

"Certainly. If the essays were made public, it would lessen their value."

"It would *add*—" Arch bit at the word and continued just as fiercely, "immeasurable value to society and scholarship. The selfish interest of those with enough wealth to own one of the volumes is an abomination, and I hope they burn for it."

Quincy only nodded her head at his strong language and then turned her gaze down toward the movement in the station. A train was preparing to depart. "What was it called, that collection of essays?"

Arch had returned to his book, and he looked up with a pained expression. "That's the greatest irony of it all. The collection was titled *Imprisoned Words*."

Quincy pushed the air from her chest, thinking it funny. "And if you owned a copy you would set them free and gain the ire of the other collectors?"

"If I owned a volume, I would beg you to print ten thousand copies on your presses and distribute them in the streets of every city in Europe."

"You'd have to show me a way to make a profit from it first," Quincy responded evenly.

Arch tilted his head and raised an eyebrow, returning to his book as he answered, "I would build an argument so enticing and passionate you couldn't deny me."

Quincy didn't bother to look at him, worried that if she did, her cheeks would burn red at his words.

A few hours into watching trains, as Quincy ran the track of her foreign expansion plan over and over through her mind, it came. Quincy's answer came. She knew where she had been stuck. Scribbling on her paper, she crossed a few things out and wrote in other key words. The pages began to sing. The movement, the flow, a business model that would allow expansion into London, Paris, New York, Rome—all based on her perfect combination of formulas. And she now knew that Paris was first and that The Q should move immediately.

Arch's barometer seemed to have picked up on the changes in Quincy's energy, and he'd begun watching her work.

"You've figured out your problem?"

"Yes." Quincy closed her portfolio and stood. "Let's go."

"You don't want to stay for the six fifteen?" Arch looked at his pocket watch. "It's due in less than five minutes."

"I've figured out my problem," Quincy said, matter-of-factly. "To stay any longer would be a waste of time."

"But the poetry." He waved his hand over the spectacle below. "Isn't that what you love?"

"I love the perfection, Arch, not the poetry."

As he gathered his things, Quincy heard him mutter that perfection and poetry were often the same thing.

————————————————

When they returned to The Q, it was a quarter to seven, and Jade was in a complete panic.

"Five editors have gone home sick. Five!"

"From what?" Quincy asked as she followed Jade through the sorter and down into the print room.

"Ellis brought shrimp in for the staff. Thankfully, I was too busy to eat any. Most of it was bad. Justly, he paid severe penance in the alley outside The Q. The idiot! They'll be miserable for the next twenty-four hours and unable to eat for the following twenty-four. Serves them right," Jade said as she brought her hand down hard on one of the machines.

The nearest mice scattered, not wanting to incur the wrath of Jade or Quincy. Quincy, however, was feeling rather calm.

"How am I to get the first print edits done in time?" Jade ranted.

"I'll help," Quincy said. "Arch as well, I'm sure. We're both fast. Pull Theodore off his mousing, and give your job over to Spense when he comes in."

"We'll never make it," Jade said, scowling as she handed Quincy the first batch of proofs. "And Ellis will never sleep easy again."

"Revenge *after* work," Quincy said, taking the proofs. "Don't waste your energy until you're on your own time."

Quincy had to dodge a cuffing from Jade, and she laughed, taking the stairs two at a time, passing through the sorter, and catching Arch in his office, preparing to leave.

"Arch, I need you to stay. Five editors have gone down with bad shrimp, and we've a stack of first prints needing immediate attention." Quincy waved the sheaths in her hand.

"I'm afraid I have an engagement at eight thirty," Arch answered as he brushed some ash from his sleeve, still there from the excursion to the train station. "But I can give you an hour, if that would be helpful."

Quincy dropped the pile of first prints onto his desk and sat in the chair opposite from Arch. "Fair's fair. I gave you no warning."

A few efficient sentences were enough for Quincy to explain the process to Arch, and he pulled a blue pencil from his desk. Quincy didn't say anything. She knew that Jade liked her editors to work in red, but Quincy was feeling generous. They each took a sheet and began. As soon as they were finished with their first stack, Jade appeared with another and whisked away the edited proofs.

Arch pressed his fingers to another page and slid it across his desk until it was square in front of him. He seemed to be enjoying the work and was fast. Quincy watched the line of his mouth as he moved his blue pencil through a word and made an annotation: it was straight, uncomplicated, and set. Pulling her attention back to her own page, Quincy caught an errant apostrophe as she was wondering what sort of engagement Arch had tonight. She imagined he was meeting his friends from law school, ready to discuss high-profile cases and the details of their work with gestures, animation, and laughter. If they could get past the theatrics of their passions, their discussions could be potentially interesting to Quincy.

"Have you decided if you will accept the Fothergils' invitation?" Arch asked suddenly.

"I can't imagine myself having the time," Quincy said as automatically as the movement of the hands on the pocket watch she'd placed on the desk between them.

"Begging your pardon, Miss St. Claire." Arch looked up from the proof sheet and waited for Quincy to connect eyes with him. "But you would do well to take time for unaccustomed activities, as nothing you habitually make time for is on your uncle's list."

His words carried such earnestness that it forced Quincy to pull out the file of honest emotion from the back of her mind, and it almost fell open. Immediately, she shut it again then replied defensively, "Why do you care so much that I keep The Q?"

"Because it's my job," replied Arch without missing a moment, his pencil still hovering above his proof, his eyes still on hers only a moment more before returning his attention to the page before him.

It wasn't his job, Quincy thought as her face screwed into an annoyed glare.

"And I know you care about keeping The Q," Arch added quietly, unexpectedly.

"So—?"

"There are some likable aspects to your personality," Arch admitted. "Perhaps I want that Quincy St. Claire to succeed."

Half his mouth had frowned as he spoke, but not as much as Quincy's. She had never really considered herself by the measurement of what was likable and what was not. There were more important things, like the new machines out of Germany and increasing the returns from the southern markets. And how she was going to keep The Q, which, Quincy admitted, only reinforced Arch's point.

Arch stayed for more than his promised hour, until the street outside his office window was hazy with falling darkness. When eight fifteen came, Arch packed up his work. Quincy watched from the far corner of her eye as he wrote a thank-you note to Spense for some fresh fruit the printer had brought to the front-office staff. Arch wrote an elegant script. That, Quincy thought, was probably considered a likeable trait—the writing of the note, that is, not the handwriting.

"Has Mr. Spenser come in yet?" he asked, tapping the freshly sealed charcoal gray envelope against his fingers.

Quincy looked toward the clock. "He won't be in for another fifteen minutes. I can deliver your," she hesitated, "message, if you would like."

Open surprise crossed Arch's face, and he nodded. "Very much appreciated."

"It's one of my likable traits," Quincy said, taking the small envelope from his fingers and setting it carefully beside her. "You can write me a thank-you card for it later. You'd better go, as I know it won't please you to be late for an appointment."

"No, my hostess will string me up, as she is counting on me to balance the tables."

Quincy cocked an eyebrow and spoke before her reserve could tell her that she didn't care, "Balance the tables?"

"Yes, you know, ensuring the same number of gentlemen as ladies."

Quincy considered the stupidity of such a thing. "I had assumed you were meeting your peers from law school."

"No." Arch looked regretful. "My obligations this evening are familial and social. The familial is always welcome. The social satisfaction varies. But, all's well that ends well."

"If the tables are balanced."

Arch gave Quincy a closed smile and then said, "Quite." He gathered his satchel and was leaving when Quincy spoke again.

"You may tell her we've a spot for an in-house accountant."

"Pardon?" Arch turned from the door. "Who?"

"Your hostess. If she can balance budgets with the same zeal as she balances society, I might even be satisfied with her work."

"I'll be sure to tell her," Arch said, one side of his mouth turned up as he pressed his shoulder against the doorframe and looked at Quincy. "You developing a subtle sense of humor isn't one of the requirements to keep The Q, but it should be. Good night, Miss St. Claire."

Quincy didn't say good night. But when she turned back towards her proof, she saw that she had missed an error.

CHAPTER TWELVE:
Society and St. Claire

"You'll go because you want to keep The Q."

"There's no guarantee it's a requirement," Quincy told Jade as they watched the perfect motions of the presses loading and printing Friday's Q. It was three o'clock in the morning, and the Fothergils' event was that evening.

"Then why is Arch pressing you to go?"

"I don't know, but it must be tied to his incompetence," Quincy said, but there was no spirit behind the sting, as he had proved himself quite competent. That was its own disappointment.

"And the only task you've accomplished has been—?"

"The butterfly."

"The butterfly," Jade repeated. "There must be something you can do that will get you one step closer to keeping The Q. We've already arrived at mid-April."

Quincy made a disagreeable noise; she had never cared for months whose names sounded frivolous. April was the worst of the lot. February was a close second.

"Go to the dinner, Quincy," Jade pressed. "Go and tell me what it's like at the Fothergils'. Heaven knows I would love to try the food there."

"If I go, I'll have some dinner delivered to the offices of The Q for you."

Jade snorted.

Quincy disappeared up into her matchbox, slept, woke, dressed, and put in two hours of work before Arch and Fisher arrived in the front office. They went about the day as per usual: the three of them setting their own tasks in order, speaking as necessary, with few extra comments on the side from Quincy. Arch and Fisher were prone to wander in their discussions—toward politics or music or what was coming out of the university. And Quincy was prone to remind them she had not employed them to be critics, nor essayists, and that they should earn their salaries.

"Fisher," Quincy said, lifting her head after she had helped a string of customers and sent their Q slips into sorting room, "would you be willing to attend the Fothergils' dinner with me this evening?"

"The Fothergils?" The blood drained from Fisher's face. "The most powerful family in the country?"

"Do you know any backwater, low-street Fothergils?" Quincy asked severely. "Of course, the Fothergils. Well?"

"I would love—well, I wouldn't love to, but I would go for you, Quince. It's just that I've already set my evening." He suddenly became very concerned with organizing his desk, which meant moving items out of place so that he could put them back again. When she didn't ask, he volunteered the information like a shamefaced informant. "I'm off to a concert at Half Crown Park with Mado."

"Mado?"

"Madeleine," Fisher replied, doing his best not to look guilty. "The girl who frequents the offices of The Q on occasion. She's French," he added, as if he felt that there should be more words in the empty space between himself and Quincy right then.

"One of *those* silly things? Oh, Fisher, you're an idiot. What have you been doing with her?"

"Concerts, a time or two," he answered as a scarlet wave washed over his face. But his defense was getting on its feet, and when he answered again, he sounded more confident. "I've taken her around the university. We've discussed history and botany and physics."

"So she's not silly is what you are trying to say. See if I believe that."

Fisher lifted his chin. "She's a governess. She speaks three languages, reads Latin, and is thoughtful, and kind, and has a heart for people. I like her very much, and frankly, she's a breath of fresh air after a day with you."

"No need to state the obvious," Quincy grinned, outwardly amused, especially since Arch had his office door open and had looked up with a creased face at Fisher's comment.

"I'm sorry, Quince. You know I didn't mean it. It's only that Mado is important to me, and I don't want you to run her through is all."

"If I am able to run her through, I see that as her failing," Quincy retorted. "She should get stouter armor. Excuse me, I have to see these to their proper place." Quincy waved a stack of papers in the air, and then disappeared into the file room.

Admitting that his words had hurt her was not important enough to take up her time, but Quincy felt the weight of it nonetheless. She had not spent a lot of time thinking what it must be like for others to be with her, just as she had never considered Fisher an impermanent feature in her life. He had always been there, and she had assumed he would always be there. And now he wasn't—because of a concert in Half Crown Park and a French governess. And that fact sat off-kilter, angled and strange, worse than his cutting comment.

Slamming a drawer shut, Quincy looked around the file room and took in a fierce breath. The Q was the only permanent thing in her life; she could guide it and keep it alive and stay on top of the market and thrive. She wouldn't lose it. And if that meant arriving at the Fothergils' alone, then so be it. And if this party did not cross something off the list, she would ring her solicitor's neck after she ran him through every one of her presses.

The Mansion Fothergil was atop Kings Cross, the most exclusive layout in its most exclusive neighborhood. They were old money, as old as one could find. No other family had had as much political sway over the several-hundred-year history of the country, and in the city of Rhysdon they were demigods. The same went for their sway over fashion and trends. Or so Quincy had unavoidably been told.

She had dressed in a coat and breeches as always, but her coat was of deep, midnight blue velvet, and her black breeches had a matching blue stripe down the outseam. Beyond this effort, the Fothergils would have to take her as she was.

When the hansom cab pulled to a stop before the Fothergil mansion, Quincy descended before the driver could open her door himself, and walked up the wide staircase without a glance at the footmen who lined the way. She assumed that one just walked into these things, so that is what she did.

A well-appointed couple walked ahead of Quincy and she followed their lead, despite the grating nature of the woman's laugh, which was high and tinkling. Quincy thought the woman's laugh should be attached to a machine that would warn you when someone particularly distasteful was at the door. She then wondered if such an invention were possible.

They entered a rather large salon, and Quincy followed.

"The Duke and Duchess of Abnersfield," a man announced to a company of gowns and suits and jewels, drinks in hand, talking as if they hadn't heard, but turning their heads just so, to indicate they had. Then the duke and the duchess melted into the gathering.

"Excuse me." The man whose occupation was, apparently, calling out names—a ridiculous way to make a living—spoke to Quincy. "Are you certain you are in the right place, young man?"

"Young woman," Quincy said, her eyes wandering the room ahead. "And if this is the Fothergils', then, yes, I am. My name is St. Claire. Quincy St. Claire."

"Miss?"

"What do you think?"

He actually smiled then. "And where is your ancestral seat?"

"The Q," Quincy replied, unsure why that mattered. She certainly wasn't going to say Lester. He cleared his throat and lifted his chin, pounding some antiquated and expensive looking staff against the floor. "A Miss Quincy St. Claire, of The Q."

The sound shifted in the room, and Quincy was met by several sets of interested eyes. She stared right back, feeling like an exotic exhibition dragged into port, until an older woman in silver materialized and stepped forward to welcome her. The woman was tall, with an abundant frame, and tight rings of silver hair curled around her head. A choker of diamonds wrapped her neck, and her shrewd eyes appraised Quincy with interest. She must be the leading Fothergil, Quincy thought, for she dressed the part.

"Miss St. Claire." Her voice was warmer than Quincy was expecting.

"Lady Fothergil, I presume?" Quincy said, sounding like Arch. This made Quincy cringe.

"Quite so. I am pleased you've accepted my invitation."

Quincy ran her fingers along the seam of her pocket. "Or so you feel at present," she replied before she could call the words back.

"Goodness," Lady Fothergil laughed. "Come, come. It's a small gathering, and we've the most astounding food. I do hope you will sit beside me so that I might ask you questions. I am a patron of The Q, you know, for anything I need. And I own a good deal of stock in your brilliant gem. Your uncle Ezekiel assured me that with you at the helm it was the most secure investment in all of Europe. He has not been proven wrong, dear man. Now." She turned away. Quincy was unsure if she should follow. But the dinner gong rang, and the party moved through a set of open doors, so Quincy trailed the rest of the company.

As she entered the dining room—a light-filled display of silver and blue and sea green—Quincy caught Lady Fothergil's eye just as a footman ushered her in Fothergil's direction.

"You will sit here, on my left, and entertain me," Lady Fothergil said. "The man on my right is the greatest bore in all of Rhysdon."

But Quincy soon saw that he wasn't the greatest bore in Rhysdon. He was extremely humorous, this lord, and was vastly inappropriate more than once. Quincy's natural dislike of anyone with a title was tipped towards the positive by his clever observations and witty dialogue. He also kept Lady Fothergil entertained most of the night. And, since he drew Quincy into the conversation only enough to provide himself an appreciative listener, she didn't mind keeping silent and focusing on the food.

"If you speak ill of any more of my guests, Ashford," Lady Fothergil stated at some point near the end of dinner, "I'll have you thrown out. You know I will."

"Don't make threats, dear lady," the man, Ashford, replied. "I've yet to say anything about your little friend's ensemble." And he lifted a quizzing glass—that had not been en vogue for over half a century—and after looking at Quincy, swung it around to amuse himself. "What are you wearing, dear child?"

"Something made by a far better tailor than was your own ensemble," Quincy answered before lifting a perfectly prepared piece of fish into her mouth. Quincy did like fish.

Ashford smiled wickedly. "She bites."

Lady Fothergil laughed. "She's right, you know, Ashford. Her jacket is pure perfection."

"The point is the jacket," Ashford retorted after consulting his wine. "You can hardly tell what she is underneath her clothing, no matter how well tailored. I mean, she's a strange little thing. Women should be in skirts, you know." He turned and addressed Quincy directly. "Who is your tailor, by the way?"

Quincy ignored him and continued gaining a better acquaintance with her fish.

"Well," Lady Fothergil laughed.

"Invite her to another foray, Fothergil. I'm determined to discover her tailor. Better yet, an afternoon tea. We can have a tête-à-tête and discover all sorts of gems about our resident representative from the world of trade."

Looking up from her plate long enough to singe the man's eyebrows with her expression, Quincy motioned a footman to her side.

"Yes, Miss St. Claire?"

"We've had, what, six different courses, not including the soup? What do you have left in the kitchens? Is there more fish?"

Ashford choked on his wine, and Lady Fothergil lifted a finger to her cheek, watching Quincy with a detached interest. The footman looked a bit like a fish himself as he processed her words, words that a guest had apparently never uttered before. He looked towards Fothergil, who gave a single nod.

"Yes, Miss St. Claire," the footman replied. "There is a generous amount of food left in the kitchen from each course."

"Good." Quincy set her fork on her plate. "I would like more fish myself now, but, after you and the others have divided the spoils you're interested in, would you see the rest wrapped up and delivered to the printing offices of The Q?"

Someone made a sound of disbelief, and Quincy realized she had the attention of every guest at the table.

"Do as she requests, Hale," Lady Fothergil said as she sent her footman away with a quick wave. "I told you, Ashford. I told you she always knows how to turn a profit. She's now fed her entire night staff from the pantry of another."

"I'm planning on paying for it," Quincy replied, wishing her plate weren't so empty.

"Marked up by twenty percent," Lady Fothergil bargained.

"Of course not." Quincy folded her arms. "Market price and the cost of delivery. If you have a minimum of ten people in the kitchen, ten providing the in between work of an evening like this, and another ten in view of your guests, the footmen, the butler, and the like—and we know that thirty active employees is a conservative estimate—and they were to enjoy the extra food left in the kitchens, they would consume a minimum of fifteen hours that could've been spent on their work. If anything, you should be paying me for having the distraction taken away."

"Bravo!" came a man's voice from down the table, and Ashford laughed.

"See what I told you, Ashford. I know what I am doing." Lady Fothergil narrowed her eyes at Quincy. "Never be afraid to surround yourself with the best."

"Unless they make it a habit of cheating you out of your own food," Ashford countered.

"Perhaps, Ashford," Lady Fothergil said with an expression that Quincy could not interpret. "Perhaps."

Quincy left the Fothergils' early. Right after dinner, in fact. The women had gone through, and the men had stayed behind, which Quincy didn't mind. Lord Ashford, she decided, was good only in small doses.

"Thank you, Lady Fothergil, for dinner."

"Why, you're not going, Miss St. Claire? We've only just begun the evening."

"I have work."

"You can't be serious. Joking, surely you are joking. It's nearly ten o'clock. No, you're not," she added. "I can tell by your face. Well then." And Lady Fothergil called to have a carriage brought round.

Quincy thanked her hostess once more, certain she should not have been looking at her boots when she did. Fothergil was polite but pulled back, already engaging the other guests, before Quincy had moved towards the door. This suited Quincy fine. She had never craved the spotlight. Nor had she asked for it.

Returning to Gainsford Street, Quincy was greeted by a print shop of satisfied employees, the only evidence of Quincy's unorthodox deal being found in crumbs and sauces spilled on the floor between the presses. They were a good hour behind in their work now, but Quincy was treated as the hero. And after a rousing cheer led by Jade, Quincy made a motion to accept the praise and then took off her jacket and got to work. Her staff followed suit, as they always did. And among the editors and the mice and the printers, Quincy felt like she could breathe. Titles, Quincy decided, did nothing but stuff up the pure air of a room, and she wanted none of it.

The drivers and morning Q boys rolled out towards their routes just as the back alley was turning toward the blue of early morning. Jade and Spense oversaw cleanup while Quincy gave a cursory glance at the mechanisms of each press.

"Saturday," Jade sighed, as if that word were the most exquisite creation of God or man. "Two days of freedom."

"Day and a half," Quincy corrected. "You're back in Sunday night."

"Don't tell me." Jade put up her ink-stained hand before untying her apron. "On Saturday morning, I'm always an idealist."

"A radical habit which only leads to misery," Quincy breathed out.

"Good morning, dear," Spense said, punching Quincy affectionately on her arm. "That was the best food I've yet tasted. I'd sell my soul to relive last night."

"Keep it," Quincy said as she half smiled, half yawned. "I've no use for anybody's soul."

She locked the back doors behind them, and then took her tired body up the staircase and into the sorting room. It was empty—and mostly clean. Quincy would finish the job later that day. She followed the siren call of the matchbox up the stairs and opened her door with a long, relieved sound.

Taking off her jacket, Quincy set it on her desk. And, after fumbling with her small gas stove, she put enough water on for a single cup of peppermint tea. She fished a leftover biscuit from a tin on her table and set it near the flame to warm it up. Then, sitting down on her small bed, Quincy rolled up the sleeves of her white shirt and unbuttoned the top two buttons. The water was not yet coming to a boil, so Quincy lay back, closed her eyes, and followed the Q drivers along their respective routes to keep herself from falling asleep.

"Miss St. Claire!"

Quincy pulled her face together and yawned rather like a cat. She smelled something strange.

"Miss. St. Claire!" Someone grabbed her shoulders and then dropped her back onto the bed. "Damnation, it's climbing the wall!"

Quincy was waking up now, still groggy from the aftereffects of a heavy sleep.

"Arch?"

The room was full of smoke, but she could see Arch crushing something against the wallpaper behind the stove. Fire. Quincy was up, fumbling with the stove. Arch beat out the fire climbing the wall—it had only gone a few feet—and Quincy turned off the gas. Arch reached for the kettle, pulling his fingers back in pain, and then he wrapped the charred garment in his other hand around its handle before taking it off the small burner. The biscuit was now a piece of black ash, smoldering, but no longer boasting an open flame.

Coughing, Quincy ran to the window and threw it open, breathing the air deeply before ducking her head back into the room.

"Dear me," she could hear Arch muttering behind her. "Are you alright?"

"Yes." Quincy had one hand on her side and was breathing hard, her pulse rattling a staccato rhythm in her chest. "Are you? Did you burn yourself?" Then she saw that three feet of wallpaper had been blackened. Had Arch arrived even a moment later—

"I got here just as the fire jumped." Motioning towards the crumpled, singed ball of fabric that he had thrown to the ground, Arch added, "I'm sorry about your jacket. It was the first thing I could find."

Quincy walked past him and, paying no mind to the jacket, lifted her fingers to the blackened wall. "I—" Quincy's hands were shaking. "I almost burned down The Q." She could only hear Arch's heavy breathing next to her. He wiped his sleeve across his forehead and stared at her. "I almost burned down The Q," Quincy repeated.

It took Quincy another moment to realize that he was addressing her, asking her something.

"Are you alright?" Arch repeated.

"I almost burned down The Q."

He touched her elbow lightly with his fingers—they felt hot to Quincy through the thin fabric of her white shirt—and he led her to the small bed. She sat and stared at the wall while he fetched the only chair in the room and sat down in front of her.

"Are you alright? No, you're in shock. Shall I fetch you a cup of tea?" He rose and picked up Quincy's kettle. "Ruined." It clanked as he set it back on the stove. "No matter. There's an old one in my office."

By the time he returned to her small room, Quincy's shock, like a typewriter, had come to the end of its row, and her internal bell had rung. She was up, removing the blackened wallpaper to see what damage the wall had sustained. It was still warm and so she had soaked the wall with the charred jacket after wetting it.

"It smells up here still—keep the window open," Arch said, "and we'll take tea in my office."

"Why your office? Why not the front counter?"

"Miss St. Claire." Arch put one hand on his waist, running the other through his dark hair, "I have just saved The Q from burning to the ground and you with it, and my office is more comfortable than your counter. Just—" He dropped his hand down into a fist. "Just indulge me."

A ragtag tea service was assembled on Arch's desk, and, using the supply of peppermint tea from Quincy's room, he poured each of them a cup.

"Almost burning down The Q," Arch said as he poured Quincy's cup and then his own, "fulfilled your second requirement. Congratulations."

"It did? How?"

Arch handed Quincy her tea and gave a tired smile. "You did something that would endanger The Q. Granted, I'm certain your uncle had something else in mind, something more altruistic, like choosing a person over the business, but I'm counting it anyway, whether he haunts me or not."

Quincy's hands were still shaking as she lifted the cup to her mouth. The stupidity of the requirement didn't make her angry, but she wasn't going to celebrate her unexpected victory with Arch watching.

"What were you doing up there anyway?" he asked.

"Falling asleep, apparently," she said. The tea was too hot, and she set it down on his desk and looked at De Vere.

"Yes, of course," Arch continued, "but why were you not sleeping at your home?"

When Quincy looked back at him, she wondered how she came to employ the greatest fool in Rhysdon. "This is home."

"What?" he half laughed. "That pathetic little box of a closet at the top of the stairs?"

When she didn't reply, his face changed. He set his cup down firmly. "You sleep here? You live here?"

"How have you not understood that fact? Fisher told you I live here. I heard him."

"I thought that was a figure of speech. I mean, who would—why would you live here?"

"People live in smaller places. People live in much worse!"

"Yes, but not people with the means you have! Quincy, your uncle's town house is sitting empty?"

"Not for long. I aim to put it on the market."

"You spend all your time here?" He was still incredulous, as if the most painful thing in life could be to live at The Q. "Alone?"

"I'm not alone. The print room runs all night, the office all day, save a few shifts at the weekend."

Arch looked at her with an expression she didn't understand, and it made her angry. It was like she was a half-drowned kitten, and he was tenderly trying to find a new situation for her.

"What are you doing here, anyway?" she snapped. "You don't work Saturdays."

"I left some personal papers on my desk. And I came to see if the rumors were true. I figured you would be working and I could ask you myself."

"You say that like working is a bad thing."

"In your case, it's obsessive."

Quincy glared. "And what rumors are you referring to?"

"That you were a splash at the Fothergils', and I don't mean that in a complimentary way. That Ashford has practically fallen in love with you, which is not a glowing reference among decent society. That you left just after dinner without so much as a *by your leave*. That you bought the extra food out of Lady Fothergil's kitchen and had it sent to The Q." He laughed, it seemed, at the absurdity of what he was about to say. "That you actually asked for additional plates of fish after licking your fingers."

"I didn't lick my fingers." Quincy said these words as if they had been on ice. She had disliked Arch for most of their acquaintance, she had thought him cold and unremarkable, but never had she thought him to be such a snob.

Arch let his shoulders drop. "Are you telling me that everything else is true?"

"The staff enjoyed their dinner," Quincy said by way of answer. "That's all I care about."

Arch was speechless. He looked at her like she was a gutter urchin caught in an aristocrat's rose garden.

"You kept pressing me into that dinner in the first place," Quincy argued in her defense. "You can't have expected me to behave differently. So what requirement did I meet?"

His usually pale cheeks were flushed. "None, dammit, you got halfway and then botched it up!"

"What do you mean halfway?" Quincy challenged.

"The requirement is for you to be invited to a dinner and then receive an invitation to return. And you've botched it! Fothergil will never have you back again." He lifted his thumb to his mouth and closed his eyes. "I wonder if it's against the rules for me to smooth it over for you."

"Smooth it over for me?" Quincy's anger was now truly sparked. "I didn't ask you to smooth anything over for me. I handled myself at dinner with enough decorum to please myself, and that's good enough. The last person I need in this world to sort out my affairs is you!"

"I couldn't agree more," Arch said, standing abruptly and reaching for his satchel. "Good day, St. Claire. I will be in Monday morning, for the sake of my own professional pride. Try not to incinerate yourself, or the office, before then."

He was up and out of The Q before she could say anything. But, as he passed by the window of his office, Quincy threw her teacup at him. It shattered into type-sized pieces against the glass and fell to the ground.

———

Fisher found Quincy in the file room Monday morning.

"What did you do to Arch?"

"Why do you ask?" Quincy grunted, lifting a box and handing it to Fisher.

"He came in just now and sent a scowl at the empty counter so hot that, had you been sitting there, it would have ended in cinders." Fisher shifted the box and looked around it to Quincy's face. "He then shut the door of his office pointedly, locked it, and has not left since."

"Good riddance—aha!" Quincy had found the file she was looking for. "Let Arch simmer for a day or so. He'll recover."

"You better hope he does. He can take The Q away from you, Quince."

"He won't."

"Only because he has a gentleman's honor."

"He says it's his pride."

"It's his honor," Fisher insisted.

"And to Arch's one virtue I trust. Now, see to the front desk a while."

"Will there ever come a day when
we are not impossible?"

ANGEL

CHAPTER THIRTEEN:

Don't Tell Me My Business

Once a year, Quincy attended a banquet held for the businessmen of Rhysdon in the grand ballroom of The Emperion Hotel. The invitation always stated *businessmen*. And Quincy always went. It wasn't a matter of principle or a statement for the women of Rhysdon. The year Quincy had turned fourteen, Ezekiel had been disinclined to show, and had sent Quincy in his place.

She had gone and had created such a stir that, had she not the street grit and print-shop drive, she might have turned tail and run. But she didn't. She had stayed and had the good fortune of being taken in by a few men who respected her uncle. Her main sponsor had been Priest, owner of *The Times*. He had enjoyed a congenial relationship with Ezekiel, as *The Q* had been picked up by *The Times*. And when he had seen the young Quincy—scrawny, small, wearing ink-stained schoolboy clothing—he took her under his all-powerful wing

The second person of note, among the business owners of the city, was Draggen, the owner of *The Rhysdon Sun*. He had not been friendly with Ezekiel, nor his foundling relation turned business protégé. Draggen had resisted taking *The Q* in his paper for as long as he could. For a few years, he had even tried to run a copycat, but to no profit.

As *The Times* was The Q's flagship carrier, Draggen had worked out a less profitable contract for his own newspaper. This did not increase his affection for the establishment of The Q. He also did not think Quincy should be invited to the banquets. He had even lobbied against it two years previous. But Priest had taken her in. And now, when Quincy arrived, she knew right where her place was. It was with the printing tycoon of *The Times* that she relaxed.

"Quincy St. Claire." Priest took a long draw on his cigar and motioned towards an empty seat beside him as they waited in the lobby for dinner. The other members of their exclusive group consisted of Tharrin, shipping king in three port cities; Blevins, railroad leader; and Clonmel, who mined copper. They all greeted Quincy with pleasure, and Blevins offered her a cigar. Quincy refused it. The smell reminded her of Ezekiel, but the taste reminded her of sooty gutters.

"What news from The Q?" Priest said slowly. "Aside from the fact that my sales are up because of it."

Quincy settled into her seat. "All my forecasts of the last year were met—"

"Crushed," Tharrin corrected.

"I exceeded my own expectations," Quincy admitted. "Expansion goes forward as planned. I've already secured a Parisian property and am assembling an office to open early autumn."

"I want to speak with you about that sometime," said Priest. "Let's compare markets and see what we can do for each other."

"And you, gentlemen?" Quincy asked, resting a booted foot on her knee. "The economy should have spurred all your interests forward."

"Copper's solid," Clonmel volunteered in his nasal voice. "I've opened three new mines and am moving towards some interests in silver."

"Railroads are as they ever were," Blevins said. "Have you seen the new engines?"

"Yes," Quincy replied. "Beautiful. Someday, I'll see how they fly. And what about you, Tharrin? Shipping profits what you expected?"

"Not what I want to see, but I have high expectations. The sea is the sea. The continent is the continent. And I've been dealing with some messy tariff business—"

"And what of the smugglers?" inserted Blevins. "I hear they've been dipping into your pockets."

"Aye, they have," Tharrin growled. "There's one in particular I'd love to set in Jane's Cellar."

"The bird fellow?" Clonmel snapped his fingers. "Hawk?"

"Crow," answered Tharrin.

Quincy smiled and covered her sins by lifting a hand to her face.

"Get the fellow behind bars," Blevins said.

"Aye," Tharrin agreed.

Priest narrowed his eyes and scratched his beard with his fingers before setting his cigar back inside his mouth. Then he said, "I believe one of our own may be dancing with the devil, gentlemen."

"What do you mean?" Tharrin questioned, looking from Blevins to Clonmel. "One of you been using his services?"

"Wrong kind of dance," Priest said. "Quincy?"

"Priest."

"Do you have anything you would like to tell Tharrin?"

"The net of *The Times* spreads far." Quincy crossed her arms, still smiling. "I know Crow. He's only an alleged smuggler."

Tharrin looked at Quincy with suspicion. "What's this, St. Claire? Do you do business on the backwaters?"

"Of course not." Quincy pulled her mouth up and eyebrows down. "When would I have time? No, Crow is a customer of The Q's."

"And," Priest interjected with his low voice and a smile.

"And a personal friend," Quincy said. "I admit freely that I enjoy his company. I find him to be—"

"A devil," Clonmel complained.

"A charming one," Quincy countered with a jaunty tilt of her chin.

"Bah! Refuse the fellow services."

"Crow is my friend," Quincy said evenly. "But, more importantly, he is a valued client, who, at this point, has never been charged with any illegal activity."

"If there's smoke—" Priest said with a sarcastic tone.

"Then put your cigar out," Quincy replied, "and leave me to manage my own business."

Quincy's friends laughed, and then they were called for dinner.

It was no surprise that Quincy found herself seated beside Priest; he had often arranged it. What was not as pleasant was that Draggen was across from her at the table. He made a point of ignoring Quincy straight off, which was fine by her. She turned to Priest and spoke quietly.

"Jade tells me your wife has been ill."

"Jade should come work at *The Times*," Priest answered. "I'll pay her more for it and give her better hours."

"Not a chance she'll have you. I give her the space she needs to do her work."

"I could match that."

"No, you couldn't. Printing is still a man's world, Priest, but The Q's print room is Jade's."

Priest grunted and returned to Quincy's earlier question. "Celine is not doing well, if I'm to be honest with you."

"I'm sorry to hear it."

"Me too." Priest finished his soup. "Speaking of the personal affairs, how are you holding up with your uncle gone?"

"If Ezekiel's goal was to make my life inconvenient, he's succeeded."

"Are you talking about that challenge of sorts?"

Cocking her chin towards Priest, Quincy eyed the man. "You know of it?"

"Your uncle asked me what I thought."

Quincy snorted. "What do you think?"

"I think he was a fool. If you want to be consumed by your business, that's your own affair."

"Amen."

Their conversation fell off, and Priest found himself occupied by his neighbor on his left. Uninterested in speaking with anyone else, Quincy focused on her food until a familiar and unwelcome voice called her out.

"Miss St. Claire, I hear you're looking to expand The Q into foreign markets."

Quincy looked up from her sirloin regretfully. "Inevitably, Draggen."

"Your in-house product does fine, deary; the country humors you.

But they will eat you alive if you try to move international. You're great-uncle stumbled upon a pretty hobby, but you don't have the chops."

Priest shifted at Quincy's left, and she saw the men around them were listening. The cigar smoke was thick, and the smell of men's lotions permeated the space around Quincy. She set her knife and fork down and lifted an eyebrow. Quincy did not need to resent Draggen's idiocy, she was confident in her own abilities.

"How many urban subscriptions did you end with this last quarter, Draggen? Three hundred and fifty thousand? How many further afield, in the country, in the smaller towns? I have your numbers, for your employees have loud mouths. I've seen your techniques. I've seen your angles, or lack thereof. Frankly, Draggen, with the resources you have available, I am not impressed. Now, I am also privy to my numbers. And my methods. And the inside of my own brain. *The Q* is pulling in several times more than *The Sun*, and for what, Draggen? News? Stories and essays and society pages? No, the money is going towards questions—a brilliant concept turned into a powerhouse operation. So, Draggen, don't tell me my business. It's clear that I do mine far better than you do yours."

The entire table had silenced itself enough to hear most of Quincy's monologue. Priest shifted towards Quincy and lit a new cigar.

"You don't belong here," Draggen replied.

"You're right, Draggen," said Quincy. "I don't. But you're apparently the best Rhysdon has to offer, so I suppose I'll have to put up with you."

"Here, here," Priest said, lifting his glass. "To Quincy St. Claire, again showing the businessmen of Rhysdon what to reach for."

Glasses were raised with the general sound of agreement. Quincy stared at Draggen as she picked up her knife and fork, then she turned her attention back to her sirloin.

"I won't tell you not to make Draggen your enemy, for you already have," Priest said later to Quincy as they left the Emperion Hotel in each other's company. "But watch your back in this city. Not all the men in business like what you do. I wouldn't trust too many of them."

"Priest, have you ever been to a foundling factory?"

"My reporters have."

"It's much more of a bloodbath than the business state of Rhysdon. I know my staff. I know my market. I know my business."

"And, more importantly, you know yourself."

Quincy looked at him. "Yes."

"Bravo," Priest replied dryly, which Quincy knew was a compliment. The man moved well in his own smoke and nonchalance—he knew how to walk quickly without looking like he had any hurry in his body, or in his schedule. Quincy knew better. The man was a machine with an internal clock, even if he wore his efficiency like a scarf.

"Speaking of knowing things and people," Priest continued, "tell me about your personal solicitor."

"Who? Arch? What is there to tell?"

"I know the man, know of the man, rather. Interesting fellow. Do you know all his affairs?"

"I know the affairs that touch The Q. Anything else is his own business. Why do you ask?"

"Keep an eye on him," Priest said, his third cigar of the evening between his teeth. "He's certainly one to watch."

"In what way?"

"Let's just say—" Priest paused at the street corner, where he would be turning left as Quincy continued straight, and looked up past the buildings of Rhysdon into the night sky. "Let's just say that I would like to make him a shooting star. Good night, St. Claire. Come by my office next week. Let's talk expanding markets."

"Good night, Priest."

Quincy sold Ezekiel's town house, moving the few furniture items she wished to keep into storage. The sale was arranged by Arch, who had discreetly lined up a buyer. The purchaser would not claim residence for two more months, giving Quincy time to select whatever possessions she liked.

"You're certain you do not wish to keep more of the furnishings?" Arch asked when she showed little inclination. Quincy was certain, and she did not grace him with an answer.

"But, Miss St. Claire, the library—?" Arch left his plea hanging in the air above the counter. He stood before her in what appeared to be nervous anticipation of the answer she hadn't yet given. Quincy had never seen Arch plead for anything.

"The library is to be sold with the rest," Quincy stated, despite his efforts.

Arch set his hand purposefully on the counter and looked at Quincy with all his earnestness, which, Quincy thought, probably signified a great deal. "Your uncle compiled one of the greatest libraries in the country, let alone Rhysdon."

"Really?" she answered, paying half attention as she reviewed the previous week's profits.

Arch opened his mouth and twisted his face. It gave him the look of a younger boy. "I would ask you to reconsider. To separate that collection would be—"

"Murder?" Quincy supplied.

"Yes!" Arch gripped the counter with both hands now, his face on the edge of hope. The image of Arch, taking such care with the street boy weeks before, tugged at the edge of Quincy's mind and she thought about feeling guilty for saying, "I will see to the dismemberment myself, Arch, so you won't bloody your hands."

Arch stiffened. "A cruel joke, Miss St. Claire."

"Notify Jackson that I will superintend my uncle's remaining possessions," Quincy added, ignoring his words. "You need not worry yourself any further. Now, I'm done discussing the matter. Please return to the work for which you are paid."

Arch set his mouth in a line and removed his hands from the counter. Before he turned toward his office, Quincy noticed that the skin beneath his left eye twitched, and it made him look sad. She felt bad. Well, she stalked the boundaries of regret, at least. But what else did he wish her to say? What use had Quincy for libraries?

To Quincy's great surprise, she was invited for tea at the Fothergils mansion. Quincy was triumphant, making certain Arch saw the invitation. He ignored her crowing and told her to have herself a nice afternoon. "Congratulations on meeting your third requirement," he stated absently.

"It doesn't matter at this rate," Quincy retorted. "It's already almost May."

He didn't reply.

At tea, Quincy and Lady Fothergil discussed business. Quincy enjoyed their conversation more than she had anticipated. The woman did have an intelligent way of understanding the world and a few other things on the side, a dry wit being one of them.

"I was wondering," Quincy said, looking around the room, "do you have many spare rooms here?"

Lady Fothergil laughed. "Why do you ask, Miss St. Claire. I admit to being nervous after the last debacle."

"It's only that I've decided to keep several crates of my uncle's belongings, and I was wondering if they could be brought here until further arrangements could be made. You've got the room, and I live at The Q. There's hardly space for anything bigger than myself there."

Fothergil's expression was one of entertained disbelief. "And storage won't do?"

"I don't want the items to be damaged," said Quincy, unapologetically.

"You are a strange child, indeed," Fothergil answered. "I would be happy to accommodate your bizarre request as long as you promise there's nothing living in the crates."

"Not that I know of."

"Fabulous. When would you like the items removed to my house? I could send my footmen to do the job."

"Tomorrow."

"Tomorrow!" Fothergil laughed. "You should have been born into royalty, St. Claire. You have an extraordinary sense of self-importance."

"If you've decided to do something," Quincy countered, feeling annoyed, "why not do it immediately?"

"Why not indeed? Hale will arrange the details with the footmen. I'll put the crates in the silver parlor of the second wing. That is where you will find them."

"Thank you."

Fothergil tapped a silver spoon against her teacup and tilted her head. "When, exactly, do you intend to buy your own establishment and claim your things?"

Quincy shrugged and took a sip of her tea. "A year or so, perhaps."

Fothergil's mouth twisted shrewdly. "So much for making decisions and seeing them through."

"That's not a decision I have time to make now." Quincy leaned back against the sofa. "My current work is more important."

Fothergil narrowed her eyes and said, "You have more gall than anyone of my acquaintance, Quincy St. Claire. I suppose I must keep you on as friend."

When Quincy packed up Ezekiel's library—with the help of Lady Fothergil's footmen—she found a small, forgotten volume in a stack of neglected books behind the door. Taking special note of the title page, Quincy tucked it into a grocer's crate printed with a singular script, so she would know where it was.

Quincy did not intend to tell Arch that she had kept the books. She told herself he didn't deserve the relief, when the reality was that she didn't want him knowing he'd influenced her.

CHAPTER FOURTEEN:
The Trouble a Man Can Come to Before Eight O'clock

"I've told you a thousand times, constable, that unless I have proof of illegal activity, I cannot share my customers' information with you, nor will I reveal whose questions are whose if they haven't themselves provided the names. Q policy."

Constable Catch, back on his warpath for Crow's scalp, breathed out with a frown that consumed the entire front office. "Smuggling is a severe problem in Rhysdon. It hurts our city's economy, and you will be held responsible for any crime you could have prevented."

"Without proof there's no knowledge." Quincy picked up her pen with a stubborn resolve, eyeing Fisher, who seemed eager to give Catch any information that he had. "Now, do you have a question for me today, constable?"

"No, ma'am, I do not." He put his hat on with equal resolve and turned heel.

Not a minute after Constable Catch had quit the establishment, Crow's tall figure shadowed the door. The bell rang as he pushed it open. "Good afternoon, love."

"Crow," Quincy acknowledged with a grin. "I didn't realize you were back in town."

"Ever a surprise. Was that Catcher I just missed?"

"Asking after you, as always."

"Humph." Crow leaned over the counter. "I've missed you, love.

Why don't you come down to The Nest tonight?"

"Can't. I'll be working."

"Why is it the bottles are always empty?"

"I told you, I'm working—"

"No, love," Crow laughed, "that's my question."

"Oh." Quincy felt herself flush.

He watched her put down his question, moving his hands over the counter before him. "Are you working late alone?"

"In the front office, yes. The back room is endlessly printing, as you know."

"What if I were to bring some dinner for you then, later? Not from The Nest—" He amended quickly. "Some decent food; good company."

Fisher guffawed.

"Why ever not?" Quincy looked up. "I could use the food, and the company. Does eight o'clock work for you?"

"A bit early for my breed, but I can make it happen, love." He rapped the counter with his knuckles. "Until then."

———

At six o'clock, Fisher rather silently packed up his desk, throwing his coat on with the air of the suffering righteous, and after securing his light brown satchel across his back, left the offices of The Q without saying a word.

Mr. Arch remained seated at his desk.

Early summer shadows began to stretch themselves out along the sidewalks of Gainsford Street. Merchants and bankers and businessmen closed their office doors behind them and walked with brisk steps toward the evening ahead of them. And yet, Arch was still at his desk, both lamps lit, the shadow of De Vere's profile on the far wall.

He came out of his office once, to fish out some paperwork from the file room, and when he came back through, pushing the swinging half gate open as he read what was in his hand, he failed to close his office door again, leaving it wide open. He showed no sign of going.

Quincy ignored him.

An hour later, Arch stood and walked across his office, where he hovered in the doorway, waiting until his silent presence coaxed Quincy away from her figures and notes. Quincy St. Claire was never coaxed.

"I've work to do," Arch began, when she refused to look up. "Enough to keep me occupied for the length of the evening. If you wish it, I could keep my door closed and stay outside of your business, but the draft coming through the open door is pleasant, as today's temperatures have been rather stifling."

Quincy glanced up at Arch. He was leaning against the doorjamb, watching her work with uncertain eyes and an expression of distant concern. For his sake, it was a blessed thing that this didn't strike Quincy as patronizing. She didn't say anything, just looked at him, tapping her pen against the counter twice.

Arch shifted on his feet and crossed his arms. "It is only that," he continued, "I have a sister, Mary. We're quite close. We try and give each other what we can, but—I would—what I am trying to say is, I would like to keep quiet and out of your way, while you entertain Crow. But, I would like to remain here."

Quincy popped her jaw and stared at him a long while before speaking. The mention of his sister had pulled at the strings of—what she was certain people assumed was—her lopsided heart. This mention of his sister called up the cold, unwanted memory of being a desperate child, not knowing how to put food into her own mouth, let alone the mouth of another. This rememberance crashed against the carefully assembled walls of her mind. She braced herself against the memory, for she could not afford it.

"Why do you think you should do that for me? Are you worried about my reputation? The lack of decorum I show?" Quincy asked honestly.

"Only that I believe," Arch lifted his shoulders and the look on his face was so unguarded Quincy surprised herself by listening, "that each one of us has times when what we need most is someone who is willing to sit quietly by, waiting for us. Not interfering, just being."

"Aren't you the philosopher," Quincy said before she could clap the words back into her throat.

Arch responded by pulling himself away from the doorjamb and standing up straight, the tenderness in his face retreating. "I would ask my sister if she would wish it, which is why I extended the same courtesy to you."

For a quick second, the amount of time it took for Arch to turn around, the amount of time it took for the hand on Quincy's pocket watch to shiver forward one sliver of a step, Quincy could only see a small blue-eyed, blond-haired girl, looking up at her. Quincy gulped and said, "Wait!"

The vision vanished. The girl was gone. Arch turned, but Quincy was not watching his face. She was looking for the face that had just been frightened back into memory, a memory she never spoke of.

"Yes, Miss St. Claire?"

Quincy blinked, gripping the fountain pen in her hand, and took a stabilizing breath. "I—well." She looked at Arch and forced herself to lift a shoulder, shaking off the ghost. "There's no sense in you keeping your door shut," she lied. "It's a hot evening. Besides, I might find it easier to finish my own reports from having your company."

They both knew this was untrue, that Quincy could have worked solitarily at the counter until Judgment Day. But Arch nodded, disappeared into the dimming light of his office, and sitting, bent himself over the work on his desk.

Quincy parted her lips, haunted by her own memory. Why Arch's words had called up such images, she didn't know, but Quincy did not have the emotional capital to afford confronting it, so she clamped her mouth shut and turned again towards her work.

Everything but work was rubbish. All of it.

Before long, lines of figures lulled her back into focus. Quincy didn't look up again until the bell on the door rang two hours later.

"Sorry, love," Crow said as he came through the door, basket in hand. "You wouldn't believe the trouble a man can come to before eight o'clock."

Tossing her head, moving a few stray wisps of blond hair from her eyes in the act, Quincy glanced at her pocket watch. It was a quarter to nine. Arch, Quincy noted, did not look up from his work.

"I hardly noticed, Crow, to be honest."

"Low compliment." He grinned and set the basket on the counter as Quincy gathered her papers and pushed them aside. He looked as he always did: long coat, high collar, windswept hair. Quincy pressed her lips together in an effort not to smile. His familiar musk filled the room, and as Quincy gathered her ledgers and stacked them neatly at the end of the counter, she remembered how much she liked it.

"I've another stool," Quincy said, slipping off her own to grab the extra stool. She lifted it up and over the counter, and Crow took it with an easy hand, setting it on the floor, and perching himself upon it, his right elbow resting on the counter, his back against the wall behind him, his legs stretched out and crossed with nonchalance at the ankles. "I see your poor solicitor is still in his office. You determined to run the man ragged? Or is he simply serving as respectable chaperone?"

"No rest for the wicked," Quincy replied. "The man has work to finish."

From her vantage point, Quincy thought she saw the ghost of a smile on Arch's face.

"Not quite how I'd imagined it, but I'll take what I can get, love." Crow opened the basket and began to reveal several items of interest. "First, bread. Good bread. None of your wispy Rhysdon fluff. Second, cold chicken and cured meats. Along with a few excellent imported cheeses and a bottle of wine." Crow grinned. "Also excellent. Also imported."

Quincy wrinkled her nose. "I don't care much for wine, so I'll let you enjoy it yourself."

"That's too bad," Crow said as he shrugged, "but I'm selfish enough not to argue."

"Where have you been?" Quincy asked in a relaxed tone that she only ever used with Crow and Fisher. "The local businessmen were asking."

"Here and there." Crow offered a half smile, unwrapping the food and laying it out on the brown paper. His fingernails were very clean, cleaner than Quincy's. "I spent some time around the continent. I may have spent time off the Irish coast."

"Allegedly?"

"Allegedly." He nodded.

As they ate, Crow told Quincy stories of different places, of nights out at sea, of ships and salt and worlds with no stable ground.

"You wouldn't like it, though, St. Claire."

"Why's that again?" she asked between a mouthful of bread.

"Because, to stand the inconveniences of the life, you've got to love the romance, and there's very little that you, Quincy St. Claire, are willing to give to a romance not covered in ink."

Quincy swallowed. "It's not really the ink."

"Oh?" Crow crossed his arms and leaned back against the wall. "Do tell me then, what it is."

"It's the machine."

Crow didn't look surprised. "The machine."

"Yes. It's the ink and the paper and the machine, coupled with an idea that can shape an entire city."

"An idea that can drain the pocketbooks of an entire city," said Crow.

"A product so perfect that it can occupy the attention of an entire country," countered Quincy.

"The power?"

"The progress." Quincy lifted one booted foot onto her stool and wrapped her arms around her knee, enjoying the easy company of the smuggler. "I understand The Q. When I turn this knob, profits do this. When I press that button, customers do that. The inside of a well-run business becomes a machine that can run above the unreliable base of human emotion."

"A rare thing you are, Miss St. Claire. It's not often I find someone with enough drive to rival my own. Why don't you marry me?"

Something dropped in Arch's office.

Quincy rolled her eyes at Crow and picked at a piece of bread. "I've yet to fit it into my schedule, Crow."

"If you don't want a local cleric, I could import one from any of the major cities in Europe or the Mediterranean."

"I'll keep that in mind," she answered dryly and he laughed.

Crow launched into another story. Quincy let an hour pass, enjoying the sound of his voice as he spoke of what he loved, before telling Crow that she had an hour's work yet and an early morning. "Will you be in Rhysdon long, at any rate?"

"Who's asking? You or Catcher?"

"Constable Catch. I've been feeding him information to feather my income."

"In that case, I'll give you an itinerary of my time. We'll see if we can send him goose chasing for several weeks."

Crow began to wrap the brown paper around the remains of their meal. His fingers were long and weathered, scars crossing his knuckles, a tarnished ring of silver around one finger. Quincy spread her own fingers: small, nail-bitten, ink-stained. They looked worse than a Q boy's.

"We carry our trades well," Crow said, following Quincy's eyes, "unlike the lily skins of the titled aristocracy. May it ever be so."

"Hear, hear," said Quincy, slapping the counter with her hand. "The world needs fewer worthless people."

"Harder than I would phrase it, love. I've a few clients among the tip shade of the city; they're not all bottom-feeders." Crow nodded towards Arch's office. "Speaking of the elite, is your solicitor hungry?"

Quincy shrugged. She had forgotten he was there. Leaning to the right, she saw him sitting back in his chair, reading, a hand lifted to his chin as he concentrated on the words before him. The street was full dark now, and the only light in the room came from the desk lamp, setting his skin in stark contrast with his dark eyes and hair. He had removed his jacket, comfortably waiting in a fitted vest over his white shirt, his sleeves rolled partway up his forearms.

"What's his name?" Crow asked. "Starch?"

"Arch," Quincy answered, lifting her eyebrows at the humor behind the error.

"Arch!" Crow called, grabbing the bottle of wine and sauntering into the office. Quincy slipped from her stool, inexplicably trepidatious about her solicitor and Crow entering into any communication whatsoever.

Arch set his book down and stood as Crow extended his hand. Arch took it graciously.

"Crow."

"Arch."

"Have you had a pleasant day?" Arch inquired politely.

"Passable," Crow said with the tone Quincy often observed men using when speaking with other men. "Nothing I couldn't handle. Are you interested in a bottle of good wine?" Crow lifted the bottle and handed it to Arch.

"I assume this was not purchased at Wellington's?"

"No," Crow said, folding his arms while Arch inspected the label with interest. "It was not."

"Forgive me, but I'm not one to support black-market work. If you brought it through a back harbor, I'm not interested."

"Take it," Crow encouraged. "There's only a glass or two left. How are you on disillusionment and the monarchy?"

Arch actually laughed. "Why do you ask?"

"Because, sometime in the last twenty four hours, the crown prince added two bottles of this particular vintage to his personal stores."

"Hardly good reason."

"Technically, under Rhysdon law, it's now an in-country product, legal as your mother's pearl earrings. Only those responsible for its import can be held accountable, and you're not paying for it, so no tariffs would be asked of you anyway. Take it home and enjoy a glass."

"Very well." Arch laughed again. "I'll send miscellaneous payment to the tariff offices tomorrow, and next time you come in, I'll let you know how it stacks up against my own cellar."

"Do that." Crow lifted his chin in a subtle nod, his voice deeper and more graveled in this late hour. "Speaking of next time I'll see you, I've run into a few situations that I need good legal advice to sort out. Do you take clients outside your Q hours?"

"Why do you ask me?"

"If you work at The Q, you must be the best."

Arch set the bottle of wine on his desk and looked past Crow towards Quincy. "I do accept outside clientele, unless Miss St. Claire finds that problematic."

Quincy dug her hands into her pockets. "What you do after hours is your own business."

Nodding, Arch looked back to Crow. "I would be happy to give you a consultation. But, I warn you that I keep myself strictly within the law. I am not a willing participant in finding ways to step around the law's intent, either."

"So you really do intend to pay the tariff on this bottle," Crow said.

"I intend to pay the tariff for the entire case. Then, the next time the crown prince fleeces me in cards, I intend to let him know I paid his taxes for him."

Though Quincy knew Arch must be joking, Crow pretended to believe him and laughed.

"You do that, Arch. Meats, cheeses, bread? On the counter."

"Thank you, but I'll have my dinner at home."

"Fair enough." Crow shook Arch's hand again. "I'll be in touch."

"Find me here to set an appointment."

"Oh, I don't think that will be necessary," Crow said, pulling at the collar of his long coat. "I know how to find anybody in this city. Good night, Arch." Crow smiled at Quincy as she pretended to be busy behind the counter. "Thanks for the company, love."

"Thanks for the food. And the stories."

"Would you like to buy the rest from me and feed it to your night staff?" He leaned towards her, his elbows resting on the counter.

"You heard about that?"

"You've become a hero at The Nest. When you come back, every man there will buy you a drink."

"My printers would be grateful for the food," Quincy replied, nodding towards the remains of their dinner on the counter, "and I'll even throw in a free question for it."

"A free question?" Crow sounded interested. "I'll use it right now. Can I see you again?"

Quincy's stomach turned, and the back of her neck felt warm. "Is this a real question?"

"It's not for your paper, that's for certain. Well?"

"As my time permits," Quincy answered as she looked at Crow's blue eyes. "I have no objections to your company."

"I'll come round during the next fortnight, when I better know my obligations. Good night, love." He leaned across the counter and kissed Quincy on the cheek before turning on his heel—the end of his long coat drawing a circle in the air—and disappearing out into the black of the street.

She stared after him, frozen in place. Quincy St. Claire didn't like being touched. Crow's mild, flirtatious approximations had been singular enough because she had enjoyed them. But this time it felt like an uppercase expression.

"Miss St. Claire?"

Quincy felt the flush across her cheeks. She pinched her lips together and realized she was clutching the edge of the counter. "Yes, Mr. Arch?"

He was again standing in the doorway, coat on, satchel in one hand, bottle of Crow's wine in the other. "Is there anything else you need from me before I leave?"

There was an extra measure of seriousness in Arch's expression.

"No. Thank you for finishing your work." She still felt flustered and realized Arch must have witnessed Crow's kiss. "I hope it's good wine."

Arch lifted the bottle a few inches, his mouth pinched, his face regretful. "I believe it is. Good night, Miss St. Claire."

After Arch left, Quincy locked the door, extinguished the gas lamps in The Q's front office, and went straight up to her room— where the ghostlike smell of smoke still lingered. Laying down on the bed, Quincy sighed and rolled onto her side. She felt a strange melancholy and was unsure why.

CHAPTER FIFTEEN:

St. Ezekiel's Day

The twenty-seventh of May was Saint Ezekiel's Day. The celebrants of this special occasion were—and had been for the last ten years—only two: Fisher and Quincy. For it was the anniversary of the day Ezekiel had brought Fisher home. The children had marked it as important, and upon an exploration of Rhysdon's cathedrals and after learning that the grim-faced statues were creatures called saints and that each saint had a day, they had begun celebrating Saint Ezekiel's Day.

Neither of them spoke about it, but come five o'clock, Quincy made a rare request from Arch.

"Would you watch the desk for the final hour and then close up the front office?"

"Certainly, Miss St. Claire. Might I ask where you and Fisher are off to?"

"It's Saint Ezekiel's Day. We've things to be about."

Arch gave a slow half nod, perhaps feeling he had missed something in his religious studies. Giving no explanation, Quincy and Fisher slipped out onto Gainsford Street.

Without discussing the established routine of Saint Ezekiel's Day, they stopped and bought cinnamon street twists and then found themselves following the road to the old town house on Linger Wood Street where they had all three once lived, the house with two point four balusters per tread.

"We were given it all, Quincy," Fisher said as they stared at the familiar door. "Finest man I've ever known, and he took me in. My whole world is now opened—wide and fresh."

"He was the finest," Quincy answered, her hands deep in her pockets, her eyes wandering along the vines climbing the face of her only childhood home. She had been so consumed with The Q—with keeping it—that she had hardly noticed that, since her uncle Ezekiel had died, the city hadn't shined in the same way. Ezekiel had made everything worth celebrating. Although Quincy had rarely agreed that anything was worth such bother, she missed the sheen he had carried with him.

"Well?" Fisher's voice broke through her thoughts.

"To the quay?"

"To the quay."

The next several hours were spent visiting all the haunts Quincy and Fisher had discovered in their first week in Rhysdon: The Quay. Henley Street, filled with vendors, where they each spent a jab, just as they had on their first visit. Queen's Park, for watching. And Fothsome House, for specialty fruit drinks that fizzed.

Fisher coaxed Quincy into a steady stream of conversations as they walked through the muddle of what the locals called Stamp Alley. It was here that full evening found them, thick with scents and color, saturated in lights and sweets and tempting games.

When night had long since fallen and they had wandered back to a now still Gainsford Street, Fisher said, apropos of nothing, "You'll get it figured, Quince. Ezekiel wouldn't have set you up for failure."

"I've only met three requirements," Quincy replied, coming to a stop before The Q's door, her fingers tracing the lead lines in the window. She hadn't confessed to anybody how her last, consuming thought every night was how she was going to possibly keep The Q.

"I'll do whatever I can to help." Fisher settled his lean frame against the stone of The Q's exterior and looked down the dark street, lit only by a scattered collection of streetlamps. Then he turned his face on Quincy. "I'll at least help keep Arch patient with you so he stays amicable."

"*Stays* amicable? He's cold as a January harbor." Which, Quincy knew, wasn't altogether true.

"He only freezes up with you, Quincy, when you deserve it. And you've got enough December in your own bones. I like him. Everyone likes him."

"I considered liking him in March—" Quincy kicked the door lightly and lifted a shoulder.

"What happened? The two of you were starting to get on. You even took him to the train station."

Quincy thought about the day she had almost burned down The Q, something she and Arch kept between themselves. Fisher hadn't asked about the burnt smell that had lingered for several days near her stairwell.

"Let's not discuss Arch," Quincy said, shaking the doorknob of The Q with her hand to hear the rattle of the lock. "Saint Ezekiel's Day is only for us."

"And in that spirit—" Fisher paused, and his left hand, graceful as a magician's despite his mangled fingers, lifted two lemons from his satchel. "I picked them up this morning."

Quincy gave the doorknob a final shake, but her face had softened. "You remembered."

"I always do."

"I know."

They slid down the door, and Quincy stuck her legs out. Fisher settled in beside her and handed her a plump lemon. It was so fantastically bright it felt like the moon in her hand. She began pressing the lemon between her palms, softening the pulp of the fruit, before breaking the rind.

Fisher was doing the same. Once finished, he pressed his index finger through the lemon's rind. A liquid spray escaped, catching Quincy on the cheek. She laughed and then laughed again as Fisher licked the sour juice from his finger and made a face. "Whew!"

"Sour?" Quincy asked.

Nodding, Fisher lifted his lemon to his mouth.

Quincy squeezed her fruit a few more times and then pressed her thumb into the faint gold peel, feeling the rush and sting of lemon juice beneath her thumbnail. The stickiness wrapped around the crease at the base of her thumb, and Quincy ignored it as she pressed the softened lemon to her mouth. The strength of the sourness was overwhelming.

"Whew!" she said, echoing Fisher, her eyes watering. "That's something."

"It certainly is." Fisher grinned as he wiped lemon juice from his chin. Lifting his fruit towards Quincy's, they toasted their spoils. "To having the money for buying lemons any time we want," Fisher said.

Nodding, Quincy squeezed the last of the lemon juice into her mouth. "That was a good Saint Ezekiel's."

"Did you ever tell him we did this?" Fisher asked.

Quincy shook her head.

"Well," Fisher threw the husk of his lemon rind across the street at a faded signboard, "he knows now."

CHAPTER SIXTEEN:
To Challenge Atlas in His Place

June came in sticky and damp. Unexpected rain joined forces with humidity like it was their business to fill the streets of Rhysdon, making the city a strange combination of unbearable and interesting. At the Q, things ran smoothly, though a slip on an order had caused Quincy to beg a day's worth of paper from Priest and *The Times*. In truth, Quincy didn't beg, and Priest didn't make the favor difficult on her, for they were both set to profit from their latest contract for the port cities.

"How did you get to the point of no paper? Don't you have extra stores?" Priest asked, waving his cigar through the hazy air of his office.

"An order slip was misplaced, and then the rail strike set back a delivery. Also," Quincy stretched back in her chair—lifting the front legs off the ground—and, interlocking her hands behind her head, she sighed, "we've taken in record Qs this month: seventeen percent above even my ambitious projections."

"Too much success. Poor girl."

"I know," Quincy grinned. "I've spoken with Blevins, and he's seeing to the trains. I'll get your bundles returned before midday tomorrow."

Priest waved his hand again and scratched his beard with his already occupied fingers. "No rush, St. Claire. I'd like to stay on your sweet side." Seeing her face, he added, "Not saying you have one. Also,

I've said the same thing to Clonmel. Don't feel too singled out."

"Your backhanded compliments are what I live for."

Priest grunted. "How's Arch?"

"Arch?"

"Your solicitor."

Dropping the front legs of her chair on the floor, Quincy brought her arms into an impatient cross before her. "Why do you even care?"

"I know the boy's father. I'm interested."

"Oh, yes, I remember. You want to make him a star in your galaxy, or something. What did you mean by that?"

"That's my business."

"He's *my* solicitor." And Quincy felt strangely possessive.

Priest tapped the end of the cigar against a porcelain dish and then left it there.

"Celine's not going to see the end of the month," Priest admitted at random.

Quincy dropped her hands to the edge of her chair. The lines of Priest's face were set at an angle too personal for friendship, at least, friendship for Quincy, when it wasn't with Fisher. She wondered why Priest found her worth confiding the pending loss of his wife. He leaned back, the wrinkles in his forehead articulating his worry as the afternoon light traced his face.

His reverie broke when Priest's distant, searching eyes found themselves on her uncertain face. "There are few who remind me of myself, St. Claire. Few with the ambition not only to build an empire but to challenge even Atlas in his place. Men chasing money, men like Draggen, hold no interest for me. But someone who aches for progress and industry and genius catches my attention. You would not stop for any man, and neither would I."

Priest's fingers reached towards his cigar, but he stopped short. "We're built of the same parts, St. Claire. That's why I mention Celine. I'm not expecting you to say anything on the matter, but I find myself wondering if—"

"If what?"

Priest grunted and reclaimed his cigar, pressing it between his lips and taking a long breath. "If I'm now finding she's the main gear. Now you see what a selfish creation I really am, wondering if the death of my wife will interrupt my work."

The cigar was pressed aggressively into the porcelain dish, and a lonely stream of smoke was all that remained.

———

"Have you seen this, Quincy?"

Fisher strode in like Apollo, the summer sun a servant to his own radiant light. In his hand was a copy of *The Times,* and he was flashing the editorial page. Quincy's own copy had already been shuffled through and discarded. She mainly kept to the business section.

"Specter. If I knew who he was, I would kiss him."

"*Who?*"

Fisher sighed, but it was with contentment, as he slapped the paper down before Quincy. "The editorialist whose been harping on public education for the better part of the spring."

"Oh, him." Quincy had glanced through his articles from time to time, thinking his pseudonym a bit silly but his arguments intelligent. She knew that Fisher had also kept track of this Specter's causes over the course of the year. She turned back to the report from the accountants.

"Guess what he took on today?"

"What?"

"He thrashed the wealth-serving culture of the exclusive universities."

Quincy had no interest in universities, but Fisher was teaching himself Latin, Greek, mathematics, philosophy, and the king knew what else every evening, so he could get in. He was hoping to take the entrance exams that winter. He had been saving for years, but with Ezekiel's inheritance, Fisher now had more than enough money for the exorbitant tuition.

"He challenged the elitism that leans more towards widening the class disparity than widening the minds of the students who enter. It's what I've been arguing for years."

Quincy picked up the paper and was scanning the essay when a besieged individual who resembled Arch entered, finagling the door with three newspapers under his arm, a mysterious package in one hand, a satchel thrown across his shoulder, and two portfolios tucked into the mess. He looked like a well-dressed junk man who specialized in paper goods.

"Morning, Arch," said Fisher.

The solicitor looked harried, yet his pleasant tone prevailed. "Fisher."

"Arch, I say, do you read *The Times?*" In his exuberance, Fisher was oblivious to Arch's disheveled state of being.

Reaching across the counter, Fisher stole the folded essay from Quincy's grasp and handed it to the solicitor, not recognizing Arch didn't have a hand for pharaoh's scepter, let alone another newspaper.

With a polite grimace, Arch shifted his package so his fingers could take the paper. Quincy opened her mouth, but Fisher moved towards Arch, so she closed it. Fisher, smiling like the day, didn't offer any help but rather leaned over Arch's shoulder.

"Cats, Fisher!" Quincy slid from her stool and walked around the counter.

"What?" Fisher sounded like a pestered brother.

"The man's drowning," Quincy said as she took the package from Arch's hand, practically knocking a portfolio loose.

"I'm fine, Miss St. Claire," said Arch, but he relinquished the package and both his portfolios with little resistance. "Thank you."

Quincy gathered these in her arms and walked them into his office. The package smelled like food. Its aroma was a siren call to Quincy, who realized she had missed her usual breakfast of biscuits and old tea. When she came out of Arch's office, his eyebrows were knit together, his lips moving in silent harmony with the black letters on the page of *The Times.*

"What do you think?" Fisher asked when he had given Arch enough time.

"Decent, but there's a type error." Arch handed the paper back to Fisher and turned towards his office door. "The closing argument could have been stronger."

"But what of the challenge in the second paragraph—" Fisher followed Arch into his office, and Quincy followed her work back to the counter.

Arch and Fisher began debating the different points of the essay until Quincy raised her voice—to what she thought was a very reasonable level—and said, "Gentlemen, I was up half the night working. If you don't have anything to do this morning, please see me for an assignment."

"He's a saint," Fisher said as he left Arch's office for his own desk, "this Specter fellow."

"He needs a new name," Arch replied.

"You both need to start working, or I'm banning *The Times*," Quincy said.

Fisher grumbled good-naturedly, but Arch looked strained as he sat down at his desk. Instead of turning towards his stack of paperwork as he so often did first thing in the morning, he placed his head in his hands and took a deep breath. Quincy thought about asking him what was wrong but decided against it. This was a business, not a nursery.

CHAPTER SEVENTEEN:

Theatre Manners, Quincy!

"And then Jack said it didn't matter and stormed out, leaving me alone with an entire box of slip biscuits."

Quincy's eyes were still scanning an updated version of several soon-to-be-expired contracts waiting to be signed, so she'd only half listened to Jade's story of her row with Jack. "You ate them, I trust?" she managed to say.

Jade smiled at Quincy. "All of them, out of pure spite. But by the time Jack came home I was ready to forgive, impatient for our biannual to be over."

"Hmm," Quincy nodded. Jade and Jack fought exactly twice a year. It was tradition. It was how long it took for the two of them to boil over, make a mess, then clean it up. Quincy didn't really care because they were never serious. If there were serious troubles that affected Jade's work, Quincy would give it her full attention. She frowned at the thought. It was not something Ezekiel would have approved of, this fair-weather concern.

"What?" Jade asked.

"Just something Priest said to me a few weeks back is all."

"Well, I better get down to the mice," Jade sighed. "We're an editor short."

"I can expect Jack's baking to arrive around eleven?"

"Isn't that the pattern?" Jade said, walking past the counter and into the sorter.

It was the pattern. For a solid week after their quarrels, Jack would arrive at the offices of The Q with baskets of baked goods before rushing to his night shift in one of the most exclusive bakeries of Rhysdon. The mice loved when Jade and Jack fought. Quincy didn't mind these biannual spoils herself. She looked at the clock. Just after nine o'clock in the evening. It was a mild disappointment that Jack's pastries were still two hours away.

The contracts in her hand were to be sent out with the Q drivers in sealed packets tomorrow, and Arch had left for the theater before Quincy could verify their readiness. She'd found the stack sitting on his desk in an even pile, Everything appeared to be in order, the numbers dancing just as they should for Q profits, and then Quincy got to the last page of the first contract.

She looked at it twice. She pressed her lips together, her eyes narrowing. That idiot of a solicitor had run off, willy-nilly, and left the contract unsigned. Quincy looked at the remaining contracts only to find the same thing, a blank where his cursed name should have been.

Quincy slammed her fist against the counter. Each contract required not only hers but also Arch's signature, and he was sitting somewhere, enjoying *Tosca*. Or *The Magic Flute*. Or something. Opera or not, her solicitor was going to sign these contracts before the early post went out. A quick glance at the newspaper reminded Quincy which theater Arch was at, and she tucked the contracts into an attaché, setting off like the destroying angel on her way to Egypt.

From the very little Quincy knew of the theatrical experience, she could not have arrived at a better time. It was just after the first act, or so she gathered, and people were moving about. Not having a ticket, Quincy informed the doorman she was here on important solicitor's business with a man called Arch. He protested her entrance five times before Quincy began to spout off every legal term she had ever heard that sounded remotely threatening and bullied her way through. She didn't like doing it, but in an emergency such as this Quincy would— what were the rich always saying?—*brook no refusal*. For The Q, Quincy would stare down Zeus.

A brief, official sounding inquiry led Quincy to the third floor, fifth box down the right side. Thinking nothing of it, Quincy walked through the elegant hallway and up three sets of stairs, where ladies covered in color and sparkle stared and whispered behind their fans. Quincy pressed on, walking down the hallway as she counted boxes. When she had found the fifth one, Quincy finally paused to register her surroundings. The carpets, the carvings, the gilt-edged *everything* made Quincy realize she was in a very wealthy section of the theater.

Too late, she thought, lifting a shoulder. Quincy wrapped her knuckles on the door and pushed in.

The scene was one from a society novella: a small, intimate grouping of the wealthy, the titled, sitting comfortably in their seats, draped as elegantly and politely as any of them could drape, diamonds and silks and clothing cut so fine they could only have been imported from the most exclusive shops of Europe. Glasses filled with something—champagne?—were in hand, and the light sounds of polite laughter dropped as all eyes turned toward Quincy.

Quincy scanned half a dozen sets of eyes, her chin lifted confidently, determined to keep her discomfort tucked away. There, in the back, leaning close to a young woman of obvious elegance, was Mr. Arch. His eyes met Quincy's, and from the accompanied expression, he was most certainly displeased with his employer's unannounced appearance.

Good heavens, were these people clients? Quincy had thought Arch to be many things, but a society vine was not one of them. And now look at him, cavorting with the nobility of Rhysdon. The thought caused unexpected pain in Quincy's chest on his behalf. Poor fool.

At this point, Arch cleared his throat and stood, buttoning his jacket. "Miss St. Claire."

"Arch."

"Allow me to introduce my friends, Lad—" Quincy interrupted before he could finish.

"A pleasure." Quincy did not smile, for the women had begun to look down their noses at her, an amazing feat, considering they were still sitting. "Arch, I have something left undone that requires your immediate attention."

Mouth still open from his attempt at introductions, the expression on Arch's face was swiftly turning into cold fury. "So pressing it could not wait, Miss St. Claire?"

"Yes."

"Very well." He turned to his companion, excused himself, and wove through the chairs to Quincy's side. Pressing his fingers to her elbow, he led her out of the box, back into the hallway.

A sound was made, the lights were dimming, and a handful of ladies and gentlemen passed Quincy and Arch.

"What in the world possessed you to hunt me down at the theater of all places?"

The roughness in his voice was uncharacteristic.

"You left the contracts unsigned," Quincy snapped back. "They're supposed to be sent with the dawn post."

"I left them unsigned because there were a few particulars that needed further review before the contracts were sent off. The delay would be no more than half a day." Arch looked behind him as more ladies passed. He took Quincy's arm, and they stepped closer to the wall as the traffic in the hallway increased.

"It can't wait."

"Miss St. Claire," Arch whispered, "I like to think of myself as a reasonable man, but this, *this* is not only highly improper but vastly rude. How you treated my friends—"

"Your friends?" Quincy snorted.

"Yes," he hissed. "My friends deserve more respect than what you have shown. And I deserve more respect than you have shown."

"Because you cavort with the graced of Rhysdon?"

"Because I am a human being!" His lips were actually quivering from white anger. "People are not numbers or quarterly reports, and I am not your slave. I give you above and beyond what is expected of my work. Now—" He took a breath and looked around, the perspiration that had gathered around his temples catching the dim lights of the hallway. "I would be happy to sign the contracts—"

"Thank you."

"—once the performance is over," he continued, "and I have had time to review my questions with you properly."

"I'm not walking back to the theater in an hour's time."

Arch swallowed an angry smile and pulled at the gloves on his hands. "I don't expect you to. There is an extra seat in the booth. Please join us for the remainder of the performance, and afterward you and I can review the paragraphs in question. The papers will be signed, and we will both be moderately satisfied."

Quincy opened her mouth and then clamped it shut again.

"My friends should not mind, and you will get your signatures no other way." He was regaining his control, looking as unruffled as he did on a quiet morning in the office.

"Fine." Quincy felt her nose wrinkle in disgust. The opera. How many times had her uncle tried to bring her? She had, of truest course, declined each time, working late to avoid the scene.

When they reentered the box, the women were whispering among themselves.

"I apologize," Arch addressed his friends. "I have invited Miss St. Claire to join us for the next two acts before we address a very pressing matter of business."

The gentlemen stood and nodded; the women waved their fans. Arch saw Quincy to a seat near the front and then returned to his own chair. A rush of notes rose from the orchestra pit, and as the curtains parted, Quincy turned enough to see Arch sitting pale and annoyed. His companion looked no happier, narrowing her eyes at Quincy with a practiced glare.

Turning away, Quincy slouched into her chair, crossed her arms, and focused on the stage before her so intently that, for the next hour, she scarcely noticed the time pass. The performance was middling; the costuming, a bit ridiculous. But there was one moment, an aria, that made her forget she was sitting in a booth of fools.

———

"Then, it's settled."

They had spent the last hour discussing Arch's concerns and sorting out the questions he had, which, Quincy admitted to herself, were valid.

The ink from his fountain pen dried, and he handed her the final contract. Quincy stared at his signature on the page: *James A. Arch* The letters were finely scripted.

"What does the *A* stand for?" she asked before she could remind herself not to say anything beyond what was absolutely necessary.

"Anton."

Quincy wrinkled her nose. "French?"

"Yes. My mother was French."

All but a few of the houselights had been put out, the stage crew had completed their work, and the few individuals cleaning the theater were almost finished. Arch shifted in his seat. He wore a suit of exceedingly fine make and looked no less respectable but more distinguished than she was accustomed to seeing in the office. His pale features were complemented by the sharpness of his evening attire. He looked distant and intense.

"If you have everything you need," he said, "I think we should be conscientious patrons and leave them to close up the theater. Would you allow me to see you home?"

Quincy shuffled the legal papers into her attaché and lifted the chain of her pocket watch between two fingers, looking at the hands on the clock. "I think I'll just walk."

"Walk Rhysdon at midnight?"

Quincy tucked the right side of her mouth down in irritation. "I've done it before."

"I am sure you have and will do so again. Please, allow me to see you home. It will save your time and mine. For how inconsiderate you have been this evening, you could at least give me the luxury of not having to walk Rhysdon with you."

"You don't have to," Quincy snapped as she stood.

"And, at this juncture, I don't want to, yet I am unmoved. Please."

When they exited onto the street, Arch hailed a hansom, and Quincy slipped inside before he could offer her any more chivalry. There was just enough room in the carriage for two reasonably sized egos, and any tendency towards Lancelotism, Quincy told herself, was to be avoided.

The silence of the drive was disrupted only by Arch coughing. His lungs must be giving him trouble again. Now that Quincy thought it over, he did looked a bit peaked. Perhaps it was the strange June weather aggravating his winter infection or whatever his sickness was. Quincy sighed. She'd been wrong. It wasn't his cough that touched her pity. Nor was it his dress that had touched her decorum. But it was the way he had spoken to her that had touched her decency, when he fiercely insisted through his hot anger, *Because I am a human being!*

So intense and sincere. Such—What was it her uncle Ezekiel called it?—righteous indignation. He had cooled back down to the winter exterior he often gave to Quincy, but she still felt pricked by her own conscience. Even a child raised in a foundling factory could understand she had been terribly rude.

"I'm sorry, Arch," Quincy said as she thought it. She had not intended to, but, since it came out, Quincy owned the emotion. She looked away from the window and into the solicitor's face. "I was rude; I embarrassed you. I am sorry."

"Apology accepted." His eyes met hers for a solid space of time before turning to watch the night of Rhysdon passing through the window. "Unexpected, but accepted."

Nothing else was said, each of them lost in the sounds of horse hooves snapping on the cobblestone streets, feeling the sway and creak of the cab. The smell of summer pollen was thick in the heavy June midnight, and it comforted Quincy for some reason.

She stole a few glances at Arch. There he sat, eyes still on the street. The silence between them felt like it ended on the sharp edge of companionship, but Quincy knew better. Pugilists always retreated to their own corners to make sure their teeth were still intact. But, before long, they would be back in the center of the ring, swinging.

When the hansom stopped before the offices of The Q, Arch descended into the street and opened the door. He didn't offer his hand to Quincy, and she didn't mind. As she skipped lightly down, she felt for the key in her pocket. Quincy turned towards Arch just as he shot his cuffs. It made him seem taller. He rolled his shoulders back and looked towards Quincy, the gaslight playing on his features in a way that made her increasingly aware of how handsome he was.

"Congratulations, Miss St. Claire, you have fulfilled two requirements tonight."

Quincy knit her eyebrows and folded her arms. "Sabotaging your social aspirations and ruining an opera in one blow?"

"Attending a performance," Arch said, "and offering a sincere apology."

"But I was only there for two-thirds of the performance."

"I'm counting it." Arch's response sounded grim. "I don't think I could endure another evening at the opera with you."

"Thursday, the sweet hour of the afternoon?"

BOY BLUE

CHAPTER EIGHTEEN:
Sweet Cakes and Innocent Romance

Crow sauntered into The Q one day while the Constable Catch was trying to grease Quincy's closed mouth.

"I'll do anything," he was saying, "if you'll just tell me what you know."

"I'm sorry, constable," Quincy answered.

The bell on the door rang.

"Catcher!"

The young constable's eyes grew so wide they looked like the marbles the Q boys traded between shifts. Quincy looked past Constable Catch to the spectacular force that was Crow. He looked more or less the same as always, but today he had a red armband wrapped around one arm of his long coat.

"Crow." And the way the name fled from the constable's throat, Quincy knew the smuggler intimidated him. "You're a right fool's mind to show your face to me."

"What do you mean?" Crow played innocent as he walked passed Catch and leaned against the counter, winking at Quincy. "Hello, love. I've missed you."

"I mean," Constable Catch said, pulling at his uniform's jacket, "that your illegal activity is written all over."

"All over what?" Crow asked, his voice so low it slid beneath Catch's nicely.

"All over Rhysdon."

Crow's eyes sparkled in a way that made it seem written all over his face.

Constable Catch pinched his face together. "Why the red armband, Crow?"

"Why not?" came the deep-voiced answer.

"I've never seen you wearing one. Is it a signal to your organization?"

"Gentlemen." Quincy wrapped her knuckles on the counter. "*The Q* has a social page, but my front office is not that. If you want to have a conversation, go down to The Nest."

"Capital idea. I'll even buy Catcher a drink."

Constable Catch leaned towards Crow and lifted his fingers. "I'm this close, Crow, and when I have the information I need, I'll be visiting you behind bars."

"I've no idea what you're talking about."

Every part of Catch's body showed his frustration. "I'll clip your wings, and then you won't be grinning like a jack."

After the constable left, Crow laughed and tilted his head towards Quincy. "He's wrong, you know."

"About what?"

"If he ever clips my wings, I'll still be grinning. Could I place a question, love?"

Quincy retrieved a Q slip from around Crow's frame. "What will it be today?"

"Red death, black bend, catch the storm's light back again?"

"That's a question?" Quincy asked.

"It is, when you're wearing a red armband."

"I'm not going to ask what it means."

It was then that Fisher came in from the sorter. He groaned audibly at the sight of Crow.

"Hello Fisher," Crow said politely, seemingly eager to impress Quincy's closest friend.

Quincy had not been aware Crow even knew Fisher's name.

Fisher ignored the smuggler politely, which sent a spark off in Quincy. Sometimes, Quincy thought, Fisher would make a fantastic aristocrat.

"Quincy," Fisher said instead, "I'm joining Mado in the park after work. Would you like to join us?"

"Occupied," was all she replied. "That's two half crowns Crow. I'll give you a special discount today."

The smuggler slipped his hand into the pocket of his coat and withdrew the exact change.

"Thanks, love. I hope to see you quayside soon." And without saying anything else, Crow flew out the door.

"You could at least say hello," Quincy shot at Fisher once the door had closed after her smuggler.

"Like you've ever said hello to Mado."

"I've spoken with her."

Fisher slipped into the chair behind his desk. "Fine."

"Fine?"

"Next time Crow comes in I'll ask *him* to come with me to the park."

"You do that." Quincy rolled her eyes. "Ply him with sweet cakes and innocent romance."

"I'm sure he needs it."

When six o'clock came, Fisher slipped out onto Gainsford Street and Quincy locked the door behind him. She watched the flood of businessmen crisscrossing before the offices of The Q, and recognized more than one accountant from the smaller Q offices down the street, before turning, passing through the sorter, and sending the door swinging open above the print room's stairs.

The mice were scurrying around their cases, Spense was arguing with Jade over punctuation, and the room smelled ripe with the promise of paper and ink and hours of preparing yet another edition of *The Q*. Spense waved Quincy down to speak with her about the night's work.

"You staying around tonight?" he asked, scratching his bald head, leaving a trail of ink on his skin.

Quincy lifted a shoulder. "Too tired."

Jade was now haranguing a mouse for a blatant error, and so Quincy slipped up the stairs, knowing she left The Q in capable hands. The stairs to her own apartment felt longer than they did most nights,

BETH BROWER

and Quincy realized how fatigued she was. She closed her eyes and climbed, her legs burning from the movement. A yawn escaped every third stair, and she pushed into her room with relief, lit a lamp, and set herself on her bed, where she removed, first one boot, then the other, throwing it across the room with the emphasis of an exclamation mark.

Her mind was still tripping over numbers and Qs, and Quincy knew that sleep was hours off, no matter how tired, so she decided to play her violin.

Quincy's love for music came from the two things she held inside the tucks of her jacket beside her heart: mathematics and solitude. The benefits she reaped after an hour of playing Mozart or Bach, or whoever, were order and inhuman company. And this night, like on so many others, these were what she felt she needed above all.

CHAPTER NINETEEN:

Arch let an even thirty seconds pass before clearing his throat and waiting for Quincy to grant him existence.

"Yes, Mr. Arch?"

"I would like to request some time off."

"Time off?" When Quincy spoke the words it sounded as if it were the first time they had been uttered together, bringing into existence a level of leisure never before seen among the human race. Her tone dripped with disapproval.

"Time off," Mr. Arch set his mouth, "is a phenomenon often heard of—and even offered—at establishments such as this. It means requesting a temporary leave of absence from one's work."

"Thank you, Mr. Arch, for your thorough explanation," Quincy said. "Why?"

"Why?"

"Why do you need time off?"

Arch looked affronted. Quincy ignored his scruples and challenged him with an expression that demanded an answer.

"My family goes to the country for a month every summer, and I request two weeks' time to be with them and the friends we are hosting. The extra hours I have given The Q should be more than enough to cover that time."

She snorted and turned back to her work.

Two weeks later, on July twenty-first, Arch cleaned his desk, set his things in order, and took a polite leave of Quincy and Fisher.

"When are you back, Arch?" Fisher asked, standing and extending his hand. Arch took it with an expression Quincy could only quantify as great relief. Well, good riddance.

"A fortnight. Not until August seventh."

Fisher nodded. "Enjoy yourself."

"Thank you. I believe I will."

"Send me a holiday post," Quincy said without looking up.

"I believe I won't."

Quincy didn't shift from her work as he left, but she entertained a smile.

If possible, board meetings had become more tiresome affairs since Ezekiel's death. First, nearly every individual on The Q's board was inherently tedious to Quincy, so that was to be expected. What wasn't expected—perhaps because Quincy had barreled through any prejudices she had encountered in the business world, usually turning them on their heads—was that certain board members had begun treating her in a very patronizing way, as if she were in over her head, a child to be tempered. Or a fly to be swatted.

The two ringleaders were Rutherford and Levins. One looked like a mole—a blind, round, self-indulgent creature—comfortable digging in the dirt. The other carried himself in a manner reminiscent of the larger rats Rhysdon boasted, the kind that you saw standing on two legs late at night just outside the pool of lamplight, testing the air for spoil and filth, hoping to strike it rich, waiting to knock a few lesser creatures about or to terrify a maid with his beady eyes. Quincy disliked both these men equally as individuals; as a duo, her instincts whispered they were insidious.

When she arrived at today's meeting, she looked for the one person whose company she could handle, Vicks, the old chair, now Quincy's assistant chair, and one of Ezekiel's friends. He was one of the ancients, the old guard. He hobbled and ranted, but, since he did both with a rather stylish cane, Quincy didn't mind. Quincy scanned the room for Vicks's bent-over, feather-headed frame. She couldn't find it.

"Where's Vicks?" she asked Hastings.

"Vicks is ill and can't make it this month. He's asked me to assistant chair in his place."

"Fine. Fine." Quincy thought nothing more of it as she sat down at one end of the long, immaculate table. The room was rented from one of Rhysdon's elite men's business clubs. That Quincy even entered proved a sore point for some of the members, one such being Draggen, fire-breathing editor of *The Sun*. Their chance encounters were never pleasant. But, Quincy thought, the club kept the room clean, so she endured Draggen and all that came with him.

Quincy called the meeting to order, asking Hastings to give the stockholders' report, which he did in a bland but pleased manner. Then he turned the time back to Quincy for The Q's finances, projections, and expansion status.

As she had done every month, Quincy handed out profit reports, showed quarterly trackers, offered a succinct, but detailed account of new contracts, and finally, explained the steps taken towards opening The Q's office in Paris. She sliced through the information like a paring knife, cutting around any unnecessary talk and keeping only the essential fruit of the matter. The reports were more than ample if the board members had any questions beyond the depths she was willing to impart in her mandatory monthly sermons on the dry health of The Q.

She didn't know why she gave so little to the board. For investors, Quincy could call up passion and send their minds down tracks fueled by not only profits and rising stock values, but also great purpose, preaching the significance of the work. The accounting rooms, the sorter, the print room, and all other effects of The Q felt the buzz of her incredible energy for the enterprise. But the boardroom was stale, like bones leached and dry. Quincy bore the meeting through with what she felt was the patience of Job.

"One last item of business," Hastings said, addressing the board, his eyes mostly on Quincy. "Vicks is not only ill but quite old, as we all know."

A few scattered whispers of agreement blew about the room like leaves in windswept park. Quincy frowned. She never felt age had anything to do with most sound decisions.

"I respectfully put a motion forward that we retire Vicks," Hastings continued, "with full honors and privileges, for having been our chair, under the brilliant direction of Ezekiel, and assistant chair to Miss St. Claire. I put the motion forward to be voted on."

Quincy pulled her face together and tapped her anxious finger on the table. Why were they forcing Vicks out?

"I second," stated Levins.

"All votes in favor say aye."

The room echoed with the stuttered trail of ayes from a dozen men. Quincy's alarm sounded.

"All votes contrary?"

"You may mark me as very contrary," Quincy said, raising a finger. "When Vicks is too old to tie his shoes or remember his name, then he might be too old to assist the board. Until then, he should stay. You're idiots to flush out the oldest institutional memory we have," she fumed. "Vicks is a sound, balanced contributor to this establishment, and he has double the experience most of you have. As chair, I ask for a recount."

Hastings looked uncomfortable but said, "Very well. All in favor, vote aye."

This time, only seven members of the board raised their hands. Rutherford and Levins exchanged a long, telling look.

"And the votes to the contrary?"

Quincy and three others, including Hastings, voted contrary. Weathers took down the votes against.

"The ayes have it, seven to four. Vicks will receive his benefits and retire from his tenure on the directors' board of The Q. We will postpone a vote for new assistant chair until the August meeting. Until such point, I will act as assistant chair."

A rumble of approval sounded, and the meeting came to a close.

Just like that, the board had rearranged the affairs of The Q. Hastings had effectively moved out the last member of the old guard. Quincy didn't like it.

"*Idiots*," Quincy growled under her breath, complaining how a board of directors was given too much power to do useless things and to botch the few important ones. She was also disappointed she'd lost the last person she could tolerate on the board.

CHAPTER TWENTY:
My Lord

Quincy slapped the packet against her knee and breathed out in irritation. A week after the board meeting, something about the ease with which Vicks was deposed still bothered Quincy. She had kept a copy of the meeting's notes, along with the details of Vicks's benefits, in a small folder. Then, the morning after the meeting, she had visited the man and had realized he had no wish to be reinstated.

"I'm old, Quincy. And with Ezekiel gone, well, I find myself obliged for the change."

"But you still believe the timing of the vote tasted odd."

"Undoubtedly."

"Why would they have pushed you out?" Quincy pressed.

"I'm like that ancient print machine down at The Q: still able but not necessary. Simple as all that, Quincy."

But she couldn't figure why they would have voted Vicks out, aside from the obvious state of idiocy most men of business resided in.

Now, days after her visit with Vicks, Quincy could still not settle.

"When was Mr. Arch to return?" she asked Fisher when the front office was empty of customers.

Fisher scratched his head but did not look up. "Yesterday, I believe, or the day before. But he won't be back in the office until Monday."

"That long?"

Fisher looked at Quincy. "You sound as if you're missing his company."

"I'm in need of his legal prowess," Quincy informed Fisher mechanically, "if he indeed has any." The additional insult was not necessary, but it felt nice.

"Then Monday should suffice."

"Yes, well—" Quincy set the packet aside and returned back to her work. Six o'clock came. Fisher stood, leaving his work messy on his desk, and slipped on his coat.

"You're leaving already?" Quincy asked.

"I'm leaving—"

"To spend the evening with Mado?" A hint of irritation crossed his face; it should have been enough for Quincy to back down. She didn't. "You know, Fisher, I really think—"

"Don't, Quincy." He held up his palm to stop her words, reached for his satchel, and threw it across his shoulders. "I don't want to hear a single opinion on how I'm choosing to live my life, and I don't want to hear you say a thing about Mado. My world isn't as tied to you anymore."

It stung. It punched. Like when Quincy pressed the keys of her typewriter too hard, and one of the steel letters shot through the paper, leaving an unexpected hole: the entire document rendered useless. Her mouth twitched, but she forced a shrug and turned back to her work, huddling over the counter, the lights glowing as evening claimed Gainsford Street.

Without another word, Fisher walked from his desk to the front door, letting himself out, the bell ringing a few moments after he had already disappeared from view. Quincy pulled at her short blond hair and looked again at the packet of papers before her.

———

She didn't know whether she had honestly tried to stay patient until Monday, but Quincy acknowledged that it made her feel better to believe she had. But, by the time noon had passed on Sunday, it was of no use. She left her matchbox room, turned the key into the back file office, and hunted through the pages of employee information. These had, on her insistence, been filed in alphabetical order, so it should not have taken her long to find information concerning Mr. Arch. But it did. Someone had tucked Arch's information sheet three-fourths of the way through, right after Spense's. Breathing out a succinct death threat, Quincy took the sheet, and without glancing at its information, slipped the file drawer back into place, blew out the lamp, and locked the door.

It was hot, as uncomfortable as August ever was in the city. The slight breeze from the harbor at least made the green feel fresh. So, as Quincy wound her way through Rhysdon, contracts and board notes tucked in with Mr. Arch's address, she stuck to the parks and the avenues most lined with trees.

She had only glanced at his address—Regent Square something or other—to be certain she was walking in the right direction, the map of Rhysdon set like a thousand rows of type in her mind. But as Quincy drew near where she believed Regent Square to be, she began to doubt she had gotten it right. These townhomes were stunning, beautiful, only a step—but no more—down from Kings Cross, where the Fothergil mansion sat as aristocratic patron to the city.

Certainly she had the wrong address. Mr. Arch, solicitor, did not keep residence in Regent Square, did he? What an odd thought. And, if it were true, what an even odder arrangement. Did he rent a room in the back? Did he work two jobs, being some sort of servant whose room and board were covered? Quincy knew nothing about the lives of upper-crust servantry, but, surely it couldn't work that way, could it? So she glanced at the paper again.

There it was, *731 Regent Square*, written out in Arch's elegant hand. And here it was, 731 Regent Square, standing in imposing white stone before her. She frowned and walked around the square twice more, before deciding she may as well chance it. After taking a sorting breath, Quincy secured her parcel of legal questions beneath her arm and stepped lightly up the stairs—five of them of rather nice proportion—then, lifting her hand to the big brass knocker, she let it fall twice. It was a peacock, the knocker. And only the noise of a scuffle in the hall brought her attention away from the fantastic bird in time for the front door to swing open.

"Clagent! We've been waiting all day!"

"Where's the scoundrel?"

A young man was staring at Quincy, with another coming up so fast he ran into the back of his friend, crying out about something, laughing. A scolding could be heard inside, coming from what appeared to be a maid.

Good heavens, Quincy thought, Regent Square had turned into a dormitory.

The young man in front seemed to recognize Quincy. His response to this recognition was to cross his arms and lean against the doorframe, clearly displeased at her appearance.

"Pardon, miss," the young man behind him said over his friend's shoulder, his eyes wandering over Quincy's ensemble. "We were expecting someone else."

"Yes. Clagent, from what I gathered," Quincy said, looking from one to the other, until the young man in front waved his friend off.

"What can I do for you?" he asked.

There was not a friendly note in his voice.

"Sorry, perhaps I have found the wrong address. I'm looking for a Mr. Arch. He's a solicitor."

The frown turned into a scowl. "Really, Miss St. Claire."

Her mouth fell open; no words came out. This tall, fresh-faced young man, hair loose, falling over his forehead, this sun-kissed specimen, could not possibly be her undertaker of a solicitor. Could it? But yes, there he was, a rather summer-filled Julius.

"James! You're letting in flies and dust. Why is the door ajar?"

A young woman—dark hair, large brown eyes, tall—came up behind him.

"Oh, excuse me. I did not see you there." She nudged Arch out of the way. "Please, come in. Really, James, you are so rude. Please, come in," she repeated.

Before Quincy could gather her troops and turn tail from the radiant energy that was 731 Regent Square, she was ushered into the spacious hall.

"You may call me Mary," the young woman said. And Mary gave a sharp glance at Arch, who still stood scowling and silent by the door. To Quincy, she gave a gracious smile. "My brother appears to have left all his manners in Hampershire, Miss—?"

"St. Claire," Quincy heard herself say.

Mary's eyes grew round, but she smiled wide and offered to take Quincy's hat. "Miss Quincy St. Claire, my friends are never going to believe that I had you over for tea."

"She's not staying for tea," came the cool voice from the door. "Business hours don't begin until tomorrow morning. I am still out of the office."

"Indeed, she is." Mary turned toward Quincy. "Ignore him. May I take your hat?"

Quincy handed over her hat in baffled surrender and reached a little self-consciously towards her hair, brushing her bangs slightly to the side.

"Your hair is as charming as was ever described," Mary appraised with approval as she led Quincy not into a drawing room but through a hallway toward an enclosed patio of sorts. "You do realize that some of the girls are quite envious? Utterly charming. And look what it does to those blue eyes of yours. You've been described as quite a strange beauty, and now I see why."

All this registered just as Quincy was ushered into the garden parlor, where three sets of eyes, belonging to a trio of young people engaged in infectious laughter, broke away from their mirth to stare at Quincy. It was too much, all of this. Too much light and happiness and newness.

Cats and kings, Quincy wondered *who* had been conversing about her hair to anyone? What a horrible thought.

"James, would you like to introduce our guest, or shall I?"

Arch stepped down beside Quincy. She hadn't realized he had followed them. There were two young men sitting with one shining young woman in pink. And toward them Mr. Arch gave a wave, "Lady Harrelson; Lord Fothergil, whom you've just met in the hall, here we call him Johnny—"

Quincy grimaced. A Fothergil. Had he been at the dinner those months ago?

"—and Scout, also known as the Earl of Straitsum."

An earl. Death could not come soon enough.

They were all staring, a bit wide-eyed and, in the case of the earl, widemouthed, as they took Quincy in. But James—*Arch*, Quincy corrected herself—kept pushing through with introductions.

"Allow me to introduce my employer, Miss Quincy St. Claire."

A general reaction of interest ran through the group, but Quincy could not quite read it. Scout, the Earl of Straitsum, jumped to his feet, pulling at his vest to straighten his rather casual appearance, and stuck his hand out in a very businesslike way. Something in Quincy thawed. This gesture, at least, she recognized. It was solid ground. She took his hand and nodded.

"A pleasure to meet the best business mind in Rhysdon."

"No need to exaggerate, Scout—I mean, Sir." She couldn't bring herself to use the slang name. "I don't believe in tin compliments."

Johnny, Lord Fothergil, laughed aloud. Scout's cheeks turned red, and he smiled. And Lady Harrelson gave Mary a meaningful look, as if she were asking her a question.

"Not tin," the earl recovered, glancing at Mr. Arch then back at Quincy. "I've never dealt tin in my life. I have it on good authority from James here that you're the best business mind in the country and the most astute employer he could possibly work for."

Lord Fothergil made some comment about work, or the lack thereof, and they all laughed. All of them except Quincy and Arch.

"Tea," Mary said, sounding a bit nervous. She rang a bell, and the chiding housekeeper from before came in with what Quincy assumed was a fresh pot of tea in the finest silver Quincy had ever seen save at the Fothergils'. Small comments were made—none of them to Quincy—as they sat in a loose circle while Mary poured and served.

"What brings you to Peacock House on such a fine afternoon?" Lord Fothergil asked with a grin, looking straight at Quincy.

"Business," Quincy said as she lifted her teacup. "I had some legal questions, regarding a few recently designed lease agreements between sponsoring newspapers in some of the expanding sectors of the country."

"Legal questions, leases, agreements, expansion—all in one sentence. Dear me." This was the earl's contribution. The women looked a little uncomfortable, which irritated Quincy to no end, as if the businessspeak would stain the hems of their afternoon gowns.

"You just can't give our poor Lord Arch a break, even on a Sunday? He's just gaining back his health, you know, and we don't want him going under any time soon," Johnny said, laughing again and receiving a cold stare from Mr. Ar—

Wait. Quincy choked on her tea. Lord Arch? She swallowed and cleared her throat.

"Yes, I've come at a bad time." Quincy set her tea down on a nearby end table and stood. "Thank you for the tea, but I'm off."

"Oh, can you not stay?" Mary asked. "We were just now to divert ourselves with a lawn game of sorts." Mary looked so uncertain as to what to do that it made Quincy think about the possibility of accepting the offer. But reason prevailed; she made her apologies and excuses and let herself out of the garden room. James—Arch, *Lord* Arch—followed her.

"There is no need for you to rush off, Miss St. Claire. I can speak with you if you would like. Though, perhaps it would be better in the library."

"No, no. You're expecting Clagent, whoever that may be—perhaps a school name for the crown prince? I do realize it was impolite of me to come to your house, of all places. It's just I—I was worried, that's all. Fisher's no good when things get bigger than his desk, and I thought you—"

The lines around Mr. Arch's face softened. "Has something happened while I've been away?"

"The contracts were an excuse to come see you—I can't explain why I feel worried, but the board meeting last week. In his absence, Vicks was sent packing with no discussion, and it felt lopsided, wrong. You know I don't trust the board, and my instincts aren't settled. It's something I would usually speak with Ezekiel about, but, well—" Quincy lifted her hat and left the packet of papers on the sideboard, where Mary had placed them. "These contracts do need your attention. If you have time to review any of them, we can speak tomorrow, Arch—pardon—*Lord* Arch, if that is what you prefer to be called."

His face turned hard beneath her treatment of the word. "Just Arch is fine."

"Tomorrow then?" She did not call him Arch.

"Tomorrow, Miss St. Claire." He let her out of the door.

With the feeling of the wettest, coldest water having been thrown into her unsuspecting face, Quincy began the long walk home. What humiliation. What foolishness. Stupid—for her to have gone in the first place, for her to have sought him out at home. She should have waited until Monday.

And that, Quincy told herself clearly, is why you do not venture out. The Q was her realm, her corner. She knew how to fight there. But in the middle of the ring it was hopeless. A lord? A *lord*? What had her uncle been thinking?

Quincy kicked an errant stone with her boot, sending it flying. Her hands were forced deep into her jacket pockets, her shoulders hunched. Bother it all, she thought.

The constant sounds—of carriages, horses, the ring of a newfangled bicycle bell—filled the air and underpinned her thoughts as she took the busier streets, the more direct route back to Gainsford. It was going to be impossible, this keeping of The Q, this weaving through silly requirements held above her head by a lord who had no business dictating her life. But what else was there if she didn't keep The Q? Nothing.

Nothing.

A shadow fell on the sidewalk and someone called out. Quincy walked through the sound, assuming it was not for her. Then the call came again, and she heard her name.

Like a spring pulled too tight, Quincy cocked her small chin up in the direction of the voice. There, in a carriage, Mr. Arch sat, looking a bit more presentable in a Sunday coat, his hair combed. The fresh color that had looked so natural and healthy on his face before now appeared out of place as he stepped from the carriage and came to a stop before Quincy. He took his hat off and held it carefully between his fingers.

"That was rude of me, Miss St. Claire. Extraordinarily rude. I am quite ashamed." He bent his head in earnest apology. "Will you please forgive my lack of manners?"

She wasn't ready for this. She wasn't yet back at The Q, where she would know where to stand and what to say and how to offer a cold acceptance, followed by an apology of her own for, once again, invading his private territory. But that was not to be done, for she was on a busy knot of Merchant Street. And here he stood before her, a lord who, oddly, worked as her solicitor, asking for her forgiveness.

She froze. Several silent moments passed between them. More than one stranger walked around their still figures. She tried to speak, but Quincy was mortified from feeling at such a severe disadvantage, something she had not felt since she was a little girl on the streets, a little girl in the foundling factory, a little girl who had sworn that she would never feel this way again.

"Miss St. Claire, I am truly sorry. Will you—" He glanced around the sidewalk and took her elbow. "Will you please step into the carriage and let me give you a ride? I know you do not need one," he said, after studying the reaction in her face. "Do this for me, please."

"There is no need to beg," Quincy finally spoke. "It's hot as Hades today."

He nodded stiffly, stepped to the carriage, and opened the door. Quincy did not take his hand, but rather pulled herself up and sat in the farthest back corner. Lord Arch followed and sat opposite Quincy, his eyes studying her face as the carriage drove on. His mouth moved to speak.

"Why did you not tell me who you were?" Quincy sprang her words at him, deflecting anything he might have to say.

"Your uncle asked me not to. He thought you might treat me different."

Quincy harrumphed. "It's the most ridiculous thing I've ever heard: a lord acting as a solicitor."

"I am a solicitor. I studied law in England and here in Rhysdon. And I am not yet a lord. Johnny likes to tease."

Quincy finally looked at his face and thought of what Lord Fothergil—Johnny—had said about Arch regaining his health. He did look better than he had before, far better than he had last winter. Yet, he still bore the marks of a long illness, and even the summer glow of a fortnight in the country could not diminish the pallor layered below.

She wanted to ask if he had gone away for his health, but that was probably impolite, so she refrained. "Your sister, Mary, is very nice," Quincy said instead.

"Yes." An expression crossed his face that seemed closer to the look he had had when he had first opened the door: the face he must show to those he knew well.

"So, if you are not *the* Lord Arch, your father is still living?"

"Still living. He is currently spending the summer in Calais. My mother is deceased these five years, so it is my father, my sister Mary, and I."

Quincy nodded.

"Shall we talk about that meeting with the board?"

"No need," said Quincy. "I've already taken you away from your guests long enough."

He seemed to make a decision then. It was quick and decisive, somehow tight against his eyes. Arch moved to the window, tapped the outside with his gloved hand, and call out to his driver, "King Spring Park."

The driver turned right farther up into the city, and Quincy said nothing. Neither did Arch, until they had arrived and he had descended from the carriage, offering Quincy his hand. This time, grumbling, she took it. It was an awkward affair.

"I thought it might be nice to walk through the park while we discuss your concerns, if you don't object," he said. "I have the time."

Quincy shrugged and, with her shoulder leading, turned into one of the tree-lined walkways. He fell into step with her.

"What happened?"

Nothing, Quincy wanted to say. Nothing that she could set her finger on. "Vicks was sick. He didn't show at the meeting last week."

"I'm sorry to hear it. Is he recovered?"

"Yes. Him being sick, though," Quincy waved a fly away from her face, "isn't my concern. In his absence, a vote was proposed. Hastings put forth the motion for Vicks to be retired as assistant chair of the board."

Arch's expression changed so swiftly that Quincy no longer felt bad for worrying. "Was it seconded without discussion?"

"Yes, by Levins. No surprise to be found there."

"He's the fellow who is a bit like a rodent?"

"Yes." Quincy didn't smile outwardly, but his mirroring observation was validating. "The vote was put forth with no argument, and everyone except myself voted in favor. I, after soundly calling them all idiots, demanded a revote, and three members joined me, obviously uncertain which force they should throw themselves behind: me or Rutherford and Levins."

"You, clearly," Arch said, his face starting to glisten from the heat of the day.

"Well," Quincy complained, "intelligence is not God's gift to every soul."

Arch looked at her, a wry smile on his face. "Neither is humility."

"It's not wholly unprecedented for a board to vote out a member—" said Quincy, ignoring Arch and letting her thought catch in the slight breeze.

"But waiting until he's absent, having no previous discussion with the chair as to why the vote would be put forth, and sharing conspiratorial facial expressions make it feel suspicious and self-serving. Not good signs," said Arch.

"That's what I thought," said Quincy.

"As the highest operating officer of The Q, you should address the issue."

"Do you think I should call a meeting?"

"Yes," Arch said, "if you feel strongly about reinstating Vicks before he becomes sour."

Quincy sighed. "He's settled with the idea of retirement."

"Then, if you really wish to know what's behind their move and reinstating Vicks isn't necessary, wait until next month. I can poke around before then and see what I can find out as far as their motive is concerned."

"So you really are my spymaster?"

He laughed. "Let us only say I am quite good at getting people to talk. That you and I having a history of—What should I call it?—*discontent* in each other's company only helps the cause. Besides, I have membership in nearly every gentlemen's club in Rhysdon, where I can meet any member of the board on safe ground, as it were."

"Why on earth would you want such obligations?" Quincy moved her eyes over his face, considering him mad for attending any club, let alone several.

"That's my own affair."

"Sounds ominous."

"It is." Arch placed his hands behind his back and then, apropos of nothing, said, "My friends liked you. They were all disappointed you had left so soon and sent their express desires to see you again, especially Mary."

"I wouldn't entirely mind that," she answered with a modicum of honesty. "To see Mary, that is. The other's might not be my sort of company."

"They're not smugglers, you mean?"

She turned, intending to round a solid punch of words at him. But he was smiling, and the look in his eye was inclusive, rather than the eternal exclusion he had given her for months—a justified protection against Quincy's barbs, she allowed.

"Smugglers," Quincy grumbled, "are easy to figure. Nobility are unpredictable and make for a painful experience in pointlessness. I never understood my uncle's penchant for their company."

"Smugglers are easy to figure," he repeated, as if thinking over what she had said, ignoring her slight to his own class. "You're a mystery to me."

"Is this conspiratorial plan—to ferret out the motives of the men on the board—supposed to be some kind of truce between us?"

Arch raised his eyebrows, as if the thought had not occurred to him but he was amenable to the idea. "It would certainly make my life easier."

"I'll think about it," Quincy said.

"I'll try not to set my hopes too high."

Quincy laughed.

Without speaking further, they walked the breadth of the tree-covered park twice. It was a posh gathering, even on this hot day, certainly more posh than the park near the wharf, which Quincy visited on rare occasions. Arch nodded politely, tipping his hat as they passed a few well-dressed people of his acquaintance.

"What am I to call you?" she said as they were walking back towards his waiting carriage.

"I already told you to keep calling me Arch."

"I don't think I can bring myself to do that knowing there will be a title there. Cats, I hate titles." She had just caught herself before saying she hated aristocrats.

"Why don't you call me James, then?"

"Your Christian name?" Quincy paused before the carriage, disbelieving his request. "I can't. That would be too strange."

"What is so strange about it? You call Fisher by his; you call Jade by hers."

"Yes," Quincy said lamely. "But that's because I don't think they were christened."

"That's the most illogical thing I've ever heard you say." He opened the door, and Quincy surprised herself by laughing again.

It was not a long ride to Gainsford Street. They spoke little, but it did seem like a real truce had been drawn. And, by the time she was stepping down from the carriage, Quincy had found her internal footing again.

"Well," she said. "I will see you tomorrow, Mr.—"

"James," he negotiated.

"Arch," she renegotiated.

"Good-bye, St. Claire. Until tomorrow."

The following morning, when Arch arrived, he nodded at Quincy, where she already sat perched on her stool, having been at work for two hours.

"Good morning, St. Claire."

"Arch," she acknowledged.

"Fisher." Arch nodded to Fisher and then disappeared into his office.

Blinking up from a book he should not have been reading during Q hours, Fisher looked at Quincy.

"What?" she said.

"What happened?"

"A truce."

Quincy slid off her stool and headed down into the print room to discuss something with Spense before he went home to sleep for the day. When she came back, there was a note on her counter in Arch's elegant script:

Congratulations on fulfilling your sixth requirement.
You made a friend.

—James A. Arch

CHAPTER TWENTY-ONE:
Love Will Make Fools of Us All, Big and Little

The next few weeks brought three changes at the offices of The Q.

The first change was with Crow, who stopped by more often than ever, staying for a few minutes before disappearing again. His conversations with Quincy had turned into a steady stream of more personal interactions.

These exchanges were not long, but enough to feel as if she were establishing more solid ground with the smuggler. He would talk, tease, ask Quincy questions. Sometimes she would answer in one word; sometimes she gave her opinion or shared a thought she would have otherwise kept to herself. Crow would listen with genuine interest, his blue eyes watching her work, his coat settled comfortably about him, his shoulder pressing against the wall as he leaned against it, confident, sure, and—Quincy felt silly for this next admission—interested in her beyond just business. She was yet uncertain what she thought of it all, but Crow did cause a reaction in her that was not unpleasant.

The second change was that the romance between Boy Blue and Angel was not only a continually blooming flower but it was also turning The Q into a veritable hothouse of emotions. The staff was over the moon for the number of Qs passed between the lovers. And Jade had to begin a second board for all their questions.

Promise me you'll not forget last evening?
BOY BLUE

Should you have spent so much, you foolish boy?
ANGEL

Would Angel please accompany me for an evening of pleasant
diversion Tuesday next?
BOY BLUE

"I can't understand it," Quincy said honestly to Fisher and Arch
one day, after Spats had come through the front offices with another
question from Boy Blue. They were sitting around Fisher's desk, having
just finished discussing the Paris expansion. "For more than a year,
they were up, down, future, no future, desperate more often than not.
But they were discreet." Quincy waved her hand through the air. "And
their discretion served as a protection of sorts. Now, their questions
come pouring in, so filled with blatant declarations, so desperate and
exposed. It's—it's selfish almost."

"Selfish?" Fisher said, looking at Quincy askance. He was packing
up his satchel, as it was the end of the day. "What are you on about,
Quincy? This has been the best two weeks of my life at The Q. Have
you noticed how happy the staff is? Have you noticed that Spense has
been whistling? Spense!"

"What do you mean by selfish?" Arch asked, forgoing Fisher's
passionate response for one of his usual, reason-based questions.

"I only—" Quincy looked at the Q slip in her hand. "Look at
them. They've lost all caution, flinging themselves out before the
world. They were coming along so steadily—for the most part—and
now, one of them is going to break the other. We all know it will

happen eventually. It always does. And someone, Boy Blue or Angel, will be discarded with all the other scraps of their relationship." Quincy looked up at their faces. "Doesn't that seem selfish to you, to encourage it, I mean?"

"You're a philistine, Quincy," Fisher replied, a half frown on his face. "In a previous life, you were some Roman goddess who followed behind Cupid and ripped the arrows right out. Ruthless, cool, dispassionate is Quincy St. Claire. I'm pleased I'll be seeing Mado tonight, just to make sure my arrow is still intact." Fisher's face brightened. "Farewell. I'm off to the land of blissful surrender and will not think of the two of you until I walk back into the office tomorrow morning. And make sure to get Boy Blue's question down to Jade. We mustn't keep Angel waiting."

He exited, and Quincy pulled at the edge of her mouth as she watched him go.

"I see the angle of your question, St. Claire," said Arch as he turned his attention back to Quincy. "But it's a strange claim: that wanting to give someone love is a manifestation of selfishness. Faith is part of any worthwhile endeavor."

"You call it faith; I call it risk."

"I do call it faith," Arch said. "Do you feel that your uncle Ezekiel was selfish for the love he gave you?"

"You mention the one person who decided to play with my fate. Yes, that was selfish."

Arch made a motion with his hand, as if clearing away invisible smoke. "No, no. Forget the requirements and remember the relationship. Was he selfish in caring for you? For Fisher? Were you selfish for caring for him? And what of your love for Fisher?"

"Yes. But blood is thick, and you can't help that, and then friendship is," Quincy shrugged, "important, though often a result of circumstance. But love?" She made a face. "It's an all-encompassing machine, with no parts but the weak human heart. You give everything to it with no promise of security in return. Why am I even saying this?" Quincy threw up a hand and looked back at her reports. "We've already had this conversation."

"But if you gamble, go all in, and the payoff comes, you've won, Quincy."

"And if it doesn't?" She looked up at him.

"Then you are left with the memory of what it felt like to win with that person in that moment, and worth every fools' hunt to have is the memory of love."

"Amazing how often the words fool and love go together," Quincy drawled.

Arch shuffled the papers left on Fisher's desk into an even pile and quoted, "*Love will make fools of us all, big and little.*"

When Quincy wrinkled her face, Arch smiled and said, "Thackeray."

"Is Thackeray another of your writers?"

"Yes."

"Keep it to yourself, Arch."

Arch laughed his silver laugh, and Quincy found the edge of her mouth flitting upward accompanied by an amused eyebrow.

This was the third change that had happened at The Q. She and Arch actually had become friends. It wasn't, Quincy assured herself, a thick-as-thieves affair, but they had begun speaking to one another with superfluous words rather than just those required to transact their business. The kinds of conversations Arch normally had with Fisher he was now having with Quincy. The proportions between them had shifted. She railed at him now just as she had before, but there was less salt in it. And he had begun engaging in return as if it were a game. More than once, he had brought her near to laughter.

And so went the remainder of August.

It was a bustling month, August, as it was the middle of an exceptionally busy quarter. The expansion plans into Paris were in full swing, and Quincy was hoping to open before October was out. London would come the following spring if all went well.

Quincy was confident in her model. She felt hopeful, even towards Ezekiel's requirements. Each night, she stared at the paper she had tacked to the wall of her small matchbox room. Of the twelve numbers descending, six of them were now filled.

1. *Butterfly*
2 *Accidental Arson*
3. *Tea (Fothergil)*
4. *Opera (Arch, unwillingly)*
5. *Apology (Arch)*
6. *Friend (Arch)*

Seven through twelve remained blank, but Quincy had stopped resisting and opened a small corner of her mind to be about the business of figuring out the remaining six requirements. Come September, she intended to make a serious study.

———

"Are you ready to hear what I've discovered?" Arch asked.

He had found Quincy in the print room, where she was eating a combination of food items hardly recognizable as a midday meal. She finished chewing her two-day-old biscuit, watching Arch watching her. She swallowed, brushed her fingers together, and then licked her lips.

"Speak on, spymaster. What treasonous tales do you bring your sovereign?"

"Are you going to come down from your throne, St. Claire, or should I kneel before you?"

"Don't be absurd, Arch." Quincy gathered her uneaten apple and slipped down from the ancient, now looking up at him. "I would make you beg before I would ever make you kneel."

"Noted. Shall we adjourn to the dungeons or to my office?"

"Sounds serious. Are you worried the presses have ears? I've no reason to suspect my machinery of being disloyal."

"Well," Arch said, pulling at his sleeve, "it's probably better that a sorter or a mouse doesn't overhear what we are saying and start a street rumor that we're nosing about concerning the board."

"Hmm. You've managed to pique my interest," Quincy said, leading the way up the stairs. "I'll dock your pay if the information is middling."

"You can't dock my pay: it's in the contract," Arch answered.

He followed her up the stairs, through the sorter, and into the front office, where Fisher was helping a line of customers.

"What if I wanted to give you a raise?" Quincy said as she walked around the Q line and into the seldom-used conference room.

"Now, *that*," Arch said, closing the door behind him, "you could do, as I am the most devoted peasant beneath your reign, however diseased, or titled, I may be—which in your mind equates to the same thing."

Grinning, Quincy dropped into the chair at the head of the table, and Arch settled himself to her right, his back to the door. "When did you develop this sense of humor, Arch?"

Arch leaned back and considered. "Probably the moment you gained yours."

Quincy didn't think this was the case; she figured he had probably just started bringing it with him to work on a daily basis. "So," Quincy said, crossing her arms, "what did you discover in the clubs?"

"Nothing."

The taste of that frustration touched the top of her tongue and she growled, "You could have said nothing in the print room and let me finish my meal, Arch."

"Was that a meal, St. Claire? I had thought you'd stolen your fare from a hungry child out on Queen's Street."

"You're choosing now to be funny?"

Arch gave her an unrepentant expression. He was unbelievable. Even though they both knew it wasn't true, she said, "I'm beginning to miss the quiet, cowering solicitor who rattled around the office with his cough in January." Then Quincy shifted her tone in an attempt to imitate Arch, "Not cowering, Miss St. Claire, only uninterested in the conflict."

Arch's face remained static save for the entertained glint that came into his eyes when she'd tried to impersonate him. "Are you quite finished with your theatrics?"

"Impress me, Arch."

"Where there is nothing, Miss St. Claire, there is always *something*."

"Now whose being theatrical?"

Arch ignored her. "So, I turned my inquiries on four people of interest: Hastings, Levins, Rutherford, and Draggen."

"Draggen? That old, useless braggart of *The Sun*? He's not on the board."

"No." Arch moved his head in a way only possible when born into title and money. "But once with Rutherford and once with Levins, I have seen him in conference he wished to keep private. It's no secret they're friends, and so, their meetings could be all smoke, no fire. But, meeting in such a way with two members of The Q's board? Well, it's something to keep an eye on."

Quincy remembered Priest's warning: *Don't make him your enemy.*

"Where did these conversations take place?" she asked.

"Rutherford was in a private room at the Gaming Club."

"And Levins?"

"Rather curiously, in a back alley off Silver Street."

Two images fought for precedent in Quincy's mind, pushing the numbers of Quincy's work aside in the same way one might hastily clear a desk. The first image was of Draggen and Levins, whispering in a back alley. The second was of Arch, following them, waiting around a corner, playing spymaster. She laughed and scowled simultaneously. "You weren't seen, were you, Arch? Cats. You are no king's agent, you lily-fingered aristocrat! You do realize this?"

"I was not seen, St. Claire. And I am quite good at following people who have no business in intrigue to begin with. I was not the least experienced of the three."

Quincy recalled the image of Arch in an opera box, his wardrobe rivaling any exquisite in town. She saw him as he looked now, dressed in utilitarian, well-cut black, ink stain on his finger, serious solicitor-bent expression on his face. Then she *tried* to see him following someone into a back alley, and she couldn't. All three images were walking in different directions, and there seemed to be no unifying point.

"Did you hear anything of the conversations?" she pressed.

"No," Arch stated, obviously not feeling bad about the failure. "I would have made myself obvious and, therefore, useless."

"Hmmm." Quincy moved her fingers to the table before her and held them there, tapping one of her pointers incessantly against the wood. "We might have stumbled onto something else entirely. It could be nothing that has to do with the Q—their own business."

"Most likely," Arch confirmed.

"But it's good to know."

"Most definitely."

Quincy stood. "If you don't mind, keep doing…whatever it is that you're doing."

Arch nodded. "I'll keep my ears open. I'm certain it's nothing to do with us, as Levins seems the sort to keep his fingers in sticky affairs he'd not want to make public, but we will monitor the next several months. In case."

"In case."

CHAPTER TWENTY-TWO:
Now This

Fisher and Quincy had never spent more than two days outside of one another's presence since Ezekiel had brought the former to Rhysdon. So, when Fisher arrived at work early, on August twenty-seventh, Quincy knew from his expression that the plane they had existed on for the last thirteen years had now shifted.

"I need to speak with you, Quincy."

Quincy set her pencil down and tucked her bottom lip between her teeth. He looked miserable and regretful, like the world had swallowed him up and he didn't know how to climb out but was determined to do it by himself. All of this meant he was doing what they had never dared to discuss out loud. He was leaving. The look in his eyes confirmed it.

Years crumbled around Quincy; she could feel the reverberation of the machines they'd worked as children, the gray of the factory, the cold stone entryways they'd slept in every night. She rubbed her cheek with the bottom of her palm, and looked towards the large clock on the wall.

"Quincy." Fisher came to the counter, dropping his satchel to the floor, and reaching across for one of her hands. "I know. I'm sorry. I'm—I've decided I'm going to start my studies, now that funds aren't an issue. Ezekiel had been telling me for years—"

"Rhysdon University accepted you? That's—I'm happy for you," she said, small-voiced, caving in to the reality she had been anticipating for thirteen years. "The campus isn't far. I'll still see you on Sundays."

"Not Rhysdon, Quincy." Fisher straightened his shoulders, pulling whatever bravery he could find into his figure. "Paris."

Quincy swallowed. Almost five thousand days of knowing that while the other person lived, they wouldn't let you starve, and now, this. "Paris?"

"It's Mado. Her mother is sick, and she's had to return home to help care for her younger brothers. And we—we plan to marry, Quincy. Soon. As soon as I finish at the university. So, it makes sense to choose a place that is close at hand, close to Mado."

"Perfect sense."

But it didn't. It didn't make any sense that their lives would shift in anything but a circular pattern, where they kept to their work, to each other, and left the phenomenon of change for other people outside the offices of The Q.

"When do you go?"

"Just over two weeks. Mado returns to France tomorrow."

"You see a future for yourself, then, with Mado?"

"Oh, Quincy." And Fisher smiled in the way he had when seeing Rhysdon for the first time. "I feel as if I'm on the cusp of every dream."

"Then," Quincy looked down, "if that's how you feel, I think you should go. We both knew you were made for things other than The Q."

"Thank you, Quincy." Fisher leaned across the counter and took Quincy's face in both his hands. She could feel the absence of two fingers and the rough, scarred skin of the hand that had been trapped in the machine all those years back. He kissed her very tenderly on the cheek, below her left eye, his face lingering afterward near hers, and she could feel his hands were shaking.

"Who would have thought of you, Fisher, being married?" she whispered. "But I think Mado's a good choice for you."

"And I think Crow's an *awful* choice for you, Quincy."

She began laughing, feeling the tremor leave his fingers. The spell was broken; she smiled, and Fisher kissed her once more before turning away towards his desk, whistling as he began his day. Then Quincy saw the transformation clearly for the first time. Fisher was no longer her fellow foundling, he was a man; ambitious, determined, with a set jaw and sharp eyes. He was what he had always wished he could become, and she was, in fact, very happy for him.

CHAPTER TWENTY-THREE:
Lazy Excuse for a Solicitor

"Arch." Quincy slammed the contracts on his desk. "I read through these before I went to sleep last night and wasn't pleased with something I found."

He looked from the contracts up to Quincy's face, doing his best not to smile.

"What?" she snarled as she sat down. She was in a tempestuous mood, as she had needed to fire a Q boy for theft. She hated firing Q boys. "It better be good or else I'll hang you in the square."

Arch shrugged and flicked open his hand. "The image of you, sitting down for a cozy tête–à–tête with Q contracts just before bed—nightclothes, a cup of tea, slippers, smiling eagerly as you dive into the paperwork before you—it's almost," he paused for emphasis, "Dickensian."

She opened her mouth, halted, and then closed it. An image that shouldn't have been funny, as Quincy had been doing it for years— without the slippers, obviously—suddenly seemed lined with humor because of how he had said it. Blasted Arch.

"I can't imagine why I ever decided to truce with you. You've become abominable under the weak flag of so-called friendship."

"I've been nothing but amicable," he defended, another smile beneath his words. "Now, what have I done wrong today?"

"You gave Fairfield eleven percent instead of nine percent. What do you think The Q is? A charity?"

Arch turned his attention, now studious instead of amused, toward the pile of contracts. Singling out the one for Fairfield Press, he opened it deliberately to the second page. "Fairfield is a smaller concern, and by giving them eleven percent, the print shop will not feel taken advantage of because of their lesser volume."

"You do think The Q is a charity," Quincy scowled. "Give him the nine percent like everyone else."

"But," Arch held up a finger, "if you look here, at the year-end accounts, he is going to pay thirteen percent instead of the usual ten. So The Q's profits will not be hindered; on a solid year, they will actually be helped. But the Fairfield Press can plan for the year-end expenses while saving money up front. I thought it a brilliant advantage for both parties."

Quincy tapped her finger against the side of her leg and glared at him.

"You see, the percentages will balance themselves out at the beginning of the fourth quarter, leaving room for additional profit for ourselves."

"I understand what you said perfectly, Arch. Cats, it makes sense, and I'm frustrated I didn't see it sooner myself. It's only that—"Quincy dropped into the chair before his desk and crossed her arms. "I have an entire team of paid accountants and my own mind—which is far better than the lot of them. You shouldn't be the one switching numbers in contracts."

"Quincy St. Claire, upset because I've improved The Q's services while bringing in more profit?"

"Of course not, you fool. I'm upset because you were the first one to think of it. I should have been willing to do that with the small population markets years ago. Let the smaller markets save more up front, have more room for investment, in return for increased payment later. It's brilliant. I thought so the moment I read it last night."

Arch settled back, placing a hand on the arm of the chair. "Then why did you come barreling in like that?"

"Just because I saw what you were doing doesn't mean you did," Quincy replied. "It could have been a mistake."

"You—" Arch's mouth pressed together, and he looked irritated. "Your arrogance can be somewhat annoying."

Quincy blinked. She uncrossed her arms and sat up straight. "Arrogance?"

"Yes. Assuming that people have stumbled onto brilliance only because they got lost in a cloud of stupidity."

"I wasn't implying—"

"But you do, St. Claire, you do. And just because I don't come to things in the same way you do does not mean I'm a complete fool. Genius I may not be, but your methods are not the only way to skin a cat." His dark eyes pinned her into her seat. She squirmed, but it was from the electric challenge between them.

"That's disgusting," she finally said, "the bit about the cat."

"It's a turn of phrase—"

"You're right," Quincy stood up.

His mouth opened for a full second before he spoke. "I'm right?"

"It was arrogant," Quincy admitted, "and I'm certain it was annoying. If you came at me that way, I would, without question, find you—oh wait—" Quincy looked directly at him, "I do find you annoying."

His eyebrows lifted in puckish reply.

"But," Quincy continued, "you've made The Q some long-term profit so I'll let you have the round, and what's more, I'll thank you for it. Thank you."

Arch shifted in his chair. When he answered, his tone was light; the expression that accompanied his words, entertained. "What generous concessions you make, now that we're friends."

"Does admitting my error satisfy a requirement?"

"No, but it should."

"You're damn right it should, you filthy rat."

The bell rang, and Quincy returned to her counter. As she was filling out a Q slip for one of the businessmen of Gainsford Street, Quincy couldn't help but see Arch's face through his open doorway. He was smiling.

A few days later, Quincy had business with Blevins, who found it amusing to have his corporate office uptown beside the hoity-toity shops of Rhysdon. The women custom of the street always looked askance at Quincy, and she hadn't yet figured out why Blevins would want to put up with them. She had come to argue out a lower fare agreement for employees taking the Rhysdon Q insert to farther locations by train. Arch came too, as always, but his mind seemed more spread out than usual.

When they arrived at the Fontblanc building, Arch said he would be in Upper Rhysdon Cathedral when she was finished.

"You'll accomplish something today that sets you apart, Arch."

"What is that?" he said, looking distracted.

Quincy scowled. "Getting paid to worship, you lazy excuse of a solicitor. Only the priests have managed that for the last several hundred years."

Arch gave her a token smile, but some thought in his mind soon clouded out the expression. Quincy entered the Fontblanc building, turning when she was just inside to watch Arch walk across the street. His concerns rested heavily on his shoulders indeed.

Her meeting with Blevins went as well as could be expected. It was the first of what would necessarily be several meetings on the subject before Blevins would willingly agree to a consensus. He preferred the drama of stretching out a decision. Quincy did not. At the end of this first round of negotiations, they exchanged news of the business world, which was as much world as either of them were interested in. Then Quincy left his office, taking herself down a flight of marble stairs, and left the Fontblanc building behind as she crossed the street towards Rhysdon's oldest cathedral.

As this wasn't the cathedral where Ezekiel's services had been endured, Quincy had not been inside it for quite some time. Built from deep stone, warm in color, cut and marked by mallet and chisel however many hundred years before—it was an architectural marvel as much as it was a house of worship. As Quincy stepped into the long aisle and scanned the shadowy pews before her, she wondered which Arch came for, the marvel or the worship?

After her eyes adjusted from the thick brightness of the late summer day, she found her solicitor, sitting two-thirds of the way back on the right side of the cathedral's nave. His eyes were closed, his head bent, fingers moving nervously around themselves like the fingers of a Q mouse on his first day.

Not speaking, Quincy slid into the pew beside him, lifting her eyes towards the myriad of stained-glass depictions of stories she didn't really know and certainly didn't understand. Ezekiel had always spoken more freely of the Old Testament. The glass works were bright, bold in the way they caught the light, claiming it for their illumination and brilliance. Quincy counted the windows. There were sixteen large panels and two rose windows: the larger in the front; a smaller above the doors Quincy had just entered through. Turning her attention back to the large windows that flanked the nave, she wondered if Arch understood the stories told there.

"Have you been in the Upper Rhysdon Cathedral before?" he asked.

Quincy started, slamming her elbow against the wooden pew, and then slamming a word—not appropriate for inside a cathedral—back into her mouth. "Ow!" she whispered instead. "Yes! Curse you, Arch; you startled me. Yes, I've been here—years ago, when I was smaller."

"Sorry for startling you."

She was still grimacing as she massaged her elbow, the sting of pain splitting in all directions like lightning. "Did I interrupt something? Were you asking God for deliverance from The Q? Or—"

"No." Arch leaned forward, resting his elbows on his knees as he craned his neck, eyes moving around the windows as if they were familiar faces to him. "I was—never mind. I was sorting a difficult problem."

As he did not volunteer anything else, Quincy didn't press. "Yes, well, keep your problems to yourself, Arch. I've no need to sort your social calendar for you. Much more important things to spend my time on."

"Certainly," Arch said in mock seriousness, but Quincy could see he was feeling better. As he turned his face back to the study of the stained glass, he looked comfortable. "That one has always been my favorite." He was pointing towards a window along the western bank of glass, towards a figure, half wrapped, being greeted in an embrace by another figure. It was a strange portrayal, as if an entombing had gone horribly wrong.

"What is it exactly?" she asked.

"Lazarus," Arch said, his manner betraying his surprise that Quincy did not know who this Lazarus fellow was.

"Who was…?"

"Lazarus was a friend of the Christ Jesus. He was raised from the dead after laying in his tomb three days."

"How?" Quincy said, instead of bursting out with the thought that she would never want to see anyone three days after death.

"The Christ Jesus spoke the words 'Lazarus, come forth,' and he came forth."

Quincy pinched the side of her mouth up into her cheek as she studied the window, trying to find the beauty that caused Arch to give it preferential treatment.

"I don't see it," she said aloud.

"You've never read the passage. Of course you would not be moved."

"I also remain unmoved in my position that we have a good deal of work to do before the office closes. Let's go, Arch."

Arch stood and took his hat from the bench beside him, carrying it in his hand until they reached the doors leading out into busy Rhysdon. Then he set it on his head with a practiced precision, adjusting it smoothly and unaware of his grace, as he pushed open the heavy doors. Quincy looked behind her one last time, at the dark cathedral illuminated with stained glass, and then stepped into the sun.

As they walked down the stairs to the wide sidewalk, Quincy said, "I never thought you for a churchgoer, Arch."

"You forced me to it, St. Claire. Some demons drive a man to the bottle, some demons drive a man to the church." She laughed, knowing she'd probably not driven Arch to do anything save repent of his agreeing to Ezekiel's terms for working at The Q.

"I do my best," she said a full minute later.

They walked back to Gainsford Street by route of the largest tree-lined streets, Arch stopping to buy a green-paper-wrapped bunch of deep red flowers.

"For my desk," he defended when Quincy glared at him.

And she snorted.

CHAPTER TWENTY-FOUR:
Peacock House

"Come for dinner tonight," Arch insisted later that week as he was rushing out early from the office for a predinner commitment. He set his portfolio, satchel, and jacket on Quincy's counter and began unrolling the sleeves of his shirt. "My father has returned to town and expressed interest in meeting you. Just he, I, and Mary will be there; no other aristocrats will be hiding in the dark corners."

Quincy made a face.

"I know Fisher is occupied with his preparations for Paris, so I won't be stealing your time with him," Arch continued. "Besides, we don't stand on ceremony at Peacock House, to the chagrin of our cook and our housekeeper. You'll find it pleasantly subtle and, most certainly, lacking the pomp of a Fothergil event."

"The last dinner invitation I accepted was a disaster," Quincy answered, pushing his portfolio off her paperwork. "And we fought afterward, remember?"

"Have you never heard the drinking song that says, 'The past we'll forgive to not let the beast live'?" Arch answered, undeterred.

Quincy grinned.

"What?" Arch asked, putting his suit jacket on.

"You, quoting a drinking song instead of poetry. Crandall just rolled over in his grave."

"You are a wit, St. Claire," he replied drily. "It looks like it might rain, but I'd guess its foolish to inquire if you'll accept a carriage?"

The expression on Quincy's face gave the answer.

"As I thought. I'll see you at dinner."

During the final two hours of The Q's day, a steady stream of customers kept Quincy from her usual work. The Q boys began trickling in, Spats—still keeping all three routes in addition to doing his training as a mouse—sauntering in the front door just before close.

Quincy followed Spats into the sorter and then left him accounting to Graves for his lateness as she descended into the print room. Spense was cursing over a machine, his grease-marked fingers exploring a hitch in the machinery. Jade was setting type and yelling at the mice to get their boards in order before she exterminated them all.

"They've begun calling me the Alley Cat or the Mouser," Jade told Quincy with the air of an amused martyr. "Jack thinks it's hilarious. Did you hear how many Qs came in from the south region for the Rhysdon paper? We're going to have to add another page entirely. *The Q* is going to be thicker than *The Times* come Christmas."

Quincy looked over the tallies tracked by her Q drivers, which were pinned to the receiving board. "Arch invited me round for dinner with his family tonight, of all things" she said as she added tallies in her mind.

"He did?"

"It's not a formal evening—just his father and sister is all—but, as it looks like I'm needed in the print room tonight, I'll not be going."

"You're not needed," Jade said sharply. "You pay employees for a reason, and if the mice can keep up, we'll roll *The Q* out in quick time. Frankly, you would be in the way."

Quincy turned from her tallies to look at Jade. They both knew Quincy could fit into any gear of The Q without causing a ripple. She *was* The Q.

"I don't want to go," Quincy admitted.

"And I don't want to split my peach crisp with Spense tonight, but I do it because we're friends. You owe Arch. See it as part of fulfilling the requirements of having a friend. What time is dinner?"

"He didn't say," Quincy replied, thinking it insufferable to be friends with someone who assumed you should know at what time everything would be. "Doesn't that class usually eat at eight o'clock?"

"I wouldn't know," Jade said, her fingers moving through the air as if they wanted to be finding type instead of talking. "Jack and I decided running with that set would hinder our low social credit, a risk we can't take."

Quincy laughed. "Tell Jack he's in no risk of that. Now, put me to work."

"Only if you promise you'll go."

"I'm thinking it over."

Quincy helped Spense negotiate the temperamental press, then set a few trays of type so Jade could run the drafts. It was a quarter past seven when she climbed up the stairs and returned to the front office. Then she saw Arch's portfolio there, the one he never came or went without, sitting abandoned on the counter. He must have forgotten it in his rush.

Complaining to herself, Quincy went upstairs, cleaned up as best as she could—there was still ink in the cracks of her fingers—and changed her clothing to a simple pair of black trousers, boots, and a finely cut jacket over a white shirt. It was the first chilly night, and a slow drizzle had begun, as her open window testified, so Quincy wrapped her red scarf about her neck and looked at the thin mirror in her room. Her hair kept falling across her eyes, refusing to conform, and Quincy knew that if she decided she cared, she wouldn't go. So she blew it away from her face and grabbed her black hat, forcing herself into deciding not to care.

The walk to 731 Regent Square felt wrapped in velvet—soft around the edges of the lamp post lights—just enough rain to round all the edges—the smells of late summer shifting in the smoke and steam smog of a city street leaning toward the fall. Quincy counted numbers in her head as she moved, content to pull up the August statistics of two previous years in her mind and compare them with the same month now over. She found, of course, she had exceeded her expectations.

Regent Square came too soon, as if it had adopted a closer neighborhood just to inconvenience Quincy's evening. Pressing her fingers against the portfolio in her hand, Quincy rather stoically approached the front door and lifted the heavy, brass knocker shaped like a peacock.

She had never been one to daydream, but Quincy imagined no one ever opening the door.

"I came and no one was at home," she would tell Arch the next day.

But this was not to be. The housekeeper opened the door.

"Miss St. Claire, what an unexpected surprise. Is Master James expecting you?"

"Yes," came the voice of a man Quincy had never met. "I believe he is, Symons. Thank you, that will be all."

The housekeeper, Symons, moved aside, and Quincy stepped into the hall and pulled her hat from her head. A tallish man—elegant, trim, richly dressed—looked at Quincy: from her short-cropped blond head to her wet, booted toes. Then his eyes rested on the portfolio in Quincy's hand, and he smiled. "Well, I'll be enchanted. Come in, Miss St. Claire, come in. The children are gone out, but, no, don't worry—I see it in your face you might be prone to do so—they are to come back shortly. Come up with me to the library. I am enjoying a fire and a drink before the entertainments of the evening commence."

"Thank you, ah—?"

"Pardon, Lord Arch, at your service." He bowed and then told Symons to please take Miss St. Claire's hat, and, oh, yes, her scarf; rather red and unusual, but he like it all the same, yes he did.

Quincy handed the scarf to Symons, and after pulling at the dull black brim of her hat, handed over it as well. She felt for the first time a hint of self-awareness for her choice of clothing.

"Good, good. Come with me, dear. There is nothing better on a rainy, September evening than a room full of books, don't you think? Or am I to really believe James that you care for numbers and only numbers and would never be swayed by the thoughts of Milton, Shakespeare, or Rhysdon's own Crandall, the great poet?"

Lord Arch motioned for Quincy to follow him up the stairs; she did so, somewhat mystified at this turn of events, Arch's portfolio still in her hand. They passed another beautifully appointed drawing room and a few closed doors before he led her into a well-crafted, well-thought-out, and well-supplied library. Had Quincy any leanings toward literary pursuits, she would have found this room a sort of paradise.

"Sit here with me beside the fire." Lord Arch motioned towards a comfortable looking wingback chair cozied up near the hearth with his own, considerably more used chair sitting opposite. A book was holding his place. He lifted it with reverent familiarity and settled himself, tapping the worn brown leather of the book's cover against his knee as he watched Quincy take her seat.

"So this is the famous Quincy St. Claire."

"And this is a Rhysdon lord," Quinsy answered, feeling the need to unsettle him in order to settle herself.

Lord Arch laughed and refused her this unspoken advantage by the way he very nearly grinned at her. "Could I offer you a drink?" he asked, retrieving his own, holding the amber liquid up to the light of the fire.

"No, thank you."

"I forget," Lord Arch took a drink and set it down after sucking his teeth, "you prefer a pint in a smugglers' hold."

Quincy sat up straighter and glared. Had Arch told him about Crow?

"No, actually," she replied with some acid. "I prefer nothing, if I have a choice, and peppermint tea, when I have none."

Lord Arch's eyes twinkled and he lifted a hand to his curious smile. "Is that James's portfolio, there?"

"He left it at The Q, no doubt to ensure I would accept his invitation. I'm not certain I would have come any other way."

Lord Arch laughed, an oval, solid sound, amusement mixed with amicable inclusion. "You come as honored guest, Miss St. Claire. You have no enemies at Peacock House, or at least that is the hope. From your end, it may be different. I've come to understand you do not think much of literature or of plays," he said easily, switching the topic.

"You're correct in that I don't think much of them," Quincy stated, "not because I deny them value but because they hold so little for me that I don't find it worth my time. I won't shade your admiration, though, by any means."

"James has said the only things you love in this world—since the passing of your delightful uncle—are numbers, progress, and profit."

Quincy lifted her eyebrows and sat farther back in her chair. "He's wrong."

"Is he?"

"Yes, about a number of things."

Lord Arch covered a smile and set his drink down, shifting his book and letting it rest against his knee in a manner that suited his title. "Tell me, then, Miss St. Claire, what else do you love?"

Quincy tapped the toe of her boot once and shrugged, "I don't wish to tell you."

"That is very fair," replied Lord Arch.

Quincy appreciated his easy retreat. He picked up his drink, opened his book to a page marked with a blue ribbon, and settled comfortably into his reading. Quincy began to look about the library. Tall windows, many shelves, a globe in a stand, a large mahogany desk, maps, a rather peculiar painting of a sea bird flung about in a windy gale with a grin on his face, and a violin inside its case, open, on a side table. Her eyes lingered on the beautiful instrument—rich red in color, well-loved, yet beautifully kept—lying contentedly against the green velvet of its case.

"Do you play?"

Quincy jerked her eyes away from the instrument to find Lord Arch watching her, his mouth drawn in a very familiar straight line.

"Only for myself, now that Ezekiel is dead," she answered truthfully.

"How delightful," he said, smiling, his handsome face giving way to the refined wrinkles of his age. "Why don't you play for yourself now, and I'll just listen?"

She half glared, half smiled. There was something about him, Quincy admitted, that she found exasperatingly charming.

"A man like you would be accustomed to the finest players both country and continent have to offer," Quincy replied. "I'm certain you'd find little pleasure in my untutored talent."

"What a nonsensical assumption." Lord Arch tilted his head. "I greatly enjoy my son's essays and prose despite having a library filled with the greatest writers of many generations."

"Arch writes essays?"

"Oh, yes. He's very accomplished in the thing. I've been telling him for years to send them into the papers or the journals. His poetry needs a little seasoning, though. He may never make a great poet."

Quincy was quite dumbfounded. She looked towards the fire, reconciling the young man she knew with this casual revelation.

"It's the evening for such entertainments, after all, Miss St. Clair. Let us have music, just you and me, a merry party."

Quincy looked back at the violin, stubbornly tempted not to play a note. She despised having people force her in any direction, even if it was one in which she wished to go. But, biting the side of her lip, Quincy felt her desire to touch the instrument sabotage her determination to resist. She had never held an instrument of real quality, and Quincy St. Claire loved quality.

Before she could change her mind, Quincy stood, walked determinedly towards the violin, and picked it up from its rosin-marked case, plucking the strings. They were in perfect tune. She spun the instrument in her hands, noticing its age, an ill-fated nick on the scroll. Yet, attentive polishing had maintained the glorious grains in the wood. The bow lay nearby, having been recently restrung, not a horse hair out of place.

"Is this your violin?" she asked.

But Lord Arch did not answer as he watched Quincy bring the violin to her chair and perch on the edge of the seat, lifting the instrument to her chin, plucking at the strings again from habit.

"You will find it impeccably tuned."

Feeling a flush on her cheeks, Quincy nodded and closed her eyes. She pulled out the first note and wished to collapse into the perfect, rich quality of the instrument she held in her hands. Quincy played one of her uncle's favorites, an English folk tune often called Kingsfoil. She soaked into the give of each string as she pulled sound from the violin, moving the bow smoothly as thick cream, while lifting and dropping each note. She played the melody once in its integrity first before adding her own flourishes the next time around. It was haunting, lovely. Quincy drew out the last note before opening her eyes.

Lord Arch sat with an expression so like his son's, so intent and thoughtful, it was startling. He did not speak, so Quincy began to play another tune: the lively French folk song Ezekiel had been wont to sing around the house. With this song, the violin truly came to life, vibrant and bright, as it danced the notes into the air. From the corner of her eye, Quincy thought she saw Lord Arch smile in recognition.

Upon finishing, Quincy rested the violin on her knee and looked at Lord Arch. He sat with the back of his finger to his lips, his thumb beneath his chin, considering her.

"Do you only play folk songs, Miss St. Claire?"

"No," Quincy said, blowing a shock of hair from her face. "For myself, I usually play Mozart or Bach. There is a composer out of France called Satie whose pieces are simple, a bit sober—certainly not Bach—but I like some of them. I played the folk tunes because you seemed to be enjoying the day, and I thought I'd cater to the spirit of it."

"Quite right," Lord Arch agreed. "But let's hear one of those sober pieces from Paris now. My wife was always attentive to anything that came from her hometown."

And so Quincy played the opening note of Gymnopédie No. 1 and gave this Lord Arch her private, honest rendition of the piece. Its notes never failed to make her ache on the inside of her chest. The song reminded her of grief, of emotions that were simpler as a child, more straightforward, that were now taken and turned into something she was hesitant to touch but could not forget. The song was not long, but Quincy played it through only once.

When she finished and lifted the bow from the strings, applause came from the hallway. Mary was standing there, clapping, with Arch just behind her shoulder, watching with a tilted smile.

"Bravo!" Lord Arch clapped his hands together as he waved his children into the library. The ease and the comfort of speaking with Lord Arch was now gone. Quincy stood, violin awkwardly hanging from her hand, wondering why seeing Arch with his family made her feel disjointed.

Mary smiled toward Quincy as she went to her father's side, leaning down to kiss his forehead.

"Did your afternoon go well?" Lord Arch asked Mary, drawing her into a quiet exchange.

As Mary responded, Quincy stepped back to the side table, taking extra care to clean the violin before letting it rest inside its green velvet casing. Loosening the bow, she slipped it into the top lid and closed the case, gently securing the clasps.

Arch had followed her and leaned back against the table, facing the rest of the room, all the while his eyes watching her hands.

"I am glad you decided to come," he said when she'd finished. "It should be a nice evening."

"You left your portfolio at the office," she replied, as if that explained her presence.

Remembrance crossed Arch's face. "I spent half an hour looking for it earlier. It's a relief you had it all along."

"And I thought it was a lure," said Quincy as she too leaned against the table, her hands catching the corners.

Arch claimed innocence, and then added, "I've always thought there wasn't a lure in this world or the next that could catch Quincy St. Claire."

Quincy looked towards him. "You're probably right."

"In any case," Arch added, "you've just fulfilled your seventh requirement. Consider me impressed."

"What?" Quincy scowled. "Coming to dinner?"

"Playing your violin for a stranger. I admit, I didn't believe you would ever do it. You've never offered to play it for me."

Quincy looked at Arch long enough for a victorious feeling to press on her lungs, and then she glanced away, watching Lord Arch converse with Mary. "Does your father know what's on the list?"

"No."

"Good. I'd hate to think you invited me out of pity."

"Never for pity; always for the company."

Dinner at Peacock House proved to be an affair entirely different from what Quincy had imagined. For starters, they broke protocol and ignored the proper dining room, instead gathering around a small round table, the sort usually used to play cards.

The room itself was just two doors from the library and was decorated in comfortable jewel tones with the most baffling collection of items Quincy had ever seen in one place. There were several unique paintings, including one of a mermaid and another of desert travelers. There was an old map, carvings, furniture of every style. There was a birdcage, filled with books; a sword, with dried flowers hanging from the hilt by a gold ribbon; a row of glass jars, filled with bright feathers; an old street placard, which said something in French; and a bust of one of the Caesars, with a dart lodged in his eye. Draperies of rich, geometric patterns hung across the windows, and rugs of equal interest and color spanned the floor. There was also a mounted butterfly, a telescope, an unstrung cello, and a large purple velvet chair, sitting decidedly in the corner, with a sea chest for an ottoman. Quincy accepted her seat, but she was quarter turned in the chair, mesmerized by the bizarre setting.

"She approves of the sanctuary," Lord Arch declared as two footmen served the first course—a peculiar looking soup—from a sideboard that also housed a strange brass frog, sitting up and staring at the occupants of the table. "The madness appeals."

"You forget that Miss St. Claire is of Spartan blood," Arch answered as he shook his napkin and set it across his lap, a refined movement at odds with the curiosities of the room. "It might be too much altogether. What do you think of it, Quincy?"

"I—"

"I think it's a bit of a spectacle, although I am partial to the sphinx in the corner," Mary said in a practical tone.

Quincy turned further, and, yes, right there in the corner was a sphinx the size of a large dog. It looked to be carved from vein cut black marble. A green silk scarf had been draped around its neck.

"I find it—" Quincy attempted again but could find no words.

"A magician's lair?" offered Lord Arch from Quincy's left.

"A bizarre exhibition," Mary said, shaking her head in embarrassment from across the table.

"I think," Arch said, smiling as he turned around, his arm resting on the back of his chair as he surveyed the room, "Miss St. Claire will say it's too loud on the eyes, too distracting, not straightforward enough. She might possibly suggest it be burned."

"I find it clean," Quincy said, looking toward her solicitor sitting at her right.

"Clean?" Arch moved his head around, the cut of his jaw sharp as the shadows from the lights.

"Clean," Quincy said, bringing her spoon to the green soup before her with some trepidation. "Crowded?" Quincy continued. "Yes. Odd? Undoubtedly. But it feels clean."

The soup tasted like mint. Furthermore, Quincy liked it.

"Well," said Lord Arch, "no one has ever accused the Arches of not being clean, so cheers for that."

Without really thinking, Arch and Mary lifted their glasses and rang them against one another, an unspoken expression of the bond this family held. As Arch was putting his glass down, he stopped and shook his head. "Not true, my lord. I was recently accused of being a rat—and a filthy one at that."

"By Johnny?" Mary asked, as if this were normal conversation. "Is he still mad about losing last November's wager?"

Shaking his head and attending to his soup before he answered, Arch said, "Miss St. Claire is the culprit."

"What?" Quincy said.

"You called me a filthy rat."

She glanced around the table before admitting with some cheek, "I've called you a lot of things."

A dimple that Quincy never quite remembered was there appeared to the side of Arch's smile. "Yes, you have."

"The question is, which ones are true?" Lord Arch rejoined. "A rat? No. But, have you ever called him an evangelist? For that he certainly can be."

"Or an exquisite," Mary offered.

"Yes, that's a good one." Lord Arch made a motion towards Mary. "James is a touch vain."

"I am not."

"A self-important academic," Mary continued despite her brother's groan.

Quincy was watching the entire interaction, wide-eyed. This was a more bizarre dinner table than she, Fisher, and Ezekiel had ever had.

"Admittedly, a tattletale," Lord Arch grinned.

Arch pointed at his father without looking at him and said, "Untrue, and you both know it. This soup is good, Mary."

"Yes, it is quite. I'll ask Cook to put it in the rotation." Then she looked directly at Quincy. "James is also a tender. He's too sensitive, St. Claire."

"Again, not true," Arch said, laughing.

"Then, what are you?" Quincy asked, grinning with the rest of them.

"What am I?" Arch said, lifting his left hand to count on his fingers while he extolled his virtues. "Vastly intelligent, too much for my own good."

Mary laughed.

"Courageous," he continued, "the pure gold sort."

"Gold from your salary at The Q, I'd imagine," inserted Lord Arch.

"Quite so," said Arch. "St. Claire pays me a tremendous wage. I'm handsome as the devil, which often goes without saying, for I am also incredibly humble."

"Very untrue," Lord Arch said as he waved his soup away.

"The handsome face or the humility?" Mary asked.

"The humility," Lord Arch answered calmly. "It's only a matter of course that I not dispute the handsome face. I am the boy's father."

"I am never inviting St. Claire to dine at Peacock House again if this continues," said Arch before thanking the footman who had placed the next course before him. "I'll never be allowed to forget any of this. She doesn't forget things, you know."

"But the secrets of Peacock House are something she'll respect," Lord Arch said, turning now towards Quincy. "You must never let on that James is handsome, Miss St. Claire. It would increase his vanity, and we cannot have that."

"I've never believed he was anyway," Quincy replied, lifting a shoulder, "so you'll not hear me repeating anything."

"There, James, we've found the antidote for your vanity: Miss St. Claire."

Arch continued eating as if he hadn't heard them.

"I told you he was tender," Mary said, smiling sweetly.

"I am not."

Quincy laughed.

⸻

Later that night, as she lay in the matchbox thinking, Quincy couldn't help but run several of the odd-sided conversations from Peacock House through her mind.

CHAPTER TWENTY-FIVE:
Secrets and Farewells

The ladder, which should have been rehung on its double peg inside the file room, was not in its place. Calling down a string of curses on the offender, Quincy looked up at the square opening in the ceiling that led to the storeroom attic. A ladder would make the task easier, but Quincy was pressed for time and walking with little patience as it had been a relentless afternoon.

She stacked some crates on the counter that ran against the wall, and balancing her small frame precariously on them, managed to swing herself up into the attic of the file room. She had a candle and a few matches in her pocket, and Quincy used what little light came up from the room below as she fumbled to light her candle and begin her search.

But before she could light it, she heard Fisher's voice, followed by the door of the file room opening. Pausing, careful not to move, Quincy waited to light her candle. She wasn't sure why. It's not that she minded Fisher knowing she was in the file room's attic. If anything, she would have usually hauled him up with her to expedite the process. But Fisher was talking to somebody, and it didn't take long for Quincy to realize it was Arch.

"That sounds reasonable to me," Arch was saying, and Quincy just sat still, half of herself uninterested in what sounded reasonable, the other half curious just the same.

"Yes. I think Mado feels the same, but I'll be honest, Arch, even when I think I know what will please her, I'm never quite certain. It's enough to drive a man insane."

Arch made an amused noise, and Quincy leaned her elbows on her knees and her chin in her hands just as he answered, "Is it any wonder the poets often write of love in a confused, albeit euphoric, manner?"

Fisher sighed. "I'm not sure a man like you should find love so difficult."

Suddenly Quincy was warm in her jacket, and uncomfortable for eavesdropping. She knew she should make a noise, call down, reveal her presence, but finding herself in the middle of a conversation between Fisher and Arch on the topic of love—a shamefully sentimental thing—was enough to keep her quiet, praying they too would pass.

"Why's that?" Arch answered.

"You're titled; you're rich; you're intelligent and a good sort of man. You're not bad to look at. I just assumed it would be an easier prospect."

"Hmmm." Arch sounded amused. "I think it's always a quandry, no matter who you are." There was shuffling, something opened, and Quincy could hear them flipping through some files. "Here's the report, Fisher. What was the other month you needed?"

"September, last year."

"It should be over there."

Quincy, listening to the sound of the search, resisted the urge to tap the toe of her boot on the attic's wood floor.

"Here it is," Arch said.

"Good," Fisher replied. A drawer closed with too much noise, and Quincy made a mental note to have the runners oiled. "Arch, could I—well, you see, Graves is already at the front desk, and I was hoping to speak with you privately before I leave."

"Certainly," Arch said.

The sound of crates shifting rose into the attic, and it sounded like they had taken a seat. Quincy cursed herself, for it was too late now to reveal her hand. Quincy began to grind her teeth.

"I'm gone in less than a week, Arch. I'll enroll in the university in

Paris, to be close to Mado, and we intend to marry once I've graduated."

"It seems like a solid plan," said Arch, sounding uncertain of what Fisher needed him to say.

"I only worry that when I leave, Quincy will be left alone."

Quincy's back went straight and she blinked, wide-eyed. Was this private interview about her?

"Quincy and I have been family since we were six," Fisher continued. "We became street partners, keeping each other alive, and when we started at the factories, our shifts were always for the same machine. Working the machines was how I lost my fingers."

There was a pause, and Quincy knew that Fisher was holding up his left hand, showing the stumps where his pinky and ring finger should have been.

"Quincy wrapped a dirty piece of her own shirt around my hand, forced me to keep working so I wouldn't lose my place. At shift's end, she saw me to a stream, cleaned up my hand, and wrapped it in a stolen shawl. And then she helped me bury my fingers, which she'd pocketed. We buried them only once she'd realized that putting my hand back together wasn't going to work. It was a mess, horrible pain for days, but Quincy saw me through.

"When Ezekiel came, he took Quincy home then came back for me, and we've been inseparable. Even when she moved into The Q and I took an apartment in the students' quarter, we've always had our days here." He took a long breath. "Ezekiel is gone, and now I am leaving as well. There's no one in the world who means more to me than Quincy. I know, I know," Fisher's voice sounded pained, "I have Mado. But, Quincy and I, we kept each other alive in so many ways, and without Quincy, I'd never have had a chance to be married or to form a career of my own making. I owe so much to her stubborn, angry, dogged determination."

"And now you're leaving her."

"Yes. I'm leaving her."

"It's curious," Arch said, sounding ponderous rather than complimentary, "you and Miss St. Claire came from the same struggles, yet you—"

"...don't walk around like a razor, threatening to gut everyone and everything that moves?" Fisher answered.

Arch laughed, and Quincy narrowed her eyes.

"I don't quite think of it in those terms, but yes."

"I'm a different person, Arch," said Fisher through a sigh. "My parents went with the country fevers when I was five, but I still remember them and how surrounded I was. I didn't feel betrayed by their deaths, just lonely. Quincy was on the streets too long to remember much of her mother, a woman who was abandoned—from what Ezekiel could gather—and left alone with a child while dying of consumption. If Quincy remembers her mother at all, it would only be a hard memory. She doesn't speak of it. Besides, we are so different, Quincy and I. I want different things; I think different things—and Quincy's a genius besides. Perhaps that much genius throws everything else off the scale, out of balance, as it were."

"But surely it's within every human being to be civil," said Arch, but his tone was philosophical, not accusatory.

"Perhaps not if the thought that you have failed someone has haunted your steps since you were five years old."

Quincy shivered, her flushed face suddenly feeling cold. She rested her head on her arm, wishing Fisher would be done, wishing she didn't know what he was planning on saying to Arch next.

"What do you mean?"

"She's never talked about it with anybody, as far as I know, but I remember the few things she said when we first threw our lots into the same game. Now, Arch," Fisher's voice quavered from the seriousness of his tone, "I've never repeated to anybody, not even to the old man, what I am about to tell you."

"Why do you wish to confide in me?"

"Because someone here needs to know why Quincy is so tied up inside, so unwilling to let anyone be important. Seeing you and Quincy now makes me think you should be the one."

"I think you misread the situation," Arch stated.

"She runs at you like hell, Arch. She's not soft, but Quincy has made a few reaches towards you that I've never seen her make towards any other person. You're the only one, I think, who can get past the edges she keeps everyone at."

"I think you misinterpret her regard for me."

"I don't think I do," Fisher said, his voice firm. "Otherwise, why would the old man have hired you with the express purpose of having you see Quincy through this year?"

"I never said he did."

"Do you deny that Ezekiel talked to you about Quincy's well-being?"

When Arch gave no answer, Quincy swore and pressed her hands to her face. Had Arch been hired by Ezekiel deliberately for this whole experiment?

"Now," Fisher continued, "what I mean to tell you is this: when I met Quincy, she had been trying to keep a younger sister alive and failed."

The ends of her fingers burned, and Quincy wanted to slam the heels of her boots against the ceiling beneath her feet. She wanted to rage at Fisher. She wanted to lock every private thought deep inside her chest and never let anybody in.

"She had a sister?"

"Yes. Quincy gave everything to keep her alive. She went bone thin and mind ragged in her efforts to provide milk and bread."

"How old did you say she was?"

"Quincy was four or five when Marie died. They had managed together for a little over a year, but when a child is already starving, and nights get cold—"

"How does a child of four keep another child alive in the streets?"

You don't, Quincy thought. You can never outrun the hunger.

"You would be surprised, Arch. It brings an old quality into your soul pretty fast, the street life, along with arresting some of your childhood fears and pain. Is it any wonder that Quincy is as jumbled and sharp as she is? It's as if her type was scattered. None of us grow up without the imperfections of life creeping into us and making us human, but we catch the errors; whether we reset them or not is up to us. But Quincy was thrown into life with no one to ever help put her back into the cases—she's done a patch job, and I think her brilliant for it. Ezekiel had often said the same, in fewer words, or rather, just different words."

"And the sister?"

"Buried near the creek in the woods outside Lester. Quincy would visit a few times a year."

When Arch spoke again, it was hushed. "She buried the child herself?"

"Who was there to help?"

"Would to God I could have been," Arch muttered, and the way he said it made Quincy pull her jacket around herself closer.

"It's all passed, Arch. Quincy's managed not only to live through whatever else in her life we know nothing of, but she also built one of the most successful businesses in the country. I don't know how often she thinks of her sister. Maybe she decided that if she kept it close inside herself I would forget, perhaps allowing her the same luxury. We've not spoken of it since we were first comrades in survival, except on the night she buried my fingers. She'd said that if you buried someone right, they could get into heaven, and so we should bury my fingers right, and I'd meet them there after I'd died. Silly, really, a child's hope, but I'm sure she'd been wondering about her sister when she said it."

Quincy buried her face in the crook of her elbow, wiping her nose on the sleeve of her jacket and feeling her eyes burn. She wasn't mad at Fisher, but she felt like he had dredged her core. For years, she had tried not to allow any memory of her childhood to create a picture in her mind. Now it was all there, behind her eyes, pressuring her head and her emotions. And Arch knew.

"Ezekiel didn't know about the sister?" Arch asked.

"I never told him. I couldn't. He'd have never forgiven himself for not finding them sooner. But he did wonder who had hurt Quincy so badly that she wouldn't leave herself to trust another person. You see, the one person Quincy gave up her entire soul to save died—horrific at any age, let alone so young—she was thrashed for it. Why, then, are any of us surprised that she thinks human relationships are the least reliable investment?"

"I don't think she'd be pleased with me knowing any of this."

Damn right, Quincy thought, her mouth turned down hard against the pain of Fisher's narration.

"I wouldn't have told you if I didn't think you were worthy of her trust. You like her and are proud to be her solicitor. You've established a rapport with Quincy. Besides that, you're a good person, Arch. With you on one side and Jade and Spense on the other, I can leave for Paris in good conscience."

"I have to tell her I know. I respect Miss. St. Claire too much to keep that knowledge from her."

"Wait until I've left for France. I don't want to find myself tied up in a sack and thrown into the harbor," Fisher said, with a laugh at the heel of his sentence.

After they left the file room, putting out the lights and leaving Quincy in the dark, she sat a good long while, fearing that if she moved, the image of her sister—frozen in her sleep—would take on too much flesh, too much form.

———

By the time Quincy again showed her face in the front offices of The Q, Fisher was gone. Six o'clock had passed. Graves had seen to the front desk, and the sorters were long since finished. The mice were well into their work, and Jade was calling out orders to the editors, which Quincy could hear above the snap and buzz of the presses in the print room. She was surprised, though, to see the lamps in Arch's office still on.

He sat at his desk, reading, frowning, and making annotations on a piece of paper. When Quincy slipped onto her stool, it creaked and called Arch from his thoughts. Upon seeing her, Arch set his book down and sat back in his chair, out of view from Quincy's counter. He sat there for over a minute, before she heard the scrape of his chair and he appeared, walking through his doorway, and catching the extra stool—now placed behind Fisher's desk—with his hand. He set it on the other side of the counter from Quincy and sat down, leaning his back against the wall.

"You're working late," Quincy said, her heart still swollen from the afternoon's events.

"I've been waiting to speak with you."

"I heard."

Arch gave her a quizzing expression.

"I heard what Fisher told you. I was in the attic when you came in."

Twisting the thin line of his mouth, Arch leaned his head back against the wall. "I wish he hadn't have told me," he admitted.

When Quincy did not answer, he continued. "It's not that I see you different; if anything, I understand you more. But we've come along in our friendship and I'd like to believe we have developed a level of respect, an enjoyment in one another's company."

"What?" Quincy said, pretending to be busy among her things. "Now you can't help but pity me as an orphan?"

"No." Arch pulled away from the wall and looked at her intently. Quincy stopped what she was doing and met his eyes. "I don't pity you," he said. "I ache for your history, yes, because you, Quincy St. Claire, have become my friend, and I worry that you will sabotage that now because I am one step closer to understanding what is inside that very thick exterior you have so painstakingly erected."

"Have I really been so bad at friendship that you all worry over me behind my back?" Quincy asked. "Ezekiel is gone, and Fisher will be soon. And, although I am fine on my own, I know you don't believe it. Well, I have Jade and Spense and—and the Q boys. And you. I know businessmen around town. I know merchants, my tailor, Crow. It's not as if my life is devoid of people."

Arch played a soundless melody on the desk with his right hand as he stared into space, listening to her words. "You do know many people," Arch conceded, "but may I ask you a question?"

Quincy shrugged.

"If The Q were gone tomorrow, who would you ever see again?"

Quincy couldn't fathom the question. It made no sense. There were too many numbers tied to The Q's existence, making up the very structures of her brain. If the Q didn't exist, neither did she. "That's an impossible question."

"Just try and answer. Remove The Q from your mind. Where does that leave all those people?"

"But the people can't exist without The Q."

He waited a moment before saying, "I think that's my point, Quincy. If The Q ceases to exist, Spense goes home to his wife. Jade goes to Jack. The Q boys go home or to the marble tournaments in the park. Graves visits her sister in Mirshire. Each and every life marches on because their stronger connections, of family and friends, are still intact. It would be a blow—I am not diminishing their work here— but everyone has a place to go."

"Except me," Quincy said aloud, still finding the image impossible.

"Except you," Arch repeated her words. "Would you go to Fisher and Mado in France?"

Quincy snorted. "No."

"I didn't suppose you would. So, that leaves me with a promise to make."

"A promise?"

"If the structure of your world ever evaporates, I will still be here." He gave her a slight smile. "I'll have you to tea the following day, or something of that sort."

"Tea?" Quincy rolled her eyes. "You? You are to be what I have left when the world ceases to exist?"

"Why not?" Arch said lightly. "We will talk business, and poetry, and whatever else we find interesting."

"I don't care for poetry."

"You will. Not as much as I do, but you'll learn to appreciate that I appreciate it. That's part of maintaining connections with people. You give yourself a little to what they give themselves to a lot. And they do the same for you."

"Sounds boring."

"I suppose it is, if you're not focused on the person you're doing it for," Arch answered.

Quincy pretended to be reading through an accountant's report on her desk a while before saying, "I don't care much for your view of the world."

"That doesn't bother me." Arch drummed his fingers and smiled.

"I don't expect my friends to be like me or to be always thinking the same things I do."

Quincy screwed her face into a question. "Then what value do you get from keeping them around?"

He laughed, a close, intimate laugh. "That's my entire point, Quincy. They are of value independent of anything else. As are you."

"I don't see it," Quincy said.

Arch stood up, slapping his hand against the counter before going into his office and gathering his belongings. It took him several moments, but when Arch had replaced his jacket and gathered his things into his satchel, he came back into the front office, his hat in hand.

"Perhaps it will help you, then, Quincy, for me to tell you that when I look at you, I don't just think of The Q."

———

After close on Thursday night, Fisher and Quincy went walking through lower Rhysdon, the neighborhoods and byways that abutted the dock and reached up in a haphazard fashion through the southern edges of the city. Quincy had always liked the way mist never trailed behind night near the docks, rather it creeped into the low streets and the dog streets just before the blue air fell into black. There weren't as many lights here as there were along the more respectable streets of Rhysdon, but those that were present, half tilting and thoughtful, hung their mystery well.

Quincy and Fisher walked through all this in silence. Silence was the most common stock-in-trade between them, and the portfolio of their friendship was thick with it. So, without words, they stepped across the streets, their feet pressing the pavement with the same sounds, their toes turned just so; they knew what life was like at each other's side. Sometimes he would speak, or she would, small offerings on the altar of their joint survival.

"Can you smell that?" Fisher said, turning his face in the direction of the dock-lined breeze.

"It smells like Fallow Shoals."

"It smells like the warehouse they locked us in after you'd stolen from that fishmonger's wife." Fisher laughed. "I was so angry with you."

"The same quick hands that got us in were the same two hands that got us out."

They had come onto an old sailing promenade at the end of the street, overlooking the busiest dock in Rhysdon. Fisher leaned over the railing, and Quincy spread her elbows out until she could feel the cool pressure of the metal through the sleeves of her jacket.

"Where did you learn to pick a lock, anyway?" Fisher turned his head towards Quincy sharply. He looked then more like a stranger than ever before.

"I never did," Quincy said. "Fallow Shoals was the first and last time I've ever done it. I just thought about what a lock did and interpreted the inside mechanisms from there."

"It saved us a beating," Fisher stated, massaging his mangled hand absentmindedly. "Thank you."

"You talked us out from underneath several beatings as well."

"You never could learn to hold your sharp end away from other people, Quincy. That got us into more trouble—"

With a sigh bigger than herself, Quincy admitted wordlessly he was right.

A bell clanged now in the full dark, and Quincy felt it tolling out the limited hours before the next irrevocable shift in her life would occur.

After some time, Fisher said, "*Per aspera ad astra.*"

Quincy turned towards him. "What's that?"

"Latin. It means *to the stars through difficulties.*"

By natural extension of the conversation, she looked up, viewing the faint points of light fighting down through a soft haze. "Does anyone make it, Fisher? To the stars?"

"I believe we have, Quince. We've seen the worst but known the best."

"It's a good thing you're moving to Paris," she said as she pulled away from the cold rail.

Fisher followed her. "Why's that?"

"You're becoming a walking proverb. I'd have to fire you."

Fisher laughed and threw his arm over Quincy's shoulders; together, they walked back to The Q.

———

The next day, Fisher's last day, the staff threw him a small party in the print room: a mild farewell, as there was a good deal of work to do for the evening. Fisher took his leave of Spense, Jade, the mice, and the printers. The Q boys stayed, in part to say goodbye, in part to eat the tarts Quincy had ordered in. Fisher's desk had already been cleaned out, and it was here, sitting in his chair, that he found Quincy after his farewells with the rest of the staff.

"I gave Arch the files needed for comparative market profits," he said as he lifted his satchel full of Latin and mathematics and philosophy: the books Quincy had watched him cart around for years, determined to make his mind what he wanted it to be.

"Good," she said.

"This is it, then."

Quincy ran her finger over Fisher's desk, like a housekeeper checking for dust. "I might remove the desk—turn this alcove into a self-help station, as it were. If someone doesn't want to wait in The Q's line, they can come fill out a slip for themselves. It would save with front counter work."

"Don't get too sentimental about my leaving," Fisher said dryly.

"The question is, how to collect their payments?"

"Quincy—"

"Perhaps if they held an account that we settled monthly, like our wealthy customers have, then they could use the desk, and we'd collect their Q slips in a file—"

"Quincy!"

"I know." She stood, wiping the nonexistent dust from her hands. "I'm only thinking. I'll meet you tomorrow morning at the station."

"The six fifteen?"

"The six fifteen."

"Tomorrow, then."

Quincy nodded. She didn't wait for him to leave before disappearing up the stairs to her room. It was late before Quincy put down her violin and lay in her bed long enough to finally sleep.

———————————————————

Quincy found Fisher waiting beside the track, coat collar turned up, satchel strung across his chest, two bags holding all his worldly possessions waiting at his feet. He looked in that moment like the brave character of some novel, a hero setting out on an uncertain fate, destined to succeed.

From the not so distant invisible line just outside the station, Quincy could hear the piercing sound of a train's brakes on metal track. The six ten was rolling in, which meant the six fifteen would be rolling out. Steam billowed into the tall architecture of the station, filling the space between Quincy and Fisher with what felt like a symbol. Neither of them brushed the smoke from their faces, rather they waited for it to waft and settle, revealing one of the last expressions they would share with each other before it all changed.

Arms crossed tightly against her chest, Quincy nodded towards the train as the rush of passengers wove around them in both directions. She kept thinking that a time like this required words—one million lines of type, laid out perfectly, with no ink stains, no backward letters—to say what should be said. But that couldn't happen, and she didn't know what else to put in its place.

Fisher adjusted the strap of his leather satchel and looked towards the train, the early morning breeze that moved through the station pulling at the ends of his hair. Another silent minute passed, and the call was made. Swallowing, Fisher turned his eyes towards Quincy, and she tried to smile in a way that told him he would get everything he ever wanted out of life.

And before Quincy even knew how, she was buried against his chest, clinging tightly to the blue coat that was holding him together. His face was bent down towards hers, his chin resting against the throbbing of her temple, pushing her hair askew. His lips pressed against her skin, and she took in the smell of his lotion mingled with the natural scent that was, as it always had been, Fisher.

A final press of his body against hers, and Fisher stepped back, all his courage bound up in the way his eyes turned into falling half-moons. He didn't give Quincy any words—perhaps too many words had been printed around them as it was—but instead lifted his beautifully mangled hand. The hand that Quincy had cared for and protected. The hand that Quincy had tried to put back together before she knew enough of this life not to try. She, in turn, lifted a shoulder. And this gesture was her own promise to him.

Without a word, Fisher picked up his bags, turned, and disappeared into the train. Then there was the sound of steam, a sign of coming momentum, the promise of power harnessed on the tracks, and a whistle split the air. In a force of noise and smoke and early morning calls, the train was gone.

Quincy turned, her hands seeking solace in the depths of her pockets, her heart seeking solace in a void that hadn't been there since Quincy was five years old. Knowing that Mado deserved Fisher didn't make it any better.

The station was filling with more movement and noise and light, as the morning sun began to bounce and rattle off the brass and glass of the building. Quincy pushed through the crowd, her eyes towards the ground, her feet guiding her out of the station. She only lifted her head when she came out onto the sidewalk. And there, before her, a familiar figure was waiting, standing with a paper in one hand, watching the flow of traffic. He saw her and waved in silence, somehow knowing it wasn't a morning for many words.

"Did Fisher tell you to come?" Quincy said, her voice sounding so unlike itself—sounding yearning.

"No," Arch replied. Then he shook his head as confirmation, as if it were an important truth she needed to know two ways. "But I knew this was his train."

"You missed him."

"I didn't come for him. I came for you."

His words went unanswered. They were too real for her. And Quincy could only pay attention to how her boots felt on her feet in that exact moment and how Fisher's absence felt in her chest. The boots were a little snug, wet from the puddles of the midnight rain. The absence in her chest felt too vast for admission.

When Quincy still didn't speak, Arch pointed down the road with his paper. "If you haven't had breakfast, I know of a place that makes excellent cinnamon twists and sweet cider in the fall."

"I haven't eaten," Quincy confessed.

"Good."

They set off. Halfway down the street, as Quincy was twisting beneath the question of what she should do with her loose thoughts, Arch said three words that set everything into place.

"Boys' names: Adam."

Quincy looked towards him, his dark eyes scanning the street rather than looking at her.

"Bertrand," Quincy said.

"Charles."

"David."

"Edgar," Arch shot back.

"Francis."

Arch wrinkled his nose, and it startled Quincy. It was as if she were looking in the mirror, for it was one of her own expressions on his face.

"Isn't Francis a woman's name?" he asked.

"No, there are men by the name of Francis: *exempli gratia*, Francis of Assisi."

Arch raised his eyebrows. "Latin, St. Claire?"

"Get on with the game, Arch."

"I had a governess named Francis," Arch explained. "A frightful creature of wrinkles and warts, gray hair escaping from her starched bonnet. She was so overpowering in my young life that I'm afraid the name always got stuck with her and that I could never pull it far enough away to attach it to anyone else."

"Now you're trying to buy yourself time for a name that begins with G," Quincy argued. Although, she hadn't minded hearing his memory, as if it were an amusing picture he had pulled out to show her.

"Don't be silly, St. Claire. George."

"My favorite saint."

"Really?"

Quincy looked at him. "He slew a dragon, Arch. Is there really any question about the matter? Harris."

"I wouldn't have guessed you knew many saints."

"Ezekiel was serious about his saints. Your turn, letter I."

"In—" Arch paused then laughed. "I can't think of a boy's name beginning with the letter I."

"Icarus."

"Oh, are we going Greek?" asked Arch.

"How should I know? You began the round."

"So I did," Arch sighed. "And I've apparently lost it. Just as well."

And as they walked the puddles that were turning pink and gold from the building sun, the streets of Rhysdon began filling with people. The scents of a city morning rose to meet the heavy and content leaves of early September. And back at The Q there was work to do. Good work. Real, solid work.

Perhaps the day would not be as miserable as Quincy had supposed.

CHAPTER TWENTY-SIX:
Pandora's Box

"Have you seen this?"

Arch extended a folded section of *The Times* towards Quincy, holding it above the array of sweet pastries and tea covering his desk. It was seven in the morning, an hour before the front door was to open.

The impromptu breakfast after the train station had prompted Arch to arrive the next morning—to Quincy's mild astonishment—with a carefully packed box of pastries.

"I thought you would be up," he had said as he closed the door with his foot and relocked it with some finesse.

"I always begin work at six."

"And usually without breakfast."

Quincy had wrapped her hands around either side of her stool's seat. "Not true," she argued.

"True," Arch insisted. "I'd like to think it was a lack of breakfast that caused you to treat me with such unpleasantness all those months."

"Not true."

Arch had stood opposite the counter from Quincy, covering the report she was reading with his box of sweet smelling temptations. They had only just come from a baker's oven.

"Where did you get this?" she asked.

With a smile and a nod towards the extra stool behind the counter—which Quincy lifted over the counter to his waiting hand—Arch answered only as he opened the parcel.

"Pandora," he said.

"What?"

"I got this from Pandora. I'm afraid that if I open the box, I will start something rather dangerous."

And so he had. Quincy now had no peace in the morning before the office opened. Every day, Arch would arrive between six thirty and seven, some sort of food item in hand. She figured that sometimes Arch stopped by a bakery and sometimes his family's cook would rise to the occasion. The food was always good, and Quincy scolded herself when she found herself enjoying it too much. Not fully giving in felt important. Quincy St. Claire did not *fully* give in.

"Why are you doing this?" she had asked one morning. "Is it because Fisher asked you to watch over me as if I were a poor, wayward orphan?"

"Poor you are not. Orphan," he cocked his head, "you once were. Wayward? So wayward it's troubling."

"You didn't answer my question."

"Maybe that's because I don't have an answer."

Now, after a few weeks of establishing the habit, both seemed to take it for granted that they would begin the day in this butter-flaked, fruit-filled, peppermint-steeped sort of manner.

"Have you seen this?" Arch repeated, shaking the folded paper just enough to bring Quincy back to the present. She had only just realized something that made her not want to look at him. This routine felt rather like something one kept after a fortieth wedding anniversary.

"Sorry," Quincy flushed. "I was thinking."

"About the board meeting later today?"

"About bad ideas," Quincy quipped, taking a sip of her coffee. "Which is also synonymous for the board meeting, I suppose."

Arch didn't respond, but he flicked his wrist and the expectant paper with it, a final warning that if she didn't take it from him now he was done holding it out.

She took the paper.

There, on the front page of the business section of *The Times*, was an article entitled *The Q, Quincy St. Claire & The Perfect Marriage of Profit and Poetry*. Quincy grimaced as she flicked her eyes across several lines in the article.

"What was Priest thinking! I'm going to haunt him for this."

"Why?" Arch asked, seemingly giving more attention to his croissant than to Quincy.

"Would you honestly want an article in *The Times* written about you?" she hedged.

Arch paused, his knife hovering above a small pot of jelly. "No."

"Exactly." Quincy tossed the paper back onto his desk.

"You're not even going to read it?"

"Not interested."

"I'll leave it on your counter, just in case you would like to wait until I'm not looking."

Sipping her peppermint tea, Quincy lifted a shoulder and decided to change the subject. "Speaking of Priest, he mentioned you to me, several months back, in a way that I couldn't quite figure."

"I can't imagine why," answered Arch. "I've never met the man in person above once or twice."

Before she could ask more questions, Arch disengaged himself by placing a third of his croissant into his mouth. He was clearly not interested in pursuing the conversation further.

CHAPTER TWENTY-SEVEN:

Paris

"It's not that I don't approve of social improvement," Crow drawled as he walked beside Quincy. "It's only that beginning with the poorest neighborhoods on the docks and leaving it there feels rather like cleaning up the trash."

It was cold, even for early October, and Crow had asked Quincy out for a late-night meal in what he considered a reputable part of town. Quincy didn't care if it was reputable or not, but upon seeing the location, she knew Fisher would care, and scream so loud she could hear him from Paris. Fisher had sent her a few letters after his arrival and even the syllabi for his courses at the university.

Crow muttered something and she looked up towards him. "Sorry, what did you say?"

They had finished eating and were now walking the streets, talking. Or rather, Crow was attempting to carry on a conversation.

"Never mind, St. Claire," Crow sighed. "I know it's a hazard to catch your attention when you've just come from work."

Puzzling her brow, Quincy replied, "I'm always just come from work."

"Exactly," he said with long-suffering. "So, then, dare I ask what's new at The Q?"

"The Paris office opened today, without much ceremony. Fully trained staff, but only one machine, as the board wishes to grow into the new market at a snail's pace."

"I don't care much for Paris," Crow said. "Filthy place."

"Says the smuggler."

"Says the pristine smuggler, who runs an exemplary operation. Allegedly. By the by, do you remember me seeking some legal advice from that solicitor of yours a few months back?"

"Yes."

"Well, he's been moderately useful, as useful as a man is who won't break the law, but I've discovered some things about him I thought you might find interesting."

As much as Quincy's interest was piqued, her personal code of conduct was not moved. "Crow, unless you've found proof he's embezzled funds from the coffers of The Q, I'm not interested."

"Every suit for every man," Crow said, shrugging it off as he changed the subject. "Do you want to end the night at The Nest?"

When they entered The Nest, a prizefight was taking place in the center of the floor. Tables and chairs were scattered, men were shouting, and a solid punch hit home just as people called Crow's name.

"Scavenge! Blythe!" Crow was through the crowd, his hands on the fighters, throwing them apart. The smuggler commenced to rail at the fighters and the bystanders, ordering the tavern be put back into order. "Cats and kings, Blythe! I told you, no more fights at The Nest. I don't need coppers in my sails!"

Quincy claimed her favorite barrel in the corner to watch the spectacle. An older gentleman, who frequented The Nest—English, but not altogether disreputable—leaned towards Quincy. "Hell hath no fury like Crow's scorn."

"What?" she said, not understanding what he meant.

"Dear me, it's Shakespeare."

Quincy muttered she wasn't interested in Shakespeare but was glad he'd considered Crow and watched as the smuggler marched the two men out the door of the tavern.

By the time Crow came back inside, the tables were back in place and the patrons were back in easy conversation with their drinks. He wiped his brow and pulled at the lapels of his long coat, greeting a few patrons at the counter while searching the room for Quincy. Finding Quincy in the corner, he came towards her with an apologetic look.

Lifting a shoulder to indicate she didn't mind, Quincy slipped from her barrel and joined Crow at the back table.

He sighed with a wolfish grin as he settled into the booth, sitting across the table from Quincy, flexing a hand now sporting a split knuckle. When Quincy raised an eyebrow, he explained, "Blythe gave me some cheek, so I gave him a reminder of whose outfit this is."

When drinks were set before them, Crow took his in relief.

"It's been a difficult month," Crow admitted at random. "I've had three shipments intercepted. It was pure silver luck I wasn't on any of those ships."

"What happened to your employees?"

"Some got away; some didn't. But they know that's part of the job and are paid accordingly. Great reward stems from great risk."

"And when caught?"

"Rhysdon smuggling laws are not kind. Years of hard labor."

The thought of Crow chained and imprisoned, stripped of his regal, backwater-prince presence, was a painful one.

"Don't get caught, Crow," said Quincy.

"St. Claire." Crow pushed aside his drink and leaned across the table, his blue eyes anchoring in hers. Quincy swallowed. "You must know I've not been simply entertaining myself with your company." Crow's deep voice turned even more earnest. "I respect you, I value your intelligence, your brilliance, and I've waited for an indication that you—"

"St. Claire!"

Quincy turned, her hand covering her eyes from Crow's scrutiny as she searched for the source.

It was Arch, of all people, winding through the crowded room towards her, looking sharper and more elite for being in a room full of sailors. Crow muttered something that may have been a curse. Quincy wasn't sure.

"St. Claire!" Arch arrived, leaning one hand against the table, slightly ruffled for the rushing. "Pardon. I ask ten thousand pardons.

Crow, I apologize, but—" Arch turned to face her. "Quincy, numbers from Paris have come in."

"Numbers?" Quincy straightened her back. "I didn't request them until the week's end?"

"I know, but Fisher stopped by the Paris office to ask after first day profits, and he sent this telegraph." Arch pulled the yellow paper from his hand and set it before Quincy with eager ceremony.

Crow watched, leaning back, arms crossed, eyes darkened and self-conscious from the interruption. Lifting the thin paper of the telegraph, Quincy opened it between her fingers. Her lips parted from shock.

"What? What does this mean, Arch? I can hardly believe—"

"What?" asked Crow.

"Apparently," Arch supplied with a victorious smile, telling the story more to Quincy than to Crow, "the anticipation in Paris was built up by not only the aristocrats but also the biggest newspaper in the city, who, I suspect, is eager for the flagship contract. People held salon parties around opening day, and thousands of questions have been flying around Paris. The scandals alone—" He laughed. "The first day was such a massive success that Fisher said he doesn't know how they will print the quantity that is required of the first edition. He also sent nearly thirty more telegraphs detailing the event—charging it to The Q, of course—and ordered two more additional presses with good faith you would approve the purchases. He also hired a small army of Q boys. You have taken Paris by storm in less than twenty-four hours."

"I can hardly—" Quincy shook her head. "You said there were thirty more telegraphs of information? Did you bring them?"

"No. I had returned to the office to resolve some unfinished work, and Jade burst upon me with the news. She said you were out with Crow, so I ventured to the first place I thought you would be, The Nest." Arch now looked around, seeing the tavern for the first time.

"I'll come now," Quincy said, sliding off her bench. "Crow, I'm sorry, but I've got to see to my work. Could we discuss—could we discuss your question another time?"

"You may have just answered it, St. Claire." Crow stood and leaned ruefully against the wall at his back. "No, don't apologize. The Q is your life's blood. Perhaps another day there will be space for my question, perhaps not."

"I'm sorry, Crow," Quincy said, relieved to not answer something she didn't know the answer to. Arch had already stepped away to offer them privacy, and Quincy, telegraph in hand, turned and followed him through the crowd and out the door of the tavern.

She and Arch half laughed, half argued as they debated what those numbers would mean in Paris. They rushed back toward The Q with the confidence of birthing a new creation—and a successful one at that—playing a heady tune in their heads.

"New presses and Q boys are just the beginning," stated Quincy. "We'll need an entire outfit of mice, sorters, printers, and a master typesetter. The space is large enough for expansion."

"Of course it is," Arch inserted. "You wouldn't have planned it any other way."

"Although I wasn't expecting this. I hope we can pull it off as a success. The problem is, I need someone there for a few weeks to set things up, but I can't possibly see how I could do it. Perhaps Fisher—"

"I'm afraid he also sent a telegraph stating emphatically that he would not be assuming any managerial positions, as he has his studies. He sends his love and says you must sink or swim without him."

"Rather charitable," Quincy complained. "Bother. As it is, the boy doesn't speak French very well. I don't speak it at all."

"I do."

Quincy halted. They were now standing on the corner of Queen's Street and Gainsford Street. "You do? Oh, yes, your mother was French."

"I could go over for a few weeks to help things get settled, seeing as how I know the business well enough. And I'm certain I could get Fisher to donate a few hours towards the cause. A few of my friends from school practice law in Paris. It would be easy to set up a very trustworthy solicitor to help manage the office."

"Hmm, there you are," Quincy said, staring at him a while.

"Meaning, you like my idea?"

"Meaning, I feel for the first time that you've made yourself useful. It's only taken you the better part of a year."

Quincy laughed, dodging as Arch pretended a blow towards her. She turned the corner onto Gainsford Street, stepping over a drunk man who had settled himself against a building for the crisp night, and continued towards the offices of The Q.

Arch followed only after he had seen if he could rouse the man. He could not, so Arch removed his own hat, setting it onto the man's bare head, before he followed Quincy down the street.

"Aren't you the model of charitable donations," she grinned, inserting her key into the locked office door.

Arch combed his hair with his fingers. "It was beginning to fray in any case."

The lock obliged, and Quincy opened the door. "This could be the birth of a new age for The Q."

"It's astounding, it really is," Arch answered, following her in.

Arch prepared to leave the next day, with a sheath of instructions from Quincy, who had told him several times she didn't expect him to do anything correctly.

"Put the fear of God and country into them. I want Paris to run as efficiently as Rhysdon. Better, even. You must set the tone." She was sitting in the chair before his desk, watching him pack the requisite documents and files. He did so with a cool, correct order.

"Do you really believe I'll fail to set the tone, St. Claire?"

"And I expect news every day," she continued. "I've sent messages round to the entire board; we meet this afternoon to catch them inside the net of what's going on. If anything interesting occurs here, I'll send a telegraph. Now, which hotel will you be staying at? I intend to bother you at all hours if I must."

"No hotel. I will be staying on Rue du Faubourg Saint-Honoré, number seventeen."

"Who lives there? Your Parisian lover?" Quincy replied glibly.

Arch looked up swiftly, a flare lifting the pallor from his cheeks, his eyes fixed on Quincy with a complex expression. "Do you really think me that kind of man?"

Quincy was startled by his strong emotion. "No, I—"

"Rue du Faubourg Saint-Honoré is where my very elderly *aunt* lives."

"Cats, Arch, it was only a joke! I've been hounding you with jokes all day and you've only laughed at them."

But Arch was clearly bothered, and he didn't speak as he finished sorting everything he needed for the trip. Quincy set her mouth in frustration and looked away, pretending interest in his bookcase, as she felt alternately irritated at his reaction and mystified by how strong it was. Of course she didn't think him that kind of man. He was Arch. He was the same person to all of his acquaintance, nothing tucked away. Quincy could feel her cheeks burning, angry for feeling embarrassed.

"I'm sorry," he said.

Quincy didn't take her attention away from the bookcase, rather she nodded absently and lifted a shoulder.

"I don't like to be teased for something about which I feel stongly, namely the erroneous convention that a man's morals may be fluid, often leaving a woman to hold the higher standard alone. And I'm sorry. I just—" Only when Arch broke off was Quincy willing to look at him. He was observing her face so intently she didn't have room not to say anything. "I want you, of all people, to think well of me, Miss St. Claire."

Quincy shifted in her chair. "I do think well of you, Arch. No need to be so—Cats!"

Arch pressed his lips together, a triffle embarrassed, but willing to laugh at himself. "You're right. And considering what you thought of me only six months ago, *less* than six months ago—" he adjusted his sentence, "I suppose we've come a long way."

"Don't go sentimental on me."

And when Arch laughed, the moment passed.

Quincy stood and walked towards the door. "We're friends, Arch, solid wood. Forgive me if most men aren't as good as you, but know that I, at very least, think well of you. Good luck in Paris. Send word when you arrive."

"I will."

Quincy knocked on the doorframe of his office once and tilted her head. "Good." Then she disappeared into the sorter to check on something that did not need any checking.

CHAPTER TWENTY-EIGHT:

Ma Chérie

Arch was gone for two weeks. He performed every detail to the letter, often before Quincy could mandate it be done. She met with the board twice during that time to keep them informed on the Parisian whirlwind. They proved not only enthusiastic about Quincy's international success but almost warm and complimentary regarding her handling of the expansion. Paris was going well.

But the list of her uncle's requirements still hung in Quincy's matchbox, like the golden fleece: unreachable, unattainable. After a sound sixteen-hour day of working in The Q, she would find herself sitting on the side of her bed at night, looking forward to the day Arch would return so that she could continue bumping into the requirements by accident and secure her Q forever.

Crow had not been by, not even to ask a question, sending his second-in-command instead. Quincy didn't know whether that was because Crow was unavailable—which was not uncommon—or because Crow was wishing to avoid another conversation after their last had ended in such a torn-off fashion.

As exhilarating as Crow's life and firm presence had always been to Quincy—providing a strange combination of the unknown and unreached for, touched by the fading scents of her former life—she found the prospect of him easing back into favorite client and nothing more a relief. Quincy's mind was—if possible—even more wrapped up in the workings of and the fight for The Q. If she wished to spend any of her expensive time in conversation, she would rather engage Arch on matters of The Q than Crow on matters of anything else.

The night that this realization fought past profit sharing and stock values to steal her attention, Quincy began to laugh. Imagine, Arch had become her preferred company, albeit his position in the company underlined the reason. Still, it came as a humorous twist in the tale. She snickered aloud for several minutes, until her brain was once again lost in her work while the clock continued to shift and spin into the early hours of the morning.

"Did you miss my irreplaceable conversation?"

Those were the first words out of Arch's mouth when he sauntered—yes, *sauntered*—pleasantly into The Q the Monday after he had returned home.

"Nothing is irreplaceable," Quincy answered, not fully looking up until she'd finished adding up her line of figures. When she did look up, he seemed...taller. She leaned over the counter to glance at his shoes, and Arch's face shifted with the question of what was she doing.

"You look taller," Quincy explained, her voice evenly spreading disinterest across the observation.

"Do I?"

Arch was pleased, standing there in his hat, overcoat, a leather satchel hanging from one hand, heavy with work and reports. Paris, Quincy thought, must agree with her solicitor. He looked as contented as she had ever seen him. "Contented as a cat," Ezekiel would have said.

"It must be the new hat," she said, "unless someone has put out a saucer of milk for you recently."

Arch shook his head, giving Quincy a friendly glare as he disappeared into his office.

"I expect a full report and strategy discussion after my appointments this afternoon," she called after him.

"I wouldn't expect any less, St. Claire," he replied with cheerful resignation. "My afternoon and evening are yours."

They worked around each other in the comfortable rhythm Quincy now expected of The Q. And when Arch returned from the print room with a cup of coffee to keep himself awake come late afternoon, he stopped at Quincy's counter and waited for her to finish with her merchant class customer—a woman searching for a reliable housekeeper.

"Did *The Times* come in this morning?" Arch asked once the woman had left. "I haven't seen it."

"So now you want to be paid for reading the newspaper?" Quincy asked as she finished the Q slip, dropped it into the basket, and reached for *The Times*, already read, folded, and tucked behind the counter.

Arch took the paper, his eyes narrowing as he focused on the print of the page before him. It was turned open to another essay penned by Specter.

"I thought only Fisher and I read Specter in this office?" he said, taking a sip and focusing on the words before him.

"Ezekiel read Specter to me when *The Times* first started printing his essays," Quincy answered tersely, as if her reading anything but the rise and fall of stocks was so far outside her personal paradigm it had to be defended. Which, she admitted to herself, was true. "I keep an eye on what's deemed printable in a number of papers."

"High compliment indeed." Arch readjusted the paper between his finger and thumb, creating a stiff half circle so he could see the entire article. "What does he tackle today that managed to catch your exalted attention? The wastes of the upper class?"

"He's taken up the cry for children forced into foundling factories," said Quincy.

"Oh," Arch responded, taking note of her serious tone. "Sorry for my jest."

"It's not halfway bad," Quincy said, returning to her work, which was her way of admitting she had found it a good balance of intelligence, insight, and sympathy.

The bell rang, two customers entered, and Arch took his paper into his office.

They stayed late, Quincy and Arch, discussing the Paris office. Well past closing, the noise of the print room rising up the back stairs, they went through numbers and personnel in great detail.

"Duval has taken to the job astutely," Arch said of his friend turned The Q's Parisian solicitor. "He works well with Lefevre and, it turns out, grew up above the print shop of his father's country newspaper. So, he knows the basics of the business in the back room."

"Good. We don't need to pay any idiots to blunder their way through."

"Certainly not. An error would be unforgivable."

Quincy, sitting in her now accustomed chair before his desk, gave Arch a fast expression. "Bygones, Arch, bygones."

"As if I'm the one with the problem," he answered good-naturedly.

Spats, who was well into his apprenticeship with the mice, came into the front office just then to ask Quincy a question regarding an illegible Q slip.

"Blast," Quincy said as she took the slip and began to decipher the rotten, half-leaning penmanship. "This is what comes of giving power to the people and letting them write their own Qs."

"You aristocratic snob," Arch laughed. "Power to the people, indeed."

"*Draperies,* Spats, that word is *draperies.* Couldn't Jade sort that out?"

"She's busy ripping into Hawkins 'bout the immutable laws of grammar or something of the sort."

"Ah, well." Quincy handed him the Q slip. "*Draperies.* And that says *Staysand Street.* A bit of a twist for the tongue, I know. Oh, Spats, before you go, how many mice are there tonight? Are you dispensable?"

"I'm always indispensable, Miss St. Claire, but your wishes take precedent."

"Grand words. Remind me to knight you later." Quincy folded her arms. "I was wanting you to run down to The Swan and find some dinner for Mr. Arch and me."

"Certainly—"

"Most certainly not," Arch interjected. "Dinner, compliments of The Swan, is not a compliment in any case."

"What do you recommend, my lord?" Quincy asked with mock reverence.

"Not The Swan. I've just been enjoying the delights of Paris. Goodness, St. Claire, take mercy, and serve me some decent food worthy of my refined palate."

She snorted.

"Here, Spats, is an address." Arch was scribbling—rather scribing—directions beneath a name. "This is an old friend, a woman who served my mother for several years. She would be happy to pull together a decent and palatable meal from her pantry. She'll not only feed you as well but also give you something to take home."

Arch handed the paper to Spats, who knew the city like Quincy knew The Q. "Not too far off by back ways and all that," Spats said.

"How much?" Quincy asked Arch.

He shook his head. "Nothing. She'll be happy to make arrangements without charge."

When Spats disappeared into the print room to tell Jade, Quincy accused Arch of being a snob. "Just because she was your mother's maid, you assume she can provide a meal at a hat's drop, with no warning and no means?"

"If I knew the woman was destitute, St. Claire, I would not have asked."

"You're acting like a beck and call," Quincy said, repeating the derogatory term for the upper class.

"The woman in question is a dear friend, whose son was unfairly imprisoned. He has been set to hang for a thievery he did not commit, and I have been defending him pro bono for the last year. We hope to have his appeal heard and won later this month. She has expressed many times the desire to do something for me, anything for me, and I find it gracious to give her the chance."

He looked at Quincy steadily, and she thought his expression strange. He was not looking at her with impatience, rather he seemed to be waiting for what she thought about what he had just said. Not for approbation, perhaps, but a quieter approval.

Quincy, not practiced in giving quiet approval, countered, "I hate taking things I haven't paid for, friend or not."

Arch leaned back into his chair, but he was entertaining a smile. "There are few things more tedious than a friend who will not graciously receive."

Quincy could have explained that nine years of poverty might have something to do with it, but instead she just replied, "You must find me maddening, then."

Arch's mouth twitched. "You, *ma chérie*, are something else entirely."

Quincy made an impatient noise, and Arch turned his attention back to the Paris report before him, not looking up when Quincy replied, "I don't speak a lick of French."

He moved his thumbnail against the corner of his mouth as he answered, "I know."

CHAPTER TWENTY-NINE:
The Cat's Out of the Bag

"The world is a mad place, and I'm tired."

This statement floated from Priest's mouth with the smoke from his cigar.

Celine had been buried not yet two hours ago, and here he and Quincy were, sitting in his parlor, Priest, comforting his cigar; Quincy, comforting a peppermint tea.

Priest had asked Quincy to meet him at his house after the dreary service. "Celine requested I not go into the office the day she was buried, so you must come to me."

They did not discuss business, though, and Quincy recognized his inviting her over as his own grieving, the faux feeling of work to get him through the day. She obliged because Priest had always been her friend and she was his.

"Have you seen this?" Priest tossed her a bent page of *The Times*. "It's Specter's latest, printed a few days ago. I expect an eruption."

Quincy took the paper, smoothed the fold, and read the title. "*Crown Prince Must Account for Own Finances Before Denying Child Charities Funding.*" She raised an eyebrow. "He's taking on the crown prince?"

"Read on," Priest puffed.

Quincy did. Halfway in, her jaw slid to the side: her equivalent of demonstrating shock. Specter was calling out the crown prince for withdrawing funding for several charities for children, instigating a roundup of the city's street urchins as a "charitable act" for the citizens of Rhysdon, and shipping them off to foundling factories against their wills. Specter was ripping the crown prince to pieces. But, what had elicited her shocked reaction was a list of the crown prince's offenses: debts, scandals, and a detailed story which outlined the prince engaging in smuggling activities outside the tariff laws of Rhysdon.

As she read further, the essay proved not only an indictment of the crown prince but also a plea to lift the homeless children and relieve them from the injustices of the factories:

Let him account for his own disregard of the law and leave the innocent— guilty only of not having the years nor the means to pull themselves from the degradations thrust upon them—to charitable hands willing to do the worthy work of the world. We, as a nation, should be carrying these disadvantaged children in our arms and lifting them on our shoulders. Let us become their nursing mothers and nursing fathers.

"Brave, to take on the crown prince," she said, not ready to part with the paper between her fingers.

Priest answered first by rearranging himself in his chair and then said, "Celine liked to read Specter's essays. She said they were the most decent part of my business."

Quincy nodded, not necessarily in agreement with Celine but from feeling the need for movement.

"I hear Paris is flinging you forward at a soldier's pace."

"We're managing despite the forced prosperity. Arch has been in Paris to see things sorted."

"He's back now," Priest said.

"Yes." Quincy wanted to ask how Priest knew this, but the hall clock sounded in four resonating warnings, and Quincy took a long breath. "Are you going to be—?"

She dropped off, and Priest gave a grunt.

Quincy stood. "I'll come by next week."

Priest's stiff, tight-skinned housekeeper led Quincy out the front door, onto the street, and Quincy walked back to Gainsford Street— one hand, settled deep in her pocket; the other, gripping the essay absently—while her mind wandered between business and death.

Quincy entered The Q's offices, dismissed Mrs. Graves from the front counter, and took her seat, sorting half-interestedly through the afternoon's Q slips in the basket. Arch was working at his desk, his door closed, head bent over his work. He enjoyed a fresh vase of street flowers despite the October cold.

Quincy had left thoughts of death behind and was fully inside the mental walls of business when the door flew open. The bell rattled and rang as if scurrying away from the force of its own shaking.

It was Crow, his faced closed in cold fury. "Where's the scoundrel, St. Claire? Where's Arch?"

"Excuse me?" Quincy was confused. But Arch, inside his office, looked up when he heard Crow's voice, and his face turned stoic.

Crow fixed on Arch's door and he marched for it, his eyes narrowing in such anger that Quincy was off her stool and grabbing his arm before he could slam the door open.

"Crow, what happened?"

"I'm sorry, St. Claire, but the devil will pay—" Crow's eyes looked frantic. "He's sold me out, and there's going to be hell for it."

Arch had opened his door, his expression set as firmly as train-rail steel. "May I help you, Crow?"

"You backwater dog!" Crow stepped towards Arch and out of Quincy's grasp. Arch, unruffled, returned to his desk, but he did not sit down.

Quincy followed Crow into Arch's office. "Crow—" she said.

"You are a Janus of the worst kind!" Crow pointed at the solicitor, taking a threatening step forward.

Arch's dark eyes burned, his arms crossed. And although he asked, "What do you mean?" it appeared that he knew full well why Crow was irate. Quincy could tell from the defiant confidence around his eyes.

"You know what you've done, *Specter*! You exposed the crown prince, and now he has taken his anger out on me. He's given the police information. I'm as good as hanged, Arch! You self-serving bast—"

"The crown prince cut his charities for the indigent," Arch cut in, raising his own voice, "and began rounding up children to work in foundling factories against their will. The king turns a deaf ear, as does our puppet parliament. I had information regarding his corruption, so I used it."

"Information given privately with a damn good bottle of wine!" Crow spat. "Where's your honor?"

"Honor?" There was a catch in Arch's voice, and his face was alight. Quincy had never seen him this angry, not any of the times she had stretched his patience. "Forgive me," Arch countered, "but I care much more about the hungry children of this city than I do about your smuggling ring! I am sorry you're on warrant. I am sorry your career isn't above board and they've got the hounds on you. It's the last thing I had imagined the prince would do. But, I am *not* sorry that I had a way to make the crown prince twist from the discomfort of public censure. I am *not* sorry I wrote the piece. And. It. Worked." There was a gleam in his eye as Arch said these words, and his hand clenched into a fist. "There was an inquest about the factories announced today, and one of the charities has again received royal patronage. There will be food in the mouths of children. Don't speak to me of honor, Crow. You've already missed your mark."

Crow stared at Arch for a full minute, the veins in Crow's neck manifesting his attempt at controlling his temper. Quincy realized she was breathing just as hard as the two men in the room, the air so tight none of them moved. Then Quincy saw something—rather someone—through the window.

"Crow, it's Constable Catch! On the street!"

"What?" The smuggler took a step away from the window as if it would burn him.

Returning to the front office, Quincy slipped behind the counter, her hands reaching for a Q slip just as the bell rang. Arch's office door slammed shut, the blinds pulled closed. Constable Catch didn't seem to notice. Quincy wondered if Arch and Crow would come to blows.

"Good morning, Miss St. Claire," Catch said. He was beaming. He looked as happy as if the final woman in the world had just declared her love for him and only him.

"Why so happy, constable? Did your ship come in?" Quincy winced at the unintended allusion.

"That," Catch grinned, his red cheeks ripe for the picking, "is exactly what has happened." From his jacket, Catch withdrew a long piece of paper, folded in half. The blinds in Arch's office quivered, and she glared in their direction before turning her attention back to the triumphant law enforcer. With a flourish and a sigh of complete contentment, Constable Catch opened the paper and set it on the counter. There it was: a warrant for the arrest of John Jones, alias Crow.

"John?" Quincy wrinkled her nose. "That's his real name? John Jones."

"Yes, and yes." Catch practically danced as he lifted himself onto his toes and then rocked down onto his heels.

"Hmmm." Quincy tapped her fingers on the counter and pushed the paper back towards Constable Catch. "Very pretty. Would you like to submit a question?"

"No," Constable Catch said too cheerfully. "I would like to ask a question. Several. Now that I have a warrant, your privacy policy is negated. By law, you have to answer my inquiries."

"That's all you want? For me to answer questions? You don't want me to turn him in or anything?"

Catch was beginning to look more serious. "Please, St. Claire. All I want from you is your complete honesty. I can apprehend the man perfectly on my own."

"If you insist," Quincy shrugged, "I'll oblige. What would you like to know?"

"What do Crow's messages mean?"

Quincy laughed. "How should I know? He came in, told me his question, flirted hopelessly," she said a bit loudly, for Crow's amusement, "and then left. I never needled him for a code sheet to decipher his secrets."

"Would he always come in person?"

"No."

"Who else would he send?"

"Men I don't know."

The constable rolled his eyes. "Could you describe them?"

"Yes."

Catch waited, and Quincy waited.

"Would you describe them to me," said Catch, not looking amused. "Please."

The door to Arch's office opened a crack, and Quincy began speaking. "Once, it was a boy: twelve or so, blue coat, brown hair, blue eyes. He had a nervous tick and would blink every thirty-eight seconds. He didn't speak much, but, when he did, it was with a Bayswater slant."

"How often did he come?"

"Once."

"And you remember all that?"

"I do."

"Who else came in?"

Quincy answered Catch's question, and then he asked more: How often had she been with Crow? Were they significant to one another?

"You've seen how many women flock around him down at The Nest?" Quincy fired back.

"Yes."

"Do I strike you as one women among many, sir?" she asked coolly.

Catch blushed. "No, indeed, ma'am. I only needed to understand if you were something more, if there was any reason he might be coming to you for help."

"Good afternoon, constable," Arch said as he stepped from his office and up to the counter, leaving his door halfway open.

"Good afternoon, sir," Catch nodded politely before turning back towards Quincy.

"You look very intent on something," Arch continued. "Anything interesting?"

Clearing his throat, Catch gave Arch a sidelong glance. "This is personal business between Miss St. Claire and me."

"I might be very useful in this particular instance, if you'd like to tell me what you're speaking about." Arch walked around the back of Fisher's abandoned desk turned Q station and began opening drawers. "I'd only be too happy to help." And he sounded like he meant it.

"He is the best solicitor in Rhysdon," Quincy added just as Crow slipped from Arch's office and began to move as silently as a cat towards the front door.

"No, thank you," Catch said rather tightly. "Miss St. Claire, have you ever received any of Crow's contraband goods or participated in his smuggling schemes?"

"He brought me dinner, and I believe the cheese was imported in an expedited manner, as well as the wine, which I didn't enjoy, but rather my solicitor did."

"Indeed," said Arch, flipping through a file. "But I did send a cheque to the tariff office, paid in full. Now, seeing that this is about Crow, would you like my help in apprehending the scoundrel?"

"No!" Catch was beginning to perspire. "I do not."

Quincy's eyes lifted towards Crow, who now stood with his back to the door, grinning, his anger forgotten in the game. He winked at Quincy, gave her a nod, and lingered on an affectionate farewell salute before opening the door.

When the bell rang, Catch pointed towards it without taking his eyes off Quincy and, assuming a customer was entering, ordered them out.

"Very well, constable." Crow said, with his lovely deep voice. "I'll come another time."

Catch's mouth fell open, and, by the time he had turned himself to face the door, Crow was out in the busy street. The shocked constable forgot his warrant on his way out and had to come back for it, scrambling and mumbling as he ran after the smuggler.

"He won't find him." Quincy set her elbows on the counter and her chin on her hands, feeling the melancholy reality that Crow had just walked out of her life.

"No, I don't suppose he will," Arch said, closing the folder in his hand. "I think it's fair that we gave him a sporting chance, though."

"Which one did we give the sporting chance?"

"Both," Arch answered, frowning. "Well, then, back to work."

"Not before we discuss this." Quincy lifted the folded newspaper left on the counter. "Are you really Specter?"

Arch pulled his bottom lip under in a rather Quincy-like manner and made a face of resignation. "I've been writing social essays under that name for the last two years."

"Who else knows?"

"My father, Mary, personnel at The Times. And now, you."

"And Crow somehow."

"Yes. Crow somehow, which means I don't really know at all who is aware that I am behind the essays."

"Do you really believe what you put here?" Quincy lifted the paper, wondering why it mattered so much.

"Yes."

"It must take a great deal of your time. Little wonder you're always ill."

Arch placed his hands on his hips and looked down. He seemed tired, Quincy thought, like he was burning from the inside and couldn't bank the fire. It was a feeling she understood well.

"I write the essays on my own time."

"I wouldn't have guessed otherwise."

Arch moved toward the doorway of his office, rubbing the fingers of his left hand together. "I had no intention to set him in trouble, Quincy. I needed something strong enough to corner the prince, but I really didn't think he'd take it out on Crow. Although, my guess is that he is quite practiced in taking care of himself. That being said, I am very sorry you lost Crow."

"So am I," Quincy said quietly. "He was a good friend. Though—"

"Though—?" Arch prompted her on, waiting, hopeful, it seemed.

Quincy shrugged and pressed her booted feet against the counter, forcing the stool onto its two back legs. "I am glad you wrote what you did. I'm not happy Crow's in trouble—deserving or undeserving—but it sounds like something might change, at the factories, I mean."

Arch gave her a hard, satisfied smile. "Just wait, Quincy St. Claire. Before long, I plan to turn this entire country on its head."

Enough light was gathered at his back from the windows that Arch was outlined in sharp relief. He looked young and hungry. He looked brave. He looked like someone worthy of the task of turning a sleeping nation on its head. And Quincy found that she had enough interest to watch him do it.

After he had gone back into his office, Quincy let her stool drop until its four legs were steady on the floor. She moved her hand over *The Times* and twisted the paper towards her, glancing again at the essay. And then it hit her, like the spark of an electric current, this was what Priest had meant all those months ago. He knew who Arch was, and he told Quincy he wanted to make Arch a brilliant star in his sky. She twisted her mouth down, but it was in approval, sanction. She felt proud of her solicitor.

CHAPTER THIRTY:

No Rest for the Wicked

Crow had gone offshore, and The Nest was shut down by Constable Catch with great satisfaction. Once, a fellow Quincy recognized came into The Q, indicating that Crow was alive and well, and so was his business.

"He sends greetings," the man said. "He says Catcher can't hold The Nest hostage because there's no illegal activity against it and there's another name on the property title. It'll be back soon off."

And, though Arch remained anonymous, word flew about Rhysdon that the crown prince was furious with the Specter.

"You have to understand why James being found out could be such a shock," Mary said to Quincy as they sat at tea. It was just the two of them, as Arch was seeing to some personal business, but Mary expected him shortly. "If the monarchy finds out James is the Specter, the prince will be angry, and, well, you see, everybody knows that the Fothergils are the Kingmakers and that the Arch family stands in the place beside the Fothergils. We are close, our two families. It has always been so. And this could make things uncomfortable."

"I didn't realize there was a strong connection," Quincy said, tapping her booted toe against the floor, not tremendously comfortable spending time at Peacock House especially without Arch.

"Oh yes. It has given my family the luxury of chasing our own whims: James, with his work in what's considered a trade; my father, with his moods, his poetry, his behavior independent of the stiff social expectations everybody else must follow."

"But you don't break with decorum."

"No." Mary shook her head. "It isn't my nature."

"Do you worry, socially, what would happen if they find out Arch is Specter?" Quincy asked. To her, this was a shallow concern.

"We keep the most secured status one could wish for. No one would slight an Arch, for the Fothergils would take notice, and when a Fothergil takes notice, it is to take action. Even for the crown prince, action against an Arch could be disastrous. My fear is more for James than society."

"How would Arch feel about losing his anonymity?" Quincy asked as Mary prepared another cup of tea for each of them.

"Disappointed. He doesn't like attention as it is, and that would make his writing more difficult, for people would not speak with him in the same candid way. I'm also certain everyone would be watching the details of his life, to see if they matched up to his ideals."

"And what would they find?"

Mary smiled, clear in her love. "They would find nothing that needs be hidden. James has always been turned towards that which would ennoble, perhaps one of his greatest virtues. He's not one for ghosts and secrets."

"Ironic," Quincy drawled, "seeing as how his pseudonym is Specter."

Mary stared at Quincy a moment, then laughed. "That is rather funny, isn't it?"

"What's his greatest flaw, then," Quincy asked, wondering what Mary would say.

Mary pursed her lips. "His greatest flaw?" She set her teacup down. "James has his own pride. Not the pride that sets himself apart from others, rather a certainty that he's right. Or, that his way is right. The difficulty is that because he so often is, he can be very blind to the few times when he isn't. Which is why watching him go headlong into battle with you has been such a pleasure for father and me. You are set so stubbornly in your own mind that he can't convince you always to do as he says."

Quincy snorted.

"Perhaps that's not fair," Mary amended. "He—" Mary paused and tilted her head. "The way you are with your numbers is the way James is with people. Very astute and concerned. So, when something turns into a puzzle without a clear solution, it vexes him. He can't control everything, and he sometimes has the mistaken notion he should."

"Do I?" came Arch's voice from the hallway. He walked into the room, carrying two portfolios and a copy of *The Times*. He nodded towards Quincy.

"James!" Mary's cheeks went pink, and she gave him a long-suffering smile. "I was rather hoping you wouldn't hear that."

"I admit to being curious." He set his things on a side table and then came and sat down on the sofa beside Mary. "I'm impressed Mary pulled you away from The Q," Arch said to Quincy.

"It's Sunday, Arch," Quincy replied.

Arch flashed Quincy a smile indicating he had remembered and then leveled a look on his sister. "Now, I interrupted an interesting conversation that I believe was about myself?"

"Of course," Mary smiled sweetly, handing him a cup of tea.

"We're talking of your greatest flaws," Quincy provided, tapping her boot on the floor, attempting to look bored although, she was enjoying the turn in subject matter.

Arch took a slow sip of tea, then looked from Mary to Quincy. "Is it because Miss St. Claire is here that you feel it necessary to discuss my less complimentary attributes? Are you trying to make her think less of me?"

"I believe it's called firing a warning shot," Mary said. "She does have to see you nearly every day."

Quincy grinned. "In all honesty, I put her up to it."

Arch scowled as he took another sip of tea. "You take an interest in my public ridicule, Quincy St. Claire?"

"Don't be naïve. I enjoy your private ridicule as well."

Arch eyed Quincy, the line of his mouth tilting upward. "Yes, I think you do. Tell me then, what are they?"

"Mary says you always assume you are right and sometimes have a hard time distinguishing when you are not."

"Only that you so often are right," Mary amended.

"So it makes you blind," Quincy added.

"Blind?" Arch fought a smile.

"Blind to the times when you are quite wrong," Mary finished. She smiled at her brother, who had creased his forehead in thought.

"Do I do it often?"

"No," Mary said.

"Probably," Quincy said at the same time.

Arch looked towards Quincy. "How did I get myself into this conversation?"

"You walked in," answered Quincy.

"Since we're on the topic," Mary continued mischievously, looking past Arch to Quincy, "he burns himself up on his interests and passions and often leaves me to manage the affairs of the house with no help. I plan an entire event, and he only arrives when it first begins and is the darling of the room. But, as that's something that only affects me, I suppose it couldn't be his greatest flaw." Mary gave a small frown and Arch shifted, resting his elbow on the back of the sofa, lifting his hand against his temple, a puckish look in his eye as Mary continued, "He despises public ridicule to an unhealthy extreme. He is more than a little vain about his appearance. He can't bear the thought of being misrepresented. Sometimes he has a temper."

"Cats and kings, Mary, I only asked for one," Quincy said.

"Pardon," Mary replied, but Quincy caught the amusement in her eyes.

Quincy shrugged. "Priest likes him, so he can't be all bad."

"Priest?" Mary's face softly puckered like a flower.

"The owner of *The Times*."

"Ah," Mary nodded. "I can't say we've spent much time in the same circles."

"Is a man to be given any time for a defense?" Arch interjected.

"Go ahead," Quincy replied. "You tell us your greatest flaws and we'll strike the current record."

"Perhaps we should start with an extensive list of how Mary could improve her character."

Just then, Symons came into the room with a fresh pot of tea.

"Were you able to finish the menus, Symons?" Mary asked.

"Yes, my lady. They're only waiting for your approval."

"I shall come now so you will not be set behind schedule. Please excuse me, Miss St. Claire. Don't let James say anything horrid before I return."

After Mary had gone, Arch shifted his head slightly so that Quincy was in his direct line of vision. "What if I don't want you knowing my greatest flaws?"

"That's unavoidable. I've practically been forced to make a study of the matter," Quincy answered, lifting her chin and blowing a shock of blond hair from her eyes.

Arch smiled then, and he waited a moment before speaking. "What do you think they are?"

Quincy rolled her eyes. "I have other things to worry about, Arch, and I'm not your priest. Cats and kings," Quincy laughed at the thought, "can you imagine?"

"There would truly be no rest for the wicked."

Quincy snorted.

"No doubt, you've a very long list." He shifted, moving his knuckles against the line of his jaw in thought. "I've often wondered if our greatest strengths are in turn our greatest weaknesses. Which is what makes them so hard to temper."

Usually, Quincy St. Claire would have given Arch a look that plainly said she couldn't care less. But today, she found herself saying, "So, your passion then makes your weakness what?"

Arch narrowed his eyes in thought and, looking down, supplied honestly, "Being overzealous and impatient, perhaps. Just as your diligence, efficiency, and rigor make you—"

"Obsessive?" Quincy hedged.

"Someone from whom I could learn a great deal, no doubt." His answer came with a sincere expression. Quincy fidgeted in her seat, away from such sincerity, and looked towards the window.

"Do you really want to know what I think, Arch?"

"Only if you'll be brutally honest."

Tapping the toe of her boot on the floor, Quincy brought her eyes back to his. "You care too much what people think of you."

Arch shifted his face in question.

"I assume you don't think so because your family has thrown off the conventions of your class and you are quite at ease with yourself in any setting. But, I think you feel the need to defend yourself if someone doesn't see clearly who you are or why you do things. You explain yourself too much, as if you owe it to the world."

Arch focused his eyes on Quincy's as he thought about her words, but he didn't speak.

"Mary was right, when she said you hate being misunderstood," Quincy pressed. "You've said as much yourself. It eats at you. You waste your energy on it."

"I care about things being clear," Arch defended.

"I care about selling *The Q*, and I do all in my power to do it. But, if someone thinks it a fool's game, if Draggen at *The Sun* thinks it a waste of time and resources, I don't care a lick, and I'm certainly not going to waste my energy trying to convince him."

Arch moved to speak, hesitated, then pulled his mouth to the side. "I do want things to be clear, to be understood. I also wonder if I'm terrified of apathy." He did not say this in his usual tone, rather something quieter, the voice one kept tucked in their vest. "I worry that if I don't fight to give the clearest picture of myself—who I try to be and what I believe to be true—I'll grow indifferent to what that vision is. A moral lethargy will set into my comfortable life, when all I want is to be afire with the cause."

Quincy didn't look away from Arch's face, and she felt something burn in her chest, the same overwhelmingly fierce pride she had felt when looking at a perfectly inked Q sheet or an expansion report that exceeded even her high expectations.

"You will never lose your passion for truth," Quincy promised.

Arch held his breath a moment, his eyes searching hers. "You say that so confidently."

"You shake with it, Arch," Quincy said, lifting a shoulder. "I suppose it's one of your greater virtues."

CHAPTER THIRTY-ONE:

Let the Cider Press Be, Quincy

"Do you smell that?" Arch said as he entered the offices of The Q. "Did you smell the air this morning?"

"No," Quincy said without looking up. "I haven't yet been outside. Business forecasts wait for no man."

"Quincy, you must!" He said it with enough passion she looked up immediately. But he wasn't looking at her, he was standing in the middle of the office with his eyes closed, a look of complete pleasure on his face.

"Have you gone mad? You look like a lunatic."

He laughed. "Walking to Gainsford Street this morning, I could smell every harvest in the entire country. The very air was singing with it. And the trees have all found their golden mark, Quincy, hovering in the perfection of their year's work."

"Which is?" Her voice sounded less interested than she was.

Arch opened his eyes. "To offer one day of blazing, unrivaled glory to all who pass beneath."

The door opened just then, the bell adding sound to Arch's internal poetry. He gave Quincy a dimpled smile as he went into his office. And on the heels of the customer came the smell of a city remembering autumn. It was rather nice.

"I'd like to place a question, please," the man said.

Quincy grabbed a Q slip. "What's the question?"

As she took down the information, Quincy watched Arch from the corner of her eye while he settled himself into the day's work. Her observation of his movements was accompanied by, well, she couldn't say what. Strange as it was, the external force of Arch had become an unknown factor. Watching him made Quincy feel...something. Shaking herself free of the thought, Quincy finished helping the customer and continued with her own work of the day.

"We," Arch announced at four o'clock, "are going for a walk."

"A walk?"

Sliding from her stool, Quincy picked up the basket of Qs, disappeared into the tumult of the sorter, dropped the questions into the sorting bin, and returned to the counter. Arch was still standing there—in his shirtsleeves—waiting for her return.

"A walk," he said as if she had not left the room at all.

"Does this fulfill a requirement?"

"Just the requirement of every human soul." When Quincy offered him an exaggerated, disbelieving look, Arch just laughed and said, "Find your jacket while I put on mine."

With Graves settled behind the counter—the former housekeeper mentioning that a raise might be in order for how often she had done that very same thing as of late—Arch and Quincy went out onto Gainsford, heading towards the high streets of Rhysdon. Arch pulled at his sleeves beneath his trim black jacket and set off down the street with his chin raised just so, his eyes bright. Quincy, in an effort to fight back a ridiculing smile, slouched.

When she asked where he was hauling her, Arch replied, "Tree-lined streets, lovely architecture, and parks with ocean views. Those are the foreordained destinations of the afternoon."

"I'm certain any foreordination includes work, Arch."

"Not all work resides in The Q, Quincy St. Claire. Come now, quit complaining, and start drawing in the draught of harvest."

They wound through the streets, talking very little, Arch leading them to the southeast rise of the city. He seemed familiar with this neighborhood. Quincy watched Arch as he listened to the rustle of life—people's feet on the sidewalks, the breeze flustering the trees. From a window came the sound of a piano, and the music made Quincy turn her head and gaze upward.

"I walk these streets late at night," Arch said, "when I can't get my mind to settle enough for sleep. Much in the way that you play your violin, I suppose."

Quincy didn't remember having told Arch that she played the violin to settle her mind at night. She wondered how he knew.

They came to a small, unattended park that was set up on a hill. The view to the right spread Rhysdon out like the palm of a hand waiting for its fortune to be told. To the left was the expanse of the ocean, with its own secrets. Its scent was a peculiar combination: salt and sea finding its way among the musky smell of triumphant autumn.

"Why Fall?" Quincy asked as she leaned over a rail that was, itself, leaning over the cliffside. "Why all this—" she hesitated, looking for the right word as she moved her eyes towards him, "exuberance?"

"Because the fall is when all good things are made manifest." Arch waved his hand as if he were the beneficent spirit of the season. "The harvests are come on, rolling into the city, a message of bounty and abundance. The trees are turning, their color revealing their most beautiful intentions, kept to themselves all year long until now." He paused, turned, and looked at Quincy with a directness she now understood to be tied to his strongest feelings. "I always feel I might be my best self in the fall; I wish to pen my best essays, listen to the purest music, taste the sweetest fruit I can find."

Quincy pulled herself up onto the rail. She didn't understand his ranting, not in a way that she could translate, but a good deal of her was willing to enjoy the late-fall light of the swiftly closing day.

"It's all the perfect verse turned crisp, Quincy," Arch continued as he walked over and leaned against the rail on which Quincy sat, looking over the ocean. "It's the press of the apple and the grape, strained through an imperfect language—albeit the poets strive for perfect expression—taken then to your presses of ink and set down for a world who will need to remember that the preamble to winter makes the cold bearable. A reminder that beauty still lingers. It's Keats, Quincy!"

"Keats?"

"Keats. The English poet." Resting against the rail, Arch folded his arms and began a recitation:

Season of mists and mellow fruitfulness!
Close bosom-friend of the maturing sun;
Conspiring with him how to load and bless
With fruit the vines that round the thatch-eves run;
To bend with apples the moss'd cottage-trees—

Quincy interrupted, "Is all poetry this long?"

Arch waved Quincy off. "You've made me lose my place. Let's see—I—I'll just begin at the next stanza."

"The next stanza?" Quincy replied with impatience.

But Arch continued, undeterred:

Who hath not seen thee oft amid thy store?
Sometimes whoever seeks abroad may find
Thee sitting careless on a granary floor,
Thy hair soft-lifted by the winnowing wind;
Or on a half-reap'd furrow sound asleep,
Drowsed with the fume of poppies, while thy hook
Spares the next swath and all its twined flowers;
And sometimes like a gleaner thou dost keep
Steady thy laden head across a brook;
Or by a cider-press, with patient look,
Thou watchest the last oozings, hours by hours.

He paused for a breath of the salt-woven, autumn-settled, soot-lined city air.

"Oozings, is it?" said Quincy in the interim.

"Let the cider-press be, Quincy," Arch said, sweeping off his hat and closing his eyes in the autumn breeze. "Let the juices of summer come oozing from the press of fall."

He had lost his head; it was all nonsense and poetry.

"Is that the end of your performance?" she asked, with a slight ridicule hanging from the words.

"There's one more stanza, if you'd like to hear it."

And, before she could tell him one way or the other, he had begun. She did not hear the words this time, for she was watching the movement of his face while focused on something he loved. It was, she admitted, beautiful. Although, she still harangued his passionate display the entire walk back to The Q.

———

Later that night, when Quincy found herself pacing her matchbox room, violin lifted to her chin, notes moving beneath her fingers like leaves scattered in the breeze, Quincy thought of Arch's face in the midst of revelation, and the memory of it made her think of the stained glass windows of the cathedral, calling to her mind the image of Lazarus being raised from the dead.

CHAPTER THIRTY-TWO:

Sharp Edges

"And then I said, 'By heavens, you have to let a fellow use his head.'"

Johnny Fothergil sat back, satisfied at having elicited a solid round of applause and laughter. Quincy sat flung over a chair in the corner, smiling at Johnny's boyish mannerisms. Scout, the Earl of something or other, made a comment about logic, and Clagent implied that Scout wouldn't know a thing about logic.

"Hush," Mary kept saying, disapproving their mild insults. She turned to Quincy, smiling graciously despite seeing Quincy's boots swinging over the armrest, and poured Quincy another cup of tea. Quincy took it, thanked Mary, and watched the room without comment.

Another young woman, an auburn-haired creature, no doubt considered a beauty, was sitting on a settee with Arch, her discussion soft, her movements intelligent. Arch was fully engaged, listening respectfully and leaning forward as he agreed or countered what she had to say.

Quincy always thought such intense, honest discussion—clearly based in trust—was like a wild animal: a foreign thing she saw happening but could never understand...or begin to know how to tame. She had never had such an exchange, not with Fisher, not with Ezekiel. Arguments, yes, a plenty. Even intimate exchanges. But soft communications, revolving around ideals and philosophies, so deeply interested in the other person's capable and complicated point of view? Not once, she thought. Not even with Arch. Whenever they began, she had derailed them.

The spirit of their interactions felt louder, the conversation more like a fencing match, with Quincy finally making an effort not to injure too quickly. The strange thing, Quincy thought as she watched the auburn girl grace Arch with a smile, was that she could picture both Fisher and Ezekiel having those slow, thoughtful, trust-filled discussions with someone else. It had just never happened with her.

Johnny Fothergil's regaling pulled Quincy's attention back to the lively end of the room, where he was entertaining Mary and the earl with a recent social blunder, one his social status could easily afford. Slouching farther into her own posture—a clear social blunder of her own—Quincy then turned her attention to the swirl of the tea inside her cup. She had not come on her own volition. Arch had deceived her into thinking the tea would only include Mary.

Upon her arrival, when she had challenged his accuracy, he had simply grinned and said, "Did I forget to mention a few of our friends were coming as well?"

It wasn't Johnny that she minded, nor Scout, despite his obvious stupidity—she had been invited to tea with them twice now, and Johnny had stopped in at The Q once, marveling at the business with sufficient reverence and curiosity to make Quincy value him as someone worth knowing—it was the collection of others, whom she had never before seen, and who all knew each other so well, that felt like a problem.

The men wore smart suits; the women, tailored dresses with skirts pulled from yards of expensive fabrics and lines pulled from France or London. Arch had introduced Quincy to the party as both his friend and employer, and she had been respectful, as polite as she could be— in the shortest amount of time possible—before retreating to her corner chair, crossing her arms, and flinging her legs to one side as she watched this pack of strange, wealthy animals.

The sound of a new voice brought Quincy from her thoughts, and she saw that Lord Arch had entered the room. He was, as ever, charming, beautiful in his age, and graceful in his movements as he worked his way around the gathering, calling each young person by name and asking after their appropriate relatives. When he arrived at Arch and the auburn creature, who-understood-the-art-of-lengthy-sincere-conversation, Lord Arch greeted her warmly, speaking with her for a good few minutes before he appeared to ask Arch a question. Standing, Arch nodded to his father—Quincy noticed they were the same height—and motioned in Quincy's direction.

Lord Arch turned to follow the motion and his eyes landed on Quincy's. She pursed her lips, half wishing she was sitting a bit straighter. Realizing it was too late to do so without betraying her discomfort, she simply flicked a hand in greeting. Lord Arch came her way—the auburn creature watching him—and bowed gallantly before Quincy, who now was most certainly righting herself.

"No need to stand, Miss St. Claire. I would join you, if I might." And he did, pulling a chair close to hers and accepting a cup of tea from Mary. "What do you think of this gathering," he asked in low tones. "I can't imagine this is what you often choose to spend your time doing."

"It's a foreign country; that's the true mark," Quincy admitted, wondering why she was willing to be honest with Lord Arch of all people.

"In some senses, yes," Lord Arch answered politely, "but, in other ways, people are people, if you can strip the lens away."

"The lens?"

"Yes. Like with a pair of spectacles." Lord Arch shifted towards Quincy, who was now sitting with half decent posture in her chair. He leaned forward, a tête-à-tête gleam in his eye. "Strip away the expensive clothing, strip away the well-placed hair, the polished accents, the appropriate social cues, and watch them interact without all those trimmings. People are what you will find, more often than not."

Quincy's expression must have looked doubtful, for Lord Arch rejoined with, "Oh, yes, you must believe me. It's true. You don't think it possible because you insist on operating outside these cues and trappings—one of the reasons I like you so much—but you must make an effort to see people for what they are, must you not?"

Johnny's loud laugh cut across the room, and Quincy looked up, catching his smile before she moved her eyes from face to face. "Lord Arch, I'm the wrong person to understand your meaning, let alone believe in it. I was just now thinking how I've never understood how any of this happens," she waved her hand, "and I don't suppose I ever will."

Lord Arch betrayed his serious interest with the lines forming on his forehead, though his tone stayed light. "What do you mean, St. Claire?"

"I don't understand how any of this happens," Quincy answered honestly. "Prolonged, sincere conversation. No—I don't know, there's no sharpness and nothing feels, well, I can't say what I mean. It's like I—" She frowned, dissatisfied. If Arch were here, he might have already guessed what she was trying to say. "Have you ever seen a glass bottle get smashed against someone's head?"

The wince around Lord Arch's eyes was perceptible when she had said *someone's*. He nodded.

"There's nothing left but sharp edges, you see; you can cut yourself on any of them. Do you see?"

Quincy was certain he didn't see, for she couldn't understand what she was trying to say herself. Were she like Mary or the auburn creature, she could have delivered a line and moved her hand in the accompanying movement to give a clear explanation, but Quincy wasn't either of them, and her hands knew how to fix presses and challenge businessmen, not emphasize polite conversation.

Lord Arch took a long sip of his tea and thought on what Quincy had said. She felt as if she could hear the sound of his mind turning and shifting her words into a formula he could understand.

"If I were to treat what you have just said as poetry—" he began. Quincy scoffed, but Lord Arch continued, "—I would say that you, Miss St. Claire, think of yourself as the smashed bottle, edges and all, and that when you look around the room, you see an unbroken set, capable of different things than you for their perceived wholeness. Have I understood right? Have I *seen*?"

Quincy did not answer, for what he had said was not what she had thought, but the echo of it was strangely familiar: as if she had an indefinable taste in her mouth and he had told her what it could be.

"Do not doubt we all have cracks, dear," Lord Arch said as he stood. "Do not think that you are so shattered. You are a beautiful, capable creation, even when you sharpen the edges of the bottle yourself."

Lord Arch dismissed himself from the gathering then, and, as if her solicitor could sense when she had braved an honest thought, Arch turned and looked in Quincy's direction, holding her eyes longer than she was comfortable with. She blinked and looked away.

When Arch had again been distracted, now by Johnny, Quincy found Mary, thanked her, and slipped away without taking leave of anyone else.

"Why did you leave without saying good-bye?" Arch asked Quincy the next morning over breakfast. The meal had come from his cook and included sausages. Quincy ate all of hers and half of his.

"Misplaced items should be returned as soon as possible," Quincy said, refraining from licking her fingers, instead burying her hands in a napkin.

"You didn't feel comfortable with my friends?"

"Johnny is right enough, the earl, Mary." Quincy lifted a shoulder. "But really, Arch, what did you expect?"

"I've seen you sit comfortable with business magnates and smugglers. Don't try and fool me into thinking you were scared off by the shirts and skirts of Rhysdon society."

"*Shirts and skirts?*" Quincy said, unforgivable underlining her words.

"It's Rhysdon slang for the younger set of the upper class."

"It's offensive on the ears. A writer should know better than to embrace such a pairing. De Vere wouldn't approve." Quincy slipped a piece of biscuit into her mouth with flair to emphasize her point.

"Your sneering isn't making me wish to be honest with you."

Quincy tried to say, "About what?" But it came out as a muffled sound.

Arch cringed. "Now who's being offensive?"

She smiled but didn't speak. Ezekiel had been relentless in table manners, but Quincy was converted to the essentials only when she wished it.

"I intended to be honest," Arch said, his eyes on her face, "and say that my father told me of your conversation: the glass bottle, the view of others as being so different from yourself."

Quincy swallowed quick, feeling an uncomfortable flush on her neck. "Speaking of poor manners. That was a private conversation between myself and Lord Arch. It was none of your business."

"My family actually speaks of things, Quincy. Granted, he shouldn't have shared the information with me if you believed it to be private. I'm sorry I was often otherwise engaged yesterday. I should have been a better host. It was my fault you were uncomfortable, and I felt sore about it all evening. Forgive me."

The contrite request for pardon was not what Quincy had expected.

"I—" She lifted a shoulder. "Forgiven and dismissed. Are you going to eat that last croissant?"

"You ate almost all my sausages."

"True," Quincy said, but Arch was already passing the croissant to Quincy.

"I intend to see you well-fed, by any means," he conceded, "so please, eat what you will."

For most of her life, Quincy would have clipped at a statement like that and made a razor-edged pronouncement regarding her own ability to feed herself. But, this morning, she only smiled, pulled the croissant apart with her hands, and offered Arch half.

October 13, 1898

Quince,

I received your last letter a few days late, for the house lady's dog had ambushed the postman and hidden the spoils. It's likely you'll have to send another, as I can hardly make anything intelligible out of the wreckage. You did ask after Mado, I saw. She is well. Her mother has finally come round to the idea of her daughter marrying a Rhysdoner, and my French is improving.

Now see here. Three times since Arch left, a Paris Q boy has arrived at my door with some emergency. I have done my duty to you and to The Q. But when I arrived, they were not emergencies at all. The French have a way of exaggerating the strain of replacing paper in a Heidelberg press, Quincy, and they have to stop coming to me. I'm barely keeping my head above water at the university as it is, and by that, I mean I'm drowning.

With all my love,

Fisher

Post Script—Jade has kept me abreast of all the Qs sent by Boy Blue or Angel. It looks like they might just make it after all!

CHAPTER THIRTY-THREE:
Questions and Answers

"Quincy, could I speak with you?"

Arch found her in the print room. It was well past seven o'clock, and she had supposed that he had already gone home for the day, despite it feeling normal that he hadn't.

"Yes." She patted the machine on her right with greased fingers. "This is one of our older machines, and I'm fixing it more often than not. I'll have to send for a German engineer."

Arch looked the machine over as if he had not seen it before. "I thought you and Spense both understood how to fix all the presses."

"We do," Quincy said. "But, if you've ever watched a company engineer tune a press, you know what love is. He keeps it tuned to brilliance. He woos it. The press always works perfectly after his touch. To this day, the occasional German engineer has been my most solid import."

"Amazing," Arch said, his eyes still on the press. "It's like you're an entirely different person. I'm now waiting for you to spout off poetry about the idea."

"Ha!" Quincy kicked the press affectionately. "This is all the poetry I need. Now, what was your question?"

Arch stepped closer to Quincy so that he mightn't be overheard. "Priest received a wire today from a progressive society in London, in regards to my essays."

"He did?"

"Yes," said Arch. "They wish to know if I might find myself in London this coming week for a series of lectures based on my work for *The Times*. It will, potentially, launch my essays into the London papers."

Despite holding his face in serious lines, he looked extremely pleased.

"You look as if I should congratulate you."

"Pardon," Arch said self-consciously. "I don't mean to. Only, it would be an opportunity to establish myself as a serious, international social essayist."

"Who cheats his employer for lack of serious work," Quincy said. "You would be gone all next week?"

"No," Arch clarified. "I would be gone next week and through the following Tuesday. I mean to catch the Thursday evening train, then a passenger boat across both channels. My first lecture would be Saturday. I would have lectures and dinners throughout the week and leave the Monday after for Rhysdon, returning on—"

"All Hallows' Eve," Quincy finished. "Are you certain you wish to lose your anonymity?"

"No."

"But it's an opportunity you can't miss?"

"It's a chance to influence change not only in Rhysdon but also abroad. The affair is really smaller than it sounds, and my name would not be making its way back to Rhysdon soon. I asked Priest to keep it out of the papers."

"Oh, so you'd already decided to go before I gave you leave?" She raised an eyebrow and gave him a disapproving smile. Grabbing an old rag from the press, Quincy passed Arch while wiping her fingers the best she could. Arch followed her through the maze of presses, mice, and the sound of Jade's voice calling out threats.

"This is a strange picture," Quincy said, tossing the words over her shoulder. "You are a future lord—quite wealthy, I would assume—who doesn't need to work as a solicitor. Yet, you do. I, on the other hand, didn't hire you but am forced to pay you a yearly salary on pain of losing my job. Now you wish to take additional vacation days—days I thought were very well spent in August—in order to be paid to lecture in another country, while I am here, passing off every requirement left on my list in vain because you won't be here to witness it."

"I feel like you're rambling," said Arch as he followed her up the stairs, and Quincy laughed. Then he added, "I don't mind you docking my pay."

"Oh, forget it, Arch," Quincy said, walking into the now closed front office. "I won't dock your pay, and I don't mind you going. It's good exposure for The Q in any sense, as I assume you will be introduced as my solicitor."

"I'll pen the introductions myself. You will be praised."

"I don't need praise. I need interest, investment, and profits. I'm hoping to storm London come spring."

"I will arrange for some version of all three."

———

Monday morning was fresh, the city outside The Q's windows looking like a crisp cutout of itself. Quincy opened the offices, wondered only a moment where Arch was, remembered, then set about her work, thinking that perhaps, alone in the front offices, she might get more work done than planned.

She accomplished less.

The day passed, customers came and went, Q boys arrived on time, save Spats—still on his routes despite his night training as a mouse—who raced in through the front door just before close, panting and handing Quincy a Q slip.

"Angel?"

Bent over for breath, Spats shook his head.

"Boy Blue, then?"

Spats nodded. Then his face broke into a heartbreaking smile.

Quincy read the Q slip.

———

Will you then marry me, dearest Angel?

BLUE BOY

———

She started to laugh and looked towards Arch's office, but he wasn't there. Just then, Jade came in, ranting about irresponsible Q boys, pausing only when she saw Quincy's face.

"What have you gone Cheshire Cat over?" Jade glared.

"This." Quincy waved the Q slip in her hand. "A proposal."

"What!" In three steps, Jade was ripping the Q slip out of Quincy's hand and staring at the question. "He's proposed. They're finally going to be married!" Jade laughed, bent down, and kissed Spats on the cheek. "We will celebrate. Run down to Averson's, and buy up all their sweets."

"You're forgetting something," said Quincy.

"What?" Jade spun to face Quincy, her tall frame taking a don't-you-steal-this-moment posture.

"She hasn't yet said yes."

"But she will," Jade answered. "I'm almost certain." But her previous three words had sounded more certain than her last three.

"She probably will." Quincy shrugged. "But we'll wait for her answer before The Q celebrates."

Jade's lips screwed themselves together in displeasure. "I don't want to wait."

"We can't celebrate something that hasn't been decided yet."

"Blast it all. Come on, Spats, let's get your questions in and get you out on the floor. I'm holding you to that, Quincy," Jade called as she led Spats into the sorter. "Next week, The Q will celebrate a betrothal!"

Quincy looked back down at her work, wondering if Boy Blue had just made a grave mistake.

———

Angel's Q came three days later. It only said, "*Yes.*"

Quincy called a meeting.

The entire staff was gathered around the ancient, where Quincy had perched, perplexed, holding Angel's Q slip in her hand. Save Ezekiel's obituary, they had never printed anything that was not a question. Ever. It was simply not done. Qs not phrased as questions were thrown into the rubbish bin.

"We can't print it," Quincy said aloud for the seventh time.

"Of course we'll print it!" Jade said for the tenth time. "We can't not print it!"

"It isn't a question," said one of the mice.

"It's the only answer worthy of *The Q*," muttered the cleaning girl.

"Spense?" Quincy asked. Everyone—Mrs. Graves, the Q boys, the mice, Jade, the sorters, even an early Q driver—shifted to look at the strong press operator.

"The Q has never before printed an answer, in all the years it's been in operation," Spense said slowly, "and I keep thinking: if Ezekiel had ever planned for an answer, what would he want that answer to be?"

It was strange to hear the print room be so silent, but this choice was a cut sharp or a bone split, as they called a hard decision on the street. Quincy tapped her foot against the old machine and looked again at Angel's euphoric scrawl. *Yes.*

If Ezekiel were to select one answer for *The Q*, it would have been something affirming, committing. It would have been the word yes.

"If this happens today, it must never happen again," Quincy ventured, and the entire staff held their breaths. "And we better hope they see this marriage through—because I refuse to waste The Q's only answer on a botched romance."

"So you're saying we're going to print it?" Jade asked, her question sounding like a challenge.

Quincy looked at the Q slip once more and released a long breath. "The Q is going to print it."

Jade whooped, catching Spense in an embrace. The mice were clapping. Mrs. Graves moved a finger beneath her eye, and Spats was grinning. Quincy felt a sudden and unrecognizable twinge that was two-pronged: one side thinking of Fisher in Paris; the other wishing Arch was already back from London.

The room had erupted into the excitement of planning how to print the answer by the time Quincy set her thoughts back down inside her mind and rejoined the conversation.

"It should be an entire page," Jade was saying, her hands spreading to form an imaginary yes in the air.

"Front page! Front page!" Spats was encouraging the mice to chant.

"No, no, no." Quincy waved her hand. "It's not an exhibition. The yes will be printed in the same section their Qs are always printed. It will be the same size as every other question. It will be private. But, it will be in italics."

Spense nodded.

Jade clapped her hands, rushing the mice back into their places. "We still have pages and pages of questions to set! Get to work! Quincy?" Jade turned back towards her. "You should be the one to do it."

"Do what?"

"Set the letters. You should set the *Yes*."

"Me?" Quincy replied, but Jade had already turned back to her work. Quincy shifted on the ancient and watched everyone in the print room burning their excitement as the fuel to get their work finished. Usually, Quincy would have thrown herself in to help, but tonight Quincy stayed where she was.

Pulling a knee up under her chin, Quincy watched the motion of The Q and its acolytes. It was, Quincy admitted, a singular beauty tied more closely to her heart than she would ever have dared articulate. And, in that moment, waiting to set Angel's answer, Quincy felt as if Ezekiel were standing beside the ancient, his hand resting near hers, pleased. It was as if he had come back to watch Quincy place the answer to every worthy question, the most affirming combination of letters ever combined.

She tucked the Q slip into her pocket, rather than pinning it onto the board.

Later, when the plate was ready, Quincy moved her fingers expertly through the uppercase italics and pulled out three letters: the S, the Y, and the E.

CHAPTER THIRTY-FOUR:
All Hallows' Eve

"Quincy!"

Quincy leaned over the jack-o'-lantern she was arranging in her window—for The Q's All Hallows' Eve festivities—and looked below. Arch was down in the street.

"You're back!"

"Only this afternoon. I just received the invite to Jade's evening mischief. Am I too late?"

"No," Quincy called down. "You're just on time, in fact. I'm about to go down to the print room, but I thought I would do something festive. How does he look?"

Arch's grin lit up the darkness. "Fantastic. He will frighten any passerby for certain, and they might send for a priest."

"Good. I've made several more for the print room. Coming down."

Making sure the jack-o'-lantern was steady in the window, Quincy then slipped down the dark stairway into the front office just as Arch was letting himself in.

Quincy grinned. She was happy to see him. She had never felt so happy to see him. As she came around the counter, he smiled, taking off his hat, and they did a strange dance of movements, uncertain how to greet one another. Finally, Arch just wrapped an arm around Quincy's shoulders and laughed.

"How was London?" she asked, extremely aware of his proximity.

"Good. That is, I believe it went well." His eyes were bright with a satisfied fire, and his cheeks were tinged with a flush of red from the cool fall air. Quincy thought nothing of it, until he coughed. His lungs, they sounded as they had at the turn of the year.

"Are you ill again?" Quincy asked as she stepped back, worried.

"It's nothing," Arch said as he walked into his office, and Quincy felt a relief to see him there again, sorting through his desk. "I was caught in the rain a few times in London, but I'd already started to feel it before leaving Rhysdon. Mary will chase it away with her odd remedies soon enough."

"Ask me why that isn't very comforting," Quincy drawled.

Arch tilted his head and raised an eyebrow. "Are you worrying over my health, St. Claire?"

"As much as I don't believe it myself, it appears I am. So, your lectures were well received?" Quincy asked, leaning against his doorframe, her arms crossed.

"Yes." Arch had taken off his jacket, leaving only his vest and white shirt, and was rolling up his sleeves. He looked up at Quincy as he finished, seemingly as pleased to see her as she was to see him. "Congratulations, by the way. You engaged yourself in an artistic endeavor with no thought for profit."

"What are you talking about?" Quincy asked.

"The jack-o'-lantern. You've fulfilled your eighth requirement."

Quincy smiled at this unexpected payoff. "There's welcome news. I might actually come off the victor."

"You will," Arch said confidently. "I'll help you as much as I'm able. It's really remarkable though."

"What?"

"Had you asked me in February, April even, I would have set a confident wager that you would fulfill no more than three requirements."

"I get what I want," Quincy said, shrugging, as if she hadn't stumbled upon most every requirement by serendipity.

"Something has happened—to you, I mean—over the course of the last year," Arch said as he walked over towards Quincy and leaned his shoulder just around the corner of the doorframe from her, standing close. "You've rounded your sharp corners. Only a hint," Arch added when he saw Quincy's face. "Don't think you've become a saint."

"I'm not the only one who's made concessions of personality," said Quincy, her words sharp, though her eyes stayed on his. "You've become less severe, more willing to jostle with me instead of taking everything so seriously."

He laughed. "Perhaps I've just been more willing to show my sweet personality, now that I'm nearly confident you won't skewer me with a portfolio or run me through a press."

"I have had that thought, I admit," Quincy said.

"It's really good to see you, Quincy St. Claire."

The noise was building in the print room, and Jade came bursting through the sorter.

"There you are. Oh, hello Mr. Arch. Did you have a good time in London?"

"Yes, Jade. Thank you."

"The cider is warm, and my Jack has lit your jacks," she said to Quincy, her eyes moving to Arch then back to Quincy with a strange expression on her face.

"Jack's here?" Quincy straightened herself. "Come on, Arch. You should know Jack, the baker, not the pumpkin. He makes amazing port cakes and slip biscuits. Better than what you've been peddling every morning."

The print room smelled like an apple bake in the fall, one of Quincy's few warm memories from her life on the streets of Lester. Every year, the farmers would gather around bonfires, and mulling spices would rise in the air as apples were baked, covered in sugar and cinnamon, as clove bread was pieced around. Now, as Quincy and Arch came down into the print room, she saw that the mice were hanging the apple string, Spense had set up the scarecrow, and Jack was just finishing illuminating the pumpkins.

"Jack!"

"St. Claire! When are you going to give my wife a few days off?"

"Not any time soon," Quincy said as she and Jack embraced each other. Jack was sincere, witty under his breath, and devoted to Jade.

"Have you met Arch? My solicitor?"

Quincy stepped back and motioned to Arch.

"No, but it's a pleasure." Jack extended his hand. "Jade speaks highly of you."

Arch shook Jack's hand, and they exchanged a few polite words, but then Timothy, one of the mice, began playing his fiddle, and their introductions dissolved as the festivities began.

Quincy, armed with a plate of port cakes, took up her usual place on the ancient. Only, this year, someone joined her. Arch pulled himself up beside her, a cup of steaming cider balanced in his hand as he settled himself. He stole a port cake from Quincy.

There, on the ancient, Quincy told Arch the news of The Q. After telling him of a strike Spats had tried to organize with the mice—a tale which had Arch laughing so hard that tears ran down his face—Quincy remembered Angel and Boy Blue.

"I have something to show you," she said, reaching into her pocket and withdrawing the now crumpled Q slip.

Arch read over Quincy's shoulder. "Yes? What is she saying yes to?"

"Oh," Quincy said, realizing he had not seen the proposal. "Last week Boy Blue proposed."

"What!" Arch threw his hand up so fast the remainder of his cider went flying through the air. He winced. "That's wonderful! And she really means to marry him?"

"She had better. I broke all Q protocol and printed the answer."

Arch did not even attempt to control his surprise. "You printed this? You printed an answer? You broke Q form?"

Quincy nodded, her stomach catching, her heart following suit. She had been secretly wondering if it was a requirement. The idea had only come to her mind the day after the answer had already been sent out, it had not influenced her decision, but she had hoped it would bring her one step closer to claiming The Q.

Arch laughed, leaning into Quincy as if they had just shared the year's joke. "I can scarcely believe it. I wish it was a requirement, but I don't think the idea even crossed Ezekiel's mind. You saved a copy for me to see, I trust."

"Of course," Quincy said defensively. "I look at it continually to confirm my brief foray into insanity."

"That's brilliant. I hope they'll be happy."

"Perhaps Crandall was right after all," Quincy said as she claimed the last port cake.

Bent over with a youthful attitude, both hands around his now empty cider cup, Arch looked at Quincy. "I'd like to believe he was."

Quincy lifted a shoulder.

"It's good to see the entire staff together," Arch said, turning the conversation. "I see even the accountants have set themselves up in the corner."

They had, commandeering more than their share of Jack's baked goods.

"Everyone is invited to All Hallows' Eve," Quincy answered, "except the board."

Arch pursed his lips, and Quincy could smell the aroma of his spilled cider mixing with the smell of whatever soap he used. "I noticed," he said. "They don't belong here, anyway. They're nothing towards the blood and bones of this place. The beauty of The Q is personified by all those who work at the Gainsford Street offices."

Quincy felt a rush of affection and elbowed Arch. "I knew you'd see why I feel the way I do about The Q."

Arch gave her a look, and she met his eye, waiting.

"I'm talking about the people," Arch said, "not the business, not the machine of it all."

"The people are an essential part of the machine," she argued. "I value them highly."

"Yes, I think you do," Arch replied. "And, if the people were separated from The Q, you would still care for them. I think that's one of the points your uncle Ezekiel was driving at, that your most valuable assets are your relationships, regardless of anything else."

Frowning, Quincy looked around the room. Admittedly, she liked the people she worked with, especially those who cared for their work in a percentage acceptable to Quincy, but why was Arch so converted to the idea of people in and of themselves?

"I don't believe that anything you can gain from a person is worth the misery that follows when they are taken away," she said at length.

Arch's reply was quiet, "Do you really mean that?"

Quincy shrugged and slipped down from the ancient. Looking back up at Arch, Quincy opened her mouth to speak, hesitated, then bravely said the words that were on her mind anyway, despite fearing how it might change the place where she and he now found each other.

"I'd like to think that I mean it, because I'm not capable of giving anything to anyone, despite what you think. And isn't that what you're supposed to do? People," she waved her empty plate towards the boisterous crowd of her employees, "they require things from you, and you may even try to give to them. But what else can you count on? Their reactions, their thoughts, their safety, their attitudes, even their lives—none of these come back at you the way you think they will." She dropped her hand and took a breath. "I can't risk not knowing what's coming back my way, Arch."

A shadow of thought passed Arch's face, and Quincy guessed he was composing a well-written thesis on human experience in his head. Leaning forward, his elbows on his knees, the empty mug still between his hands, he gave Quincy a long look. "Come to my house Saturday for tea."

"Can't," responded Quincy. "I'm busy avoiding human connection."

"Come," Arch insisted, dropping off the ancient and resting his hand on it, while staring at Quincy. "Mary has been wanting to see you, by any way, and I can make you a promise."

Quincy cocked her head. "What?"

"I, as a flawed human, am promising to give you just the outcome you expect: that I will be there and that it will be nice."

"I might be in a horrible mood, which wouldn't be nice, proving your formula flawed."

Arch leaned towards her, his lips almost brushing her ear, and spoke quietly with an intonation that gave Quincy no room to disagree. "That only proves your own formula flawed, Quincy."

Without waiting for a response, he stepped through a game of jacks that the Q boys had put half crowns and jabs on, and disappeared up the stairs.

CHAPTER THIRTY-FIVE:

Beija Flor

When the day came for The Q to print invites to the Fothergils' ball—to be held on the tenth of December—Lady Fothergil purchased an entire page of the Rhysdon edition. And Quincy was, as Arch was quick to point out, on the list of those invited.

"You must come to the Fothergils' ball," Arch said as he reviewed the invitations from the opposite side of Quincy's counter. Just as the extra chair in his office had become Quincy's, the extra stool floating around the counter had become Arch's. Tonight, even though they were an hour past close, Arch had not rushed away, but stayed, casually reading through the invitations.

"Why?"

"It is *the* event of December. Everybody with title, influence, or prestige is there. The talented, the interesting…"

Quincy balked. "You speak as if you expect that to make me say yes."

"Priest will be there," Arch said, half invested in their conversation, half occupied with the paper before him, still reading through the list of the prestigious invitees.

"And yet, I am not swayed."

"If it's a matter of not knowing how to dance—"

"I know how to dance, Arch," Quincy said through gritted teeth.

She now had his full attention. Arch looked up with mild suspicion before his lips parted in amused disbelief. "You, Quincy St. Claire, Q baron and business magician, know how to dance?"

She had surprised him, and Quincy wasn't sure why this fact pleased her. Her jaw relaxed into mere disapproval. "It was not a voluntary education, Arch. Fisher made me learn so I could practice with him. He thought it would help him woo refined women. And where did it get him? Courting a governess and living in Paris." Quincy wrinkled her nose at the distasteful thought.

"Which dances do you know?" Arch asked, as if he could catch her out admitting she only knew the Wharf Square.

"The Marianne, the Classical, and the Queen's Waltz. Granted, I learned them from Fisher. We must have looked like the Bulgarian circus."

"You know the Queen's Waltz?" Arch now looked dumb and rather like a farm animal, Quincy thought, with his mouth open like that.

"The Queen's Waltz is easy if you think through the counts."

"This is too rich. I'm going to sell it to *The Times*."

"You don't believe I can dance," Quincy said, spreading her hands flat against the counter and leaning forward. "I can see it in your face. You don't believe me."

Arch was laughing now. "I just can't imagine you, of all people, learning to waltz."

"With Fisher," Quincy stated, furrowing her eyebrows as if it were an obvious obligation.

"With Fisher," Arch repeated before running into another peel of laughter, the image cementing the joke.

Quincy picked up her pencil, muttering, and continued the inventory. She didn't like being teased; it felt like someone else stubbing your toe.

"Forgive me," Arch sighed, his eyes bright. "Peace, Quincy. I'm sorry for making a tease of you. But now you really will have to indulge me."

"Never. Go home, Arch. You've worn out your welcome."

"Please." He grabbed her hand, and Quincy was so startled she dropped her pencil.

"I'm not waltzing in the front office of The Q," Quincy insisted, picking the pencil back up again.

"You're not waltzing anywhere, apparently." Arch withdrew his hand. "Indulge me."

"No."

"I'll put a prize on it. You dance with me, and I'll leave home early enough to bring those honey slap cakes you like from the bakery off the quay for breakfast tomorrow morning."

Quincy gave an involuntary smile. She did like the honey slap cakes. Very much. "And?"

"And what?" Arch said, pulling his face into a disapproving glare. "That's a very high offering."

"So is my dancing."

"Fine, I'll ask the cook for a selection of breakfast meats. She'll skin me for it, you know. It means she'll have to get up early."

Quincy nodded with approval. "I will strike that deal, if the slap cakes are still hot."

"You devil."

Quincy laughed and tapped the end of her pencil against the counter.

"I'm ready," Arch said.

"What, now?"

"Yes." Arch looked at the clock. "If I'm going to be home to ask Cook the favor, I can't dally over the social page of *The Q* all evening."

Feeling the muscles of her mouth tighten, Quincy dropped from her stool, came around through the half gate, and stood before Arch stubbornly, her arms crossed. He rose, pulled his vest straight, and held out his hand, waiting, a grin fighting with the line of his mouth.

She stared at his waiting hand, the thought of touching Arch in this way feeling strange. Fisher had been such an extension of herself, she had never given space or thought to their physical interactions. But Arch was very outside of herself. Arch was complex and very present each time he entered the room.

"The Queen's Waltz?" she heard herself say, still staring at his hand.

"The Queen's Waltz."

"I'm not trying to prove I can dance as much as I'm trying to prove you wrong," Quincy said, placing her hand in his, aware. So very aware. "And to finally get what I want for breakfast." Her other hand moved towards his shoulder, and she was blindingly certain he was touching her waist. Amid this strange sensation, her eyes found his and he smiled.

"I don't enjoy dancing," said Quincy.

"I wouldn't have expected any less, St. Claire. Now." He began to count under his breath—"one and two and three"—and led her into the dance. If Quincy had thought she knew the Queen's Waltz, she realized now that it had been a thinly shaded mimicry of the dance.

Arch was perfect. In a way that Fisher never could have accomplished. Arch moved flawlessly, the lines of his dance articulate, confident. Quincy had no difficulty following him. For music, Arch was lightly humming, keeping the notes in the monochrome tone of practice, rather than in outright melody. Dancing with Arch felt like playing the violin. And something under her skin responded to the art.

They completed the Queen's Waltz, and Arch took Quincy right into the Classical. After a few times through, Arch became conversant. "This variation is sometimes made among the younger set." And he spun Quincy at an unexpected time. "Good, good. Just like so."

Next, they went through the Marianne and then returned to the Queen's and the Classical. He then taught Quincy a dance called Beija Flor.

"Meaning *hummingbird*, or *to kiss a flower*, in Portuguese," Arch explained. "My mother said it's a longtime favorite on the Iberian Peninsula."

As Arch instructed Quincy in the steps, his hand tightening about hers, he pulled her body closer to his. It was like nothing Quincy had ever imagined. She had to close her eyes and listen intently as Arch counted out the steps. As it turned out, the Beija Flor was not only Arch's favorite but Quincy's as well.

"It's sweet—" he began.

"It's less wasteful, less showy—" Quincy argued.

When they each realized they were speaking over one another and that she was somehow still pulled close to him, her face just inches away from his, Quincy stepped back. And the impromptu dance experiment ended. Quincy was feeling flushed. She rubbed her hands on her trousers and retreated around the counter while Arch sat back down on the stool. She glanced towards the large clock on the wall behind Fisher's empty desk and saw that they had been dancing for three-quarters of an hour. Her hands were shaking.

"You were right," Arch was saying. "You do know how to dance—very well, in fact."

"I need to pull something from the file room," Quincy said, speaking over the end of his sentence.

She disappeared into the file room and closed the door behind her. When the latch had clicked and the door was secured, Quincy leaned against it and took a deep breath. Her entire self was trembling: her mind, her fingertips, the walls she had maintained around every human emotion. Quincy crushed her fingers into her hair, forcing it back from her face, and wrapped her other arm around her ribs.

She couldn't understand. Closing her eyes, Quincy reached for something to anchor herself to. She was soon muttering through number sequences—3, 9, 27, 81, 243, 729, 2187, 6561, 19683, 59049, 177147, 531441, 1594323, 4782969, 14348907... She could see them stretching out on the slate board of her mind, lining up in perfect order, static, unfeeling, secure. But at some point in her counting, Quincy would again remember feeling the sensation of Arch just before her face or would smell his aroma on her clothes—a hint of Peacock House—and the numbers would jumble in a way they never had before.

She could hear him now, waiting for her, pacing in the front office, but Quincy would not move. She let the sounds of his soles on the wood planked floor rattle off the numbers in her head until, finally, the sounds moved to his office, then across the floor, ending with the locking of the front office door as he left.

Quincy waited in the silence, counting two up two up two up—1, 2, 4, 16, 32, 64, 128, 256, 512, 1024, 2048, 4096, 8192—until she was certain he had gone. Shifting her weight, her muscles resisting the movement, Quincy placed her hand on the doorknob, twisted it, and came out into the front office.

It was all but dark. Arch had extinguished all the gas lamps save one. Quincy looked at the looming clock. It was nearly ten. Arch had paced for well over an hour, waiting for some evidence that Quincy was lined with normal, human feelings. But she wasn't.

Quincy ignored the soothing sounds of the presses, running the next morning's *Q*, and, after extinguishing the light, dragged herself up the stairs and into her matchbox. She crumpled into bed. As she lied to herself—saying she was sleeping—Quincy's mind entertained three questions: How was she ever going to apologize to Arch? How was she never going to see him again? And how was she going to forget the pressure of his hand around hers?

CHAPTER THIRTY-SIX:
Old Blood

Waking was a messy affair. Quincy was twisted inside her clothing, uncomfortable. Her eyes felt swollen; her mouth, sore. Dawn had yet to break, and Quincy had yet to find any true rest. But she rose, stripped away her clothes, bathing herself in a washbasin of two-day-old water before pulling clean clothes over her resistant body, and then she flung open her window.

The night air, anxious to shift aside and make ready for the dawn, flooded Quincy's room and her jumbled senses. She leaned over the window's ledge and took a long breath. It had been how many days since she had leaned over it and called to Arch in the street, so pleased he had returned? So pleased to see him back in his place as part of The Q?

Now, in the golden shadows of November, tripping over things she didn't understand—like the way he had been looking at her and the way she had been looking back—Quincy was wishing Arch had never returned at all.

She descended the first few stairs with some trepidation, worried she would find Arch, dutifully attending to work in his office, the box of promised breakfast waiting. But when she reached the bottom of the stairs, the room was dark.

Setting the lights and pulling herself to the business she had left scattered on the counter the night previous, Quincy noted the time. Five thirty seven. Early. Too early for Arch or anybody. The print room would have sent out the Q drivers, and Spense would be seeing to the final arrangements of his work and then roll on home to his wife and his children.

Sitting at the counter, rearranging papers, Quincy did what she knew well, she lost herself in her work.

"Quincy!" Spense burst in from the sorter at a quarter after six. "Thank heavens you're up. Down, into the print room. Now!"

"What?!" Quincy almost tripped as she rushed to follow Spense through the sorter and out onto the stairs, looking about her. The print room was empty, clean. "What's happened?" she asked at his back.

Spense was clanking down the stairs at such a speed that Quincy felt frightened the entire staircase would come off the wall it was bolted into. "Griggson found him, just after the last wagons rolled out. He was in the back alley. I sent Griggson for a doctor."

"Who did you find in the back alley?" Quincy demanded as she tripped after him.

Spense brought Quincy around by the back door. There on the floor, unconscious and bloodied, lay Arch.

"Arch!" Quincy was at his side before she thought about how to get there. His face was whiter than fresh print paper, and he was bleeding. His left eye was bruised and swollen, with cuts across his face. She shook him, but he gave no response. "Is he breathing?" she cried frantically.

"Only just," Spense answered as he wiped his forehead, his red face more flushed than usual. "I didn't dare drag him farther without a doctor. He's been taken to pretty bad."

Quincy undid Arch's necktie and collar. His clothes were ripped, and she was certain he had taken more blows than just to the head. "Arch, are you alright? What happened to you? Arch!"

"Don't shake him too hard now, Quincy." Spense bent down, resting on the balls of his feet, running a nervous hand across his forehead.

Quincy pressed her hand to Arch's face, but her hand came away with the red stickiness of old blood. "He's cold. He must have been out there all night! He can't do that, Spense; he gets sick!"

"When did he leave the office?"

"Not until late. We were—he didn't leave until late. Someone must have jumped him and dragged him around back through the alley. How did the Q drivers miss him?"

"Why? For money?" Spense asked, referring to possible muggers.

Quincy felt Arch's pockets. "Where's his satchel?"

"I'll go see," Spense said, disappearing out the back door. He returned only a moment later, Arch's satchel in hand. "It's still latched, everything settled just tight. It doesn't look like anyone's been in it."

"Why would they jump him? If it were for money, they wouldn't have taken him so hard. Look at him, Spense! They were *trying* to hurt him. No street mugger would have done this."

Arch's coat was ripped, and as Quincy pulled it back, she could see that he had taken a knife across his chest. Although it had left only a shallow line, he was bleeding again from having been moved, the blood sluggish and slow, sticky and cold on her fingers.

"It's no good," she repeated aloud, over and over again, feeling terrified he would go cold before the doctor was fetched. Quincy's hands were shaking as she took off her own jacket and pressed it against the gash beneath his torn shirt. "Where is Griggson with that blasted physician?"

"I'm here!" Griggson shouted as he burst through the back door. "I've got a doctor. He's coming up now."

After a moment a doctor, out of breath but with his bag in hand, came through the back door of The Q.

"What's this?" the doctor asked, rushing to Quincy's side. He was not as old as she had expected, but his hair had gone towards the gray. This comforted Quincy. She trusted experience.

"James Arch is my solicitor," Quincy said quickly. "He was found in the back alley this morning. He must have been set upon after leaving work late last night."

The doctor was already taking in Arch's condition, pressing his fingers to Arch's chin and tilting his face towards the light. He then worked his fingers around the clothing Quincy had tried to loosen.

"It looks to be quite bad," he said, looking back up at Quincy. "Is there a clean place in these offices where I can work on him?"

"Up the stairs," Quincy said authoritatively. "There's a bed. Spense can carry him up."

"Carefully," the physician warned, "and as quickly as you can. You, young lady, boil some water, gather some clean rags."

Quincy was instantly up, yelling for Spense to hurry as she ran up the stairs, through the sorter, and up her own back stair into her matchbox room. She had a kettle of cold water sitting on the stove, and Quincy lit the gas and struck a match with practiced fingers. Then she gathered several clean shirts, ripping them into strips. And by the time Spense came into her room, carrying Arch in his arms, Quincy realized she had been muttering a prayer beneath her breath.

Arch's pale face made no movement when Spense laid him down. The physician, a Dr. Latham, was bending over Arch and unbuttoning his shirt.

"This fellow got on the black end of someone," the physician said as he pulled Arch's shirt away from him. His abdomen and chest were red, his skin raw, bruises spreading in strange shapes and directions. The knife wound was clean, but he had lost a good deal of blood, the thin layer of fresh red soaking into the aged mess of the night before.

"Only one knife pull, Quincy," Spense said as he watched the doctor. "I'd say they were trying to scare him, not kill him. Teach him a lesson. Rough him up."

"It could be a costly lesson if infection sets in," answered Dr. Latham. "If they went too deep."

"Spense." Quincy snapped her fingers. "I need you to go to Arch's home. Get his father and his sister. They live at 731 Regent Square." She didn't bother registering if Spense had heard her or not, for the physician had called for the water, which was now boiling.

For the next hour, Quincy did something she never did, she turned her mind off, she stopped thinking ahead, and she focused only on the person before her. When the physician spoke, Quincy acted immediately and efficiently. Other than that, she was pressing her hand against Arch's brow, frowning at the cuts and bruises across his face. He must have fought back for them to have smashed up his face in this way. Lifting one of his hands in hers confirmed it; his knuckles had bled and were now swollen and bruised. The fool, Quincy thought.

While Quincy was downstairs, writing a message for Jade to come back as soon as she could and open the front office, Dr. Latham had finished removing Arch's clothes and had wrapped him in a blanket.

"His knee was hit with a metal pipe of sorts," Latham told Quincy when she returned. "It's swollen, and, along with his infected cut, this knee will trouble him a great deal. He shouldn't walk without a cane for a significant amount of time. It could bring permanent damage."

Quincy was bent over Arch's face, her thumb investigating the torn skin by the corner of his eye, when Mary came bursting into the room, followed by Lord Arch.

"James!"

Quincy jumped back, slamming against the wall as Mary came to her brother's side and took his hand.

"James? Why, he's not even awake!"

"I'm afraid he took several blows to the head," Dr. Latham said to Lord Arch. "He's not yet come to."

Lord Arch's face was drawn and stern. Having never seen him be anything but convivial, Quincy marked the anger-lined concern. He asked a few well-placed questions, receiving naught but broad answers, and then thanked Dr. Latham, who said there was nothing more immediate that he could do.

"I can return within the hour."

"My own physician is Dr. Tremmle. Do you think it wise that I call him in?"

Quincy could see that Lord Arch was not so much asking but telling Latham that he was grateful for Latham's attendance and that his own doctor would take it from there.

"Yes. Dr. Tremmle is a colleague and very respected, a good man. If he has any questions for me, send him my way."

"Thank you, doctor."

Mary's eyes met Quincy's after the doctor left. "What happened? How did he come to this?"

"Spense found him this morning," Quincy said. Although Quincy's arms were crossed, her fists balled tight against her chest, her hands were still shaking. "He'd been lying in the alley, behind the ink crates. It must have happened last night, late, after he left the office."

"What time did he leave?" asked Lord Arch with a hard voice.

"We'd finished our work and were—" Quincy waved a hand. "It wasn't quite ten o'clock. He left, and soon afterward, I went to bed."

And while she had slept, the cowards had dragged Arch into the alley and left him to the mercy of the cold night. How could she have not known? How could she have stumbled through sleep with such a heavy heart and not realized that he needed her?

There must have been some sign of these words on Quincy's face, for she felt a hand on her shoulder and started. It was Lord Arch.

"It's not your fault, Miss St. Claire."

Quincy reset her fists against her ribs and nodded, but she couldn't speak.

"Mary, go down, and send that Q boy after Doctor Tremmle."

"But—!" Mary gripped Arch's shoulder and shook her head.

"Go. I have some words for St. Claire."

Mary's brown eyes looked up pleading, like her body would unravel if she walked too far away from her unconscious brother. She rose dutifully, not willingly, and shut the door behind her in exclamation.

Lord Arch was still standing at the foot of the bed, and Quincy backed farther into her corner, feeling tight, ready to spring, to shuttle out whatever words he might require of her as fast as she could. But he didn't say anything. Lord Arch just looked down at his son and brought a hand to his eyes, drawing his fingers together from across the opposite ends of his face. With his other hand he motioned to Quincy.

"Come here, Quincy St. Claire."

She didn't move. He continued to motion until his persistence made her step towards him. Then Lord Arch pulled Quincy in close, wrapping Quincy in his comfort. And Quincy, as she felt her cheek press against his chest, thought that this must be what having a father felt like. She had never wondered before.

"Tremmle will tell us more, but I should think James will come out of this fine."

Quincy couldn't look at the still solicitor, especially under Lord Arch's scrutiny, so she turned her head and looked towards the window.

"You doubt my prognosis?" Lord Arch asked.

Closing her eyes, Quincy saw only the dead body of a lifeless girl. "Her eyes hadn't moved," she had told Fisher all those years ago.

"What?" Lord Arch interrupted her thoughts.

Quincy hadn't realized that she had spoken these words aloud. "He hasn't moved," she said.

"He will."

Nodding, Quincy let a sad sound escape her lungs. She felt so young.

"But you, Quincy St. Claire. Will you be alright?"

Quincy did not respond, and Lord Arch did not ask again.

CHAPTER THIRTY-SEVEN:

Lazarus

Mary brought their family's physician up not long afterward. Quincy retreated, claiming her place on the top of her bureau, and looked down on the street as Dr. Tremmle, Lord Arch, and Mary conversed urgently around the bed. Dr. Tremmle was deeply concerned that Arch still remained unconscious.

"If he does not wake soon, I'll worry about damage to the brain. But—" He held up a hand as Mary made an angry noise. "I expect he will come round, now that he's warm and well taken care of." Tremmle tsked over the bruises that were deepening in Arch's face, and he gave Mary instructions for a poultice after seeing the bruises in Arch's abdomen and chest. But he looked relieved when cleaning the knife wound, saying, "Rather shallow. I'm more worried about the blows." Then he grunted when he studied Arch's knee. "He might not walk the same, especially without a cane."

Lord Arch swore under his breath and stepped away, leaning against Quincy's table, fixating on her worn violin without seeming to really see it.

Tremmle continued to give instruction to Mary as to Arch's care. "I've another patient to see to, then I'll return. If he hasn't woken within the next hour, there are things we can try. There's not much swelling in the most sensitive parts of the head, so I am feeling optimistic."

"How would be the best way to transport him home?" Mary asked.

"Moving him is out of the question until I've seen him awake," Tremmle said firmly. "Unnecessary risks shouldn't be taken."

"We can't possibly keep him in this dreadful storeroom," Mary said, looking around Quincy's matchbox warily.

Quincy, who had been watching the movements of Gainsford Street out the window, felt a sting in her eyes. She was shaken, rattled from the night previous as it was, and now, she turned her head to face her room with fresh eyes. It was a place for filing papers or for storing the unwanted. She remembered Arch's disapproval when he had first seen it. This was another thing that happened when you let people in, she reminded herself: your important places were desecrated or, perhaps, simply shown for what they were.

"Mary," Lord Arch said in reproof. "We are thankful to Miss St. Claire, as we have put her out of her comfort. It is clean, ordered, and single-minded. If anything, it is better than what James would find at home."

"This is your room, Miss St. Claire?" Mary asked, looking at Quincy in alarm, understanding. "I did not mean to imply—"

"It's no matter," Quincy said, setting her face. She dropped from the bureau, and the sound of her boots on the floor sounded spare—as spare as the rest of the room. "If you need anything, I'll be downstairs. If you can't find me, you can ask for Jade." And before Lord Arch could speak, Quincy was through the door and down the stairwell.

Jade, tired rings beneath her eyes, looked up at Quincy with worry but couldn't speak, for she was helping a customer. Quincy walked past Jade, through the still empty sorter, and dropped down into the print room. Just as she had thought, Spense was still there, sitting on a chair, asleep, his head tipped back, his mouth open.

"Spense!" Quincy punched his arm.

"What!" Spense sat up and wiped his mouth, too tired to care. "How's Arch?"

"Unconscious," Quincy answered, grabbing a nearby stool and climbing onto it. "Dr. Tremmle, their family doctor, thinks he'll wake up soon."

"Good," Spense wiped his eyes. "Good."

"Before you go home, tell me how you found him."

"Oh." Spense yawned and blinked. "I was finishing sorting the print room. All the Q drivers had rolled out, and Jade was off, so were all the mice and printers. I had shut down and was running some of the rubbish out, when I saw a shoe beneath a paper."

"A newspaper?"

"Yeah, someone had covered him in paper so he couldn't be seen easily."

Quincy glared past Spense, knowing this was no regular mugging. Someone had been targeting Arch, waiting for him. Slamming her hand against a nearby press, Quincy slid off the stool.

"You should get home and sleep, Spense. I need you back tonight, but I'm keeping Jade here until Mrs. Graves gets in. She'll be coming in late for her shift, so you'll have to direct the mice. Go see your family and sleep."

Nodding, Spense stood up. "Send for me sooner if you need it, Quincy."

"I will. Thank you, Spense." She put her hand on his arm.

"If I hadn't have found him—" Spense left off.

At those words, Quincy's heart made a noise she had only ever heard it make twice before.

After Spense left, his coat in hand, his shoulders bent from the long shift, Quincy went into the back alley to investigate. There, behind the rubbish bin, were crumpled pages of *The Times*. Quincy picked up the closest page and checked the date. She had thought so. Reaching for the next sheet, Quincy smoothed the corner and looked. The same date. Refusing to leave without reinforcing her theory, Quincy checked every bit of crumpled paper. Each page was printed on the same day, the day that Arch had published his essay condemning the crown prince.

Quincy lifted the page that held Specter's crumpled essay, noting the expletives written around it, and tucked it into her pocket. She then searched the alley, finding Arch's portfolio near the street, flung open, its pages with his elegant scribbles scattered, drifting in sad abandon towards the street. Gathering as many as she could find, Quincy tucked them back into the portfolio and returned to the front office of The Q.

Jade turned to face Quincy with a relieved face. "He's awake."

Quincy took a step back, catching herself on the sorter door, her hands flat against the wood.

"His sister was just down," Jade continued. "He seems cognizant, asking for water. The doctor left, and Mary just sent out for broth."

"He's awake," Quincy repeated. She opened her eyes, not realizing they had been closed. "Has he said anything?"

"I don't know. You should go up."

Quincy shook her head. "I don't want to be in the way of his family, and I need to move, to walk, or I might—" she hesitated. "Do you mind staying until Graves comes in? Then you can come in late tonight. Spense can start the mice. I've already told him you would be back a bit in your hours."

"I don't mind Quincy. I understand. Go."

Without further explanation, Quincy placed Arch's portfolio on his desk and disappeared out The Q's front door into the crowd of Gainsford Street. She wandered for an hour, not spending any attention on her whereabouts. As she walked, Quincy didn't focus on her anger for whoever had dared hurt Arch. It only mattered that he had woken up. It only mattered that he would still be himself. Finding the villains would come after he recovered. And then, she would be not only angry—she would be vengeful. Quincy kicked the sidewalk at this thought, happy that it made her foot hurt.

It was cold, too cold, even for late November, and there was a winding breeze that kept lifting the ends of Quincy's hair—she had forgotten her hat. Spent leaves had escaped the parks and been blown down every avenue of the city as if in a declaration of something. Quincy tucked her shoulders forward, hands in her pockets. She didn't know what nature was trying to declare; that was Arch's job: to explain things Quincy didn't understand.

She must have intended it all the while, for when Quincy found herself entering the offices of The Times, she already knew what she wanted to say to Priest. She ascended the green marble stairs and let herself into his office. Priest's secretary saw Quincy, but before she could confirm or deny if Priest was available, Quincy was through the door. The smoke told her Priest was in and had been all day.

"Don't you ever breathe regular air, Priest?" asked Quincy, as she waved her hand and looked through the dim light of the curtained office.

"It's bad for my lungs," Priest said from the other side of the room. She saw him now, standing near the bookcase, a volume in hand, a cigar hanging from his mouth.

"I'm going to have to stop doing business with you. It may kill me," Quincy complained, sinking into one of the large leather chairs that were waiting before a dead fireplace. "You're office is cold."

Priest snapped his book shut and studied Quincy a moment. After setting the volume back in its place on the shelf, he walked over and sat down opposite Quincy.

"You're in fine form, St. Claire. What? Did Draggen pull a fast price?"

Quincy flared, not at Priest but at what she was about to say. She pulled the folded essay from her pocket and handed it to Priest.

"So, you discovered your solicitor to be the loudest social conscience in Rhysdon. Doesn't excuse the foul, albeit creative, language you've added to his work."

"I didn't add it, Priest," Quincy snapped. "I found it where they left his body in the alley last night."

"Body?" Priest took the cigar from his mouth in one quick movement. "Is he dead?"

"No." Quincy took a long breath. "He's only now woken up, but the doctor thinks he'll recover, a permanent limp for his pains."

Priest looked again at the essay. "Glorious hell, he's touched a nerve."

"Yes."

"And we both know whose," Priest stated before rolling his abandoned cigar between his fingers.

"There may be more than one suspect."

Priest tossed the essay back to Quincy and sat back. "We're scheduled to print another piece by Specter tomorrow. Should I hold it?"

The question hit Quincy at an odd place, as if it had sunk between two ribs when it was meant to strike bone and drop off. "I couldn't say, Priest, but I don't think Arch would want you to change anything. He strikes me as the 'words are power even when they beat you for it' type."

"We all are in this business," Priest said instantly. "The power of words."

Quincy lifted a shoulder. "Print the essay."

"I will. And I also intend to do something else that will give Arch a bit more protection."

"What?" Quincy asked. She was suspicious, defensive of anybody doing anything for Arch that she didn't approve of.

"I'm going to print his name, announce him as Specter, make a show of it."

"People already know he's Specter. He's been lecturing in London."

"In London, yes. That's because a colleague there wired me for his information. But this news is not yet known or spread in Rhysdon."

Quincy wasn't sure why Priest thought this would help. "I don't understand."

"Someone willing to hurt Arch knows he's Specter. They've threatened him through physical harm, with their greatest weapon being the ignorance of the city. If everyone knows Arch is Specter, as beloved an essayist as *The Times* has ever had, they will all be watching out for him. If he gets hurt, the people will get angry. And when the people get angry, heads roll. His notoriety will serve the office of protectorate."

"I can't tell you if he'll approve of that or not."

"He won't." Priest raised an eyebrow. "But, as he writes for my paper, I am making this decision for his well-being, approval or no. Send round a Q boy this evening with news on how he fares. I want to be kept abreast of his condition."

Quincy left, worried she may have set something into motion that Arch wouldn't approve of. She was so distracted as she thought about Arch's identity being published that she didn't see the flower vendor until she had nearly run the woman over, which at Quincy's height, was not an easy task.

"Sorry."

"Pardon, miss." The vendor straightened herself and her basket. "Would you like flowers? Late mums. In just this morning."

Quincy shook her head, her eyes wandering over the bright pink blooms that should have long been faded and gone.

"They's my November, miss. Nobody else in Rhysdon knows 'em, as they come up from the South. The last of the blooms before Christmas holly and the like."

Had Arch been with her, as he should have been, he would have purchased a bunch.

"How much?" Quincy asked, feeling foolish. She had never purchased flowers from a shop, let alone on the street.

"Two half crowns."

Snorting, Quincy drew the coins from her pocket and took a bundle of pink mums. Impulsive actions were always foolish, and this one was no exception. But Arch might like them. Flowers in hand, certain the entire business class of Rhysdon would see her, Quincy disappeared into a park, where she sat and then paced and then sat again.

Two hours later, she returned to the streets of Rhysdon for more aimless walking, knowing she should return. But Quincy was worried that Arch would be worse when she did, and she wouldn't know how to handle it.

The afternoon moved as it always did, one minute at a time, shadows shifting into longer shapes with the late fall sun. It was cold, and Quincy's flowers were curving their heads down, limp. She was still a ways uptown, and the afternoon was nearly over when she passed in front of the Upper Rhysdon Cathedral.

Tired, feet sore, Quincy climbed the steps and went in.

She was alone, the stained glass not even making a strong showing against the coming of the gray evening. Quincy slid onto a bench, set the flowers beside her, and wrapped her fingers into the ends of her jacket. A movement near the front, among the combination of altars and pillars, caught her attention. It was an old man, a priest, moving in silence, lighting a long row of candles as the light outside faded. They illuminated the space around him and made him look set apart, or chosen, in some way.

Quincy didn't know much about the tenets of any particular religion, but she sensed in this man a devotion she thought Arch would appreciate. The candles lit the darkening space, sending a faint glow onto the stained glass windows full of stories. Her eyes wandered, wondering, until they rested on the strange image of the man wrapped in white, standing beside another. Lazarus. That was what Arch had said, that it was a man named Lazarus, raised from the dead.

As Quincy studied the window, she felt an overwhelming feeling of relief and, in its wake, a tremendous desire to see Arch, to be with him, to do whatever she must so that he would be well. She grabbed her limp flowers and disappearing into the evening street, turned toward Gainsford and all that waited for her there.

CHAPTER THIRTY-EIGHT:

Indispensable

It was dark when Quincy arrived at Gainsford Street. The Q had just closed, and Mrs. Graves was cleaning the front office. She greeted Quincy with the discreet attention of a practiced housekeeper.

"Everything went off well, though a message was sent from the board, wondering why you had missed the meeting this afternoon. They assumed something had come up at The Q and held the meeting in your absence, requesting that you send the profit reports for Rhysdon and Paris by Q boy."

"I—I forgot we had moved the meeting to today," Quincy admitted, sniffling, her fingers cold from the walk. "It wasn't even in my mind."

"Oh, course not, deary." She took the flowers from Quincy's cold hands. "I'll see these get in some water, then I'll bring them back out to you."

After watching Graves disappear with the flowers, Quincy turned her attention towards the narrow staircase which led up to the matchbox—and Arch. Quincy, full of purpose and honesty only thirty minutes prior, now felt sheepish about ascending the stairs, uncertain what she would find there. But as fate's humor would have it, Lord Arch himself came down before she could do anything about her uncertainty.

"Miss St. Claire! Very good to see you returned. I suppose you've heard that James has awakened and seems to be doing well?" Although he sounded polite, Lord Arch had a strained expression on his face.

"Yes," Quincy answered. "I didn't leave today until I'd learned so."

"Yes," Lord Arch said, looking at her. "Yes, well, Tremmle is encouraged, though James can hardly move for the pain. The doctor has asked he remain here for now, possibly a few days. I was just coming to find you and ask, does this put you out?"

"No." Quincy shook her head and pushed a hand stubbornly into her pocket. "I'm anxious about moving him. I'd be—I'd be more than pleased to help in his care. I even have one of Ezekiel's old canes in the storeroom if Arch should—not that I see him up anytime soon, only—"

"Good, good. Do come up. He's sleeping now—doubtless he will the night through, as Tremmle has given him a draught—but do come up."

Nodding, Quincy followed the lord up her stairwell and into her room.

Arch was indeed asleep, Mary sitting on the bed beside him, looking tired, her eyes heavy, her face flushed and soft.

"Miss St. Claire." Mary stood, until Quincy waved her down. "Were you able to get your work done today?"

Quincy nodded. She had accomplished nothing.

Lord Arch offered Quincy the single chair in the room. She didn't take it, and they both remained standing.

"Did the doctor say anything else?" Quincy asked him.

It was Mary who answered Quincy, repeating what Lord Arch had said then adding, "James woke several times today, body sore, but his mind was clear. I'm rather encouraged. He asked for you twice, but Jade said you were out."

Quincy felt a twinge of guilt, and she realized how she must look—dirty and disheveled—as she had been in the street all day.

Lord Arch was leaning against the wall, his arms crossed, one hand rubbing the fine material of his jacket absently. "Mary, we must be home now," he said at length.

"Papa! I'm staying with James through the night, should he need anything."

"Mary." And his voice was stern. "Miss St. Claire is here, and you need your rest if you are to nurse James at all. I'll not have you take ill for foolishness. We will send food—soups and fruit—and everything he might need while you're absent."

"But, if he wakes up and needs me—"

"Quincy has said she will see to him."

Mary opened her mouth, looking from her father to Quincy and back.

Quincy interpreted Mary's hesitance and then said, "Spense is in the print room all night. Between the two of us, we can carry the task."

Resigned, Mary pressed her hand to her eyes. "Alright. Let us go then, and come back tomorrow first thing."

"Yes," Lord Arch said, as if leaving had been Mary's idea. "I'll call the man to bring the coach around."

Mary fussed over her brother before standing reluctantly. "There's broth there, on your little stove. It's cold but good, if you would like some."

"No, thank you," answered Quincy. "But I'll keep it warmed in case Arch wakes up."

Mary nodded, her eyes lingering on the singed wallpaper above the stove, her expression not entirely trusting of Quincy's culinary ability to keep soup warm. "Well, I should go."

Quincy followed Mary down the stairs, and they found Lord Arch, waiting, the coach just driving up. "I'll be locking the door," Quincy said, walking over to Fisher's desk and finding his abandoned Q key. "This will see you in or out at any time you need."

"Thank you, St. Claire. Please send round if anything worrisome comes up," Lord Arch said. "And, again, thank you."

As Mary walked out the door, she again assured Quincy—or herself, rather—that she would be back first thing come morning so that Quincy would not have to worry about anything difficult. Lord Arch then interjected, saying, "Mary, Miss St. Claire has far more experience caring for the ill and the wounded than you do. Let her be."

Quincy wondered what Arch had told his father.

Saying nothing, Quincy locked the door behind them. Then, lifting the ink-can vase of flowers that Graves had prepared off the counter, she climbed the stairs to her room. Being left alone with Arch in the capacity to care for him was bizarre, dreamlike. To Quincy's judgment, Arch looked worse now than he had when they had first found him that morning. Dark bruises puddled terribly around both eyes; his left cheek was swollen and raw down to the edge of his jaw; there were various scrapes on his face, a gash from a ring leaving a fresh, angled line beneath his right eye. But his breathing was solid; it sounded rounder somehow, and Quincy took comfort in this. So she claimed her usual bureau window perch and watched empty Gainsford Street entertain itself with a few windblown newspaper sheets.

"Quincy?"

Like an arrow long held in a drawn bow, Quincy released herself towards the sound of Arch's voice so quickly she tumbled to the floor in one clumsy movement, albeit landing on her feet.

Arch winced; she couldn't tell if it was from the fear she would tumble or from the sound her boots had made.

"Careful," he said weakly.

"Sorry." Quincy was now standing at the foot of her bed. She brushed a piece of hair from her eyes, buried her hands in her trouser pockets, pulled them out again, and then folded her arms across her chest.

He attempted the slightest of smiles. "Do you always land on your feet like a cat?"

Quincy didn't know. She lifted a shoulder and returned her hands to her pockets. Fidgety things hands were.

"You're up," she said. "Your father said you would sleep through the night."

Arch shifted enough to grimace, tilting his face towards hers, the dark bruises emphasized in the lantern light from Quincy's table. "I've been hoping to see you. Have you been downstairs this entire time? Mary kept saying you were—" he twisted from the pain of speaking, "not available."

Quincy shook her head. "I didn't want to be in Mary's way up here, but I couldn't get any productive work done without wearing the front office out with worry. I walked Rhysdon instead."

"Where did you go?"

"I don't know. The park, the cathedral, various places."

"The park?" This caught Arch's interest. "For how long?"

"I don't know. Two, maybe three hours."

"What dragged you to the cathedral?"

Quincy lifted a shoulder.

"Did you work?" Arch moved his head to the side so he could see her better.

"I thought to," Quincy snapped. "Though, it was highly unproductive. I operated at less than twenty percent capacity worrying over you. I missed the board meeting this afternoon. Clean forgot it was today. A message was sent around: they'd gone on without me, assuming I was dealing with a pressing matter at The Q, and asked, 'Would I be so kind as to send copies of our profit charts to the members of the board at my earliest convenience?' and 'What about the Paris reports?' Cats, I haven't had a day so derailed since Fisher caught his hand in the machines."

"That's good," Arch smiled again, and it was a tired thing, "that you spent some time off today. The flowers are nice," he said as his eyes wandered to the defiant pink blooms in the ink can.

"You're always buying flowers for your desk, so I figured you might want some until you're moved back home."

"Thank you, Quincy St. Claire. They are beautiful." His eyes were closed, though, and Quincy knew he must be tired from the time he had spent with Mary. "If I'm not mistaken," Arch said through his tired haze, "you've fulfilled three requirements, all today."

Quincy didn't care a king's death if she had. She was still terrified that Arch wouldn't wake up the next morning. "I'm not going to trust you on that, until your mind clears up. If it clears up."

"I'm not anticipating any permanent damage." Arch swallowed. "Come, sit beside me, Quincy St. Claire."

"Why?" Rather than wait for an answer, Quincy pulled the solitary chair to beside the bed and sat down. "In case you're wondering," she said, as he moved his head to the side, meeting her eyes, "those sheets are very nearly clean. They'd just come in from the laundress two days before."

"I'm not worried about that, Quincy. I've been very comfortable, considering."

"Not such a bad place after all? Not quite a 'pathetic little box of a closet at the top of the stairs'?"

"It's very nice." And his voice was almost too quiet. "I like hearing the sounds of Gainsford Street through the window. I like how quiet it goes after six o'clock."

Quincy looked towards the dark window. "After six, I can hear a single person walking the street because of how the sounds echo off the buildings."

"Yes." His swollen face shifted. "I like it."

"I like it, too."

"Thank you, for letting me stay here."

"Peacock House would be far more comfortable, I'm sure."

"But—" Arch closed his eyes, as if it helped him focus on the words he was about to say. "You wouldn't be there, and I'd worry about you."

Quincy's lungs hovered for a moment, and it was all she could do to not breathe in too loudly.

"Do you mind if it takes me a few days to get back on my feet?" Arch continued. "I don't yet feel ready to do my work."

The absurdity. Quincy wouldn't let him near his work until he was significantly better. "The Q survived before you became an employee, Arch."

"I like to think of myself as indispensible."

"No one is," Quincy grumbled, for the first time not feeling it was true.

Arch smiled, and it looked rakish for the bruising on his face and the slight rumple of his hair. "I still like to think I am."

"Are we going to talk about what happened?"

The lines of his mouth turned down. "Tomorrow. I'm quite tired." When he said tired, his hand moved to Quincy's, where she had absently rested it on the corner of the bed. He wrapped his fingers around her own, catching the cuff of her jacket in the tangle, and then closed his eyes, falling to sleep with his hand around hers.

CHAPTER THIRTY-NINE:
I Don't Care, I Really Don't

Quincy woke, her neck stiff from sleeping in the chair. Her hand was once again her own, his resting nearby. Arch would probably not wake soon. It was still dark. But Quincy could hear the noise from the presses coming up the stairs, so she wiped her eyes with the heel of her palm, stood so as to not make any noise, and left the matchbox and Arch to their sleep.

Jade was whistling as the final load of *The Q* was being carried out the back door and set atop the wagons. They were in the final dregs of the mad night's workload, and Quincy expected both Spense and Jade to be exhausted from the events of the last two days. Spense looked it—worn, all yawns and blinks—but Jade was fresh and lively.

"What are you so happy about?" Quincy asked, pinning Jade's happiness into place, like a bug, so it couldn't move too much, couldn't crawl about on her tired skin.

"I can't help it." Jade pulled the alley door closed then wiped her hands on her apron. "I told myself I wouldn't say anything, but now that Arch isn't in so much danger, I can enjoy my secret to its fullest drop."

"Do I even want to know what you're talking about?"

"You. And Arch," Jade answered matter-of-factly. "The other night, I went into the sorter to see if there were any un-gathered slips—there had been a mislaid stack of Qs the night before."

"And?"

"And I saw you! Quincy St. Claire. You were dancing with Arch. *Dancing*. I could hear him counting the rhythm and couldn't help but peek through into the front office."

Quincy felt the back of her neck tingle from embarrassment, but instead of scowling, she gave Jade a hard smile. "It was part of a wager. He still has to pay up."

Jade shook her head and leaned with one hand against the press, the other hand resting on her waist. "I don't care how you came to be dancing, Quincy. I really don't. But when I saw the two of you and the look on his face, I was ready to die a happy death. Bury me now, for life could not get better, nor more surprising."

"What do you mean 'the look on his face'?"

"Quincy!" Spense's voice cut across their conversation. "Can I ask you a question?"

"We're not finished," Jade said over her shoulder as Quincy escaped to Spense.

After sorting through a scheduling error with Spense, Quincy avoided Jade and slipped back up the print room's stairs. In the sorter, she paused, folding her arms, pacing the long room, trying to make the nervous pain in her stomach go away.

She didn't want anyone to talk about it.

She didn't want to think about it.

CHAPTER FORTY:

Father v. Son

The following day, Lord Arch called what felt to Quincy like a war council. Dr. Tremmle had just dismissed himself, declaring that Arch shouldn't be moved until Tremmle could be certain there was no internal bleeding.

"I don't take chances," Tremmle said, waving a finger at Arch to emphasize his medical expertise.

Arch looked a picture. For, though the swelling on his face was beginning to go down, the bruising had taken on an even bigger life of its own: black and green, with purple rivaling the dark of his eyes. His left eye was still mostly closed. Earlier, when Quincy had delivered the early morning *Times* to his sickbed, informing Arch that Priest had revealed his identity to all of Rhysdon, Arch had closed his right eye with a sigh, the angled cut on his cheek pulling against the act.

"I want to know," Lord Arch said after the doctor had left, "who was behind this."

"Who would have reason to be angry, James?" Mary said softly.

"The smuggler you mentioned?" Lord Arch asked.

"It wasn't Crow," Quincy said from atop her perch on the bureau. "He wouldn't have settled a score like that."

"Dear me," Mary said, obviously finding Quincy's friendship with a smuggler appalling.

"It wasn't Crow," Arch confirmed quietly.

Lord Arch shifted in his chair and lifted a finger to his lips. "You know who it was?"

"Yes."

"Who?" Mary asked, her wide eyes defensive.

Arch did not want to say, that was clear water to Quincy, but his father's gaze pressed it out of him. "The crown prince wasn't pleased I called him out publicly. He sent some diplomats, as he called them."

Lord Arch stood so fast his chair slid across Quincy's wood floor with an awful sound.

"It's true," Quincy said, looking directly at Arch. "I found this where you'd been left." She reached into her pocket and brought out the folded page with the essay.

Lord Arch stepped over and snatched it from Quincy's hand. After scanning the page, both the essay and the new additions, he looked up, angry. "Ladies, could I please speak to James alone?"

Quincy tapped one foot then the other once against the wood of the bureau and then slid to the floor. Mary had risen and was looking now from her father to her brother.

"Come on, Mary," Quincy said. "I'll put you to work. Someone in your family has to earn your brother's salary."

She could hear Arch giving a pained laugh as she closed the door behind them.

The yelling in the matchbox began soon into the private interview and continued in fifteen-minute intervals. While customers were helped by Quincy or Mary—who was so pleasant that she often pulled an extra question from them—they could all hear an occasional shout and then a weak rebuttal rattling down the stairwell.

"My solicitor has been dealing with some illegal activity," Quincy would say as she efficiently helped customers and sent them on their way.

During a break—both in the stream of customers and the yelling—Mary returned from the sorter with the empty Q basket and gave

Quincy a satisfied smile. "There is so much happening here. The sorter, the maps on the walls of the print room, the routes, the machines, the mice just coming in; I'm understanding why you throw yourself into your work the way you do and why it's all-consuming. How could it not be?"

Quincy felt more enthusiasm at Mary's comment than she meant to. "I should thank you for listing my passion as an asset rather than an emotional liability. Write what you just said down for your brother to see."

Mary smiled. "I'm going to have to convince James to convalesce longer so that my foray into the world of trade can be extended."

It was not long before Lord Arch descended the stairway, unhappy. "He thinks he can do anything, with no consequences. Mary, James is resting, and we best be going before I send the boy to his permanent rest."

Mary's cheeks tinged with pink, and she looked towards the stairs. "I—"

"St. Claire is here. She has already said she would take care of him." "I will," Quincy said.

"But are you sure there is enough food? And what if he needs—"

"Leaving Arch at The Q isn't like leaving him in the Himalayas," Quincy said, her eyes rolling. "You've brought enough food for a small army, and I'll see that he eats and is comfortable. Spense can help Arch with anything else he needs."

This thought seemed to appease Mary. "I will be back in the morning. We mustn't derail your work too much, Miss St. Claire."

Not long after Lord Arch and Mary left, it was time for Quincy to close up the offices of The Q. After a cursory visit to the print room, to ensure that Jade, Spense, and the staff had everything in hand, Quincy found herself knocking quietly on her own matchbox door.

"I'm awake," Arch said, and Quincy pushed the door open. "And alive, despite the verbal beating I just endured."

He was changed into a fresh nightshirt Mary had brought and was propped up on Quincy's pillow. From what she could tell, he had not been asleep but, rather, thinking. Had his face not been so battered, she would probably have seen lines around his eyes.

"Your father said you were asleep."

"I pretended to be tired so he would leave."

"Are you hungry? I promised Mary I'd feed you. She doubts my ability to take care of the wounded. I also suspect she thinks The Q is riddled with mice, but she's not said it aloud."

Arch shifted and then grimaced before saying, "Anyone who can tuck their friend's fingers into a pocket with the intent to sew them back on later can heat up a bowl of soup."

Quincy wrinkled her nose. "Why would you have paired those two images? Really, Arch. I've lost my appetite. One would think *you* had grown up in the street."

Arch laughed, and Quincy set about heating up the soup. She did so in silence, feeling the strangeness of Arch watching her in such a domestic task. When it was heated sufficiently, Quincy poured it into two tin cups and served them without ceremony.

"I am afraid I keep things simple in the matchbox. No fine china or anything."

"I'm quite partial to the rituals of this matchbox of yours. I might commandeer the place and send you back to Peacock House, where the cook can fatten you up."

Quincy handed Arch his soup and sat on the side of the bed, facing him. "I have too much work for a commute."

She could see that Arch was tired, that it was difficult for him to lift the cup to his mouth. "Let me help you," Quincy said with the impersonal tone of business. Setting her own soup aside, she took the cup from Arch's hand and lifted it for him to drink.

It was a slow process and felt so vastly personal that Quincy thought perhaps Mary was right. Each time Quincy's fingers brushed against Arch's jaw, now two days past a shave, she wanted to think of an excuse to leave before she disappeared into it. Touching him felt painful. It felt like someone had opened an endless cavern they had no willingness to fill. It brought back the emotions she had felt after they had waltzed—the stupid waltz that had kept Arch late, that had led to him being beaten—it was the feeling of being at sea with no anchor.

"Are you alright?" Arch asked, interrupting Quincy's thoughts.

She started, spilling the last of his soup onto her hand. "Yes," she answered, cleaning her spill with a rag. "Are you finished?"

"Yes, thank you. I've been trying to feed myself all day, and it was too painful, but I didn't want to admit to Mary how much it hurt. I'm afraid they have broken my ribs."

"Bastards," Quincy muttered.

His eyes shot to hers quickly. Of course it was a word no young women of his acquaintance would ever say. She paired a cringe with a dismissive half shrug. Arch simply watched her with a warm expression.

Quincy tapped the toe of her boot against the floor.

"I'm sorry, but can you help me lie down?" Arch asked, and the question struck an odd humor in Quincy.

She laughed, so tired she couldn't help it. "Yes."

Quincy didn't really help shift him as much as give him something to hold on to as he forced himself away from the pillow. Quincy readjusted the bedding beneath his head, and he thanked her as she sat down next to him again.

"You've not yet told me what happened," Quincy said, aware of his weight pressing against the mattress beside her.

"I was leaving Gainsford Street, when they grabbed me, dragging me down Queen's and into the alley."

"How many?"

"Three, a fourth keeping watch on the street."

"And you fought back?" Quincy indicated the deep red marks across his knuckles.

This made Arch smile, and he lifted a hand to the bruise on his jaw. "I got a few punches in before they had me down."

Quincy made a noise that sounded suspicious. Fighting was not something she could see on the résumé of James A. Arch. "It looks like they bashed your knee with a rod or a pipe and kicked your ribs a time or two."

"The rod took me down. I couldn't say when I lost consciousness."

"And the knife cut?"

"I can't remember."

Quincy wanted to swear again, but she refrained. She looked down. "I'm sorry."

"Don't be, Quincy. It wasn't anything to do with you."

Yet, she was the reason he had stayed so late. "You scared me, Arch. The blood was dried and sticky; your face, pale as death—"

"He wanted to frighten me is all; the thugs took it too far."

Quincy looked up and met his eyes. "Are you frightened?"

As best he could, Arch gave her a steeled smile. "Not enough to make me stop."

CHAPTER FORTY-ONE:
Why Not, Indeed

Under Dr. Tremmle's directive, Arch stayed three more days at The Q. Mary came each morning—bringing Arch a fresh nightshirt and his shaving paraphernalia—and Quincy worked feverishly to accomplish her work. For as soon as the offices had closed and Mary had gone home for the evening, Quincy found herself upstairs, asking Arch if there was anything he needed, and ended up sitting on the end of the bed, discussing things Quincy had never bothered discussing with anyone. She even played the violin for him.

"You play the violin with such evident love of the music," Arch said. "Why don't you attend the symphonies?"

"Sitting in a booth with too much perfume and the endless sounds of women's fans is not how I like to consume my music."

"Rent your own booth." Arch spread his hands. "Rent your own theater, for heaven's sake, you've got the capital."

"I wouldn't know who was worth seeing."

"That's simple enough—I would. Next time a musician of any note comes to Rhysdon, I'll take you."

"I thought you never wanted to sit through another performance with me again?" Quincy said, resting her violin on her knee, calling to his mind the disastrous night at the opera.

"That was the opera." Arch grinned, his eyes lingering on her face.

He then began coughing, a side profit from his night on the street. His lungs had had a bad reaction. Quincy waited it out, and offered him a cup of water when he finished, unwilling, or perhaps unable, to verbalize how hard it was to watch him in pain.

———

The next evening, Arch asked about the foundling factories, and she told him. He asked her about Fisher and loneliness. He asked about her mother, and she told him.

"I only remember her trembling as she tried to light a candle so she could sew through the night." Quincy lifted a shoulder. "It was always cold, and there was never enough money for food and coal. Some days we ate; some days we kept a stove. I suppose she must have weighed which one would help us sleep easier each night. God knows what she died from. She hadn't moved come morning, and I tried to wake her, but her face was hard, her hands stiff and frightening. I took Marie, went begging for bread, and never went back to the room we were renting on the back of the milliner's shop. I don't know who found her," Quincy admitted with guilt, "nor how long it took."

In the dim light of the matchbox, Arch's eyes looked like night layered inside a wider, deeper darkness, giving him a nocturnal aspect wholly unsuitable for someone who resided in Regent Square.

He looked at Quincy for a long while before saying, "And what did you feel for your mother, Quincy St. Claire?"

Quincy looked up at the ceiling and reached into the farthest corner of her mental file room. What did she feel for her mother? A fierce defensiveness. A confusing resentment. An all-encompassing sorrow that she had not known how to understand her mother's life or her death. A heavy taint of shame, for not having had the courage to return to the still room shrouding the even stiller corpse. A wish that she had not delivered her sister to the same cold fate.

"She was too big for me—to bury, I mean. I couldn't comprehend how I could solve that problem before me, but leaving her was an ultimate betrayal. I swore with a streeter's wish that nothing would ever be too big for me again. For years, I believed she must have woken after I'd left and wondered where we had gone."

"But she had died."

"Yes, but your Lazarus came forth." Quincy looked down. "Why not her?"

"Why not, indeed," he answered softly.

"And then," Quincy continued, more for herself than for him, "when Ezekiel found me, I gave everything I could to The Q, and her ghost finally left."

"You found something big enough to force the pain out."

Quincy's lips parted, and she looked up at him. His battered face seemed to hold two emotions: concern and something Quincy could not understand. Shifting, Arch pulled himself up and reached for her hand, his other hand wrapping around Quincy's forearm, pulling her toward him.

Quincy shivered involuntarily but moved closer, feeling his hand move from her arm to her waist as she drew near. She leaned towards Arch and kissed him. It was simple, spare, her lips on his then gone, but Quincy was trembling when she pulled away, unwilling to look at anything but the visible pulsing beneath the skin of his neck. His hand was on the side of her face now, and he kissed Quincy again, longer, less simply. It frightened her how endless her own pain felt beneath his fingers. The sounds of the presses in the print room underpinned the moment. And, when Quincy pulled slightly away from Arch, she felt her own blood pulsing with the same power of the machines below.

"Quincy St. Claire," Arch whispered, both his hands now on her face, his forehead pressed against hers, his eyes closed. "Please give room for me."

He kissed her again, a patient expression, and then let go.

———

Arch returned home the following afternoon. She was at the offices of Hewitt, Hewitt and Hewitt when he left. Although knowing he would think otherwise, Quincy had meant to be at The Q when Arch left, but Mary must have seen Arch to the carriage too quickly, taking him home to Peacock House with all its respectabilities. Quincy didn't know if he had waited to say good-bye, but when she came back, she found only a hastily written note.

Quincy St. Claire,

You have given me much to think about during my long days away from The Q. Thank you.

Your faithful solicitor, and bludgeoned admirer,

- James A. Arch

Quincy folded the note and tucked it inside the interior pocket of her jacket. Mrs. Graves had been watching the front desk, so Quincy sent Graves into the sorter, reclaiming her own stool and helping the steady stream of customers that came in while she reviewed the latest numbers from Paris. Once closing time came, Quincy slipped down into the print room, discussed the current issue of *The Q*, and then disappeared out back.

The alley was quiet, dark, hovering in stillness. But Quincy walked it twice and then returned to the front counter, wishing she had seen Arch and been able to say good-bye.

CHAPTER FORTY-TWO:

December

Arch did not come back to The Q for a week. After so many years alone in the matchbox, Quincy laughed at herself for feeling lonely there and berated herself for the distraction. She looked up at the list she had pinned above her bed, a lopsided reaction around her heart as she looked at numbers nine through eleven.

1. *Butterfly*
2. *Accidental Arson*
3. *Tea (Fothergil)*
4. *Opera (Arch, unwillingly)*
5. *Apology (Arch)*
6. *Friend (Arch)*
7. *Violin (Lord Arch)*
8. *Jack-o'-lantern*
9. *Procuring Flowers*
10. *Sitting For An Hour in The Park*
11. *Missed a Meeting with The Board*
12.

Arch had written the last three once Quincy had been certain his mind wasn't addled by the attack.

"You have but one requirement remaining, Quincy, and then The Q is yours," he had smiled. "I knew you would do it."

It was strange for Quincy to realize how far the requirements had felt since Arch had been hurt. Now she stared at his elegant handwriting and wondered what it would finally take to secure The Q. Arch had told her he would make certain she would finish on time, and Quincy was inclined to believe him. Quincy was also inclined to cover her face whenever she thought about him touching her, wondering if he now wished he hadn't, wondering if she now wished he hadn't.

Quincy didn't know if the delay in his return was due to the orders of Dr. Tremmle, Lord Arch, or Mary, but when Arch did come back, she could tell the days as an invalid in Peacock House had been wearing on him. He took to his office as if it were the first room containing air that he had seen in days.

He smiled at Quincy and uttered his relief at being back, "Busy, with more purpose than keeping my sister happy."

They didn't speak of the kiss, but Quincy thought Arch moved differently around her, as if he always knew where she was without having to see her. It was like watching the mice before the type cases, their fingers knowing exactly what they were reaching for.

Quincy herself had thought of Arch so much during the past week, she had left some work undone, and for the first time in ten years since coming to The Q, she felt there might now be another thing that she was reaching for. As foreign as the feeling was, Quincy found herself daring to hope he meant what he had said to her—about giving a place for him.

Arch still looked the worse for his injury's wear, and the cane he now sported did little to ease the pain of his battered knee when he moved about. Yet, when Quincy was leaving for a meeting uptown, Arch insisted on going with her.

"Arch, you can hardly walk. I saw you hobble into the office this morning."

Arch held up his cane: a sleek, black ebony affair. "That's what this modern contraption is for."

But Quincy knew what had been done to his knee, and she didn't think he should be walking on it. "You'll slow me down," she said.

"Maybe that's the last requirement," Arch said, grimacing as he stood, his body still sore. "Now, we can leave ten minutes earlier, and you will still arrive on time. If it's bothering me too much, we can call a hansom."

"When Mary serves my head up on a plate because you've made yourself worse, remember it was all your fault."

"Mary has nothing to do with my work decisions," Arch scowled as he went through the arduous process of getting onto his feet. "Let's keep my family out of this."

"I take it your father has been after you about the essays?" Quincy said when they were on the street.

"Yes," Arch replied, his face drawn as he limped. "I apologize for being snappish to you in the offices."

"Were you?" Quincy tucked her hands into her coat pockets. It was a cold day. "I hadn't noticed."

The corner of his mouth curved. "Because it's your natural habitat?"

"I can see I've become a bad influence on you," she said virtuously.

A gang of schoolboys, let loose on the city streets, burst around Quincy and Arch like a whirlwind, one slamming into Arch, who grunted. Quincy reached out and steadied him.

Without a pardon, the boys scattered in their laughter. Quincy recognized one of her Q boys among the assailants but didn't comment, pretending instead she hadn't noticed him. It had been careless but an accident nonetheless. Children—with the exception of a lazy Q boy— were given Quincy's patience. She remembered too acutely what it was like to be one of them, in a world full of adults unable to see past their own lives.

Arch wrapped his hand around hers tightly and was grim faced, a shimmer of sweat appearing just beneath the brim of his hat.

"This is ridiculous," Quincy muttered. "I'm calling a hansom. How can you expect to make it uptown if you can scarcely walk?"

"I don't need you as my nursemaid, Quincy," Arch stated, forcing every tone but politeness from his voice, even as his fingers dug into her hand from the pain.

"I'm not. I'm being practical." As Quincy spoke, she grabbed his wrist with her free hand, for Arch had begun to sway.

"Thank you," he said, wincing.

"The Q can pay for a hansom, and you can give your knee time to heal properly. Having a permanent invalid for a solicitor won't benefit me in the years to come."

"Do you really mean that?" he asked, his eyes still closed. "Cats, this hurts."

"Of course The Q will pay for the hansom. You don't imagine that I would?"

"No." Arch let a half laugh slip through his pain. "I mean, that you intend to keep me around beyond this year?"

"Why ever wouldn't I? You've just started to become useful."

He looked at her. "I've just started bringing you breakfast every morning, you mean."

If he weren't already injured, Quincy would have kicked him.

"If you can be smart, you can hold onto your cane while I hail a hansom." But Quincy let go of his hand carefully, making sure Arch had his balance before she walked to the edge of the sidewalk. It took a few minutes, but then an available hansom pulled over, and Quincy helped Arch into the cab.

The driver took them to the Fontblanc building, near the Upper Rhysdon Cathedral.

"You can go sit with Lazarus while I'm in my meeting," Quincy said.

After Quincy crossed the street, she watched Arch limp towards the cathedral, stopping to buy the day's editions of *The Times* and *The Sun*. Knowing Arch would have something to take his mind off the pain, Quincy entered the building. She could still feel the pressure of his hand in hers.

———

When Quincy finished her meeting, she had anticipated finding Arch sitting calmly on a pew inside the cathedral. She was not expecting to find an incensed solicitor pacing haltingly along the sidewalk, mumbling beneath his breath. He looked far more upset now than he had that morning.

"Arch?" Quincy came to a stop next to the distracted solicitor.

"Can you believe some people?" He waved *The Sun* at Quincy as if it meant something.

"What?"

"Read it." He waved it at her face again then proceeded to explain the content without giving her the paper. "There's a critic, a fellow who usually writes snide articles in the society column of *The Sun* or reviews the most popular entertainment. He's going after my essays only because it's me. 'A petty prince of manners, amusing himself with the poor,' he says. 'A silk-made dandy, who must certainly hire out for coherent thought, as he has none himself.' 'A boy pushing religion and conscience like a country doctor with his eye set on a profit and a warm dinner.' Oh, yes, and here's the favorite: 'of all the afflictions brought down on man, it is the preacher, whose words and ideals are forced into your consciousness, that is the most intolerable. Leave preaching for the churches; better yet, leave preaching alone entirely. We do not want it, and we do not need it.'" Arch crumpled the paper and tossed it to the ground. "There's more, if you wish to join in the ridicule."

Quincy was more concerned for Arch's knee than for his ego, but she understood his ire.

"I refuse, Quincy." He cut his hand through the air. "I refuse to be silent when I know of an injustice and am in a position to make it known. Enough preaching? Not wanted? Not needed?" He motioned towards Quincy. "I say: Preach! Preach! If you know of a higher ideal, if you see a better way for mankind to exist, then preach! Don't sit quietly by because of your own imperfections! What happens when a set of imperfect people spend their time talking about becoming better? Chances are one or two of them might actually choose to become better. Unless we buy the hedonistic drivel of the day, what keeps us from it? Are we so scared of failing? We're human! We fail. We fall."

He looked at the cathedral, and added emphatically, "We sin. And yet something calls us towards perfection. Do you know why? Because we're good for it. We have the capacity to examine our lives and improve, to change. But we can't do it just on our own. So, preach. Don't you want it?" he asked fiercely. "I do! And I'm not going to let a self-indulgent critic, who is more concerned about popularity and amusement than humanity and improvement, derail my course. I will preach, dammit, and I will improve my own character with the same determination, so help me God."

He paused now, breathing hard, leaning on his cane, his face glistening. Passersby glanced in their direction and then continued to move around them. As much as Quincy had learned that Arch was willing to speak up and speak out, his external shows of loud anger were still rare enough that it was like watching a comet burn against the sky, and she couldn't keep her eyes from his face.

When he motioned, inviting her to respond, Quincy gave a matter-of-fact lift of her shoulder. "Don't listen, then. Write your essays. Publish. No sense in being small because someone else doesn't have the courage to measure up."

For a moment, she thought Arch hadn't heard her, that he was still twisted up in his own righteous indignation, but then he smiled, laughed at himself, and tilted his head, the brim of his hat casting a shadow across his face.

"Thank you."

"For what?"

"For listening to my—*preaching.*"

"I've been doing that for a year now," she said. But her expression was set in pride, and she gave him an encouraging nod before turning towards the street to hail a hansom.

CHAPTER FORTY-THREE:

Cats and Kings

When the next several days passed without either of them mentioning what had taken place the night before Arch had left the matchbox, Quincy felt foolish for having spent time thinking about it.

On the ninth of December, he arrived at The Q in time for the offices to open, but no sooner. Blame couldn't be placed on Arch for not upholding their newfound routine, Quincy reminded herself, for he could hardly move himself along the sidewalk, let alone carry a box of breakfast pastries. But this change gave Quincy something to feel frustration with, however unjustified.

As painful as it was, Quincy found herself being curt and sharp the few times when Arch asked her a question. He had given her an odd expression in return, staring at her as if someone had moved the type cases to the side; as if Arch kept finding an X when he had expected a Q.

After that, Quincy made an effort to speak with the same comfortable banter they had established the last several months, but it wasn't comfortable. Arch, in turn, relied on humor and cajolery to absorb the strangeness.

He explained that he would need to take an hour to visit the tailor.

"I have my final fitting for the Fothergils' ball."

"You're not going, are you?"

"Of course I'm still attending the Fothergils' ball." Arch scowled at the obviousness of her question, swinging his cane in a confident way to underscore his words as he sat on his stool across the counter from Quincy.

The cane had become an elegant extension of himself, and he used it with such nonchalance that Quincy was worried he might start something among the upper class—that all the young, idiotic aristocrats with nothing to do would soon be walking the streets with canes, and moving about Rhysdon would prove more difficult for everyone else.

"You can't dance," she said meanly.

Arch sighed. "Clearly, but my friends will be there, and it's not an event I care to miss. By any means, I would have thought your interest piqued, Quincy, as *everyone* is going to be there."

"Your point, Arch?"

"I was hoping you would see my trail and follow it for yourself," Arch said. "It serves me right, when I know you're so literally minded. My point is that everyone in Rhysdon will be there, including the crown prince."

Quincy stopped, the blood in her veins waiting a full count before moving on. "The crown prince? The scoundrel who sent fists after your once handsome face? I'd like to take my fist to his, but I fear it would make an improvement."

Arch gave Quincy a lopsided smile. "You think I'm handsome?"

"You were," Quincy retorted, "but now I think your nose is a little crooked."

"My nose is perfect."

Quincy rolled her eyes. Aristocrats. "What are you going to say to him?"

"Nothing."

"Nothing? I don't believe you."

"Come with me to the ball, and see for yourself. I had thought you would want to be an extra brace of intimidation at my side."

"You think I could intimidate the heir to the throne?" Quincy snorted and tapped the edge of her pencil on the counter.

"I think you could intimidate anyone you wanted to."

"Except you, apparently."

"Mostly true." Arch twisted his fingers around a string he plucked from the edge of his jacket. "I've given myself permission to see you as human, a vast improvement. When I look at you now—" He paused, suddenly becoming preoccupied with wrapping the string perfectly around his finger. "Come with me. I will fetch you myself, and we can have a pleasant drive to the wolf's den together."

"Does Lady Fothergil know it was the crown prince behind the beating?"

Arch winced, but not from pain. "I prefer to think of it as a fight. Three against one, and I gave one of them a broken nose."

"Until I see a set of three for-hire beats limping about Rhysdon together, I'm calling it a beating."

"You're so cruel."

"You didn't answer my question."

"Yes, Lady Fothergil knows. My father let it slip. I find it all rather irritating."

Quincy grinned. "I like your father."

"Which I find strange," Arch lifted his cane, "for he's far more different from you than I am."

"You think you're like me?" Quincy countered with a snort.

"Only your very best qualities."

"Ha!"

"Also, I have a sneaking suspicion that Lady Fothergil means to seat me directly across from the crown prince at dinner."

Quincy looked at Arch, her curiosity roused. With the swelling gone, his handsome face was again balanced by his cheekbones. His nose, by some miracle, wasn't crooked. And the cut beneath his right eye gave him a jaunty look of confidence to go with the deep bruising still under his left. He looked calculating and dangerous.

"And what are you going to do—to the crown prince, I mean?"

"Me?" Arch, in an instant, managed to look cherubic despite the bruising. "Nothing. Fothergil is the one for the games."

"What do you mean you aren't going to do anything?" Quincy

challenged. "You write social essays to change the world, Arch! Don't tell me you mean to do nothing?"

"I will do something," Arch said, now watching the end of his cane as he let it hover above the ground. "I intend to keep writing my essays for the improvement of Rhysdon."

"But to the prince?"

"To the prince, I intend to turn the other cheek."

"What?" The word flew so fast from Quincy's mouth that Arch flinched.

"What would you have me do, Quincy?" Arch asked, leveling his gaze in earnest question. "Would you have me humiliate him? Would you have me play his games and catch his ire again? Or, would you rather have me use my time and energies calling out greater injustice when I see it? There are too many other words to write for me to settle a score of one. I owe my energies to more than just myself."

"Then you let injustice win!"

"No, I will still address the problems of state and the abuses of power, but in the right way and for the right motivations," Arch answered. "I will serve the good of more than just myself. If I reduce myself to fighting his petty game, I'll have given up my moral position in a grander battle. Besides, I don't just look at the stories depicted in the windows of Rhysdon Cathedral, I believe them. I will cry truth as I see it, and truth will out."

Quincy felt a flash of anger at Arch—and for Arch. Her eyes stung, and she mumbled against his stupid ideals as she pretended to be absorbed in the work before her.

"That being said," Arch added, "I believe half of Rhysdon will be watching our interactions. You blood thirsty set should have plenty of amusement, I'm sure."

Quincy looked up to see Arch in the middle of a puckish smile, and her curiosity overrode her pride. "Fine. Then I suppose I'll have to come. Someone will need to tell the crown prince off if you won't do it yourself."

His smile deepened. "Good." He began to change his tone and, therefore, the line of conversation with great effort. "I was hoping you would still come, as I've already asked Lady Fothergil if she would pair us."

Quincy didn't understand what he meant, and her face reacted before she could. "Pair us?"

"Would you rather be paired with someone else, sit beside someone else at dinner?"

"Well, no," Quincy admitted.

"I thought not. Also, would you like to be seen as an eligible debutante of sorts, waiting for the unmarried men to pay their attentions?"

"What are you talking about?" Quincy wrinkled her nose. "I've never even heard that word."

Arch shook his head and moved his hand towards hers, stopping short of actually touching. "In case you haven't noticed, Quincy St. Claire, you are very intelligent, interesting, and beautiful. Lord Ashford has publicly declared you his muse, and the aristocracy, usually so snide about those in trade, has gained great interest in you. Probably," one side of his mouth lifted in a smile, "because you are oblivious to their social dynamics and have never been seen as a vine climber. As my dear godmother, Lady Fothergil, would say, you've caught the imagination of the *ton*, and, when one catches the imagination of the *ton*, one receives attention. So—" Arch paused for a breath, and Quincy realized how fast he had been speaking. "I asked Fothergil to pair us, formally and informally, to make it seem we are a sort of couple and force the admirers to keep their distance." He was not looking at Quincy now but rather focusing on the end of his cane.

Quincy felt an astounding combination of embarrassment and, well, an uncertain rage. A handful of kisses, not spoken of since his return, did not a pair make, and she disliked his presumption. "I'm quite capable of taking care of myself, Arch," she said icily.

"Blast it, Quincy. Do you think I don't know that?" Arch lifted his eyes to hers, his eyebrows furrowing. "Do you think I don't realize that you don't need anybody or anything? Even if it appeared a week ago that you felt different than you obviously do now!"

"I—"

"Is it good for you?" Arch continued, hitting the floor lightly with his cane, releasing his own frustrations over her silence on the matter of their kiss. "No. Do I wish you would stop treating human intimacy as the plague? Yes. Do I wish that you would realize that I'm being selfish in wishing you paired with me at the ball? Yes. I am being selfish, Quincy, and I want to be with you because I *want* to be with you. But don't you dare think for one moment I don't consider you the most capable person of my acquaintance."

"I—" Quincy halted, looking away as she pulled at the end of her hair just above her ear. Quincy wanted to say he wasn't quite being fair, but when she looked at Arch, he had a strange expression on his face. "We haven't even— Have you once thought about," she hit the end of her pencil against the desk, "what happened?"

Arch gave her an exasperated smile. "It's all I've been thinking about."

"I thought you had forgotten."

"Forgotten? Forgotten that? You're the most difficult person I know," he said with a self-conscious laugh, ungenerously and deservedly.

Quincy flushed. "There is no law that says you have to put up with me."

"But don't you see what I'm trying to get at?" Arch pulled his mouth down. "You're so astute in business. You catch every detail. Yet you don't, or you pretend you don't—" He paused, turning on his stool until his shoulders were squared up with hers. "I am going to say something I may endlessly regret."

Then don't say it, Quincy wanted to shout. Instead, she sank down between her shoulders and waited, her elbows resting solidly on the counter.

"You are someone I want in my life, and—"

"I am," Quincy pressed her fingernail into the wood of the counter. "We work in the same office."

"You—" he pointed a finger at her, looking like he would throttle her where she sat. "You are going to either kill me or turn me into a saint. Cats and kings, Quincy!"

Quincy was tempted to tell him she had renewed her vow of human isolation. For whenever you dragged people into anything it became unclear. The lines moved. Sometimes daily.

But Arch had become more to Quincy than she had imagined possible, so she tried to understand, worrying full well she already did. "I'm sorry. What are you trying to say?"

"That at the Fothergils' ball, I *want* you to be paired with me. I want people to see you and me as—" He began to laugh. "You know what people are saying about me since Priest revealed me as Specter?"

Quincy thought the question odd and out of context, but she lifted a shoulder and waited.

"They've been calling me the most articulate man in Rhysdon: absolutely untrue, but encouraging. Yet, within a matter of minutes, you can dismantle all my language so I don't make any intelligent sense. Let us just leave the conversation where it now stands. Does that sound agreeable?" He seemed to be asking himself this question as much as he was asking Quincy. "I'm determined to have a good night at the Fothergils' tomorrow, and you have said you will come with me. Shall we just leave it at that?"

"What else have we been talking about?" Quincy asked, sincerely wanting to understand exactly what Arch was trying to say.

But Arch took it as some kind of joke at his expense and said, "Exactly my point."

Quincy felt herself blush and looked down. She didn't know how to do this, any of this.

"Seeing as tomorrow is Saturday," Arch continued, "I won't be in the office, but I'll be by in the evening, to pick you up. Nine o'clock?"

"Yes, of course," Quincy replied, feeling foolish for the whole botched conversation.

Arch nodded, looking uncomfortable but amused. "We will be quite the pair: me, with my blackened eye and newly acquired limp, and you, by just being you."

A thought crossed Quincy's mind, and she panicked. "I'm not wearing a dress."

She didn't even own one.

"I'm not wearing one either," Arch laughed. Then he stood and limped into his office rather elegantly despite the cane.

At six thirty, a hansom arrived to take him home. Quincy was working at the counter as he left.

"Tomorrow, then?" she said.

"Nine o'clock."

"Arch."

"Yes?"

"I really—I'm not sure how to understand any of this, but I don't mind."

He waited.

"I don't mind being paired with you," she said.

Arch looked down, let himself hint at a smile, then raised his eyes to Quincy's. "I don't mind it either."

"Then its settled, I suppose."

Arch looked at her, almost as if he would limp back to the counter, but he stayed at the door, and said instead, "Would you make me a promise?"

"Depends what I'm promising."

"Please don't hound me about confronting the crown prince," Arch answered. Then he opened the door—pain from the effort evident in his face—and added, "Even if he is a bastard."

———

Quincy waited an hour after Arch left before she fled to the print room. The time for self-containment was past, she told herself stoically.

"I need to speak with you, Jade."

"Now?" Jade turned from the block she was setting for *The Q*'s front page. "I'm in the middle of a slug."

"Ask one of the mice to finish," Quincy prodded, rather than ordered, a show of tremendous restraint. Instead of leading Jade back up the stairs and into the front office, Quincy walked the length of the print room and pulled open the door of a closet where they kept the crates of ink, brooms, and whatever Spense couldn't stand sitting about the floor. There were no lights, and so Jade hesitated at the door, then she shrugged and entered. Quincy followed, claiming a place on

THE Q

the floor against the wall. She could see, just as the door was closing behind them, that Jade was leaning against a stack of crates.

"Jack," Quincy said in the dark.

"Jack? You dragged me into a dark closet to tell me what my husband's name is?"

"Tell me about you and Jack."

Silence.

"How did you and Jack become you and Jack?"

A long pause, and then a laugh. "This is about a certain solicitor we both know?"

"This is about you and Jack. I need to know why you decided he was worth your time."

Quincy didn't really mean to phrase it that way, but it was the least vulnerable position she could take, and Quincy was not going to be more vulnerable than she already had been. It was why she had chosen a dark closet—she needed to protect her facial expressions.

"It was during my second year working as a mouse at The Q. I started dropping by a bakery every morning at the end of my shift, and he was one of the apprentices, often up front at the counter during the busy hours. I stopped by four or five times a week, but we never spoke beyond the usual. One morning, I was late because Davies had dropped three cases of type on the floor. Do you remember him?"

Quincy did. She had fired him.

"Anyway, I was late, so he wasn't at the counter. I took my bread and set out just as he was leaving the bakery. We fell into step and began to discuss our work and the city and everything." Jade took a breath. "Do you know in the evening, when the street lamps begin to light all over Rhysdon but the daylight hasn't yet faded, and something in you wishes it could be like that forever? Well, that was how it was being with Jack. Whenever we were walking and discussing or laughing or disagreeing, I felt happy. It was comfortable, and I realized that I liked him better than anyone else I'd ever met. So I began to wait for his shift to end, and we spent nearly every morning together. We lived close enough that it never put either of us out of our way."

Quincy made a noise. Love seemed as much a matter of convenience as anything.

"But," Jade continued, "when he finished his apprenticeship and acquired work at the bakery farther uptown, I was there on his first morning, waiting."

The darkness became the only noise between them, until Quincy let an audible sigh escape. She was worried about something going wrong when she wasn't certain she was comfortable with it going right.

The door to the closet flung open, and Quincy lifted her arm to cover her eyes.

"What the—?"

It was Spense.

Quincy scrambled to her feet and Jade was grinning.

"Important meeting, Spense," Jade said.

Spense pulled his red face to the side and scratched his chin but refrained from asking. "I need some ink," he said at length.

"By all means," Quincy said, moving past him, feeling Jade following on her heels. When Jade started laughing, Quincy was grateful because it made her smile and it dissipated Quincy's nervousness for the evening ahead.

CHAPTER FORTY-FOUR:

The Fothergil Ball

Arch was, as per usual, on time. He descended slowly from the carriage, showing a great deal more pain than he ever did when in front of Quincy. She was watching him from the darkness of the matchbox, perched on the bureau. He said something to his man then disappeared beneath the eaves, letting himself in.

Quincy made a nervous sound and looked at her clothing. She had always made her own small statements in fashion, and tonight was no exception. Quincy was wearing a new ensemble that Favreau, her tailor, had insisted she wear even before Arch had convinced her to go with him. Favreau had heard not only that she had formed an alliance with the house of Fothergil but also that she was invited to the ball. He'd cornered Quincy on her next appointment with the piece already made.

"I'm probably not going," she had said to Favreau.

"I designed it especially for you, and you will wear it," he had stated stiffly. Its jacket was made from black velvet with all the modern lines, yet it was altogether more feminine than anything she had worn. But it was the trousers that had given Quincy pause. They were dark purple, a black ribbon sewn into the outseam, as he had done on her other costumes. They were a statement piece.

"The boots I've had made—" Favreau had said.

"You've ordered me boots?" Quincy complained, eyeing the trousers with a suspicious eye.

"Yes," he sniffed. "Now be quiet, you dreadful girl. They rise up with a heel and feature a sharp toe, with buttons all the way up. None of your schoolgirl laces for the Fothergils' ball. Wear this shirt, with a bit of lace showing out, and I expect you to be the eye-catcher of the entire event."

It was an order, not a favor. Quincy had grumbled about "blood-sucking tailors," and he had shaken his head in uninterested pleasure.

"I expect a report of the ball when you come for the fitting of your new jacket."

"My clothes should last longer than they do," Quincy had grumbled.

Favreau had looked down his nose, which meant he liked her and was about to say something he thought was funny. "Then stay away from ink."

Quincy hadn't laughed.

"Quincy?"

Hearing Arch's voice on the stairs pushed Quincy out of her thoughts.

"One moment." She didn't want Arch waiting at the bottom of the stairs so she waited, listening. Once she heard the door to his office open, Quincy came down, feeling overdressed.

Seeing Arch immediately resolved this issue. He was standing at his desk, leaning on his cane, one hand stretched over the report he was reading soundlessly. She almost didn't recognize him. Had she thought him elegant at the opera, it was nothing compared to his attire now.

Everything about Arch's appearance was perfect, not a hair out of place. His suit was magnificent in every line, deep black, endless black; it matched his eyes. The suit was inventive, while keeping a strong anchor in tradition and class. It set him apart from his surroundings. Favreau had finally outdone himself, and Quincy was glad it had been for Arch.

"There you are," he said, looking up. "Why are you smiling?"

"I'm relieved you won't embarrass me," Quincy lied.

Arch laughed, and Quincy guessed he was very aware he looked perfect, even with the severe bruise still beneath his left eye. "Seeing you, helps this make sense." He held a pocket square between his fingers; it matched the dark purple of Quincy's ensemble. "In my final fitting this morning, I mentioned to Favreau that I would be accompanying you to the Fothergils' ball. He reamed me out for over an hour, saying that we had not "given him the proper consideration," and his apprentice delivered this just before I came to fetch you. You didn't tell me he'd already supplied you an ensemble for the ball."

"What, you wouldn't have begged so hard?"

"I would have begged harder."

Quincy lifted an eyebrow and swept her eyes over Arch's suit. Favreau's creations already looked like they were designed with each other in mind. Where Quincy's was smart in design, Arch's carried a masculine shadow of the same lines; where hers was feminine, his was elegant. Now, with the touch of purple over his heart, they were a complementary set. It made Quincy think of a well-designed font.

"As ever, you look arresting, Quincy St. Claire," Arch said as he came out into the front office. His assured walk—forced, Quincy now knew—made the cane appear a mere decoration for personal style. "Shall we?"

—————————————

The Fothergil mansion in Rhysdon was smaller than their properties in the country, which was to say, roughly the size of the king's favorite palace. Upon their arrival, Quincy realized there were two entire wings she had not even realized existed. Every window was lit, and the grounds were immaculate. Music floated down into the main courtyard, where carriages moved in practiced grace.

"Why are you grinning like a ghost?" Quincy asked Arch, whose eyes were reflecting the torchlight along the drive as he looked towards the mansion.

"Aside from this being one of my favorite evenings of the year? Anticipatory humor, I suppose. Things have been set in motion that I can't stop but that I do expect to play out in the social climate of the evening. It should be amusing."

Quincy said, "What things?"

"Pardon?" He moved his eyes to hers.

"What things have been set in motion?"

Arch let out a quick, humored breath, his eyebrows lifting. "The most powerful creature one can let loose among the elite, Quincy. Someone has given birth to several rumors regarding my invalid state. It will not be a comfortable evening for the crown prince."

"You've gone turncoat rather quickly," said Quincy, leaning back with her arms crossed. "Only last night you were too righteous for retribution."

"Oh, I didn't start the rumors, Quincy. Though, as I've heard variations of what's making the circuit, I find I must be honest with you," Arch said as their carriage finally came to a stop before the grand staircase. The carriage door swung open, and, as Arch descended, he looked over his shoulder and said, "A few of the rumors revolve around you."

"What? Arch!" Quincy scrambled out after him, glaring. "What've you done?"

"Nothing. I told you—I don't peddle rumors," Arch said as he and Quincy walked up the long staircase in the company of the silent servants and flickering lawn torches. "That being said, rumors are more valuable than money among those with significant social power, and the crown prince will find his name on everyone's lips. I didn't encourage it, preferring to enjoy the fullest measure of the evening's entertainments, rather than being the evening's entertainment. But, in case you fear the prince will not receive his comeuppance, this public censure should be enough."

"Ooh, public censure," Quincy said, as if that weren't a flimsy threat.

"One hundred years ago, speaking ill of the prince would have been considered treason."

"And now?" Quincy asked as they came to the marble portico leading up to the open doors of the Fothergil mansion.

"Now, it's simply a demonstration that the crown prince can't silence the people, let alone a family tied so closely with the Fothergils."

"The Kingmakers."

"The family that placed the prince's family on the throne to begin with."

"If the Arches have been so close with the Fothergils," Quincy replied, "I'm surprised you weren't the ones placed on the throne."

Arch tapped the top of his cane with his finger and paused just before entering the grand hall. "They did offer it to us. We didn't want it."

She looked at him sharply. Quincy knew Arch too well to think he was exaggerating. Now, in the contrasting lights, the brightness from the mansion before him, and the darkness of the portico at his back, he looked like he could have been raised a prince.

"Good thing," Quincy said, lifting a shoulder. "You would've made a terrible sovereign."

Arch laughed and shifted towards Quincy, lifting his free hand to her back as they entered. "It wouldn't have given me what I want."

Quincy did not move away, walking near him as they passed through two sets of ornate doors that were flung open. Ahead of them, a duke and a duchess were announced by Fothergils' crier, who then recognized Quincy. Arch fished in the pocket of his fashionable jacket and then handed a card to the man.

The crier, who clearly knew Arch, looked disapproving until Arch gave him a serious nod. Clearing his throat, the crier called the attention of the room and said, "Quincy St. Claire and her solicitor, James Arch."

The sounds of hushed conversation moved in time with the rustle of the women's gowns, a refined sweeping noise, turning towards the door. Arch performed splendidly. The entire room watched as he, cane in hand, led Quincy down the steps with apparent ease. His face was clear, open, and handsome. He nodded to those he knew and gracefully limped towards their hostess, who stood at the far end of the room beside Lord Arch and none other than the crown prince himself.

The prince's lips were full, raspberry pink, complementary to the golden tones of his hair and skin. He glared at Arch with a haughty malice, Arch, on the other hand, only looked more congenial.

"Why is he here so early?" Quincy asked.

"Hmmm?" Arch moved his head towards Quincy's. "Oh, Reggie doesn't enjoy the shadow of his father and always arrives early enough to make his own shining entrance, before the king makes his. We are actually quite late."

"Reggie?"

"Yes, unfortunate, isn't it."

Reggie was watching them approach with a show of amusement. Quincy narrowed her eyes and quirked an eyebrow when the prince looked at her face.

"James!" Lady Fothergil kissed him. "Dear me, what has happened to you?" she exclaimed over the deep bruise under his eye.

"My scribbling has apparently made someone angry," Arch laughed. "But, no matter."

"Hmmm, yes," Lady Fothergil pretended disinterest. "The soonest way to deal with a fly is to swat it and forget it was there. Pay no worry to the matter. Keep scribbling. You know the crown prince, of course." Lady Fothergil motioned gracefully in the direction of Reggie. "I believe you both were at school together."

"Your majesty," Arch said, bowing to a respectable measure.

Quincy noticed Lord Arch pull a disapproving face as he watched the interactions of the prince and his son.

"Arch," the crown prince said, his eyes passing from Arch's face to the cane in his hand. "Starting a new fashion, I see."

"I actually believe this was one you started," Quincy interjected, her arms folded across her chest. Arch made a surprised sound as the golden tone of the prince's face turned purple.

Lady Fothergil looked on dispassionately. "This charming creature," she said, "is the famous Quincy St. Claire of The Q. Miss St. Claire, the crown prince."

"Charmed—" Quincy and the crown prince both spoke simultaneously, and neither sounded like they meant it.

"Do excuse us," Arch said, his expression caught just before a laugh. "There are a number of acquaintances I wish Miss St. Claire to meet, and I do not wish to monopolize either the time of my hostess or that of my sovereign."

"Certainly," the prince said, considering Quincy now with even less apparent interest than he had shown before. "I believe that is how your sort gets by, Miss St. Claire, pleasing your betters so you might steal from their pockets?"

"I couldn't say," Quincy answered. "I haven't yet met anyone I'd consider my better, especially not at a gathering such as this." She then leveled her gaze at the prince. "Obviously excluding your hostess, the Lady Fothergil."

Lord Arch made a surprised noise, but Quincy detected a hint of pleasure beneath his face. Quincy flashed the prince a brilliant smile and turned to follow Arch, who was eagerly leading her away.

"No rules of proper conduct for Quincy St. Claire," Arch said as they moved towards a gathering boasting Johnny Fothergil's company.

"What are the rules, then? Let someone insult you without fighting back?"

"Are you trying to get me beaten again?"

"He wouldn't dare."

As they moved forward, Quincy took time to study the room. It was large, immense, with gilded detailing, cream walls, and blue and ice green complements: a stunning affair that opened up onto a larger ballroom. The dancing there had already begun, from what Quincy could see through the doorways.

"Arch! St. Claire!" Johnny greeted them, lifting up a glass of gold-colored liquid in soundless cheers, and the circle moved apart to include them.

"Fothergil, you know my esteemed superior, Quincy St. Claire. Quincy, let me introduce you to our friends. Here is Lord Beddles. The Earl you know." Scout nodded his head. "Henry Clagent you have met. Here's the incorrigible Wakefield, and this is Lord Tines. Gentlemen, Quincy St. Claire."

This evening could easily prove as uncomfortable as Quincy had feared, her trailing behind Arch as he played society darling. After the round of introductions, she fumbled through a motion she believed would translate into recognition of them all. They were a different breed—comfortable in their family money, handsome expressions so natural on their faces, exquisites about their clothing—all of them. Arch seemed oblivious of Quincy's discomfort.

"We've heard all the rumors, Arch." Wakefield motioned towards the cane. "Now, tell us what this is all really about?"

"Yes, what is this all about?" Lord Tines added, but his gaze was on Quincy. She crossed her arms and settled her weight on her right leg, reminding herself not to glare. He had not, after all, sounded unfriendly.

"Clagent, here, thinks it was the smuggler," Lord Beddles joined in, "while Tines suspects you, dear, placid Arch, of a love affair."

Quincy looked sharply at Arch, wondering if this was where she came into the rumors that were gaining such momentum among the upper class of Rhysdon.

"It has nothing to do with smugglers, nor an illicit affair," Arch said, pulling at his cuff as he smiled.

"And everything to do with a certain set of social essays and a crown prince?" Lord Beddles asked.

Arch did not confirm this, but he gave a reluctant smile, the kind that lies flat, turning up only at the last possible chance.

"Of course it runs in that direction," Quincy said, glaring over her shoulder towards the prince, who was now surrounded by a flock of female admirers. "Look at the fop; no mystery he had to hire four street fists to do his dirty work for him."

Johnny Fothergil nearly lost his drink in a frantic sound between a sputter and a cough, and Lord Beddles laughed. Lord Tines said something rather droll, from the looks of it, but Quincy couldn't hear, as everyone but she and Arch were now laughing.

"So this is a Fothergil ball?" Quincy balked, her voice barbed from feeling self-conscious. "The gentlemen all stand in insipid circles amusing themselves?"

Quincy thought she heard an audible groan from Arch, but it was Lord Tines who answered her. "This, Miss St. Claire, is only the preliminary. The first hour is spent in gathering, gossiping—"

"Drinking," Johnny Fothergil inserted.

"Quite so," Lord Tines rejoined. "We prefer to give the young ladies plenty of time to decide whom they intend to ensnare. Soon, we filter into the ballroom for an hour of dancing, and then dinner is served in stages. Dancing, revelry, games—"

"Gambling—"

"And the occasional clandestine meeting," Tines continued. "It all continues 'til dawn. So, you see, Miss St. Claire, there is a great deal of time for insipid circles before the games are afoot."

"Then it's a good sight that the graced of Rhysdon don't actually work. With a night like that ahead, we're all going to make ourselves useless for three days."

"Quincy," Arch said, but he was laughing.

"One of the graced apparently keeps himself amused with work," Henry Clagent said, motioning towards Arch, his eyes on Quincy.

"Quite so," Lord Tines added with curiosity.

Now Quincy's glare came on in full force.

"That, gentlemen, is our cue to greet the other guests," Arch said, his hand reaching towards Quincy as he smiled at his friends. "See you in the rounds, gentlemen."

"Those are your friends?" Quincy complained once they had begun weaving through the room.

"Have I even once been disparaging about Crow?" Arch asked in a light tone, but his face indicated a stronger emotion.

"No," Quincy admitted. "You let Fisher have that territory."

"And I did some work regarding his more legal activities because he was your friend." Arch slowed to a stop and turned to face Quincy directly. "Will you extend me the same courtesy? This event is important to me. I want to share it with you, but I need you to be amicable. I need you to try—"

"To thrive outside my natural habitat?"

"Yes." Arch grinned, his teeth looking extraordinarily white against all the black in his evening attire.

The light, the music, the heat of the rooms, the crystal, the sound of dresses moving across the floor—none of this belonged to Quincy in any meaningful way. She had spurned the very notion of it, miles away as it was from her typesetters and gears and ledgers and gritty streets conquered by even grittier souls.

"All this really means something to you?"

"Many of the people do," Arch motioned, looking about. "The tradition, the customs; the Fothergils are practically family. She is my godmother, after all."

"Understood, then."

"Understood?"

"I'll try to see what you see, though it's never been a strong suit. Cats, Arch, it's never even been one of my suits at all."

"Thank you," Arch said, and he looked like he meant it. Then he kissed Quincy on the cheek.

All sound stopped, or so Quincy thought, but as they made their way across the floor, Quincy realized it was not the din of the noisy room that had disappeared momentarily, only the heartbeat inside her chest. It did not help matters when he took her hand as they wound towards a group of Mary's friends, Quincy feeling the gait of his limp through his fingers.

It was one thing, Quincy thought, one massively terrifying thing, to kiss Arch in the secrecy of The Q. It was another to know that he still felt the same desire to be with her, to touch her, before everyone of his acquaintance. Instinct, built from years on the street, told Quincy she had never been in more danger than she was now, but hope argued against it. And Quincy was surprised, for she had never been one to invite hope in. It must, she decided as she felt her hand trembling in his, be Arch's fault.

The next hour proved an exercise in all of Quincy's self-control. She did not want—no, she was determined not to let Arch down. He had taken a risk, he had speculated wildly on Quincy St. Claire, and she found herself wishing to come through, to prove herself wrong. The simplest solution, she thought as she and Arch met with endless guests, was to say little or nothing and to avoid breathing in extraordinary amounts of perfume, which Quincy was certain reduced one's intelligence.

This strategy, however, had to be amended each time a direct question was asked. Quincy tried to appear interested in the questions, but her own answer usually came out blunt or nonplussed.

"I'm trying," she whispered to Arch when they had found a respite against the walls of the ballroom, where the early hours of dancing were taking place. "When she asked me why I enjoyed living life pretending to be a man, I couldn't think of anything to say but something to set her off. As if I would ever want to be a man. They are as insufferable as most women. I really did think my response a model of restraint, considering."

Arch closed his eyes with a grimace. "You mean, when you answered that if men were to continue making better use of their time than women, you would continue to dress like a schoolboy and run a business?"

"Had I thought she actually knew anything or did anything worthwhile, I would have refrained from calling out her stupidity," Quincy rebutted. "I run a printshop, Arch, and have no practical use for skirts. Believe me, I've been making a massive effort."

"I know." Arch's shoulder touched hers as he leaned in her direction. "I can see plain as day that you are being monumental. But you keep making judgments about people you know nothing of and responding from those judgments."

Glaring, Quincy snorted. "Says the man who writes essays on the very same thing."

Arch shook his head, moving the drink in his hand in a small, slow circle. "I hope that I wait until I know where the issue stands before I make my opinions known. And, I only call out individuals who hold political or social power and abuse it scandalously. Lady Childs, who you have assumed does, knows, and is nothing, has actually spent most of her life caring for an ailing mother, an addle-minded aunt, and a younger brother, whose gambling habits have caused strain on her social and financial position. She finds the clothing you wear particular and confusing because she's never even thought of what a printshop would be like. If you were to spend one teatime in the woman's presence, you would find her sympathetic, understanding, and loyal."

"Spare me," Quincy replied, but her expression gave concession to Arch's words. "I don't know how you exist as you do. Isn't it exhausting, to think well of so many people?"

"Quite the opposite, Quincy St. Claire," Arch said, a light smile on his face. "I think people are the most worthwhile use of our time, which is why someone like Lady Childs will always have my admiration and encouragement. She has given her life to caring for others and, therefore, has really accomplished something."

"You preach too much."

"Preach back. I can handle it. And, if I'm wrong, I can change."

"I don't want you to change."

A strange expression crossed Arch's face, a mixture of deep satisfaction and mystification. "But what is love if it's not wanting the best for the person you care about?"

"Not love," Quincy said as if she knew anything about it.

"You are trying to change for me tonight, trying to keep your sharp edges away from people, making an effort to act in a way different from the harshness to which you are accustomed, all because you know I would be grateful. How is that any different? I'm not asking you to cease being Quincy St. Claire, but have I not asked you to be a better version of Quincy St. Claire on my behalf this evening?"

Quincy let out a sharp breath and crossed her arms. Two problems had arisen in her mind. First, she wanted to accuse Arch of not taking her as she was. But Quincy knew that he had taken her at her worst and still treated her decently. He had taken her as a mix of good days and difficult days and had managed to maintain his bizarre idea that she was worth having in his life. She could not accuse him of wanting perfection. He was far more accepting of her in reality than she was accepting of any imperfection or human flaw in the operations of The Q.

The second sliver beneath her skin was that he had used the word love, as if it were an assumption, as if whatever caring they had for each other could be considered worth spending that word on. With terms like that, Quincy was not just frugal, she was a miser. She didn't know how she felt about someone assuming she was willing to spend it when she'd never really let it leave the vault. Though, Quincy did remember what she felt when she first saw Arch unconscious on the floor of the print room, and it was a great deal more than just care.

"And there she is. My, my, my."

Quincy looked up. It was none other than Lord Ashford, the society scoundrel she had bantered with at the Fothergils' dinner in the spring.

Stiffening to what Quincy thought was formal intimidation, Arch looked at the man with a formidable politeness. "Good evening, Ashford."

Quincy hadn't moved, but rather crossed her arms and brought one booted heel up against the wall behind her, probably damaging some gilt rococo nonsense. She nodded at Ashford despite the tangle of thoughts still in her head. "Ashford."

"Have you no other words for me this evening, Miss St. Claire? I was hoping you would come. Do you dance? That would be amusing indeed."

"I do dance, as a matter of fact." Quincy knew she looked bored. "But, in sympathy with Arch, here, I'm declining the exercise."

"Ah," Ashford said, his eyes traveling the lines of Arch's frame, ending on the black shine of his cane. "I heard you and Reggie had boxed it out. I couldn't say you'd won until I saw you both here tonight. You have, decidedly, found the best tailor. Did St. Claire spill her secrets on the cut of a fine jacket to you? Now that I've opened the question," Ashford's smile was lurid, "has St. Claire spilled all her other secrets to you as well?"

Quincy's hands formed fists, and she glared. Arch lifted his chin, the contrast of his face and eyes dancing in anger, his lips drawn tight, his gaze narrowed. "Ashford, I am not above breaking a man's nose. I've done it before."

Laughing, albeit taking a step away, Ashford was saved from any further conflict by a footman arriving to inform James Arch and Miss Quincy St. Claire that they were to come to dinner.

Quincy pushed herself away from the wall, and she and Arch walked around Ashford without so much as a second glance.

"I thought you were practicing the turning of the other cheek, Arch," Quincy said as they walked towards one of the formal dining rooms. "Threatening a man's nose doesn't seem in line with that philosophy."

"Yes, well," Arch stepped stiffly, his face still set, "you tend to bring my folly out in spades. Besides, where I may not raise a hand for myself, it would be a cold afternoon in hell before I wouldn't do it for you."

She burned, her heart most of all, and Quincy clipped the edge of her lip between her teeth and looked away, brushing a lock of blond hair from her eyes.

Upon entering the dining room, Quincy found herself with the most exclusive dinner set of the evening. Not only were Lady Fothergil and Johnny in attendance, along with Lord Arch and Mary, but there were also among the elite party none other than the king and his son, the crown prince. The king had arrived while Quincy and Arch had been wandering through one of the outer rooms. They had heard but missed seeing his appearance.

This was, Quincy realized, the first time she had ever even seen the king. He was old, just older than Lady Fothergil, yet he still stood straight, and his eyes were clear. He was just being shown to his seat, at the opposite end of the table from Lady Fothergil, when Quincy and Arch entered the room.

Arch stopped and bowed respectfully as the king's eyes fell on them.

"James," the king waved his hand, "you look a bit worse for wear. Has Mary been giving you difficulties?"

Quincy's eyes drifted towards the crown prince, who was looking down at his empty plate, uncomfortably seated at Lady Fothergil's side. Everyone was watching, trying to understand if the king knew or not. From the look on Lord Arch's face, and her own instincts, Quincy decided he had not yet heard.

"If she had, it would be just deserts, Your Majesty," Arch replied.

"Come, James." Lady Fothergil was still standing, waving at Arch. "You will be seated at my right. And the prince is here at my left. You see, I have reserved the most handsome men for myself."

Johnny made a funny noise of disagreement, and the king laughed.

"You, Miss St. Claire, are to be seated at the king's left," Lady Fothergil continued. "Yes, don't look so startled. I know James had asked for you, but His Majesty heard you were in attendance and simply changed the table on me."

Quincy's skin jumped—or felt like it did, anyway—and she glanced towards the king, fully aware that she should be bowing, or something, instead of just staring.

"I don't bite too often, Miss St. Claire," said the king, his clear eyes watching her with interest, then he took his seat. Quincy made an acknowledging movement, feeling the whole affair was starting off badly, too informal, too strange.

Arch nudged her and gave her a reluctant parting smile, as if they weren't going to be sitting at opposite corners of the table a mere eight feet away. Lady Fothergil must have seen it, for she started to laugh without explaining herself. Then a footman led Quincy around the table and waited for her to be seated to adjust her chair. It had such a high back she felt she had grown even smaller.

Quincy frowned, guessing it would be rude to let her eyes wander the table without addressing the royal problem to her right first. She set her hands on the arms of her chair, sighed audibly—an accident— and looked towards the king. His brow was creased, eyebrows turning down at the bridge of his nose, and his lips moved in interest.

"Forgive my lack of etiquette," Quincy said baldly. "I wasn't prepared and never anticipated this—Your Majesty."

"I can see. It is customary to wait to be addressed before you speak. It is also customary to curtsy or bow, as the case may be, before you sit."

Quincy lifted a shoulder and pulled her mouth to the side. "Is it customary to be simply flattering? Or does Your Grace expect any kind of intelligent conversation?"

He blinked, stared a touch long, and then began to laugh. "Are you so confident you can provide the latter that we should skip the former?"

"I can. Can you?" The rest of the table had gone into a temporary lull and caught Quincy's words. Arch grimaced, and even Lady Fothergil's eyes went a touch wide. The crown prince gave no reaction, as he was speaking in flirtatious whispers to the woman on his right. "Can Your Grace, I meant to say," Quincy amended, not thinking there was anything inappropriate about asking a direct question.

"Certainly," the king said just as the soup was being served.

Quincy then commenced to have a sprawling conversation with her sovereign through the next seven courses of the meal. He asked about her work, The Q, and the rumors he had been hearing of her Paris success. She, in turn, asked about his work—how he spent his day, his time—his relationship to the parliament, and whether he agreed with the latest antitrust legislation being pushed through.

"That I cannot say," the king replied. "I am to remain neutral on all matters of politics."

"So, you can't effect real change," Quincy stated, devouring the rosemary and honey chicken before her.

The king's bejeweled hand paused in its motion, his rings catching the light, as he disagreed. "It would be faulty logic to assume that you, as a business leader, could not effect political change. You must not think I am incapable of the same."

"You're right," Quincy said. "I'm just curious, then, how you go about it. Not in the manner the prince does, one would hope." She snapped at the end words as they came out, cursing under her breath, wishing she had not been so utterly stupid.

"Pardon?" the king said.

Quincy set her fork and knife down and looked towards the king with resignation. She now knew enough about the man to understand he wouldn't allow the cat to be put back into the bag, no matter how it might scratch.

"Explain your meaning, Miss St. Claire," the king pressed.

"I'd rather not."

"I don't care." And the informal courtesy, which he had been game to try, evaporated in the underlying condescension of his tone.

Quincy's hackles rose. "James Arch is sporting bruises and a cane because your son sent four street toughs after him; the small man's way of making change, in my opinion." She lifted her fork and placed a piece of chicken in her mouth, chewing rebelliously as she watched the king's reaction.

His face did not move. Only his eyes flickered to the other end of the table, from his son to Arch and back. He did not say anything further to Quincy, and when the next course came and she started to speak, he cut her off. "I have no more interest in conversing with you, St. Claire."

Lifting a shoulder, Quincy reached for her goblet and took a sip. "And the relationship between proletariat and sovereign disintegrates," she mumbled.

"There never was a relationship," the king said, lifting a fork full of food into his mouth, "nor do I wish there to be."

"Hear! Hear! At least that's something we can agree on." Quincy lifted her glass, and the king, to her slight surprise, lifted his.

"To the end of something that never was," he said, wiping his mouth with his napkin.

"To the end," Quincy replied. Their glasses clinked, and Quincy noticed they had gained some attention from others down the table. Arch sent Quincy a confused look, and she just shook her head. No need to complicate matters further. Let him think she and the king had left on the best of terms.

"I do feel I bring out the unorthodox among the nobility of Rhysdon," she said to Arch later. "It never quite goes as I'd expect it to."

When it was nearing three in the morning and Quincy had heard enough music, watched enough dancing, and juggled enough conversations with people she cared nothing for, she was given a pleasant surprise, a breath of dirty industrial air, as it were. Priest made an appearance.

"Priest!" Quincy surprised herself and him by throwing her arms around his neck.

"Have you really been stuck on this island of aristocrats for so long you're feeling sentimental about me, St. Claire?"

"Yes."

Arch's friends had asked if he would like in on a game of cards in the library. Arch had looked like he wanted to go but had declined. Then they had seen Priest.

"James Arch." Priest extended his hand. "Pleasure."

"Mr. Priest."

"I trust you're recovering well."

"Yes."

"Good. We've not yet discussed that I printed your name. You see why I did it, though?"

Arch nodded.

"And you're still reluctant to fill the shoes of known public essayist. Well, I understand."

"When did you arrive?" Quincy asked.

"An hour back." Priest's fingers looked restless without a cigar. "I was hoping you'd be here. Do you have time to talk business?"

A flood of relief and joy threatened to knock Quincy over. "Can we? My good behavior is nearing an end, and I think Arch has been wanting to play cards in the library but was too polite to abandon me."

Priest's face creased with interest as he addressed Arch. "Do you gamble?"

The side of Arch's mouth smiled, and he leaned against his cane. "Once a year, at the Fothergils' ball. No more, no less."

"Do you win?"

"Always."

Priest grunted. "Good. Good. Off with you now. St. Claire and I will be down the hall, in one of the drawing rooms."

Arch gave Quincy a smile, the ends of his fingers touching hers, and then he was gone.

"Fetch me a drink, St. Claire—if you would—and I promise to smoke only one cigar."

They found a room where a fire had been set but that was otherwise uninhabited, and they spoke business casually, in long, stretched out thoughts. It was less of a business meeting and more of a refuge, two creatures outside their habitat, finding comfort with a bird of their own color.

"Why did you come at all if you were going to be this late?" Quincy asked, sitting with her feet pulled up under her as she leaned against the arm of the expensive sofa.

"Fothergil has invited Celine and me for years, and it was always her—Celine's, that is—favorite event of the year. Oh, she loved the arrival, the food, the gowns. By heaven, she loved the gowns enough to drive a man out of his head. I found the thought of dining here without her to be—" he took a long draw from his cigar and released the smoke into the dim light of the extravagant room, "—taxing."

Quincy nodded in understanding, her eyes heavy, lulled by the comfort of the fire, the company, and the soft, feather-filled pillows. She shifted into a less decorous position, remembering the nights when she would sleep in Ezekiel's library as he read.

"It appears that you and Arch are—?" Priest let the question hang next to the cigar smoke about his face.

Quincy shrugged as best she could, her face half buried in a pillow. "I don't know what to say."

"Do you care a great deal for the boy?" Priest asked, scratching his temple while expertly holding the cigar with the same hand.

Quincy took a long breath and closed her eyes. She intended to give an honest answer—if she could stand it.

"You can tell me it's not my damn business."

"I don't know, Priest. It's not an easy thing to make sense of. But," Quincy blinked her eyes and looked at the fire, talking aloud to herself as much as to Priest, "when Spense brought Arch in from the back alley, all bruised and bloodied, it felt worse than when Ezekiel died."

Priest grunted but didn't speak.

"Do you miss Celine?" Quincy asked. The smell of cigar smoke filled Quincy's nostrils.

"Work has been a bit flat."

And Quincy understood what Priest meant, what Celine had meant to him: that the shine was now gone out of what he had thought would always consume him. With these thoughts in her head—and moving dangerously towards her heart—Quincy St. Claire fell asleep.

⸻

It was the sound of a pulse, the double beat of blood moving, that woke Quincy. She moved her cheek and felt soft fabric and beneath it, the reverberations of a heart in the shell of her ear. Her eyes were still closed, but she knew it was Arch she was curled up against, his arm around her. She could smell his lotion and his skin. Quincy sighed and shifted, nestling against his chest. His arm moved in response, but he made no effort to rise, and neither did she. It wasn't long before she returned to her dreams.

CHAPTER FORTY-FIVE:

He's a Good Man, Arch

"Time for a late breakfast," Lady Fothergil declared as she began opening the curtains in the drawing room. "Up, up!"

Quincy wiped the night from her eyes, fighting a yawn. Arch tightened his arm around Quincy and then let go as she sat up. He shifted in the corner of the sofa, wincing at the noise and light as Lady Fothergil fully opened the curtains.

"Breakfast will soon be served, James. It's time you took yourself upstairs."

"Yes," Arch said sleepily. "Pardon me, Lady Fothergil."

Wrapping his hand around Quincy's for only a moment, he stood and—limping—quit the room.

Quincy brought herself to her feet. Cats, she was tired. "I should go," she half yawned to Lady Fothergil.

"Stuff and nonsense. It's ridiculous to run off into the streets without a proper breakfast," Fothergil insisted. "The rest of the guests have been turned out, but the Arches are family. James is upstairs, to wash and change, and there's no reason why you shouldn't do the same. He has a room with fresh clothing for whenever he stays," Fothergil added.

"I don't have anything to change into," Quincy argued, lifting her hand to her face, her head splitting from the night of revelry. "It would be better if I just returned to The Q. I have an evening of work ahead of me."

"More nonsense. It's Sunday morning; you've no need to rush off. Hortense!" Lady Fothergil called a maid into the room. "Please take Quincy upstairs to the cherry blossom room, and see her changed. I've ordered some clothes for this very purpose," Lady Fothergil said as if ordering a wardrobe for a distant acquaintance were a normal thing to do. "Don't grimace, child. James always stays for breakfast, and I knew you were coming with him."

So Quincy followed Hortense upstairs, finding herself ushered into a light, flower-like room of soft white and faint pink. The furniture was deep brown, and Quincy indeed felt like she was in a blossom-laden cherry tree. There had been a grove outside of Lester that Quincy's mother had taken her to see one spring and she had never forgotten the memory.

"My lady says that she regrets not knowing the name of your tailor, or she could have ordered a set of clothing like you usually wear, but she has commissioned a few pieces for your use, whenever necessary." Hortense pushed Quincy towards the bed before facing the armoire, and pulling the doors open. Quincy took in a long breath and shook her head. No, no she would not change. The armoire was full of nothing but dresses.

"No."

Hortense pretended not to hear, pursing her lips and considering Quincy's coloring as she selected a few gowns and laid them over the bed. "The plum, I think, or the blue," she said in her thick French accent. "The pink would be lovely, but I imagine you would put up a fight."

"No fight," Quincy stated, "as there will be no dress."

"Why ever not?" The maid turned in distress, the expensive gowns falling gracefully over her arm.

"I've never worn a dress in my life," Quincy said as if this were reason enough to refuse.

"But, you will be spending the morning in the company of Lady Fothergil and the young gentlemen. You will not wish to be the only one in soiled clothing."

"There are worse things." Quincy worked at The Q. She always ended up in soiled clothing.

"Miss St. Claire, you would look lovely."

"I would feel the fool, Hortense," Quincy said honestly, with a hand covering her face. "I would."

Hortense smiled the kind of smile that held secrets at its corners like bunches of rosettes. "I will take you in for a bath, and then we will see how you feel about the dresses. You will at least indulge me one look."

When Quincy had resided with Ezekiel, she had often bathed. The Q did not have such amenities, and in her tired state, she couldn't oppose. Hortense led her into a small chamber, where a warm bath had already been prepared.

"Take your time. The gentlemen won't be down for three-quarters of an hour, I imagine, so you should not rush."

She didn't rush. Sinking into the warm water, Quincy leaned her head back and promptly fell asleep.

Hortense woke her, urging her to use the scented soaps. "And this is for your hair. Under the water. Go."

Quincy washed her hair and then stepped out into a soft robe. A fire had been set in the cherry blossom room, and it was warm when Hortense began to dry Quincy's hair.

"Such a lovely color. Do you cut it yourself?"

Quincy nodded.

"How?"

"Using the mirror in my room and a pair of scissors."

"Hmmm. Lovely. You must let me style you this morning. Now, I've taken the liberty of sending your underpinnings to be washed and have clean garments for you to wear."

Quincy frowned and closed her eyes, searching for patience, but she slipped into the white, lace-edged articles without speaking. It wasn't until Hortense pulled out a coutil corset that Quincy felt fully awake.

"No. Absolutely not. I am not a society strumpet."

Hortense was undaunted. "You promised me you would let me see you in one dress." Quincy was certain she had not made such a promise. "And you will *not* be able to wear any of these pieces if you do not have a corset. Now," Hortense's tone turned indomitable, "turn around while I lace this up."

Quincy stood with her arms crossed, resting on the heel of her left foot, staring the French maid down. Hortense, however, was not some mouse at The Q and did not back off. She glared right back and lifted an eyebrow. "I am ready to force you, Miss St. Claire, if necessary. I ask that you trust me. Now. Turn. Around."

Quincy waited long enough for Hortense to *know* that she was choosing to cooperate and then turned. Hortense placed the corset around Quincy's waist and ribs and then began to work the ribbon through the back, pulling it tight.

"This is ridiculous!" Quincy gasped as the maid pulled tighter and tighter. Quincy breathed in as deeply as she could, her hands on her now greatly diminished waist. Never had she realized the sanity of her own wardrobe, until now. When Hortense had finished, Quincy was ready for the world to end; for if she remained in this corset for much longer, her world certainly would.

"Now, purple or blue? Or, will you brave the pink, which is my favorite?"

"What do you have in black?" Quincy asked, her forehead folded into lines.

"Black is not for the morning. Yes, there is one gown of black, and it's a delicate piece of lace that you would most certainly not want to wear to breakfast."

Quincy sighed as much as was possible while bound in such a barbaric contraption. "Untie the corset. I'm putting my own clothes back on."

"Oh—" Hortense paused, an apologetic look crossing her face. "I sent those off to be cleaned."

Quincy set her mouth, incensed. Fothergil was a master manipulator, she had taken the round, so Quincy had to cede her this small victory. She would certainly be more cautious in the future.

"Fine," Quincy said through gritted teeth.

"Purple? Blue? Or pink?"

Quincy muttered a string of low-street curses—Hortense did not flinch—and then turned towards the bed, where the gowns lay. The blue gown was so lace-adorned, with bows and frills, that Quincy discounted it out of hand. The purple was well-trimmed, sharp, but the color was suffocating, sugary: thick and sweet. Quincy then considered the pink. It was in the fashion of the day save that the sleeves were Grecian and delicate, rather than being a monstrous display of fabric. The layers of its skirt, though gathered, fell gracefully to the ground, with no bows and a more sophisticated line.

Quincy touched it with her fingers and resigned herself to the unanticipated fate that had befallen her. "Fine. The pink."

Hortense pinched back her smile and lifted the gown, pleased with herself. "You will look a picture, Miss St. Claire."

She helped slip the garment over Quincy's head. Quincy closed her eyes, her hands clutched, as Hortense settled the gown in place. "One moment, a needle and thread will tuck this in, and the fit will be perfect."

Quincy snorted and kept her eyes closed, feeling the line and pull of the thread as the dress was tailored to her waist.

"Now," Hortense said to herself as much as to Quincy, "the buttons."

Quincy felt the gown take shape around her; the proportions felt strange, spare or bunched in the wrong places. When Hortense pushed Quincy over toward the mirror, the skirt was so loose and strange on Quincy's legs she felt indecent. She was changing as soon as she could get back into the safety of her matchbox wardrobe.

"Here," Hortense said, moving Quincy to face the mirror.

Quincy gawked. She looked a different person altogether. Her carriage was forced into a different aspect: her shoulders back, waist emphasized, skirt falling full to the ground. The women's clothing she had seen in the streets was often made of a sturdier material, a heavier fabric, but this was made of filmy, soft stuff—what a woman of great luxury would be accustomed to.

"Ridiculous," said Quincy.

"Lovely," Hortense countered. "Now, let me address your hair and send you down. They will be waiting, *ma chère*."

Quincy cooperated, but only just, as Hortense set her fingers in a jar of something and began pulling the ends of Quincy's blond hair. She styled Quincy's hair with confidence, and, Quincy admitted, it was flattering. When the maid had finished, Quincy asked after her boots.

"But, I have—"

"You can't have washed my boots," Quincy insisted. "I don't intend to wear anything but."

Hortense muttered something in French, but she disappeared and reappeared with Quincy's boots. They were heeled and buttoned, as Favreau had wanted, and didn't look particularly strange when Hortense forced them onto Quincy's feet.

"See, the dress covers them anyway," Quincy grumbled. She tried to slouch, but it was impossible in the corset. What nonsense.

Hortense let a gleeful laugh escape then said, "If you're wearing the boots, then I insist on one more thing. Sit."

Quincy waited as Hortense ran a black ribbon through Quincy's hair and tied another black ribbon in a charming knot around her wrist. "There. Now the boots will look like a statement of fashion rather than of sheer stubbornness."

When Quincy finally found her way down to the breakfast room, she was greatly relieved, for she had nearly tripped over the skirts three times. "Rubbish," she grumbled as she pushed into the door. And there they were, Johnny and Arch, speaking about something—Johnny with a piece of breakfast cake halfway to his mouth. Arch glanced up as Quincy entered, and, without even consulting the expression on her face, he began to laugh.

"What?" She crossed her arms, but this emphasized the cut of her dress, so she dropped them to her sides, fists ready to throw a punch.

Johnny stood, food still in his hand, mouth open. "Quincy, you look a picture."

"A picture indeed," Arch grinned as he also stood. "A picture of manipulated compliance. Look at that scowl. Here," he walked around the table and pulled out a chair. "Sit, and I'll fetch you a plate of breakfast."

"Breakfast?" Quincy shot her eyes to the clock. "It's noon. You lot are the most worthless people I've ever known. Dancing, eating all night, playing cards, breakfasting when half the work of the day should be done. Wastrels, all of you."

Arch had started humming, deliberately blocking out Quincy's words. Johnny was laughing, though, beginning to list the extravagances of his class with a condemnatory glee.

Quincy could see the consequences and, admittedly, the charm of having spent the entire night at entertainment. Both Arch and Johnny seemed to be in a satisfied mood. She sat perched on the edge of her seat just as she had been so critical of women sitting before, because she found her clothing left her little choice. The lace edge of her neckline—Neckline? Was that what this was? Quincy thought not— was scratching against the curve of her skin. She wanted to rest her elbows on the table and put her head in her hands. But she couldn't. She was too restricted.

Arch was going on about something—Was it cards?—as he filled a plate full of breakfast foods. And Johnny answered him with some smart comment. Bending her thoughts back to their conversation, Quincy saw that Arch looked fresh, happy, despite his limp, like he hadn't missed any sleep.

Quincy thought about waking that morning, her cheek pressed against his chest, his arm about her waist, and she lifted a hand to her temple, closing her eyes. Things were spinning far beyond what a usually controlled Quincy St. Claire found acceptable. The situation was apocalyptic. In the last twelve hours, she had insulted the king, confided her emotions to Priest, woken to the heartbeat of Arch's body, and was now wearing a corset and a dress. She had never been one to read the bible, but she was certain there was something about the end of the world between its pages. Well, call Quincy a prophet, and give her a pulpit, for the end was certainly near.

"Are you alright?" Arch asked, setting the full plate of food before her and sitting in the empty chair at her side. He leaned his elbow against the table and rested his cheek against the knuckles of his hand, watching Quincy with a worried expression.

"No." She opened her eyes. "I'm exhausted. I've a headache. And I'm starving." Arch motioned at the plate of food before her, and she snapped, "To fit into this corset, I had to choose between my stomach and my lungs. I decided to breathe and, therefore, have no room for eating. Is it any wonder that society women are so dull? They spend all their energy on basic survival. My admiration for them has grown to no bounds, and I rescind all my previous commentary regarding their useless existence. Every day is a matter of life and death. Give them each a medal."

At the mention of the undergarment, Johnny looked uncomfortable, but Arch merely smiled, his eyes exploring her face as if she were a pleasant memory. "Eat what you can, and I'll see that Harris delivers the rest to The Q, where you can eat in the freedom of your own wardrobe."

"If the females of this city ever find out how uncomfortable their clothing really is, Arch," Quincy said, stabbing her food with her fork, "there will be riots in every quarter. It's nearly bad enough for me to join the women who march in Rhysdon Square and shout at Parliament. I understand now why they're all so angry."

"Votes for women," Arch responded wryly.

Quincy couldn't help herself, and she laughed, then she ate what food she could.

Johnny disappeared after a few minutes. And, when Quincy pushed her plate away and turned towards Arch, she found him as attentive as before.

"Thank you," he said, "for coming with me. It meant a great deal, and I deeply enjoyed sharing the event with you."

Quincy simply replied, "Only for you."

The words seemed to hit Arch softly. He closed his eyes a moment before moving towards Quincy, and, resting his fingertips in a line down her neck, he kissed her.

Quincy was aware of how his hand moved each time they kissed, and of how he now rested it gently above her collarbone, his thumb anchored against her pulse as his fingers wrapped gently around the curve of her neck. As she asked more from his kisses, she lifted her own hand to his wrist. Just then, Arch pulled back, dropping his hand and resting his forehead against her shoulder, rather than looking at her.

"I think it would be best if I said good-bye now, Quincy St. Claire. I should not follow you back to The Q today."

Quincy took a long breath, or she tried to. His nearness was like lightning, and she needed it even as she was certain she wanted to run from the storm of this companionship that so startled her, despite not knowing how.

"It's Sunday, by any means," Quincy said, catching her breath. "There's no work for you to do, until tomorrow morning."

Arch laughed and looked up at her face, his dark eyes bright. "I wasn't worried about getting carried off by the allure of the new contracts, Quincy, I assure you."

Lady Fothergil, as it happened, was planning to visit a friend and offered to drop Quincy off at The Q once she came to understand that Arch would be returning directly to Peacock House.

"We'll go together, Miss St. Claire, and brave the cold of the town. Dear me, you can't go out without a covering, a thick shawl or a coat."

"How about my own clothes?" Quincy delivered this line with a hint of sullen challenge.

Fothergil laughed. "Yes, Hortense and I were larking all morning over the plan. And see how it turned out? You look lovely, and I got to see you dressed properly at least once. Oh, I know it will never happen again, but that's all the more reason for toying with you. The cherry blossom room is yours now, for whenever you have need. The dresses are yours also. You might find yourself wishing to make use of them once or twice."

The notion of volunteering to wear such contraptions again was enough to finish shaking the very foundations of Quincy St. Claire. She looked forward to her return to The Q with a fervor she had not known before.

When Hortense appeared with a matching pink, floor-length jacket, Quincy refused. "Let me borrow one of your coats," she said to Arch.

"It'll drown you."

"One could only hope."

And he laughed.

A few minutes later, Quincy was sitting in one of the Fothergil carriages, Arch's jacket wrapped around her as she watched Rhysdon pass by her window.

"I had a few words with our beloved prince."

Quincy gave Lady Fothergil her attention. "And?"

"I don't think we need to worry about his methods any further. I don't play the bully, St. Claire—those methods are beneath my attention—but I don't mind reminding him that, after deity, I rule the day."

"Good."

Fothergil tilted her head and met Quincy's eye. "You and James have become quite the talk of the *ton*."

Quincy snorted.

"It was confirmed before the party, of course," Fothergil said, her mouth setting decidedly as she glanced out the window. "You were seen in the street, apparently. And I've heard other reports of a similar nature. It's no surprise to me that James has serious intentions towards you."

Quincy shifted in her seat and moved Arch's jacket slightly. "Intentions for what?"

"Do you not know what that means?"

"No," Quincy said slowly. "Should I?"

Lady Fothergil shook her head, the sparkle of her diamond earrings playing with the various points of light coming in through the carriage windows. "Dear me, child, sometimes you make me want to ring Ezekiel's dead neck. He should have brought you to me years ago, the old fool. Intentions. *Intentions.* They are saying that James has it in mind to ask you to become affianced to him."

When Quincy did not shift her blank expression, Lady Fothergil brought the fan in her hand down onto her knee. "Marry you, child. Marry you."

The sensation Quincy experienced then was similar to that of a typewriter being pulled apart and thrown down a stone staircase. "That is the stupidest thing I've heard all—ever, actually." She delivered Lady Fothergil a sharp look of disbelief. "Why would you or anybody—? It's just—when Arch does have intentions, as you call them, they will certainly be towards one of the lace-edged, sweet-minded things he takes to the opera. They won't be for a girl with ink-stained hands and a mind for nothing but figures and business, who has tortured him for the better part of a year, walking about in clothes reminiscent of a twelve-year-old boy. I would hate to put Arch through the embarrassment of having people actually think that he would."

Quincy made an angry noise. "And what if I don't want to be *intended*? What if I have my own opinions on the matter? It's a remarkable thing, how many contracts are assumed without consulting both parties. Cats and kings!"

Quincy was on her feet before she even realized she was, stumbling out of the carriage as it was held up on the corner of Queen's Street and Gainsford. She pulled the foolish skirts behind her and, with her cheeks flaming from embarrassment, wrapped the jacket closer as she barreled down the street. Quincy felt blind, her head pounding, her eyes unable to focus.

That Rhysdon's elite had speculated about a permanent alliance, watching her last night as if she had signed a legally binding merger, was—

Quincy slammed into someone. "Sorry," she muttered, stepping around them.

"Whoa, whoa." An arm wrapped around her and pulled her back. "I'm sorry, love. But, after all these weeks offshore, you're going to have to greet me better than that." The rich, sonorous voice was a welcome sound after a night of tinkling conversation.

"Crow!"

"Yes, it's me, love," he said into her ear, for Quincy had thrown her arms around him, pulling the sea-breeze smell into her nostrils.

"But what are you doing here?" Quincy stepped back, looking up into his cold blue eyes and weather-fresh smile. "On a Sunday, no less, when there's not much crowd to hide you?"

"What, for a dog's breath, are you wearing?"

Quincy pulled Arch's jacket tighter around her and glared.

"You've changed, Quincy St. Claire."

"No, I haven't," she spat back fiercely.

"Well, you need to. Come on. Do a man a favor, and hide him from the police awhile. Let's find you some decent clothes, and I'll take you out for a drink. I think you need it."

"I don't want a drink. Cats! I just want quiet. And brusque, clear manners. And trousers. And—and peppermint tea! Is that such a strange thing? Is that too much?"

She stepped around him, pounding away towards The Q. He turned heel and followed at her side, careful not to trample her hemline. Crow didn't answer her questions but was watching her with a worried face. And when she came to The Q, she swore at the lock, and he laughed.

"I forgot my key," Quincy raged. "Last night, I left it sitting in the matchbox because I was so—"

"Lucky you're with me, then, love." Crow lifted a few metal pieces from the pocket of his long coat and stood next to the door, easing his way through the lock with a smile on his face like a person calling a cat to cream. It didn't take him long.

"Impressively fast," Quincy muttered as she swept past him into the cold, empty front office of The Q.

"I won't deny that I've opened this door for my own purposes on more than one occasion."

"Crow!"

"Quincy!" he replied, mimicking her tone. "Now go change. I'll wait here. We can find some off-path tea shop, and you can tell me what all this," he waved a hand at her, "is about."

"But what about Constable Catch?"

"Catcher is visiting his mother in the country. Besides that, he spends every Sunday morning in church."

"And so you crawled out of your sea?" Quincy said, as she slipped behind the counter and towards the stairs.

"Oh, I'm much more comfortably established than that."

"That makes one of us, at the very least."

The stairway sponsored more echoes than usual as she stomped upward, holding the foam of pink froth out of the way of her black boots. When she arrived in her room she slammed the door and it felt good. Then Quincy fell onto her bed in a more dignified manner than she would have liked to. She could hardly bend forward enough to reach her boots, eventually pulling her leg up and only just snapping the buttons open with her fingers. They were stubborn beasts, but she managed one and then the other, though she ended out of breath and patience. She shrugged off Arch's jacket, threw it at the bed, and then realized she had no possible way of extracting herself from the dress and its accompanying corset.

Quincy gave a fierce cry as she tried to pull the gown over her head, with no success. She could hear Crow laughing below.

"Do you need my help, love?"

"Do you have a knife?" Quincy shouted, followed by a grunt as she tried to shift the dress once more.

"Yes."

"Slide it under the door."

She could hear his heavy steps on the stairs. Then a small knife, bent over itself in an ingenious way, came sliding under the door.

"Ha!" Quincy said instead of thanking the smuggler, and she reached her hand around the knife triumphantly. As Crow descended the stairs, she could hear him whistling a sea chantey.

Pulling the knife open, Quincy considered the dress in her small, chipped mirror. She didn't want to waste a perfectly well-made piece of clothing, even if she never meant to wear it again. Exploring the back with her hands, she realized she was buttoned in all the way up and that, if she pulled, the dress would tear before the buttons would give. Holding the knife in her hand, Quincy slipped it beneath the lowest button and forced it up.

She felt the pop, heard the sound of the button hitting the floor, and felt the gown give slightly. Encouraged, Quincy twisted her arm again and popped the next several buttons off in the same manner. They were now beyond her reach, but she was able to set the knife down and, using her hands, pull the rest of the back apart without damaging the dress too much. She slipped the dress off and threw it onto the bed triumphantly.

The corset proved an easy fix, as the knife simply had to cut the ribbon holding it all together. It took a deep breath, loosening around Quincy as if it were just as relieved as she was. She let it drop to the floor and ignored it, opening her own armoire and finding a clean, but worn pair of trousers, her own assortment of undergarments from the bureau, a plain shirt, and one of her thicker jackets.

Changing felt like a miracle. She relished every breath. And, once her clothes were in place, her jacket on, and an old pair of lace-up boots on her feet, Quincy claimed her red scarf and left the remnants of the morning scattered across the matchbox, fleeing to the familiarity of the front office and Crow.

"Here's your knife," she said triumphantly.

"Keep it," Crow grinned. "You might need the same escape route the next time you're cornered into such a mess."

Quincy's face testified there would be no next time, but she pocketed the folded blade as if it was her most prized possession.

"You forgot this." Crow reached a hand out and pulled the black ribbon from Quincy's hair. With the ribbon gone, he mussed her hair with his hand and smiled. "There you are, Quincy St. Claire."

She wrapped the red scarf around her neck and buried her chin in it, saying, "Let's go."

Crow led them through several blocks of back alley streets, coming out in a small, lower middle class shopping district. Most of the shops were closed, but there was a corner tea shop and bakery with its windows glowing. They ducked inside and settled themselves in a corner, Crow where he could see both the street and the door.

Tea in hand, bread and pastries cozying up on the plates before them, Quincy began to relax.

Crow's smile, as he looked at her, was quizzical and entertained. "The fates are kind, St. Claire. I wouldn't have missed that debacle for anything. Now, are you going to explain the odd circumstances? Or do I have to speculate?"

"I attended the Fothergils' ball. It's the biggest—"

"I know what it is, love," Crow laughed as he cut her off. "Did you actually dance?"

"No."

"I thought not," he said, lifting the cheap-street teacup to his mouth.

Quincy glared. "I can dance, actually. Arch says I dance very well."

"Does he?"

Quincy looked down, embarrassed, wishing she had not spoken at all.

"Don't play coy with me, St. Claire. You never have before. It's clear as morning you're rattled. Tell it straight out."

"I'm not playing coy," she shot back, her words hot. "Don't assume I am just because you've seen me in a dress."

"Fair enough," Crow said.

So Quincy told Crow. She spoke about the evening, the people, the endlessness, the exchanges. He grinned, laughing more than once, and was an easy audience.

"So, why were you marching up Gainsford in such distress?" he asked.

"I'd just escaped from the Fothergils' carriage."

"Why?"

Quincy had not been specific in regards to her interactions with Arch, but she could feel the weight of it on her face and decided to make a clean confession. "She'd insinuated that Arch might have intentions for me."

"Intentions?"

"Yes, it's when—"

"I know what it means, love."

"Good," Quincy snapped, "because I didn't."

"Hmm." Crow crossed his arms and looked thoughtful. "I see why you're spooked, even though you do care for Arch."

"What makes you think I do?"

"I know the price of something when I see it, love. It's my trade."

And asking questions was Quincy's trade. No wonder she felt afraid of the answers.

"If Fothergil said it," Crow reasoned, "then there must be a basis of truth, and that would imply a most serious affection between you and Arch."

"I couldn't say," she answered, lifting a shoulder.

"You're frightened," Crow said, the tone of his voice turning toward wonder. "Quincy St. Claire, I have never seen that emotion cross your face."

"Is my fear justified?" she asked candidly, picking at a pastry.

"Yes."

Quincy moved the crumbs on her plate with her finger. "What do I do?"

"What do you want to do?"

What one wanted to do was not the kind of equation Quincy was accustomed to performing in her own head. It's not that she didn't do exactly what she wanted most of the time but that she had never verbalized it in such a way. Quincy took a breath. What did she want?

"I want James Arch," she said decidedly and then, with equal force, added, "I don't want the trappings that go with him."

Crow's mouth moved slightly, and his face flickered with a thought. Waiting for it to come through, Quincy tapped her finger twice.

"No one has ever managed that feat, Quincy St. Claire. It isn't possible, and it isn't fair."

"Then I just figure out what I can live with?"

"Or live without."

A woman brought them a new pot of tea and some fresh bread. Quincy watched as Crow poured them each another cup, and she took hers gratefully. The scent reminded her of Ezekiel, of Thursday evenings in his library, sitting before the fire. For the first time, she not only missed Ezekiel but also missed his house, the old house and the new house. The matchbox didn't quite feel like enough anymore. She grimaced, even the thought making Quincy feel disloyal.

"He's a good man, Arch," Crow admitted, setting his cup down and turning his eyes thoughtfully towards the street. "And he's in a place in society where he wouldn't make his feelings public if he weren't intent on giving his life to you."

Quincy closed her eyes for the pain of it. How did people speak of this as if it were a wonderful thing, the process of letting someone become your heart? "What if I don't know if I can take it?"

"That," Crow drummed his fingers on the table, "is what you're discovering. It's a journey, St. Claire. You can't set the type once, print the issue, and be done with it."

"It's like a daily newspaper, you mean, not an single edition?"

"Sure," he shrugged.

"What if—" Quincy lifted her hand to her mouth, her finger and thumb glancing along her lower lip. "What if I don't know if I can risk losing it someday?

"Losing what?"

"What I would gain by choosing him, knowing that, at some point, he won't be there anymore."

Crow breathed out and cocked his head to the side, thinking. He weighed what she said for a few moments then said, "Have you lost my friendship, even though I've left Rhysdon?"

"No."

"Or Ezekiel's love because he's dead?"

Quincy shook her head. She had lost him but not the memory of what she was to him.

"People have been giving themselves to each other for thousands of years now, Quincy St. Claire. I shouldn't gamble they were all wrong, if you're counting the cards, that is."

Crow walked Quincy back to The Q and paused at the door. Looking down at her, with an expression of camaraderie, of affection, he said, "Be brave, Quincy St. Claire."

"Come see me again?"

"When I can. And don't worry, I'll have my lines keep an eye on you. If you need me, I'll see myself to your door."

"Or let yourself in?"

He grinned.

Quincy hugged the smuggler and took a long breath to keep the memory of Crow sharp. He kissed her on the top of the head before stepping away, turning his back, and pulling his collar tighter against his face as he whistled down the street.

CHAPTER FORTY-SIX:

Be Brave, Quincy

Quincy worked that evening in the print room, keeping Jade entertained with accounts of the previous evening. What caught Quincy by surprise, as she decided to take Crow's counsel to be brave, was that she found her sense of The Q felt stronger, more secure, as if being brave with people gave something to everything else you loved.

"You have only one requirement left before The Q is yours?" Jade asked at some point.

"One more," Quincy said, holding up a finger. "Arch has promised he'll help me get there."

"Of course he has," Jade smiled.

Later, before falling asleep, Quincy realized she still had the black ribbon tied around her left wrist. Lifting her fingers to work it loose, she paused, and decided to keep it in place as a reminder, as a talisman of some sort.

Quincy slept soundly, woke early Monday morning, and focused on her work. She didn't expect Arch to come in early, but neither had Quincy expected him to come in so late.

"I apologize for being late," he said distantly, standing at the counter, his fingers abusing the corner of *The Times*, his eyes anywhere but on hers. "I had a meeting first thing this morning that I didn't know about until late last night."

"I wasn't worried," Quincy said. "Had you only slept in, I wouldn't have held it against you, for all the upper class extravagances of the weekend."

She had said this in a tone meant to elicit a smile. He gave her a brief one, watered down and polite. Quincy creased her brow but said nothing.

"Please excuse me, but I have a significant amount of work to do today and must prepare some things for the board meeting tomorrow."

Quincy had forgotten the meeting. "Of course. I didn't remember it myself. I've my own numbers and profits to report as well as those that came in from Paris yesterday afternoon."

"Then we should see to our work, with no further ado." With that, he withdrew into his office and closed the door. The hinges complained, making a long noise; the door was so unaccustomed now to being closed.

Quincy sat stock still for ten minutes, so shocked she couldn't even feel the pain of his sudden indifference. Her fingers moved to the ribbon on her left wrist, pulling at it nervously, wondering what she had done wrong.

He didn't leave the confines of his office all day but worked with his head bent, his jacket thrown over the back of his chair. Deep lines edged his eyes. A few times, as Quincy fumbled through the numbers of her reports or looked up after helping a customer with a Q slip, she thought she saw him watching her through the window of his office door, holding a strange expression on his face, his eyes on her, the end of his pen resting against his bottom lip.

When the wretched day came to an end, Arch packed up his work and tucked it in the portfolio beneath his arm, saying good-bye with little more than the tip of his hat and a few polite words. Quincy locked the door after him.

She stood inside the door for a long time, her mind blank, not understanding a single interaction from the entire day. The noise of the press room starting up was too much for her in this state of realizing she had been right all along: that people were never worth it. Quincy grabbed her scarf from the matchbox and left the offices of The Q behind. She disappeared through the back alley into the dark streets of Rhysdon.

Be brave, Crow had said, Quincy, be brave. Be brave so that when someone closes a door you thought was open you could save face? Be brave so you could experience the other end of someone's regret? Be brave, Quincy.

Be brave enough to go it alone.

Quincy hit the lower streets, places that no self-respecting citizen of Rhysdon would be seen. The streets were wet from a flash of early evening rain that, though now departed, had left the low town atmospheric and smoke-stained. Quincy skirted the streets along the inner quay, and each time she stepped, a swirl of fog rose around her black boots. It looked like the ghost of Rhysdon itself, rising out of the streets to go haunting. The fog was all-consuming—it matched the bent of her own mind—and she was willing to give herself over to it.

Be brave, she thought, be brave enough to be nothing.

CHAPTER FORTY-SEVEN:
A Great Mistake

Arch didn't even make an appearance at The Q the following morning. When four o'clock came, and his office still sat empty, Quincy pulled herself together—along with her files—and set Mrs. Graves at the front counter while she trekked uptown by herself. It was almost dark, the light leaving earlier now that winter had come.

Quincy arrived at the building and without giving herself space for thought, passed through the lobby, went up the stairs and down the hallway to the board room, looking neither to the right nor to the left. Then, with her head ducked, she pushed open the door.

Arch was already there, sitting in a chair away from the table and against the wall. Quincy pulled her shoulders straight and lifted her chin. Only half of the board had assembled thus far and Quincy cursed herself for arriving a few minutes too early. She glanced at her pocket watch then silently took her place at the head of the table, aware that Arch was sitting just inside the peripheral vision of her right eye.

Quincy pretended to be engrossed in the profit reports she had prepared, paying no mind as the board members began to gather in the room, greeting each other, speaking casually. The reality was that all of her energy was going towards the survival of this meeting—and then the survival of the rest of her life.

The quiet around the table called her back from the reports, and

Quincy stood without ceremony, acknowledging the board with a few brisk words before opening the business of The Q. She began with the finances of the last month, both in Rhysdon and in Paris, and, when she reported triple the expected profit margin in the two and a half months since Paris had been opened, she expected the board to acknowledge this victory with some outward satisfaction.

They remained still, stiff, more of them watching the table than looking her in the eye. Quincy thought it strange, but she had been so disoriented that nothing felt in order, and she moved on.

It was not until all the business had been attended to in this same uncomfortable, silent manner and Levins had asked to bring forth a final matter for the consideration of the board that Quincy began to care that the very air of the room seemed to be sitting wrong. She had assumed it was her own internal barometer affecting her perception. But the way Rutherford turned in his seat when Levins spoke and Harris's refusal to make eye contact with Quincy made her sit up straighter in her chair.

"What is it you wish to bring before the board, Levins?"

Levins nodded and stood. He pulled at his coat and cleared his throat. "Miss St. Claire, you have been a valued *piece* of The Q now for almost ten years and have accomplished an extraordinary amount for one so young. Still *nineteen*, I believe."

Quincy leveled a gaze at him and tapped her fingers once on the table. "And?"

Levin's cleared his throat. "The board feels The Q is at a pivotal point in its journey as a growing concern. With the success in Paris, we are now poised to do the same in London—"

"I know," said Quincy, her words cornered and compact. "I wrote the prospective."

"Yes, and very well done indeed. The board feels, as I said before, that, as we are growing to become a continental power, possibly bicontinental, as New York could suit us very well—"

"The format would have to be adjusted for the Americans," Quincy inserted, sitting back in her chair. "I've already drawn up a proposal on the issue. I mean to bring it to our January meeting."

This made Harris clear his throat, and Levins look uncomfortable as he gave her a disingenuous smile. Quincy knew he was trying to be patronizing, and she was not allowing him to do it.

"Wonderful. And the board will consider what you have put together and then rely on more expert minds to decide how The Q should move forward in the future."

"What do you mean 'more expert minds'?" Quincy asked, confused about whom he was referring to.

"I mean that The Q has outgrown your capacity," Levins said firmly, although he was now looking at the table. "The board would like to put forth a motion to phase you out of operation by the end of the year, letting a more experienced hand take over management of the company."

"But—" Quincy halted, wondering who in this world they were thinking understood the nature of this business better than she. "You mean to suspend my role as chief officer of operations of The Q? Of my own company? And keep me filing reports while someone else botches up my job?"

"No." Levins tilted his head, perspiration gathering at his hairline. "We mean to buy you out of your remaining stock and remove you from the company. The compensation we've discussed would be immeasurable. You will be as comfortable as the king, I daresay."

"Compensation?" Quincy snapped. "I own most of The Q stock."

"Forty-seven percent," Harris inserted deftly. "You own forty-seven percent. As it was, you owned twenty-five percent before your uncle died. He once owned thirty percent, but sold eight percent of his shares to Vicks."

"Vicks?"

"Yes," Harris continued. "And, two months ago, the board purchased said eight percent from Vicks for a rather generous price, which means fifty-three percent of the stock is now publicly traded. By Rhysdon law and the company charter, if the board votes by three-fourths majority, you will be forced to exchange your stock for a generous compensation and relinquish any tie to the company."

Quincy took half a breath in complete astonishment. "I still don't understand."

Levins was beginning to get impatient. "It's clearly explained in the documentation Mr. Arch has prepared. We discussed the terms at the November meeting—where you were noticeably absent—and have asked Mr. Arch to draw up the transition documents. Mr. Arch? Do you have them with you?"

Quincy spun around in her chair, knuckles white from her grip on the edge of the table. Arch wouldn't look at her.

"Yes," Arch said after a pause, as he stood with the papers and his cane. "I have prepared the documentation, just as you asked." He took some papers from his portfolio and limped towards Levins, handing them over with what seemed to Quincy, a detached interest.

Levins glanced at the papers and nodded, a smile coming into its own on the side of his lips.

"Splendid, Mr. Arch. Well done."

Arch gave no verbal response, rather his jaw tightened, and he gave a sharp nod.

Quincy watched this exchange from a hollow place inside of her, disbelieving it. Arch wouldn't have done this to her. He wouldn't have taken what was most precious away from her, without a warning, without a fight.

Arch pressed his lips together and limped gracefully back to his chair in the shadowed corner of the room. And Quincy watched him. Arch still wouldn't meet her eye, no matter how her eyes pinned and prodded.

The strange sensation that she had never seen him before crawled up her back; he looked foreign, distant, strangely separate from where she sat. Quincy had been beaten, starved, pummeled, and bludgeoned. She had been cold, exhausted, and nearly defeated. But she had never been knifed in the back before. She now knew what it felt like, and she was stunned as much as betrayed, for she had given him all her confidence—and all her courage. It hurt deeply, even in places she had believed were only shallows. It hurt more than she could ever fathom.

And Arch would still not lift his eyes to hers.

Quincy's focus was snapped back into the present moment by something Guthries was saying. Conversation among the board had begun in low voices, and Quincy gritted her teeth. Arch would still not lift his eyes to hers. Well. No matter, Quincy turned to face the board. She would not look at James Arch again. He deserved nothing from her.

"Here we are," Levins was saying, looking down at the papers in his hand.

Quincy listened, silent as death, as Levins read the document that would forever separate Quincy St. Claire from The Q. It was a document perfectly crafted. A black gift. Cruel and empty. And the ramifications of such a gift rattled around the inside of Quincy's heart, like the broken lock of a door.

"We should vote now," Rutherford was saying, "as it's already been discussed."

"But we're not all decided on this course of action," Guthries interjected. Quincy looked towards him, holding an angry breath.

"I think," said Fraey, motioning towards Quincy, "we should give the board more time to make a sound decision. Ezekiel would not have wished us to rush such a thing, and Miss St. Claire has yet to prove whether she is still worthy of the helm. This needs time and discussion. It is December the twelfth. I say we disperse, review the matter in full, then reconvene on the twenty-sixth to make our final decision. If the board still feels compelled to vote for St. Claire's removal, then she will have one week to settle her affairs and be out by the first of the year."

"But—" Levins began to protest.

"Wise. Very wise," Waits said, looking at the watch in his pocket. "It's late."

"Matters like these are sensitive," Rutherford interjected, "and should be dealt with immediately." Then he began a monologue about courage, about "being men of determination and action," and about "moving forward into the future."

Quincy pushed back on her chair, balancing on the rear legs, her arms crossed in iron stubbornness, her pulse pounding like a war drum.

"Fraey's meeting on the twenty-sixth would be sensible enough," Waits interrupted.

A round of agreement moved despite Rutherford and Levins.

Then Arch spoke from the shadows, and Quincy fought the instinct to cringe at the sound of his voice. "It is well to remember that Rhysdon law forbids any outside discussion of these events. They can only be talked over between members of the board until after the vote on the twenty-sixth. No members of the staff may be made privy to the question at hand."

"Yes, yes," Levins said, looking perturbed.

"Do you wish to say anything, Miss St. Claire?" Fraey asked.

"By all means." Quincy let the feet of her chair smash to the floor. Be brave, Quincy. Be brave.

Quincy stood, leaning forward, her fingers extended on the table to hold her weight as she narrowed her gaze on the men that sat in front of her. "I find the facts, gentlemen, to be interesting. All of you here are beneficiaries of my taking the helm of The Q. Less than a third of your positions existed before I did. I have turned this business into a giant and your names, by association, into gold. Now look at you," she glowered, piercing the men with her eyes, "a confident body of fools, who've *never* been a quarter as successful as I've been."

Her words settled wrong in their faces. They took exception. She didn't care, her calm exterior slipping towards internal danger of a machine spinning out of control.

"Now you suppose," Quincy continued, "that all you have to do is depose Quincy St. Claire, get rid of her, recruit the weak-spined solicitor to draw up a couple of contracts, and off you ride, to expand the empire beneath the steady hand of the all-knowing board of directors."

Rutherford scoffed. "Hundreds of businesses thrive without Quincy St. Claire."

"The Q won't." Quincy straightened, folding her arms and resting her weight on one foot in a challenging stance. "As if you could rip the heart from the body and expect it to live."

"Ezekiel was the heart," Fraey replied staunchly. "The Q stands for his vision, his dream."

Quincy rounded on him. "Ezekiel was the midwife!" she shouted. "Ezekiel was the mother! He gave The Q its body; he set the blood in motion. But, *I* brought it into maturity. I made demands and expected perfection! I pulled it through adolescence, where so many endeavors get lost, get lazy, get distracted. I enlisted and trained this powerful, intelligent force that is taking city after city, and you will regret killing the general if what you want is to win the war!" She was shouting, shaking, emotion rising as she pounded the table with a fist. "The *Q* stands for *Quincy*, you fools!"

No one uttered a word, and Quincy, breathing hard, could only look at the lines in her fisted hand and think this was surely the worst day of all days.

"*Q* stands for Quincy," she repeated aloud, disoriented in the wash of anger. "*Q* is for Quincy." Releasing her fist, Quincy stepped away from the table of vipers, brushing a lock of displaced blond hair from her eyes. "That's all I have to say."

Perhaps someone spoke—the entire board could have exploded in objection—but Quincy heard nothing. Away from the table, she was out the door before her ears could remember their intended function.

An image came bursting at Quincy as she disappeared down the hallway. It was the face of one of Ezekiel's friends, an old war hero from England, who had once described in detail seeing a man hit directly at short range with a cannon ball.

"A spectacular mess, horrific and utterly obliterating," he had said. "I was standing thirty feet out, and it damned well stained my uniform."

Ezekiel had ended the conversation abruptly; no doubt after realizing that his wide-eyed great-niece was sitting by the window. But Quincy had seen enough grit before to have experienced the picture of that man's death in her mind. It was now vividly before her again as she shot down the stairs, trying to breathe. Quincy St. Claire was gone, and there were now only pieces, stuck to the various panels and curtains and carpets and to uninspired men, who would wipe her blood from their suits, mark this as a good story, and continue telling it to their friends for the next thirty years.

When Quincy hit the street, she was greeted with a moving wall of white and black, overwhelming, thick. It was snow. Rather, it was a wet sleet. She closed her eyes, unable to weld a coherent thought together.

It felt like a grand relief, the nothingness that now pervaded her vision, which had already begun eating at her mind the night before.

Someone moved around her, pushing her shoulder. Quincy didn't care. She opened her eyes and ignored the storm as she moved in whatever direction she now faced, walking anywhere, for direction didn't matter. Bodies don't matter once the heart has stopped.

"Quincy!" a voice shouted through the December wind, but Quincy wasn't interested. "Quincy! Stop!"

She didn't.

A hand grabbed her arm and pulled her around almost violently. Arch was breathing hard, his face admitting the pain of having chased her through the streets. "I'm sorry, Quincy. Please. I couldn't speak with you about it, and I only found out yesterday morning. I couldn't—I couldn't bear to look at your face, and I hated the fact that I couldn't say anything. It's the law, Quincy."

She just stared at him, this distant creature, whose ties with her had been severed the moment he had handed the transition documents to Levins.

"You did it," Arch breathed, "the last requirement. Quincy, you fulfilled Ezekiel's list. He wanted you to say 'Q is for *Quincy*.' He wanted you to realize that you were enough. Quincy—"

Quincy's mouth moved to form a word, but instead she stopped and just stared, her eyes drilling into Arch's with disbelief. What did any of Ezekiel's requirements even mean at this point? In two weeks, they would vote her out of The Q regardless, and she would be left utterly bereft of all that mattered. And Arch wanted to celebrate that she had won the silly game?

"Quincy?"

In two weeks time, she would cease to exist.

"Quincy, say something." James Arch leaned on his cane, his face still pale despite the cold, a curtain of iced-over snow keeping them apart. "You can't mean to let things lie like this between us. Do you— are you not going to say anything?" When she didn't answer, he drew his face together. "Do you mean to leave it at this?"

Quincy gave a stiff nod, turned, pulling the collar of her coat up to shield her neck from the spitting snow, before she went barreling down the street.

He followed.

Struggling to keep step beside her, Arch looked as if he wanted to say seven things at once. Wise, Quincy thought, that he chose not to say any of them. She didn't look at him again but built a fortress, ignoring the outside of her mind, fighting her awareness of Arch's uneven gait as he kept time at her side. If his knee gave out she wouldn't stop, she wouldn't even look back.

Quincy walked and walked, black boots slapping the puddles, shoulders pushing against anyone who found themselves accidently in her way.

"Excuse us. Excuse me," Arch was muttering, offering apology for each of Quincy's miniature altercations. "Forgive me."

Quincy blocked him out harder, further, along with the noise of the streets and the moment when the sleet turned a brighter white and started to fall softer onto the wet pavement. She ignored the gaslight, the streams of Rhysdoners hurrying to be out of the storm. They faded away like ghosts, and she walked. She walked for what seemed like hours. Nothingness spread out before her.

"Where are we going, Quincy?" Arch finally asked, catching her arm with his hand again and swinging her around to face him. The movement of him bringing her back to herself made Quincy dizzy. She blinked, and there was Arch, his face wet, his cheeks a fierce red, his hair dripping. When her reply was a numb shrug, he frowned and didn't release her arm, saying, "Come with me."

Either her pride or her exhaustion or her disdain for Rutherford and Levins—and the whole lot of them—kept Quincy from opening her mouth to protest. She didn't care anymore. Arch could be walking her to the docks to throw her in, and she wouldn't fight it.

The snow grew so thick that Arch was holding his arm before his face. As he was leading her along the roads, Quincy again disappeared into her thoughts. Down several more streets, around a corner, and up a few stairs, Quincy stumbling in spite of herself and then there was a knock. A door swung open, sending light out into the snow.

"Master Arch! Heavens be."

"James!"

Arch was protesting that he was just fine, and Quincy was startled by the sudden warmth. She looked up. But before Quincy could turn tail and disappear, she was ushered through the hall, past Symons and Mary, and into the drawing room of Peacock House. A fire was lit.

"Child! She's frozen," Symons cried, following them in.

"She's in shock," Arch hastily explained.

Quincy was dragged to a sofa; her wet jacket peeled from her shoulders; a warm cup placed in her hand by someone. It spilled, burning Quincy's skin. Quincy looked down. She hadn't realized she was shaking.

Arch crouched down before her, grimacing, his cane forgotten, his hair and clothes still dripping wet, the cold red of his face fading into triangle shapes on his cheeks. Quincy lifted her free hand—which was shaking more than the other—to her brow and looked up and sideways, coming to herself, horrified at the attention. For the first time in her life, she felt like she was going to break, to shatter. Her mind would snap, and there would be no way to bring her back.

He must have seen this, or sensed it, for Arch stood and whispered something to the others in the room. Anxious voices came in response and then an ushering out. The lights were turned down, leaving only the fire and a few candelabras of ivory candles. Arch himself then sat beside Quincy, his jacket removed, a cup of hot tea in his cold hands.

"Damnation," he muttered.

Quincy hadn't bothered to lift her own cup of tea to her mouth. She just stared at the pattern of the carpet before her. Her fingers and her feet ached in the heat of the room. She sniffed.

The door opened. Someone set down another tray of tea. The scent of peppermint asked for Quincy's attention. She ignored it. Arch took the cup from her hand and stood. She heard the sound of silver on china then a crash. Arch repeated his earlier exclamation, and the sounds of preparing a cup of tea began anew. He sat down again beside her and set the fresh cup into her hand, resting his own hand now on her back. His fingers were cold and she flinched. Arch pulled away as if he had burned her, his mouth moving into a straight line.

After several minutes of neither of them moving, he finally said, "Have you finished with your tea?"

Quincy handed the undisturbed cup to Arch, and he placed it on the table beside his own.

"Are you warm enough?" he asked, sitting up, the red from his own cheeks fading away, leaving his complexion stark against the black of his eyes.

Quincy said nothing. Her jaw felt too taut.

Rather businesslike in his movements, Arch reached for Quincy's hand and pressed her fingers between his own. "Your hands are still cold." His left hand traveled up to her face, touching lightly her cheek, then her chin. "Your face has warmed, though."

What an unbelievable thing, Quincy thought, determined not to flinch or turn away however different she felt about him touching her now. Her gaze shifted, and she was staring at him, hardly breathing.

"Quincy, I couldn't speak to you of it."

Her eyes felt rounder as an unaccustomed pressure rimmed her lower eyelids.

"Levins sent me a note Sunday night," Arch continued. "He asked me to meet with him first thing in the morning. He asked about the process and how the documents would be drawn up. By law, I couldn't say anything to you."

She released a burst of air, as if she would laugh. But her voice, when she finally spoke, was graveled. "You can keep your law, Arch."

He opened his mouth in consternation then closed it again.

"You couldn't have planned it better," she muttered, seeing the last year in a new light altogether. "Bring Quincy to the point of being within reach, bring her as close to The Q as possible, then rip it away. What satisfaction you must have now, Arch. You won."

He moved back, his eyes staring. "Why would you say such a thing?"

"Because it's nothing, none of it," Quincy cried. "And you're—all you had to do was warn me. You didn't. You fed me to the wolves! You dropped me in, and now I've lost The Q. You are the reason I've lost The Q."

"Are you saying this is my fault?" he replied, his expression bewildered. "As if your own ill-temper and arrogance had nothing to do with the board wanting you out?"

"And I'm going to be out! Be happy! You won the game." She lifted her clenched fists. "Then, you tell me I made the last requirement? It was a cruel trick, Arch."

Arch looked baffled and was making an effort to return to his patience. "Quincy, you have two weeks. We have two weeks. I can help you sort this out. I can't speak to the board, but I can support you; I can help you prepare arguments. If we can win even a few votes—"

"*We?*" Quincy stood, her fists now anchored to her sides. "What do you mean you can help me? I'm done, Arch. I fulfilled the requirements. You're gone. You're nothing. I don't need you! I never wanted you in the first place, and you were foisted—"

He flinched.

"—foisted on me. Now I can do what I've wanted to all year. I can fire you! You're finished. I never want you to walk through the front door of The Q again." Quincy slowed herself down to emphasize every word of her next sentence, "I don't want anything to do with you."

He was frozen, unmoving, his lips parted slightly, his hands resting before him. He looked up in obvious pain, as if she had shot him. But then in his eyes came the fire she had seen before, and her words burned any softness out of his face.

He stood and stepped away, looking down at her with the practiced air of the wealthy. His voice came out hard, "The joke is still at your expense, St. Claire. You can't fire me during the process of corporate restructure. I still represent the board, and I *will* do my job. But, have no worries, I don't intend to walk through that door ever again while you are still part of the company."

"Good."

Mary entered just then with a tray of food. "Oh, Quincy, are you quite recovered? Don't rush off. I've brought food for you both. It's late."

"And I still have some work to finish at The Q," Quincy replied, not minding the edge in her voice.

Arch folded his arms. "Mary, would you please ask Symons to

please bring Miss St. Claire's things?"

"Certainly," Mary said, her eyes moving from Arch to Quincy.

Mary disappeared, and James Arch walked past Quincy to lean against the fireplace. He didn't look at her but, rather, stared down the flames.

Quincy stubbornly watched the door.

He should have said something, anything to prepare her.

Symons came in with Quincy's jacket, which was still wet through. "There, my dear. Not very dry. It won't suit for a walk through town, so I've called the carriage around for Master Arch to see you back home."

"No," Quincy said.

Arch said nothing.

Mary, who had followed Symons into the room, opened her mouth to speak, but Quincy was faster on her tongue. "I've no need to inconvenience Mr. Arch any further. I'll walk."

"Take the carriage, Quincy," Arch said darkly.

Quincy turned fiercely on Arch, "Why can't you understand that I don't need anything from you! I trusted you—" Her voice broke. "A great mistake."

"You have made yourself perfectly clear." His lifted his chin. "Good evening, Miss St. Claire." He walked past Quincy, reaching for his own coat, laid over the back of the couch, and left the room. Without a word to Mary—who had started crying—Quincy threw on her own jacket and thrust her hands into its wet pockets, deserting the drawing room, passing through the hall and out into the cold.

She felt wretched.

The storm did not abate.

When Quincy got home, she cried.

CHAPTER FORTY-EIGHT:

A Damned Shame

Quincy spent the next two weeks visiting every member of the board who would agree to meet with her. She argued, she reasoned, she pled for their votes. Every time she left a meeting, Quincy knew she had lost. It was self-immolation of the cruelest sort, this fact that she kept trying.

Waits was the one who finally gave Quincy an honest piece to the puzzle of her deposition.

"There's simply more to it, St. Claire," he frowned, sounding uncertain of his words. "Other considerations. I might very well vote for you—all of Rhysdon knows your brilliance—but most of the board has been swayed by a different source of profits. And they feel The Q is secure enough to follow it."

Quincy narrowed her eyes. "What do you mean?"

Waits pulled at his mouth, and then made a decision. He raised his eyebrows in a helpless expression. "Bought out, as it were, Miss St. Claire. The owner of *The Rhysdon Sun*—"

"Draggen?"

"Yes. Mr. Draggen has offered the board an incredible sum if The Q gives first preference to *The Sun* over *The Times*. He wants his to be the flagship paper, and he's prepared to give The Q a greater profit for the privilege of being the host newspaper, along with stock in *The Sun*.

Among other things."

Quincy shifted in her seat and tapped her booted toe against the floor. "Is he offering the members of the board money to see this through?"

Waits turned red. "That would be highly illegal and—"

"Is he, Waits?"

"I don't think there would be any way for you to prove it. You'd just look like you were turning over stones to have your way."

"So the board pushes me out, turns *The Sun* into the flagship paper for a pretty penny, and the members of the board are paid off by Draggen, who probably hopes to benefit from the profits of the foreign market." She collapsed back into her chair, sinking her hands into the pockets of her jacket. "He's bought their votes."

Opening his mouth as if to say something, Waits then thought better of it, and closed it again.

"You do realize Draggen is no great mind for business," Quincy stated, staring Waits down. "He's good, but he's not much better than that. And now, he's swaying all of you with his numbers that he may not have the acumen to back up." She snorted and stood up. "Priest won't suffer if *The Times* is a secondary rather than the flagship paper. He's too brilliant for that." She sighed. "I was right. You are a bunch of fools. Selfish fools."

Quincy stopped visiting members of the board after that. She knew she had lost.

Jade was worried. Spense was worried. But Quincy continued to say nothing. She did her work and stayed up late, often falling asleep at her counter in the early hours of the morning. When she did manage to climb the stairs to the matchbox at the end of a day, she would lie awake in bed, looking at the space on the wall where she had ripped away the list of requirements before burning it. After sufficient time had passed, Quincy would rise, change her clothes, and return to the front office and her work.

Arch was true to his word—he always was, Quincy thought—for he did not come back to The Q. She had no knowledge of whether he had met with any members of the board. She figured he had.

What Quincy hadn't anticipated was that, as much as she hated this cruel fate of being ripped from The Q, she was haunted by what she had said to Arch in equal measure. He, in some ways, felt just as irreplaceable, and she could hardly bear either loss.

"It's a bad business, St. Claire. Cutthroat and weak."

Crow leaned against the side of a dark doorway in one of Rhysdon's dog streets, where one of Crow's minions had led Quincy.

One of the smuggler's sailors had arrived just before close, and had said that Crow was waiting for her. She had closed the office and followed him, finding the smuggler, with a serious bent in his expression, hiding in the shadows of an abandoned building.

They stood in silence for a long while before Crow spoke again. "I hear things, Quincy. It's my work."

Quincy nodded.

"I think I've sorted out the truth of it, but will you tell me how it happened?"

Quincy let out the breath she seemed to have been holding for days and scuffed her boots against the stone of the doorway. If Crow already knew, it at least gave her someone to speak with. So she began in stilted sentences, each one tearing her heart a bit more. The board meeting. The fight with Arch. The days of realizing that each member of the board had turned against her for his own profit. The numbness. The disbelief. The complete loss of self. It came out like infection from a wound.

"Damned shame," Crow said several minutes after she finished.

Quincy didn't say anything in response, just stood there, crouched in the corner, staring into the darkness.

"And Arch?"

She shook her head and lifted her shoulder in a careless way. "I said things, and—well, he's certainly glad to be rid of me now. It's no use; I've been broken for too long. And he shouldn't have to—"

Crow must have heard the crushing weight beneath what she said, sensed the piercing blow of what Arch had done in her voice, for Crow didn't ask her anything else about the affair.

Then they parted; Quincy, towards The Q, Crow, into his underground exile.

———

The rest of December was like a wild horse, determined to sprint forward with no regard to the pain it was causing Quincy. She did her work, watched each day disappear, and then locked the door, saying good-bye to another moment of still knowing who she was. A daily disappearing act—that was all the process was.

CHAPTER FORTY-NINE:

This Mysterious War

Two days before Christmas, on the twenty-third of December, Quincy received a card. The handwriting was familiar but not telling enough to keep her from opening it. She immediately wished she hadn't. It was from Lord Arch.

> *Dear Quincy St. Claire,*
>
> *I write to invite you for a Christmas morning tête-à-tête. My children will be out until four o'clock, and so the coast is clear of enemy bombardment. I promise you a cheerful few hours, with no great inconvenience to yourself. I don't mind playing turncoat in this mysterious war so that I might enjoy the company of one I deem a friend. We won't tell James I had you over.*
>
> *With sincere regard,*
> *Lord Thomas Arch*

Quincy set the invitation aside with no intention to answer it nor to make an appearance. How could she ever set foot in Peacock House again? Arch had betrayed her, had sacrificed her on the altar of the law. And she had said such horrible things. She had lacerated the one person in this world that she cared for the very most. Returning to Regent Square would be a great imposition to both the Arch family and her own fractured state. It would be better if she just disappeared.

On Christmas Eve, the pressroom was still, the employees gone home, for no issue of *The Q* would be printed until the evening of the twenty-sixth. Quincy sat in her matchbox, perched atop one bureau, her feet resting against the other, watching the furious exhibition of snow gathering in the deserted street below. The gaslight stretched the shadows from the large flakes, making Gainsford Street seem otherworldly, strange, with tucks of sinister shadows in the darkness. She slumped her shoulders and leaned against the frame of the cold window.

In her hand was a letter from Fisher. He had heard from Arch, who had indicated things were precarious at The Q and that he might want to know how Miss St. Claire was faring. Fisher had guessed the cause, indicating his disbelief that it might be true.

Quince,

I can only gather from Arch's words two things: First, that you are in danger of losing The Q to the board of directors. And since he said you've fulfilled the requirements, this is the only option I believe. What are they about, Quince? You have brought The Q all the success it has. Scoundrels! Every one! It makes sense now why they forced Vicks off the board. He would never have voted against you.

Second, Arch is worried about you but is unable to know for himself how you are. You must have quarreled, and for that I'm sorry, as it seemed you'd become fast friends. Quincy, do you need me to come home? Will you write and tell me the state of things? I would come. I would always come. I promise you, I would try to sew up any part of you that is ripped away.

You're probably laughing at me right now, having already picked yourself up and brushed yourself off after swearing off the entire human race.

Write to me.

Fisher

Quincy didn't feel like she needed to be brushed off and set on the pedestal of devil-may-care courage—she just wanted someone to sit down in the mud of the whole affair and tell her it was alright to be broken. That's all Quincy wanted, to be sad and be told it was just fine.

And be told that she would be just fine.

CHAPTER FIFTY:
Merry and Bright, and All That

Christmas morning was as bright as any day had been all December. The new snow, white against all the sooty expectations of a smoke-filled city, was dazzling, reflecting and refracting a cacophony of colors, too loud for Quincy's eyes. She pulled her hat down and slouched into her thick, red scarf.

Black boots, dark blue breeches with a black silk ribbon along the outseams, and her sharp-shouldered jacket, all covered by the mass of red scarf wrapped several times around her neck and over her chin—Quincy, despite the misery of the month, still looked herself as she stepped towards Henley Street.

She was in search of an open market where she could buy peppermint tea, a handful of candied caramels, a loaf of country bread, a bag of nuts, and, if she were lucky in the find, a lemon to suck on. This had been Quincy's Christmas feast ever since Ezekiel had brought her to Rhysdon and had given her money enough for anything she had ever dreamed of eating on the holiday.

Henley Street was rich enough to have variety and poor enough to be open a half day on Christmas. Some shops stayed open even later. Ezekiel always disapproved, preferring Quincy to stay home. But each December twenty-fifth, there Quincy would go to secure her own personal brand of yuletide cheer.

"Quincy!"

Her chin shot out of her scarf so fast the cold air rushed down her neck. Reaching to pull her scarf closer, Quincy looked down the street to see a tall figure waving. Jade.

"What are you doing on Henley?" Jade grinned from behind the lapels of her woolen army coat. She held up a box of candles. "Jack and I thought we'd throw candles all over tonight for our lavish," she rolled her eyes for effect, "Christmas dinner. With pudding, of course. And friends. Anyway." Jade blew some hair out of her face. "You're coming this year? Mentioned it weeks ago, if you remember. Now, I know you didn't come last year, or the year before that, but I insist. Really, Quincy."

"Thank you, but no," said Quincy, finally getting a word in. Not that she had been in a rush to, at any rate. "I'm—"

"But Quincy—Ah, look, there's Jack with a rabbit, a rabbit of all things. Adorable, but I'm not cooking it, so I hope he is." She made a face. "Eight o'clock, then? Be sharp, and I'll even let you—"

"I've been invited to spend the holiday with Lord Arch," Quincy blurted out before she could even think to stop. She paused then clamped her mouth shut. What had she just committed herself to? Jade, apparently, was asking herself the same question, for her eyebrows came together with a fierce pull. "I'm here on Henley, searching for a gift I can take," Quincy lied, "and I'm having a terrible time of it. I don't suppose you've seen anything?"

"What? Like a gold-plated spoon? Perhaps a diamond-studded collar for the dog?"

"I don't think that's the kind—"

Jade's face melted into a grin. "I'm pulling at you, Quincy! You're really going to spend Christmas as a guest of Lord Arch? Will you see *our* Arch? I hope that means you've forgiven him for whatever happened between you. I've never seen you happier than when with Arch," Jade said just as Jack stopped beside them, tipping his hat at Quincy.

"Miss St. Claire."

"Hello Jack."

Jack held up his rabbit. "Are you coming tonight?"

"No. Sorry." She turned back to Jade. "I'm supposed to be there by late morning."

"Then I better let you get on your way." Jade smiled as she took a candle from her box, handing it to Quincy rather ceremoniously. "Happy Christmas, merry and bright, and all that."

Quincy nodded as she took the candle and tucked it inside her jacket. Once Jade and Jack were down the street, Quincy stopped in at the bakers for the country bread, found a small pastry shop that sold the caramels, and, at last, patronized a grocer's shop, where she found her peppermint tea and a handful of Brazil nuts. They even had lemons. Quincy bought three.

With each step, she cursed herself for her stupidity. Jade would inquire about the day and be hurt that she had been brushed off, lied to. Quincy threw a stubborn caramel into her mouth as she walked back to Gainsford Street with her Christmas parcels and couldn't believe she was considering Lord Arch's invitation. Of all things, sneaking behind Arch's back to spend Christmas Day with his father and then to be gone, neither he nor Mary any the wiser—this was not the sort of thing Quincy St. Claire did. But Jade.

"Too late now." She gritted her teeth, and instead of turning left towards Gainsford, she hailed a hansom and gave directions to Regent Square.

———

Symons answered the door. "Well, Miss St. Claire! What an unexpected surprise. Is Master James expecting you?"

"I am," came the voice of Lord Arch from behind the confused housekeeper. "Happy Christmas, Miss St. Claire!" He greeted her with an enthusiastic handshake. "Would you mind if we settled in the library? I never like to be too far from my books on Christmas. You understand."

Quincy lifted a shoulder. No, she didn't.

The elegant face of Lord Arch shifted into amusement. "Ah, of course you don't. You are incurable."

"I have always liked you in that red scarf," Lord Arch continued as he and Quincy ascended the staircase, her parcels still in her hand. "Now, if Symons can keep our secret, it should be quite the jolly party."

If ever a room were created for Christmas Day, it was the Arch library. The rich colors, the fire, the green chairs by the fireplace. Someone, in the German tradition, had placed a tree, a real tree, in one of the corners, and it sparkled with candlelight. The scent reminded Quincy of being a child, and she felt the chill of winter up her spine despite the fire.

Lord Arch motioned for Quincy to claim one of the honored chairs before the hearth and poured her a cup of peppermint tea. "You see, I haven't forgotten your first visit and asked Symons to always keep peppermint tea in full stock. That," he handed her the tea with the same slight flourish she had seen Arch use from time to time, "is my way of saying you are expected and wanted at Peacock House."

Quincy snorted, and Lord Arch's eyes twinkled as he poured himself a cup.

"And just what are you clutching so tightly?"

Quincy looked down. "A few Christmas indulgences I've become accustomed too."

Lord Arch laughed for a good minute. "This is too rich, too wonderful. Do tell, Quincy St. Claire, what are your Christmas *indulgences*?"

"If you must know," grumbled Quincy, "country bread, peppermint tea, caramels, Brazil nuts, and lemons."

"Lemons for the tea?"

"For sucking," Quincy admitted unabashedly.

Lord Arch threw his head back and laughed again. "Is that why you've nothing sweet to say to my poor James these days? Lemons, indeed."

Quincy could feel herself being baited for a fight. "It was my understanding that James had no part in this gathering. Wherever he—" Quincy stopped and looked over her shoulder, which made Lord Arch laugh. "Where is Arch anyway?"

"He and Mary went to church and then will spend a good deal of the day at the Fothergils'.'"

"But you'll not join them?"

"Later this evening, there will be a gathering here. Lady Fothergil, Johnny, other close friends. Christmas is the favorite time at Peacock House; it always has been. The weeks of December are filled with various parties, entertainments, music, and every good thing you can imagine, and we partake of them all. But, on Christmas, everyone wishes they were here. It is the merriest of parties; it is the grandest of evenings—enough sparkle and magic and music for all."

Quincy pressed her hands against the teacup—an antique number of cream, gold, and emerald green—and looked about the library.

"You didn't stay home because of me, did you?"

"No." Lord Arch settled back, crossing his legs as he looked towards the fire. "I requested to have the day to myself, a day to think and to remember. You see, Quincy St. Claire, it was on this very day, Christmas, six years ago now, that I lost my wife."

"I'm sorry." And Quincy meant it. It felt easier to console Lord Arch than it had been with Priest. Perhaps six years felt like a safe distance to assuage someone's pain. It wasn't as fresh. It wasn't still contagious.

"So am I," Lord Arch replied, his eyes moving with the fire as it lapped the wood. "It's not ruined the day; it's made it more profound. All the same, I like sitting in my library, thinking of her. James is very much like her in the important ways."

Quincy set her now empty teacup on the floor. "She was French?"

"Yes. Intelligent, kind, as beautiful as any woman you've ever seen." He shifted and looked towards Quincy. "I'll never forget the first time I saw her: hair, dark as a raven; her eyes, just the same. And yet—" Lord Arch lifted his hands gracefully. "There is a certain slant of the light, Miss St. Claire, just as morning is shaking off night, when the shadows are still deep, but the sky has given way to ivory and rose, the clouds tumbled out in all their glory. That's what it was like to be with Isabella Brielle De Vere. So beautiful in spirit it was painful for me."

"De Vere? Like the essayist?"

"Certainly," Lord Arch said, setting his teacup on the side table, the china rattling against itself in the pretty sound of a flat bell. "De Vere was her father."

"De Vere?"

"Yes, the social injustice that burns my son comes from the De Veres. The poetry, from Crandall, my mother's grandfather. James has words so thick in his blood he can scarcely breathe without them. And, clearly, he thinks them worth dying for."

Quincy leaned back in her chair and pressed her hands into her jacket pockets, realizing she was bothered Arch had never told her. "Why did he never say so?"

"James's love for his heritage, especially for his grandfather De Vere, is so intimate, so, well, holy that he doesn't speak of it often. As to why he did not tell you, perhaps he felt you would have no compunction using it against him if you were angry."

Quincy flinched.

In the market on Henley Street earlier that morning, Quincy had seen the fishmongers gutting their doomed catches, and that was how she now felt: like Lord Arch had run a knife through her. She had no self-control to keep it from her face.

"I should not have said that, Miss St. Claire." Lord Arch softened his tone. "That was unfair, an assumption I had no right to make."

"You had every right," Quincy said, realizing her face was burning. She pressed the back of her hand to her cheek and grimaced.

"Let me say this, if nothing else is said, you've changed him, Miss St. Claire."

A tumble of panic came, and she pulled her shoulders up defensively, waiting for the judgment.

"You see, I believe he's a better man now," Lord Arch stated unequivocally. "Certainly more passionate about his work and his writing for having been a student of your own qualities. Before meeting you, all his grand thoughts paraded around in his head, and he was getting a few places with it, his essays catching on. But he rather fell in love with the way you worked, the way your mind relentlessly turned every stone until what you had created was perfection itself. Your ethic, your courage, your determination. He's been working to match his own character to the virtues you own since he started in at The Q, and I can attest that he's better for it. Thank you, Quincy, for that."

Quincy set her mouth. "I'm not sure I believe you, as he's always lecturing."

"James does like to lecture." Lord Arch grinned, eyes twinkling. "A forgivable folly, I suppose."

Raising her eyebrows, Quincy almost snorted.

"Ah, dear child." Lord Arch tilted his head patiently. "For a young man who values honesty and a young woman who delivers her opinion with such frank direction, I find myself curious why you two can do neither with each other. I'm not saying this month hasn't been its own special disaster. James, let the record show, has been an absolute terror these last weeks. At home, he's a black cloud, and abroad, he burns beneath the false pretense of enjoying himself. He can't fathom a way to convince you that he is worth letting back into your fortressed world and fears he's spoiled it for good."

"Now," Lord Arch continued lightly when Quincy's panic consumed her face, "enough of this. It is a day without James that I promised you. We must enjoy ourselves, and James must suffer as he chooses. Really, St. Claire, what is he to us on such fine a day?"

Quincy laughed, her embarrassment not quite dissipated.

"It's Christmas, after all, Miss St. Claire. Let us have music, just you and me. Do you know any carols?"

She did. Ezekiel had loved carols more than anything. She stood up and walked to the violin case, opening it with an unexpected anticipation.

"Ezekiel came to Peacock House for several Christmas parties these last years."

"I don't remember him mentioning it," Quincy said as she was tuning the violin.

"You, I recall, were occupied with business."

"Likely."

Quincy returned, violin in hand, settled on the edge of her seat, and began to play one of her uncle's favorites, "The Coventry Carol". The violin responded as if it loved Christmas Day above all else: bright and bold, yet lingering. Quincy followed her first selection with the lively French carol "Patapan". Then she pulled the notes straight into "Jesus Christ the Apple Tree": sweet, lilting, and sad enough to make the listener feel heartbreak between each note.

Another hour passed: Quincy, pulling from memory every carol she could remember, and Lord Arch, being the attentive and appreciative listener.

"Play "Patapan" once more, for me, with the same flair, of course."

And so, Quincy played, tapping the drum with her toe, dancing on the very top of each note: light, puckish, frosted on one side, fire bound on the other. When she finished, an eager applause came from the hall. Symons's face turned red when Quincy almost jumped from her chair.

"I'm sorry, Lord Arch, Miss St. Claire, it's just been a long time since I've heard such music in the house."

"Yes," Lord Arch rejoined. "There's been very little since my wife died. She was the real musician. You play like her."

"Indeed," Symons said, lifting her apron to dab at her eyes. "I'll be seeing to a brunch for you just now."

Quincy spent what could only be termed as an amiable day with Lord Arch. They spoke or sat in silence. She played more carols on the violin, watched the fire, and almost forgot the messy days previous. It was nearly three o'clock when she prepared herself to leave.

"Only if you're certain you don't want to stay for the festivities. You could ignore James the evening through, I'm sure of it."

Quincy pulled her mouth to the side with a regretful twist. "No, I have—something important is happening tomorrow I would like time to prepare for."

"James indicated there would be a rather distasteful meeting with The Q board, but he said nothing further."

"Well, come tomorrow afternoon, you will know it all." Quincy's voice came off these words with such sadness that Lord Arch's expression turned tender.

"It can't be as bad as all that."

"It's worse," Quincy said, strapping her emotions tight. "Happy Christmas, Lord Arch. Thank you for inviting me."

"Don't forget your lemons." Lord Arch helped her gather whatever Christmas indulgences the pair of them had not consumed.

When Quincy stepped down the stairs of Peacock House, she let a long sigh trail behind her, wishing tomorrow had already passed.

CHAPTER FIFTY-ONE:

The Art of Mourning

The board meeting lasted less than ten minutes. Quincy sat at the head of the table, stoically staring into the distance that wasn't there. Levins called forth the motion. They all cast their votes to "release Quincy St. Claire" from her obligations to The Q.

The only contrary vote was her own.

Levins asked for Arch to bring over the paperwork. Arch moved from the deepest shadow in the room, where he had been watching the entire affair. When he set the contract before Quincy, for her to sign, his hand was shaking.

Quincy stared at the page, passing her eyes over the words. The financial recompense was substantial. Adding that amount to what she had already inherited from Ezekiel, Quincy would have no financial worries her life through. She was to vacate her post before Monday, January the first. Also, she could take nothing from the offices of The Q, as it was all the property of the company, except for a small list of her own assets. Quincy skimmed the list, noticing among the wreckage that she had been given her own bed. How generous.

Quincy picked up the pen Arch had set on the table and signed her name to the paper with what Quincy could only accuse herself of being a numb flourish. Levins let out an audible sigh and smugly signed his name beneath hers. Then each member of the board did the same.

Arch handed Quincy a copy of the contract and said something in regards to the transfer of funds to her own accounts.

She gave no response, confident he would take care of it. With nothing else to be said, Quincy stood and left the board behind.

———

Quincy knew she wouldn't find sleep. Stark reality was always the most effective drug for keeping one awake. Donning her jacket and scarf, Quincy was down the stairs and out the front door of The Q. The dark streets of Rhysdon did not counter her conscious melancholy, but they gave her enough space to spread the heartbreak out.

Quincy found herself at the park overlooking the ocean, the one where Arch had brought her to hear him recite poetry. The railing was all but ready to fall headlong off the rocks and into the endless black depths, nothing visible in the dark night. Only one sound came up to testify that there below, the ocean was refusing to be forgotten, persisting in its melancholy waves. With each rush, it was living; with each retreat, dying.

Quincy sighed. Her chin quivered, and she could feel the ends of her mouth drawing down, fighting. How she had cried these last weeks. How she had sorrowed. It was not just The Q; it was everything buried beneath what she had now built her life on: It was her mother, her sister. It was hours of fear, which robbed children in the fiercest way. It was Ezekiel and Fisher and the endless bent of fighting for The Q to live and live well.

But now, tears did not come. She couldn't give it anything more. Quincy was bone dry, having aged years and years since the hour she had signed away The Q. She sat now, perched on the bent rail, aware of the distance dropping below her, a relief to finally have the earth doing what she felt her soul had been feeling through the whole miserable mess. And Quincy, as she sat, her coat pulled around her, her red scarf the only real guard keeping her from the bitter winter wind off the sea, could almost hear the sound of Arch's feet as he himself paced somewhere about Rhysdon. James Arch, sleepless and awful and— Quincy sighed, deflated.

The salty wind came strong and even. Salt was a preserver of sorts, Quincy had once heard. It kept things from going rotten. It also, Quincy knew, could erode the metal parts of a good machine. The pieces of Quincy's mind—not interested in philosophy—still thought it strange how something could destroy so and yet preserve at the same time. Quincy wondered if the salt wind of this Rhysdon midnight would rust her away or keep her from deteriorating into nothingness.

If she wasn't nothingness already, Quincy wondered, her thoughts mixed in rue, her heart beating with stronger stuff, bitter and abandoned. And sad.

What difficult internal pallbearers carried her grief. This loss of The Q and everything she had been willing to give her life to. This loss of The Q in the legal shadow of Arch, his part in the play, and his absence now as the finale came to ruin. She thought of his face as he'd stood in the parlor of Peacock House, wet and in pain from having followed Quincy all about the city, angered and hurt at her words. Retaliating with his own.

Perhaps it was the wind, strong enough to blow the unbearable weight away from Quincy's shoulders—which were now shaking from her having sat still for too long—but Quincy could feel him now, the shadow of Arch at least. And she saw how difficult it must have been for him. Arch could have warned her; he *should* have prepared her. But he had felt bound by law in his ability to speak, and had he broken, given in—whether for pity, which Quincy didn't want, or loyalty, for which Quincy yearned—he would have ceased to be James Arch.

"I don't want you to change," Quincy had told him once. Well.

Her own regret soon muddled the clarity, and Quincy slid from the railing to the pavement, back into the mess and disappointment of it all.

CHAPTER FIFTY-TWO:
Fools and Their Windows

Arch sent Quincy his resignation the following morning, along with a note saying he would see to the details of the contract with the board by courier and that he had informed the board of his departure from The Q. Arch also wrote that he did have several worthy candidates if Quincy would like a list of possible solicitors to set in his place.

Quincy stared at the page, tracing the elegantly written words. Her eyes drifted to Fisher's empty desk, towards Arch's closed door, and then back at the note in her hand.

The bell rang as a customer entered, and Quincy put the resignation into her drawer.

"Welcome to the offices of The Q," Quincy said, picking up her fountain pen.

News of the buyout spread through both The Q's staff and the city. The reasons given varied: Miss St. Claire was cashing out to add to her immense fortune, Miss St. Claire had made a few bad investments and needed to sell, Miss St. Claire was ousted by her own board.

"How could they?" Jade gripped the handle on a press in disgust. "You've made The Q what it is, and they just vote you out? It's criminal, that's what." She slammed her hand down. "I'm not working for the likes of them. They'll see. We're all loyal to you, Quincy."

Quincy had not told Jade which rumor was true, but Jade knew. She had guessed, as had all the staff at The Q, and they felt what Jade verbalized.

"Thank you, Jade," Quincy said. "No need for you to leave a good job over me."

"We'll see about that." Jade blew a piece of loose hair out of her face, her hands smudged with ink. "Priest has been after me for two years now. Maybe I'll defect. He's promised better hours."

Quincy lifted a shoulder.

"There was nothing Arch could do about it?" Jade continued. "Can't he file a suit or something?"

"No, there is nothing Arch can do." Quincy heard the flatness in her own voice. "Besides, he has left The Q as of this week. Another opportunity must have come up, and I wish him well."

Jade stood stock-still, staring Quincy down. "I am sorry, on both counts."

"Thanks, Jade. I'll be here through the end of the week, before the board puts me out."

"Will you be moving out of your room, then?"

"Yes."

"Where?"

"I'll set myself up at The Emperion in a day or so. Then next week, I'll look about for a place. There are houses enough for sale. Financially, I have my pick." Quincy pulled her mouth to the side. "Well, I've a lot of work to finish before I'm done with The Q, so I'll take my leave later this week."

Jade did not look happy. "Let me know what you need from me, me or Jack."

———————————

"Are you certain you don't want a cigar?" Priest asked.

Quincy smiled ruefully. "Something stronger may be the order of the day."

Priest grunted and leaned back in his chair. He had sent for Quincy and when she had been too busy to leave The Q, had ordered her to come anyway.

"It isn't easy," he said.

"What?"

"Dealing with most of the people we come into contact with. Especially in business."

"Have you heard from the board?"

"Oh, yes. They can't break their contract for another year, and then, if they want to give the better contract to *The Sun*, they can—and hang in the process. We both know *The Times* will be fine. We both know you'll be fine, as well."

Quincy looked away.

"Oh, don't doubt yourself now, St. Claire. There's no reason for you to feel the world is falling off your shoulders. You'll come across something, think of an idea, and before long, it will become the talk of Europe. Don't think yourself defeated."

"It takes heart, Priest," Quincy stated. Then, giving her chin a shake, she looked towards the fire, her jaw tight. Hers might be all gone.

"It takes grit. It takes decision and determination." He took a long draw from his cigar and blew the smoke out through his nose. "You didn't survive the foundling factory to give up before you'd even lived through two decades. Miles stretching out before you, St. Claire. Trust that you'll know what to do with them."

She didn't mention Arch, and—praise whatever powers may be—neither did Priest.

———

The next evening, after a long day of hard work, Quincy went upstairs to the matchbox and emptied all of her belongings into a trunk in the corner. It was time to leave the matchbox behind. Quincy knew it would be better if she left now, tonight, before the week was out. Saying good-bye to the matchbox before she had to say farewell to The Q.

They all fit, her things, with room to spare. Even the violin. When she closed the lid, Quincy sat down atop the trunk and stared numbly at the furniture. What would they even do with this small room? What would it become? She didn't know. Quincy turned off her lamp, leaving the room in darkness, and climbed atop the dresser, perching beside the window one last time.

Fools and their windows—these words came back into her mind as clearly as her uncle had always said them: "Fools and their windows. They while their lives away, when they should step out. Then the adventure begins."

Quincy didn't agree with him; she felt strongly about windows, fiercely about them. Perhaps, at times, it was foolish. But, at other times, they felt like salvation. That was always what Quincy's window had been to her.

Several minutes passed, then several more, and Quincy knew that if she remained, her gears would slow down like an unwound clock, and stop in their place. As Quincy needed all the bravery and motion she had to leave her matchbox, she told herself it was time to go.

So, reluctantly, she dropped to the floor, threw on her coat, and pulled at the side strap of her trunk, leaving her matchbox sanctuary forever behind.

She hailed a hansom out on Queen's Street, and it was not long before she was dropped at The Emperion. The hotel was tall, with grooved columns of white and green marble. The manager insisted on putting her in a suite. Quincy wished to throttle the man, claiming she would prefer a simple room.

"Only the best for Rhysdon's famous Miss St. Claire," he insisted again, claiming he would cover the extra charge if she would tell all of her friends she was staying at The Emperion.

Quincy rolled her eyes. No one would be knowing she was at The Emperion.

The suite was a haze of mauve. And if the manager had not been so efficient in leaving her alone, she would have demanded he take her out of the ridiculous chamber. It looked like a boudoir where guests were strangled with flounces as they slept. The carpets were too soft, the bed too big, the curtains too filmy and too many.

Quincy pulled out her pocket watch and glanced at the hands to make certain its gears had not been choked into silence for all the fluff in the room. A fire had been set, and the room was so warm Quincy pulled her scarf from around her neck then flung herself onto the bed.

A maid came just then, asking if she could see Miss St. Claire settled. No, she did not wish to be settled. But, before Quincy could prop herself up on her elbow and scare the girl away, she realized she was on the most comfortable bed she had ever lain down on. And she could not move, even if she wished to.

"Yes," she told the maid, and it was not long before Quincy had fallen fast asleep.

Quincy woke to see full mid-morning chiding her from outside her window. Of all the ridiculous things. It was Friday and she had slept late.

Quincy pulled herself off of the bed, stripped away her worn clothing, washed, changed, doing whatever she could to look presentable, then slipped into her jacket, scarf, and hat and was out the door, down the stairs, and racing past the front desk before she could be greeted in any way. Taking fast to her heels, Quincy ran all the way to Gainsford Street.

Someone had better have unlocked the door.

Jade was sitting at the front desk, helping a line of three customers, when Quincy stepped into The Q. Breathing heavily, Quincy nodded towards Jade, who met her eyes and smiled.

Quincy took herself directly into Arch's office and closed the door, sitting down—she noticed—in the original chair that had belonged to the desk. His own chair, the one Arch had brought with him, along with his busts and paintings, was gone.

When had he come and taken them away? Quincy frowned, counting the few times she had been away from The Q. Wasn't it only last night that she had left? Had he come then?

Had he, perhaps, climbed the stairs to the matchbox and found her gone?

The office door was pushed open.

"The customers have been seen to," Jade said. "Don't worry. I stayed late after my shift to finish a bit of extra work, and when it was time to open, there wasn't a soul in the front office. Now I've seen everything—where were you?" Jade asked in a disjointed tone, as if remembering and inserting the question too quickly over her already existing words.

"The Emperion." Quincy stood and walked out of the office and past Jade, claiming her stool behind the counter.

Jade followed. "You moved out, then?"

"Just last night. They gave me an atrocious suite, with more gauze and glimmer—"

"A suite?" Jade was incredulous. Then she laughed.

"Forced upon me, much like everything else."

"Jack and I have always wanted to have a night at The Emperion."

"Happy New Year, then." Quincy waved her hand at Jade while yawning. "I'll see you get a night or two when I vacate. Now, go home and sleep. I'll see you this evening."

"Deal," Jade grinned, "on both counts."

A messenger delivered a parcel of legal papers—from Arch, of course—to be reviewed by Quincy that afternoon. For the first time in her life, Quincy worked with only half her heart, reviewing the endless legalities with a stabbing pain, and a rising anger. She wished someone could understand how desperate she was feeling. How fast it had all turned on its head, Quincy's life.

The bell rang, and Quincy looked up to see a young boy in an expensive coat and breeches, the spitting image of a royal footman. On his pocket, embroidered with silver, was the mark of the Fothergils' house. She would have recognized the Fothergils' livery regardless, both for its coloring and for its out-of-date grandeur.

"For milady," he said, pushing the note in his small hand across the counter. His eyes carried such a singleness of purpose that Quincy half wished to buy him out for a Q boy.

"There's no milady here," Quincy said. She opened her drawer, pulled out a coin and tossed it to him. This was, apparently, unexpected, for the boy's eyes went wide as he lifted his hands to catch it. "Are you to wait for an answer?" she asked when he continued to stare.

He nodded.

"Fine." Quincy broke the seal, unwound the rich, cottony paper and read the fine script. Lady Fothergil was demanding Quincy over that evening for dinner, to reassure her that her investments were safe. It was an order.

Quincy wanted to tell the entire lot to go hang, but Lady Fothergil was a loyal customer of The Q, and her concerns were valid.

"Yes," she told the boy. "Tell her I'll be there."

"Eight o'clock, milady. A carriage will be sent to fetch you at The Emperion." He bowed, turned tight on his heel, and marched out of the office.

Quincy glared, feeling invaded. How, in all below heaven, did Lady Fothergil know Quincy was staying at The Emperion?

The day passed, as it always did.

Quincy took herself away from the office just after seven, returned to the hotel, changed her clothes for a slightly more formal version of the same, polished her black leather boots, made a note to have the heel repaired, and then prepared herself for a long evening of legal explanations and appeasement.

CHAPTER FIFTY-THREE:
What Can You Live Without?

The carriage arrived neither a minute before nor after eight o'clock. This, at the very least, pleased Quincy as she slapped her pocket watch closed and entered the rococo monstrosity that was the Fothergils' formal carriage. Sitting far back into her seat, Quincy tried to keep hidden from the curious faces watching the carriage pass.

It wasn't long before Quincy was staring at the grand exterior of the Fothergil mansion. She disembarked before the footman could properly do his job and walked up the front steps just as the doors opened and a small army, consisting of the butler and more footmen, welcomed her in.

They took her hat, and Quincy, brushing her hair from her face, was ushered into the gorgeous sitting room, where, to her chagrin, she heard a familiar laugh. Lord Arch, *the* Lord Arch, was sitting with Lady Fothergil, all smiles and charm.

"Miss St. Claire!" He stood, graceful as always, and, in the matter of a few steps, was greeting Quincy wholeheartedly. "It has only been four days since you were with me at Peacock House, and yet I feel it has been much longer." The way he searched her face—noting, perhaps, the circles forming beneath Quincy's eyes—made her feel, for the first time all week, that she could again weep.

"Here, here! Miss St. Claire." Lady Fothergil had raised her ample silver frame and was now waving them over. "I do not intend for you to stand by the door all evening. Come and sit, there's a good girl. Thomas, bring the poor girl near the fire."

Quincy almost shot back that she wasn't aware there was a poor girl in the company, and that, due to an undercutting board, she was wealthier now than she had ever been. But the fire did look nice, and both of them were in pleasant spirits, so Quincy pressed her mouth shut and sat down, keeping her melancholy to herself.

"How are you, dear girl?" Lady Fothergil asked. Lord Arch poured Quincy some tea—peppermint—his mannerisms too much like his son's.

"I would like to allay your fears, Lady Fothergil," Quincy stumbled through the words, "and answer any questions you have, regarding your investments in The Q. It will remain a viable—"

"Oh, hush." Lady Fothergil stirred her tea before meeting Quincy's eye. "I've no worries about The Q. I know my way around my investments, and the business world is no mystery. They do not call the Fothergils the Kingmakers for nothing, deary."

Quincy's mouth was open. She took great pains to shut it—and keep it so.

"Now you are angry." Lady Fothergil laughed. "We invited you up for a night with friends, to relax, to lift the burden off those tiny shoulders for a few hours."

Before Quincy could level an accusation, Lady Fothergil continued, "Why the deception, you ask? Thomas and I are not fools. You would not have accepted an invitation had it come any other way. So we played on your sense of duty to The Q to get you inside the carriage and up that hill."

"Forgive us, Miss St. Claire." Lord Arch smiled warmly, his elbow leaning against the arm of the chair, his fingers stretching from his temple to the end of his jaw. "Surely, you cannot fault our reasoning?"

Quincy rolled her eyes as she took another sip of the tea and acknowledged the fact ruefully.

"Good." Lady Fothergil laughed. "We will eat as soon as the others arrive."

"Others?" Quincy felt her eyes go wide, to the apparent amusement of Lord Arch.

"Only my son," Lady Fothergil said, waving a hand. "And Mary. And James, of course."

And before Quincy could gather her wits sufficiently to incinerate them both and run, the doors opened and Johnny Fothergil walked in, followed by James Arch.

"Hello, Mother!" Johnny said. "Do excuse our late arrival."

Arch met Quincy's eyes only a moment, flinching before following Johnny to Lady Fothergil, taking her hand, and greeting her with understated civility. He turned away, to smother a cough, and Quincy wondered how long he had again been sick.

"And is Mary not with you?" Lady Fothergil sounded affronted. "I do hate uneven tables; they unnerve me."

"I stepped on Mary's hem, and the maid is seeing to its repair," Johnny admitted.

"Walking too close, no doubt." Lady Fothergil pretended to be put out.

Lord Arch laughed, and Johnny flushed. "No doubt not close enough," Johnny muttered as he turned around to greet Quincy.

She welcomed the hint of a smile on her face, for the idea of any affection between the pair was certainly news to her.

"Miss St. Claire." He took her hand with a bow and settled into the chair beside her. "James will have to fend for himself, as I plan on monopolizing all of your time until dinner. He's told me of the events at The Q these last weeks. Well," Johnny corrected himself, "he has, rather, clarified which rumors were true and untrue. It's been very distressing for him, to be sure."

"Has it?" she replied flatly as she looked across at the cut, trim figure of Arch paying his respects to Lady Fothergil. His manner was polite, but his expression wasn't happy. Something beneath Quincy's ribs twinged. He looked so tired.

Johnny continued conversing about nothing really, and Mary entered soon, greeting Quincy more warmly than she deserved. And without much ceremony, the intimate group went in to dinner. Quincy was seated at Lady Fothergil's left. Lord Arch was seated opposite Lady Fothergil, at the end of the table. Mary and Johnny were across from Quincy, and Arch, silent as ever, was at her left.

The meal began with Lady Fothergil turning towards Mary, at her right, while Johnny and Lord Arch spoke—longer than was usually considered polite—about the last opera they had attended. This left a pointed silence between Quincy and Arch. Neither seemed to be inclined to disrupt the arrangement, so Quincy pretended he wasn't there.

After Arch had received a threatening expression from nearly everyone at the table and ignored them as long as possible, he leaned slightly towards Quincy and said, under his breath, "I suppose I should say this is a pleasant surprise, but, truth be told, I knew you would be here."

"Well, you're a surprise to me," she retorted, noting how the others were speaking even more animatedly with their partners, creating the illusion of privacy. She sipped a spoonful of the soup, a flavor she didn't care for in the least.

"You received the papers I sent over today?" he asked as his own soup, virtually untouched, was cleared away by a silent footman.

"I reviewed most of them this afternoon," Quincy answered, pressing her fingers to the stem of her goblet, so very aware of him. "You've done excellent work. I'm sure the board will be grateful for your loyalty." Her words had more vinegar than she meant, and Quincy berated herself silently for it.

Arch turned more fully towards her, and she could feel his eyes searching out hers, waiting to see if she would say anything more. She didn't. Arch turned away and moved a hand across his face, a motion that confirmed he was deeply tired. It made Quincy want to be someone else, someone who felt less anger, someone willing to tell him he was going to get through the week. But Quincy didn't know if she would survive the week herself, let alone the years following. Why should she give him any of her lean reserves?

The dinner continued with more of the same, only a few lines shared between them to ward off the near stifling pressure of their dinner companions. Quincy's simmering temper was edging towards a boil. Finally, just before a berry caramel soufflé was to be brought up from the kitchen, Lady Fothergil threw her napkin on the table.

"This won't do, this won't do at all. If the two of you will not speak to each other, we shall have to amend our plan."

Arch almost choked on his glass of wine, leading to a series of coughs. When he had regained his voice, he said, "I beg your pardon?"

Mary, to her credit, was the only person at the table who looked properly mortified.

Lady Fothergil reached for Quincy's hand—an unpleasant turn of events—and glared at Arch. "It is hard to believe you two are turning Rhysdon on its head, as you seem perfectly incapable of carrying on adult conversation." She waved her bejeweled hand. "Sort this out, or I'll ruin you both."

Neither Quincy nor Arch moved, but his jaw was taut, and Quincy could see he was trying keep his temper from getting away from him. The silence hung as heavy as one of the Fothergils' chandeliers. Nothing in the room seemed to move except Quincy's heart, pounding out a disorganized rhythm.

"Hopeless," Lady Fothergil said to Lord Arch after a few minutes had limped passed. "Let us walk through then, all of us. No, not you." She pointed sternly at Arch when he shifted. "You will stay here and clear up this mess. Godson indeed. There's your spiritual direction."

"My dear Lady Fothergil," Lord Arch said, "it is hardly any of our business, now is it? Look at poor Mary, she's about to swoon. Johnny, would you?"

Quincy shot Mary a look. She really was ready to swoon. And Johnny Fothergil was more than willing to offer her his arm. Quincy knew Lord Arch was trying to draw the attention away from Quincy and his son. While the others fussed over Mary, only he glanced towards Arch then swept his eyes to Quincy's. She blinked and looked away, gripping the edge of the table as the rest of the party made their way to the drawing room. The sound of their leaving was muted, for Quincy could scarcely hear anything through the pounding in her ears.

Once the staff withdrew and the door was closed, Arch made a noise, rumpling his napkin in one hand, tossing it onto the table as he stood up, his eyes looking everywhere but in Quincy's direction. A year ago, even five months ago, she would have left before now. Standing without a word, Quincy would have passed by the drawing room, gone out into the hall—retrieving her scarf from some startled footman—and let herself out the front door. Even the thought of returning to the dreadful Emperion would have been better than the jolt of this disaster.

But they were caged now, not by the room or by Lady Fothergil but by the words they should have already spoken and hadn't, by what had passed between them, both before the betrayal and after. She had felt sharply the rejection of Arch's silence that morning after the ball and rage for his subsequent part in the maneuvering of the board, but she also still keened inside over the words she had flung at Arch's face. They had hurt him deeply; even Quincy had seen that. She remembered very clearly his expression when she told him he was nothing.

Her heart was now juttering as she leaned towards the table, resting her elbows, cupping her face in her hands. James Arch was not nothing. He was more than Quincy dared to acknowledge. But they were so very off balance, the two of them. And every line that was crooked caused the entire page to be off-kilter. When in the print room, nothing stopped Quincy from coolly putting away the type and beginning the difficult, tedious business over, until everything was perfectly in place. She accepted no less. But to do that between yourself and another person? To straighten out a misunderstanding? An offence? Who was mad enough to even try? Why should she rip herself up to set him aright?

As she heard the sounds of his feet pacing at her back, his silence as pointed as hers, Quincy answered her own question—and it was her own voice speaking inside her head, not Ezekiel's, not Jade's, not Priest's, not even Arch's—and the answer was this: because when someone means something to you, you need to see them aright. Even if you are angry. Even if you feel abandoned. Even if it is only to set them on a path that will lead away from you.

And James Arch meant a great deal to Quincy. Despite it all.

Grasping at any grit she had left inside her, Quincy pushed back her chair and stood, crossing her arms as she glared defensively in his direction. He was ten steps across the room and paused in his pacing, half turned towards her, his dark eyes burning. Pulling her mouth to the side, Quincy stared Arch full in the face and organized a long breath. She would set this right and then leave it behind.

"Listen." She let the breath go sharply. "I'm sorry, Arch. I really am." As she spoke, he bent his head down but kept his eyes on hers. "Whatever you may have deserved, it was beyond the mark to say you were nothing to me." Quincy's voice grew thick, and she cleared her throat, fighting any aberration to her plan. "You're not worthless; you're not nothing. You're a great deal, and I want to thank you for— for everything. I'd rather say good-bye having said my piece, and there it is."

If she thought her words would lessen the tension between them, smooth it out like fresh ink, she was wrong. He had winced when she'd said the word good-bye. It was almost undetectable, but the sight of it made her feel as if someone had dropped her heart.

His mouth opened once, then twice, but he didn't speak. She watched him wage his own personal war—the battle playing out on his face clearly enough. What she couldn't see was what he was fighting himself for. He hadn't lost anything.

Through all this, Arch was keeping a concentrated watch on her face. Quincy stared back, feeling her messy emotions roiling around the beating of her heart. When he finally pulled his shoulders back and lifted his chin, looking more like himself, Quincy waited for him to walk out the door without a word.

He didn't leave, as Quincy was preparing herself for. This was confusing, threatening to Quincy. People left you, didn't they? Wasn't that how it always ended? But he merely shook his head and set his face in a tight expression, one thousand words behind it, none of them yet spoken.

Quincy found herself turning her hands into fists then releasing them again, waiting for the moment when the tension would burst open into something more wild. She still hadn't looked away from his face. And the trace of misery she saw was heartbreaking. But not enough to call Quincy off from guarding her own besieged emotions.

"What?" she finally dared Arch, unable to endure his scrutiny any longer.

"What do you want, Quincy St. Claire?" he said, and it sounded less like a challenge and more like an invitation.

Quincy dug her heels into the carpet and frowned. An invitation for what? When she didn't answer, he lifted a shoulder, just in the way she always did, and Quincy felt like she was looking into a mirror.

"What—" His voice halted only a moment. "What must I do, Quincy St. Claire, to be good enough for you?"

Quincy's stomach dropped, like the final break of an old press. "What are you driving at, Arch?"

"I can't figure you out." He spread his hands, the dark circles under his eyes accentuated by the lamps of the dining room. "You're unsolvable, Quincy St. Claire. I have tried, but now I've let you down again, in the worst way either of us could have imagined. I know that. I failed you, and you're angry with me, and I can't even think what I could do to make it right."

Quincy blinked. "No," she shook her head. "No. You don't get to say that. No one gets to just say that."

Arch lifted his hand, bewildered, and said sharply, "Why not?"

"Because it's not true," Quincy clipped. "It's cheap. It's unfair. Besides, you always do everything right—"

"It's not cheap, and I don't do everything—"

"You do!" Quincy flung out her hands before her. "You don't break. You don't rust. You couldn't even taint your honesty by telling me what the board was planning."

His face came together at her words, his eyes narrowing like he was in physical pain. "I'm so sorry, Quincy, but I couldn't be dishonest, even for you."

"Well, of course you couldn't," said Quincy, unfolding her arms and sinking her fists into her pockets. She had already spent the hours thinking about it, so Quincy laid the words out now as if they didn't mean anything to her. "I understand why you couldn't tell me. About why you didn't," but her voice flickered like a candle, "why you didn't say anything. I know why you, James Arch, chose not to. I only—"

The contrast of Arch's face was strong as his expression turned sharp. "You wish I were a different person."

"No." The word shot out like a bullet from a gun as Quincy pulled her hands from her pockets. "I don't think you should be different. You're like that blasted polestar Fisher was always obsessed with when we were children. Never moving, constant, always in the correct place. You do what you say you'll do. I think—I think that's why I've been willing to trust you. I only wished you'd not been so—" A wash of shame caught Quincy, and she closed her eyes tightly, making an angry sound and bringing her hands up to her face, her fingers tense and curved.

"What is it, Quincy?" Arch said, his voice losing its asperity. "What is it you're trying to say?"

Vulnerability was not Quincy St. Claire. Laying yourself bare was not Quincy St. Claire.

"Please tell me, Quincy."

Be brave, Quincy. Be brave. She clenched her jaw, pressing the heels of her palms against her closed eyes, and then forced the words out so low she almost couldn't hear herself. "I kept feeling I had done something wrong, the day after the ball. You wouldn't even look at me, and I thought you'd realized the mistake you had made, that I wasn't reliable enough for your trust." Her voice caught. "Then, at the board meeting, you ended up knowing everything—"

"Quincy." Arch was across the room, wrapping his hands around her wrists, pulling her hands away from her face.

When she opened her eyes, he was there—the same sincere expression she'd seen hundreds of times as she sat at her counter or walked the streets of Rhysdon. She did her best not to look away.

"Please believe—I did all I could. Seeing you the morning after the ball, and knowing what I knew, knowing what they would be taking from you—knowing that I couldn't do anything to stop it—" He made a noise, like his words had fallen and he had to pick them back up. She blinked against the weight in her eyes. "Quincy, you're the last person I want to see hurt or cheated or wronged, and I didn't know—"

Quincy wrenched her wrists free, taking a jagged breath. There was no stopping the mess and clatter now. "I'm so angry with you! Just let me say it. I'm so *angry* at what happened, for your part in it and for my own blindness. So you weren't going to tell me. Fine. All you had to do was be there." Quincy spat out the words, stepping backward. "All you had to do was look at me. Sit beside me. I don't know, Arch, hold me together? Would I have listened? I don't know. Would I have felt you were on my side? I can't say. But you could have done *something* so that, when it all came falling down, I would know—"

"Know what?" he asked earnestly.

"That you wouldn't leave when everything changed," she burst out, trampling over her own words. "Everyone leaves, Arch, everyone leaves me behind. And I thought you'd promised me, in a thousand ways, that you wouldn't—" She broke off, wiping her eyes with her sleeve. "I'm so angry at the whole wretched mess."

His face froze at her words, only the line of his mouth working back and forth. He was silent for a long moment, the thoughts building up behind his eyes, until he let out a slow breath and dropped his head, hands on his hips. "You're right, Quincy. You're absolutely right. Oh, I botched it badly. Dammit."

Arch shook his head and lifted his head enough to bring his eyes to her face. "I did abandon you. I just couldn't bear—I should not have been so absent those days before the meeting. And I should have come and made you see me afterward. I was so upset by it all, and I thought you really meant it, you know, everything you said that night: I was merely a means for keeping The Q, and the Q was gone, so I was to be disposed of. Cast aside. No longer needed by the great Quincy St. Claire." His words were edged. "It was—I admit, my temper kept me from wondering if you really meant it. It also kept me from trusting that, perhaps, you didn't."

"You don't want to keep me in your life, Arch. I'll never come through for you. Not really."

He turned away from her and took a few steps in a slow circle. The thought crossed Quincy's mind that he might be deciding whether he should trust her. He shouldn't. But part of her wished he would. It might give her the courage to trust herself.

"Besides," Quincy continued, set on winning him over to her way of thinking, "I saw the look on your face, when you decided you didn't want anything to do with me."

Arch jerked his head around and looked at her, taking a step closer, his jaw working. "That's not how I feel."

Quincy made a noise. "Yes, it is. It should be. What if it's true, what I said? What if you were only a means for keeping the Q?"

Quincy knew it wasn't true, but she said it anyway. Arch was scowling now, and he walked to her and gripped her shoulders, holding on as if he would sink. "We both know that isn't true, Quincy, but I need to know what you want."

"What I want? I want to scream," Quincy admitted fiercely. "I want to war. I want to beat something and curse and be angry. And I want you to—"

"What?" His grip tightened. "Anything."

The way he said the word anything gave Quincy courage, the courage to tell him what she had been wanting from him all along. Her voice almost dropped to a whisper, "I want you to tell me that, somehow, something can be unbroken."

"Yes," Arch insisted, nodding more to himself than to her, like he was figuring something out. "It can. I don't think you will feel it possible until you've made it through this week, Quincy. But, afterward, when it's over and you've found your bearings, you'll see that it's all ahead of you. That it can be unbroken."

"I don't believe you."

"Then trust me that you'll believe me soon enough," he insisted. "Will you, at the very least, believe how sorry I am for all of this?"

"Yes."

"Are you still angry with me?"

"Yes," said Quincy.

Then the door swung open, and a maid gave a startled noise at the sight of them. Arch let go of Quincy and stepped away, the lamps catching the glint of sweat on his temples.

"I beg your pardon," the maid stammered, her eyes wide.

"No," Arch replied, his face flushed. "We were just leaving. Please don't let us be in your way. Quincy?" His eyes caught hers. "Won't you come with me?"

"Where?"

"I don't know. The library? An abandoned parlor? Anywhere the others are not. The last thing I can endure this evening is more meddling from my dear godmother."

Quincy closed her eyes and gave a messy laugh.

"Here." He handed her a handkerchief, which she accepted, and then, hesitant at first, he reached out and took her hand. Quincy gripped his tightly in return.

A fire was going in the library. Instead of sitting in a chair, Arch stretched himself out on the rug before it, propping himself up with his elbow, disregarding the press of his evening clothes. Quincy dropped down beside him, her arms crossed on her knees. Her face felt stiff now from the disloyal tears that had spilled onto her cheeks.

"I'm sorry, Quincy," Arch said, not looking at her. "I didn't know how to bear it." Silence sat heavy between them until he added, "I didn't know how you would bear it."

Quincy shook her head. "I don't know if I will."

Several more minutes passed, neither speaking, just the snap of the fire and the sound of a clock in the hall outside.

"I had a Christmas present for you—" Arch said after a while, watching his fingers follow the pattern of the carpet rather than looking at her, "before I swore I'd never have anything to do with you again."

"What was it? A horse whip?"

Arch laughed, and it was the silver sound she had grown accustomed to. "I should have. I would have used it too, whipped some sense into you after I'd used it on myself." He paused. "No, I actually secured a box for an exclusive violin concert this Sunday night, New Years Eve, as it happens. Pierre Despain is the greatest violinist of our age, and he only plays each city once. This Sunday, he comes to Rhysdon for one of the final performances of his career. I heard him in Paris years ago. My mother took me, and I've never forgotten it." He coughed and then continued, "I had thought you might like to go."

Quincy dared a sad half smile, "I might have."

"But not now?" Arch's eyes looked towards her, vulnerable. "I didn't cancel the box, even when I wanted to box your ears. Come with me. I'll bring the olive branch for my sins."

"I'll go," Quincy answered. She had always wanted to hear a violin virtuoso. "If your chest cold doesn't put you under before then."

Arch laughed, but it was graveled. "It won't. It'll go away soon enough. I haven't been sleeping well is all, and I'm afraid stress and little sleep aggravate it."

"But is it something that will go away?"

Arch raised his eyebrows and nodded. "The doctors say it would if I was willing to take better care of myself."

"I've been worried about it," Quincy admitted as she picked at the carpet. "A great deal, actually."

Arch smiled as he quickly breathed the air out of his lungs. "I'll set a strict regime," he answered, somewhat teasing. "After the concert, that is."

"I'm serious, James Arch," Quincy whispered.

Arch looked up at Quincy, and he held her gaze, until Quincy saw that he understood what she was unwilling to say aloud. With an earnest nod, he said, "I promise, Quincy St. Claire."

She wanted to say thank you, but an overwhelming shivering sound was all that came from her lungs.

His fingers found the end of hers. "How have you been holding up, Quincy? Honestly."

Quincy leaned forward, her elbows now on her knees, staring at her ink-stained fingers touching his. She knew how messy the emotions of the last weeks had been; stripped down, bare, all the inner workings exposed. And the truth she had found there was that Quincy had mourned for Arch as much as she had for The Q. A different grief, but a mourning nonetheless.

Quincy had done many things that most people wouldn't know how to do. But she didn't know whether she could be honest with herself about how—after pushing aside the spare parts and broken pieces from around her heart over the last week—Quincy realized she had found one thing that would not move: Arch.

"I'm afraid to be honest."

Arch did not reply; he merely waited. So she told him the truth.

"I don't understand yet what it will be like to live without The Q. I don't think I will until I leave behind my key and walk away. And it might not even register until weeks after, what it is that I've lost. But," Quincy looked at Arch, spending all her bravery in this final transaction, "I do know what it means to live without James Arch. And I don't think I can bear having lost you both."

"Quincy." Arch sat up, pulling himself beside her, placing a hand on her back. "You don't have to."

"But we—"

"What's happened between us that can't be fixed?" he asked, lifting his other hand to her face, turning it towards his own. "If you care for us, for me, as much as you care for any one of your presses, we will be fine. You will doggedly keep us working."

Quincy blinked and lifted a single shoulder. Arch's eyebrows slanted and he shook his head, leaning forward. "Quincy St. Claire," was all he said before he wrapped his hand behind her neck and kissed her, as if he were trying to tell her something he didn't know how to say, something he didn't want to risk she misinterpret.

His touch felt like coming back, and Quincy realized she had been waiting for it. When he pulled away, both of his hands now on the sides of her face, his eyes searching hers for an answer, Quincy nodded then wrapped her arms around him. She pressed her face to his chest, and his response was to gather her to him, saying something she couldn't hear.

And there it was, the heartbeat she had heard the night of the Fothergils' ball, pulsing again in the shell of her ear. Quincy closed her eyes from relief. It gave her the same comfort the sound of the press gave her. It was a familiar machine.

"I had a Christmas present for you," Quincy admitted sometime later, when she and Arch were sitting close, their backs to a long sofa, his shoulder pressed against hers. "It's here, if you'd still like to see it."

"Here? At the Fothergils'?"

"I didn't have room for it in the matchbox."

"Really?" Arch said, his face hovering between caution and pleasure.

"I think you'll like it."

The hallway was dark, but Quincy stole a candle from the library, frustrated there was not a ready lamp. She retraced her steps from her previous visit, leading the way.

"Where are we going?"

"The silver parlor in the second wing."

He followed Quincy through the hallways, and when they arrived at the closed door of the parlor in this cold, unused portion of the house, Quincy gave him the candle and let him walk into the room before her.

Arch entered and then stopped. The room, a moonlike creation of elegant shadows and pale silver paper, was filled with the dusty smell and shape of crates. He looked back at Quincy in question, his eyebrows drawn together. When she didn't answer, rather folded her arms and leaned against the doorway, he stepped towards a stack of crates and, angling the candle, peered down into the darkness.

Arch gasped. He dropped before the crate, his fingers reaching, running along the leather, gilt-edged spines of the books before him. His mouth was working as he set the candle down on a nearby table, pulling a volume from the crate and lifting the spine to the light so as to see the title. His fingers ran reverently over the cover, and he opened the pages with care, noting the publication details to be found there. He went through every book in the crate, then wordlessly tucked them all back into their places before he moved the crate to the floor and began to sort through the crate beneath.

He said nothing, lost in his search, muttering and remarking to the shadows until his single candle had nearly melted, flickering in warning. He set down the volume in his hand and gave a long, contented sigh. The candle melted into its self, suffocating the light, leaving only the smell of smoke lifting in the room.

Without a word, Arch rose and walked to where Quincy waited, her hands now in her pockets. Before she could speak, he caught her up in an embrace so strong it lifted her to her toes and she had to wrap her arms around his neck to not feel as if she were falling. Through the layers of his coat, she could feel his heart drumming.

"Ezekiel's library," was all he said.

Quincy couldn't reply, the overwhelming presence of Arch enveloping every thought. And she now understood—Fisher and Quincy had always stood by one another, Ezekiel had pushed her forward, but Arch was consuming Quincy as she was consuming him, keeping her close, tucking her against him until she felt she was becoming a new creature, one that would thrive with him. She dared not open her eyes, but rather buried her face in the lapels of his coat, trusting she wouldn't fall backward, trusting they were enough to hold each other up.

"What are you looking for?" Arch asked, when they returned to the crate library with a lamp.

"It's something I've been saving for you, that possibly not even Ezekiel realized he had." Quincy moved several crates to reach the last one set in the corner, marked with a faded grocers script. She sorted through the books until she found a small volume in faded green leather. The one she had tucked carefully away months before. Arch set the lamp on a nearby table as Quincy held the book out to him, and he took it with marked interest. Turning the book in his hand and seeing the title was worn off, Quincy watched as Arch flipped it open to the title page.

Quincy had always thought the most beautiful sound she knew was the rhythm of the powerful Q presses, but the way Arch exclaimed with sincere joy was more immense than her body could hold. She had to look away from him, as he stood holding a volume of De Vere's *Imprisoned Words* in his hand.

It was the foreign sound of the clock that woke Quincy come morning at The Emperion. The sound was a stranger, for it was different from the clock she'd paced her life by since Ezekiel had first brought Quincy into the offices of The Q. The clock in The Q had helped raise her, a relentless governess. The Emperion clock sounded weak-willed, and unimportant. The sound broke Quincy's heart. Time, of all things, had never been unimportant. The purple haze of the room made the morning sunlight stuffy rather than clear. She pushed her blankets away and realized she'd fallen asleep in the clothes she'd worn to the Fothergil's the night before.

The Fothergil's. She'd left late. Arch had seen her back to The Emperion, quiet, his hand enveloping hers, an expression of baffled pleasure around his eyes as his other hand gripped the one volume Quincy knew he would love, the small book she had found in Ezekiel's library all those months before, tucking it away with the intent to gift it to Arch.

Reliving the moment, Quincy's eyes wandered around her room at the Emperion and she smiled. She was so overwhelmed by the evening, so off balance. Or rather, centered in a different way. Quincy covered her face, from the sun, and the inevitable confusion of trusting someone, of caring for someone, and forgiving someone who had forgiven you. It was a wonder to Quincy, how one could feel so utterly heart-broken and bound up simultaneously. She opened her eyes to the window and thought of the stained glass Lazarus. She wondered if it had been more difficult than he had let on, to be called back from the dead.

CHAPTER FIFTY-FOUR:

For James Arch

When Quincy left The Emperion, there was a note waiting for her at the front desk. It was written in a tired, yet eager hand.

Quincy,

I have spent the night devouring the Imprisoned Words essays. I can't express what this means to me and that you were so generous to have kept it, to have kept all the books. I will be waiting for you this evening at The Emperion come 6:30. Dinner out?

Quincy slipped the note into her pocket with a slanted smile and then, stepping into the bright sunlight of the winter day, she set her mind towards work. It was Saturday morning, and there was more to do than she was capable of in the time given. She could not waste minutes. In all honesty, Quincy had anticipated working through dinner, but she would stop for James Arch and go back later.

Jade and Spense were still in the print room, tinkering with the largest machine, when she arrived.

"We had problems with it last night," Spense said, his face red from exertion, his hands black with ink. "I think I've sorted it right, but perhaps you should take a look."

"Perhaps you should sabotage it," Jade suggested.

Quincy put her hand on the press defensively then began to move her fingers through the dismantled portion of the machine. "Don't take it out on the presses, Jade."

Jade laughed. "Well, Jack told me to not take it out on him yesterday, so you're denying me all my scapegoats. Is it Arch, then, I can blame?"

Quincy felt the flush on her cheeks as she worked. "No."

Spense had slowed in wiping his hands and looked away, but Jade made no effort to hide her pleasure. "Quincy! Does this mean you and our solicitous aristocrat are back on speaking terms?"

"I am not going to answer you."

"But he's off your blacklist. I can see out the side of your expression."

"Go home, Jade. I'm rather busy today."

From the corner of her eye, Quincy watched Jade's eyebrow tilt up as she smiled. "As you say, St. Claire. Oh, Quincy, I have a type question regarding Tuesday's *Q*, as we won't be printing an edition for New Year's Day. Since I won't be in tomorrow night, I'll stop by this evening, after Jack and I see a late matinee. We would be by around seven or eight."

Quincy grunted as she reached inside the inner works of the press and righted the errant apparatus. "I won't be here that late. You better ask it now."

Jade had never looked utterly perplexed in her life. Impatient, confused, frustrated? Yes. But, perplexed? Never.

"You won't be here?"

"No, I'm leaving at six and won't be back until late." Quincy pulled away from the machine and stole the rag from Spense's hand to wipe her own. "That should set you right, Spense. Do a test run now, and I'll give you overtime. Jade, what's your question?"

Quincy turned towards Jade, who now looked curious.

"You are leaving at six? Tonight? With all the work you have and only today and tomorrow to accomplish it?"

"I'm not a slave of the board." Quincy lifted a shoulder as she moved past Jade towards the stairs. "Thank all of heaven for that."

Following, Jade made a disbelieving noise. "Yes, but you are a slave to your own perfection."

Quincy was up and through the sorter, Jade at her heels. Once they were in the front office, Quincy spun around and put her hands out, indicating that Jade's opinion on what Quincy was about to say was not welcome. "James Arch has invited me to dinner, and I am going to go."

Jade did the best she could to not react—by Quincy's estimation, at least—but her lips tilted dangerously. "I'll let you get to your work, then."

"Don't you have a question about the type?" Quincy called, as Jade was already halfway back through the sorter.

"Not anymore," Jade threw the words over her shoulder. "You're busy. I'll figure it out."

Quincy looked at the large clock on the wall. Eight o'clock in the morning. Quincy slipped onto her stool, spread her hands across the counter, and, being careful to step around her heart, continued the painful process of surgically removing herself from The Q.

The day passed as she knew it would, too fast, with one task coming right after another. Quincy cursed Levins and the entire board in one thousand creative ways; she not only blamed them for stealing The Q, she blamed them for Arch not being in his office. His help would have been invaluable.

When six o'clock came, she set her reports and the operating notes she had begun to write out on the side of the counter, and turned off the light, leaving the office locked and alone.

Arch was already at The Emperion when she arrived, sitting in the lobby, pouring over the small volume of essays, his mouth moving quietly with the words on the page.

"I have read through it twice and find myself unbearably anxious to begin again," Arch told Quincy as they sat at dinner an hour later. "Ever since my mother told me the story, I have dreamed, dreamed, Quincy, of finding a copy and printing those essays. It has been the closest desire—" He closed his eyes and lifted a hand to his face. "I still can't believe it. I've already contacted Priest. He's going to do a serial, and then we'll prepare the book for publication. He thinks the London and Paris papers will pick them up as well."

"And you'll receive another beating, but by the collectors who hold the other editions."

"I won't even complain when it happens," Arch grinned. "Besides, maybe they'll go after Priest first."

Quincy watched his joy with a sad smile on her face. His dream was just before him, and hers was fading. Arch must have had a similar thought, for his expression turned wistful. "Strange to consider that, by Monday morning, you will be finished with The Q."

Strange to consider indeed.

CHAPTER FIFTY-FIVE:

Q is for Quincy

Sunday was quiet as Quincy set her house in order. The file room was cleaned, the ledgers, up to date; and her hastily written manual of operations was waiting cautiously on the counter as if it wondered whether things would operate at all after she left. Quincy was grateful for this small bit of loyalty. She would not yet say good-bye. That would come later. Only after the concert would Quincy return, so she could leave it all one last time. Arch came for Quincy in the carriage and took her back to Peacock House for dinner before Despain's concert. Lord Arch and Mary were both out.

"I didn't think you would mind," Arch said, "as I didn't think you would want to talk."

She didn't, and though she didn't answer, he knew she was grateful. They ate at the small table of the family dining room, surrounded by its oddments and tucks. And Quincy felt that everything, even the black sphinx draped in the green scarf, was in her corner.

The concert hall was buzzing, filled with energy and laughter and calls. Arch looked sharp, his limp improved, his cane still in his hand. Earlier, he had asked Quincy if she needed time to change into an evening gown first and then had burst out laughing, as if he were the king's jester.

"You've been under too much strain these last weeks if you think that's funny," Quincy had said, not giving him the satisfaction of a laugh. But she couldn't hide her wry smile. "I'm quite comfortable as I am."

The concert was more than Quincy had imagined it would be. Despain was a magician. Watching him play the instrument caused such a feeling of desire in Quincy that she had to lean forward, her fingers wrapped around the balcony, wondering what she could now do with her own life that would rival the beauty of this man's work. She ached for excellence, craved it. She ached for the excellence she was leaving behind to lesser hands with lesser ambitions.

When Despain made his violin cry, Quincy felt as if he were simply releasing the sorrow she felt filling the contours of her bones. Arch reached his hand to her knee and kept it there, while she folded her arms across the balcony rail, her face buried in the sleeves of her jacket, her sadness buried in the music.

"Let's walk," Quincy said into the frigid air as they left the concert. "Is that fine? Will it bother your knee?"

"I don't mind," Arch replied, pulling his collar up around his ears. "It seems apropos for the final night of the year. I'll come with you, to close up The Q one last time."

One last time.

Quincy pulled at her bottom lip and nodded, falling into step beside Arch, grateful he was willing to come. Despain had ended with a sad encore, quiet and unassuming. Its melody now haunted Quincy's thoughts.

"It isn't long now," Arch said, tilting his head to get a glance at his pocket watch in the patchy light of the gas lamps. "Twenty-five minutes to midnight. About as long as it will take us to get back to The Q. And what a year it has been."

Quincy only nodded in reply. What was it Ezekiel had said one year ago? He disliked endings, but beginnings were—what? The best of adventures? It was something like that. Quincy wondered what Ezekiel was thinking now.

The cold pressed up through Quincy's boots and into the balls of her feet, a wintry burn each time her feet came down on the frosted pavement. Everything was deep gray, the gutter pushing itself up onto the sidewalk in slush and puddle. Arch offered Quincy his arm and she took it, finally admitting that her uncle had been right: she really did need a proper winter coat.

The walk back through the city was quiet. Revelers were to be found on all the streets Quincy and Arch avoided. They walked through the quiet avenues and side streets, crossing a snowbound park before coming onto Gainsford Street the back way. And there, clear enough for anyone to see, hung the signboard of The Q. Quincy felt for the key inside her pocket and pressed her fingers around its shape.

She had lost The Q.

"Let's slip inside," Arch said before Quincy realized she had stopped, and was staring at the door. "It's cold out."

Pulling the key from her pocket, Quincy thought it strange that the lock didn't feel different now than on any other night she had returned to The Q. Pushing the door open, the bell's chime spread itself over the quiet front office. It looked just the same. She had been expecting, well—what? A sense of finality, of ritual ended, of significance? For the building to know, perhaps, that she was entering it for the last time and that, from here on out, although everything else remained, all would be different?

"It's quiet."

"It is," Arch replied.

Quincy passed the counter, her fingers running along its edge, and pushed the door to the sorter open. She frowned. Light was coming up from the print room.

"The light to the print room is on, but the staff shouldn't be working tonight." Quincy cocked her head, confused. "We don't send out an issue on New Year's Day."

"Perhaps someone came in to clean up." Arch folded his arms and leaned against the door of his former office.

Shrugging, Quincy took five steps across the sorter and turned the knob on the door.

A loud cheer met Quincy full in the face.

As she stepped out onto the stairs, Quincy saw that the print room was full of people. She turned around to see Arch, grinning—actually grinning—standing behind her, looking down on the crowded room. More cheers, and someone called her name, and Arch nudged Quincy down the stairs.

Jade stood at the bottom, arms folded, brown hair piled atop her head, smiling like a devil. She threw her arms around Quincy. "We had to have a party for St. Claire!"

A violin started to play, accompanied by a pennywhistle. Drinks were passed around, and someone had started dancing.

"They've all come, Quincy," Jade spoke loudly over the erupting noise as she looked about the room, her arm still around Quincy's shoulders. "Jack and Spense, the printers: the entire staff, actually. Spats, even, and a few other naughty Q boys who snuck out their windows. Lady Fothergil—well, everyone." Jade squeezed Quincy again and winked at Arch over Quincy's head.

Like a coil, Quincy sprang around to face the solicitor. "You knew about this?"

But before Arch could answer, Jade laughed. "Knew about it? It was his idea. Come on, get a drink and some food, and start making your way around the crowd."

"Quincy!" Spense brought his large hands down on Quincy's shoulders. "Dear girl, tonight will be a good night." He pushed her through a crowd of mice. "There's a lot of people waiting on you."

The faces were all familiar. Mice, Q boys, Q drivers, long-term clients. And then the one face that always reminded Quincy what the fabric of her heart was made of. Fisher.

She was in his arms, and Fisher was smiling, both of them talking so fast neither heard what the other was saying until they pulled back, tears in their eyes, laughing so hard Quincy wasn't certain she wasn't sobbing.

"You came all the way back from Paris!"

"When Arch sent me the telegraph, I knew I had to come. Mado is here with me, somewhere. She'll be happy to see you."

"And I, her."

"*The year is young, Midnight just rung*," Fisher quoted as he slipped his mangled hand into his pocket and pulled out a New Year's penny, for luck. He kissed one side, and Quincy kissed the other. Then they flipped for it. Quincy won. "For luck," Fisher said, handing her the penny. "Now go get a drink, and settle in. We'll be here half the night, I am sure, plenty of time to find a corner and talk about your next adventure."

"Yes." Quincy could not see over the people. "Which direction is the punch?"

"Punch? Wassail!" He lifted his cup and nodded towards the back. "Crow's set up on the side wall, on the ancient."

"Crow's here?"

"I hunted him out myself."

Quincy clapped Fisher on the shoulder and then wound her way through the gears of conversation until she saw the tall, dark smuggler leaning against the ancient, talking with one of the keeps from The Nest, who was jovially serving the thirsty crowd.

"Crow!"

"Love!" Crow set down his glass, and, in two steps, he had lifted Quincy off her feet and kissed her soundly on the cheek. "You've quite the party here, gorgeous."

"But what are you doing, being seen by so many people? Did you get an appeal to come through?"

"Not a chance." Crow ushered Quincy to the counter and motioned for a drink while taking up his own. "I'll disappear before dawn quietly enough."

"It's a shame Constable Catch wasn't invited."

"Muddy shame," Crow said. "I heard rumor he may be transferred."

"Meaning?"

"Meaning a bit more freedom for your favorite smuggler."

"Alleged smuggler."

Crow shook his head. "I'm afraid my profession is set in the law books now. Smuggler it is."

"Keep yourself out of reach, then."

"Cheers to that."

Dancing had claimed most of the open floor, and those not participating were now standing around the presses, talking, laughing, trying to get a chance to speak with Quincy. They all did. They all wanted to talk with her, and she—to her surprise—wanted to talk with all of them.

Lady Fothergil was dressed to the nines and, in the company of Johnny and Mary, stayed long enough to wish Quincy well, to take a turn around the room, and upon Crow's urging, to consume a mug of the wassail.

"Who is that handsome creature, Miss St. Claire," she asked as Quincy escorted her to the exit.

"That, Lady Fothergil, is Crow, an infamous smuggler, hardly appropriate for your attentions."

"Oh, dear." Lady Fothergil turned her head back and looked again. "Oh, dear, he is a catch, isn't he? You're certain you want James?"

Priest also made an appearance, which, of course, meant his cigar accompanied him. "If this were happening in my print rooms, I would have a heart failure, St. Claire."

"I always told you The Q was a special place."

"If you weren't leaving, you'd be having one as well."

"I suppose Spense and Jade will have to worry over it now," Quincy replied.

"Well, I'm going to treat myself to more of that wassail and go home. I can't keep this up, these all-night shindigs. I'm getting too old for it." He took his cigar from his mouth and let out a long breath. "Come see me this week, St. Claire. I want to discuss your future."

For most of the evening, Quincy couldn't see Arch. She was surrounded by conversation and noise and laughter and everybody asking her what she was planning for next. Did she know? What had her brilliant mind decided to set out on?

"I'm not quite ready to say," she found herself repeating time and time again.

And Quincy, who had been only focused on The Q, began to look through her mind to see what thoughts were to be found there.

Despite being quite late, or early rather, the party continued. Quincy climbed the stairs, a mug of wassail in her hand, and settled herself on the top step, staring down at the print room turned party hall.

Crow and some of his associates were sitting on barrels with an inebriated Q driver, singing sea songs; Fisher and Mado rarely left the dance floor, Jade and Jack would move from group to group, from dancing to conversation then back.

And there was nothing orderly about it, but it was full and rich. And Quincy felt remarkably at home. She reached for her pocket watch to check the time and then reached again, padding her empty pocket in confusion.

"Is this what you're looking for?"

Quincy's watch dropped before her face, swinging on its gold chain. Her eyes followed the chain up to the hand of the person that held it up. James Arch. He dropped her watch into her hand and sat down beside Quincy on the top stair.

"Where did you come from? And where did you get my watch?"

"I asked Crow to steal it from you so you would, for once in your life, forget the time."

"You asked Crow to pickpocket?"

"Yes."

"Wonder of wonders. I hope he didn't swipe anything else."

Arch pulled the key to The Q's front door from his pocket and set it into Quincy's hand.

"He did, love."

She laughed upon hearing Crow's accent coming from Arch's mouth.

"Where did you come from just now?" she asked him.

"I was sitting up by the front windows, enjoying a respite from the noise." He waved a hand casually over the crowd. "I assure you, the last party I hosted was a far cry from this."

"I'd imagine. Thank you, James Arch."

Arch's black eyes searched hers. "I found myself worried you thought all you had was The Q, and I guess I wanted you to know that it wasn't true, that you have so much more than that." He looked down over the revelers. "Ezekiel would be pleased with this, Quincy. He would have loved tonight."

Quincy tapped a boot toe on the stair. "Yes, I think he would have."

"Miss St. Claire!"

Quincy looked down the stairs to see Lord Arch standing there, hand on his hip, jacket removed as if he had been on the dance floor. "I've it on good authority you dance quite well, dear girl. Do come and show me how it's done!"

"I don't dance in public," Quincy replied.

Lord Arch laughed. "Marvelous. I'll not make a big fool of you on your first go. Come down. No embarrassment, as it's coming on four in the morning, and no one will remember having seen you try."

"That's hardly a comfort," Quincy said to Arch before she stood and took the steps lightly. "How about another mug of wassail instead?"

"Done. I am quite grateful to you, Miss St. Claire," Lord Arch said as they moved towards the ancient. "That's as pleased as I've seen James all month long. All year long, perhaps."

Quincy's eyes flickered up toward Arch, his silent, observant figure enjoying the view while his mind was probably spinning a web of words together.

"When you know him as I do, you'll see it," Lord Arch said. "It's a gleam that settles and how he carries the slightest squint around his left eye. And the healthy flush of color in his cheeks."

"Now you're teasing me."

Lord Arch laughed.

—————

The first light of morning was dropping into Gainsford Street when the last guests let themselves out the back door. Fisher and Mado, promising to see Quincy the next day, rushed off to find sleep, as had Jade, Jack, Crow—who had slipped out before anyone knew he had— and everybody else.

It was New Year's Day, and the offices of The Q were a mess. Quincy looked across the print room at Arch, who stood in his shirtsleeves, the white sleeves rolled up to his forearms, his hair askew, broom in hand, tie removed, and collar unbuttoned at the neck. It was the most indecorous she had ever seen him. And her tired heart, worn wide and thin from the events of the night, pulled itself tightly around the thought of him.

Once all was done—the ancient looked again respectable, the garbage had been set out back for collecting, and the lights were extinguished—Quincy and Arch sat at the front counter, half tired, half exhilarated, staring out onto the quiet New Year's Day street.

"I could sleep all week," Quincy yawned, rubbing her eyes with the heel of her hand.

"You should, but you won't."

And Quincy, looking at him, thought James Arch had a smile that looked like the sunrise. She turned her attention to the patterns of light making room for themselves on the worn planks of the floor, and she knew, from years of watching, the way the sun would move itself up the wall. She felt the wood of the counter beneath her hands and looked at the doors, the windows. Quincy thought to herself that, if she somehow listened carefully enough, she could hear every word that had ever been spoken in the front offices of The Q.

And she was ready.

"Shall we go?" She looked over at Arch, who was fighting sleep valiantly—and losing.

"If you're ready." Arch stood, retrieved his coat, and began to put it on. "I'll walk you home."

"Home?" Quincy thought of the depressing hotel room. "Where's home?"

Arch finished securing the buttons on his coat and then reached for Quincy's jacket, which was lying across the far end of the counter next to her red scarf. He handed them both to Quincy.

"Home is anywhere you want it to be, Miss St. Claire. But, until you decide where that is, I figured you could stay with us, a guest at Peacock House. If you'd like. I could send round for your things at The Emperion."

She looked up at him, watching as he straightened his shoulders and shot his cuffs. Seeing he was under her scrutiny, he looked at her, then to the floor, smiling.

Yes, home could be where he was.

"I would like that," Quincy said as she slid off her stool and threw her jacket on. "And you," her fingers moved quickly along the buttons, "as my solicitor, could help me find a suitable residence in due course, one with enough space for our monstrous library."

"Oh?" Arch raised his eyebrows as he watched her wind her scarf around her neck, burying her chin and lips in the vermilion wool. "The great Quincy St. Claire wishes to retain me as her personal solicitor?"

"I can't fire you. It's in the contract."

And now he laughed, really laughed, and as they left the counter, he picked up Quincy's stool with one hand and, limping, brought it with them.

"I figure your next venture will involve a counter of some sort, and you'll need this."

"But I can't take anything from the offices."

"Well, Quincy, I wrote the final contract, and when Levins and Rutherford study it closely enough, they will see that this," he held the stool up very seriously, "is listed among the personal possessions of Quincy St. Claire. Legally, it's yours. Happy New Year."

She had never smiled so hard. "Thank you."

"You are most welcome. Now, I can manage the stool, if you'll carry my cane."

Arch reached for the door, turning the knob, and stepped out into the street before her. For this, Quincy was grateful, because he knew she needed to look back at an empty space and to be the last person to touch the knob the final time she left the offices of her beloved Q. As she did so, she thanked her uncle for bringing her here and thanked The Q for being the haven she had needed it to be.

With a set face and a quick nod, she stepped out onto the street and pulled the door shut behind her, locking it securely one last time. Then she slid the key back through the mail slot and heard it drop onto the wood floor of the front office. Her heart fell with it.

They walked up Gainsford Street in silence.

"What next, Quincy?" Arch finally spoke as they turned left onto Queen's Street, his limp only just evident.

"Next? A bath, a long sleep. Breakfast, I suppose."

He waited, knowing she had not answered his question.

"I do have some ideas," Quincy continued, "some business ideas that might be worth pursuing. I would like to schedule an appointment with you to discuss them, perhaps after dinner, in the library."

"I'll be attending a concert this evening."

"Oh."

"But, afterward, I would be happy to hear your plans. You could come with me, you know; you wouldn't want to miss this performance."

"Where is it?"

"Coincidentally, in the library. A concert by Quincy St. Claire should just about cover the cost of a consultation."

She heard herself grumbling about extortion, but her own words were lost in a yawn.

James Arch slowed his step and gave a more earnest reply, "I'm very eager to hear your plans, Quincy."

Quincy linked her arm through his and glanced at the stool he was carrying. He knew, this James Arch, how to get her through.

———

Later that day, when Quincy was curled up on the window seat in the Arch library and feeling the cold drift off the glass, she opened an envelope Arch had given her. It was a letter from Ezekiel, to be given Quincy at the year's end.

"I've no idea what he wrote to you," Arch said as he handed it to her. The envelope was of a thick cream paper, the kind of paper Ezekiel had always said was endowed with its own soul. Bringing her finger beneath the fold, she broke the seal and pulled the letter out. There was his familiar, wobbled slant.

Quincy, my dear little pixie child,

I write this with great faith that you have accomplished the task I set before you. It is, I admit, a bit nonsensical for me to do so, but, Quincy, I want more for you than what The Q can offer. I want for you a wider world and all the joys in it. You don't see that now. You have just stormed off, without a proper winter coat, not knowing that it's important to know how to buy a bunch of flowers on occasion or how to wonder at a butterfly. You swatted at it, didn't you? Just as I suspected.

I don't ask you to give your heart to everything the way I do. But I do want you to experience hints of beautiful things, bits of color and conversations, so that you might discover what you can love, even if they are not the things on the list I've set before you. The world will go on if you miss a board meeting; the world will not go on if you have not found people to give something for. Did you manage it, Quincy girl? Did you stumble your way through the list of requirements without stubbing your toe too many times?

I told Arch that he could not help you in any way. I also told him that, if you did not succeed, it would be forever on his head and that I would haunt him in this life and hold him accountable in the next. He takes things too earnestly, that boy.

Quincy smiled.

Someday, I hope you have the courage to leave The Q behind. You have done brilliant things with it, but there is more to be done elsewhere. What else, I wonder, is Quincy St. Claire capable of? In the not too distant future, I hope you will have the courage to find out.

With all my love,
Your great-uncle Ezekiel

P.S. I do believe, if you were to really know James Arch, you would find him a loyal friend, someone who could keep up with you, someone worth having in your life. I only ask that you think about it.

ACKNOWLEDGEMENTS

To write a book is to turn ex-patriot. Upon arrival in your adopted country, you unpack your cases, check the nibs on your fountain pens, and begin scribbling down everything you see. It is daunting, and engages the soul in a way nothing else ever quite does. You are very aware of and endlessly grateful for all those who support you in this endeavor.

There were those willing to pack their trunks and visit Rhysdon, to walk through the story and tell me what they thought. A handful of dear friends, most of my siblings, my parents, were all able to make the journey. {And I count it a great victory that I found Caitlin in the offices of The Q well past her curfew. Twice.} All of you were insightful and encouraging, and this story is better for having traveled with you. There were others who wrote letters, keeping me tethered to home and to life, all the while encouraging me forward as I discovered how this yearlong experiment of Ezekiel's would end.

A few special thanks go to the following: Alena, for helping me to clean up the print room a few drafts into the tale. Ben, ever the magician, who fixed the presses over and over again. Kevin and Kim, who were willing to let me crash at The Emperion of their house as Kevin helped me figure out just how to wrangle this world into black and white. Julie, my fantastic copy editor, who set herself to the task with a dedication that even Quincy would approve. Kip, from the first minutes of encouragement to his last minute help. I will always take you to the train station with me. And an especial thanks to Allysha, my substantive editor, who has spent hours at The Q, venturing occasionally to Peacock House, or uptown into Rhysdon's cathedral, or to The Nest for a pint with Crow. As always, passport in hand, you are willing to make the trip, taking up residence in whatever city I am in, coming to know all the characters I am trying to write. Thank you for the months you have spent in Rhysdon. We had fun pretending that we were locals, after all.

ABOUT THE AUTHOR

Like many of my siblings, I would sneak out of bed, slip into the hallway, and pull my favorite books from the book closet. I read my way through the bottom shelf, then the next shelf up, and the shelf above that, until I could climb to the very top shelf, stacked two layers deep and two layers high, and read the titles of the classics. My desire to create stories grew as I was learning to read them.

Subsequently, I spent my time scribbling in notebooks rather than listening to math lectures at school.

I graduated with a degree in literary studies, and have spent several years working on the novels that keep pounding on the doors of my mind, as none of my characters are very patient to wait their turn. I currently live in Utah with my wonderful chemist husband, and books in every room of the house.

Made in United States
North Haven, CT
24 October 2023

43127081R00286